Thy Mother's Glass

From David to
Jonathan — biblically! —
with the author's affection
David

Thy Mother's Glass

A NOVEL BY

DAVID WATMOUGH

HarperCollins*PublishersLtd*

I wish to thank the Canada Council for a projects grant and the Banff Centre in conjunction with the writing of this novel.

 For information address HarperCollins Publishers Ltd, Suite 2900, 55 Avenue Road, Toronto, Canada M5R 3L2.

First Edition

Canadian Cataloguing in Publication Data

Watmough, David, 1926-
Thy mother's glass

Hardcover ISBN 0-00-223887-X Paperback ISBN 0-00-647399-7

I. Title.

PS8595.A7T5 1992 C813'.54 C92-093396-3
PR9199.3.W3T5 1992

---

92 93 94 95 96 ❖ RRD 5 4 3 2 1

For Floyd and our forty summers

"When forty winters shall besiege thy brow and dig deep trenches in thy beauty's field...Thou art thy mother's glass, and she in thee calls back the lovely April of her prime...."

William Shakespeare, Sonnets Two and Three

"It is the nature of all greatness not to be exact."

Edmund Burke, Speech on American taxation, 1774

BOOK ONE: MAMA

CHAPTER ONE

1916: Fog. Mustard yellow—but blackening the glass as it swirled against the compartment window. With difficulty she read the letters Y L N O S E I D A L *in green as they appeared from her seat inside the slow-moving suburban train. Alone in the carriage, she spoke the inverted legend aloud. Pretended it was the name of some Russian village favored by the czar and his family for recovery from the wounds of that 1914 defeat at Tannenberg. It had been a terrible disappointment—the Russians losing to the Germans so early—but what could you expect from a nation of serfs?*

She sank back against the antimacassar protecting the plush velvet seat. Of course, it didn't matter any more. With the might of the British Empire, and with America about to join the Allies (according to the newspapers), the last great advance would now, after twenty-nine cruel months against that withered-armed kaiser, finally see the defeat of his armies, which had raped and pillaged their way across Belgium and France.

It was odd, though, she reflected, as the train crept past the peasouper darkness of Stratford Junction, that those three—the king, the czar and the kaiser—should be all so closely related, all so tied to her whom Poppa invariably referred to as The Old Queen.

The woman gingerly raised a beige glove to wipe condensation from the window of the Ladies Only compartment to see where the train had brought them. But her mind was now away. She thought of how displeased The Old Queen would've been to know her family was quarreling in public. How many times Poppa had told her Queen Victoria valued loyalty above all else!

Thinking of her father brought her immediately if reluctantly to that first day she had started work as an analytical chemist.... Russian soldiers, frostbitten and weary from the defeat by Hindenburg, the work girls had chorused, had been seen by night as down the length of England they had marched—with snow still on their boots.

Loud pistol-cracks pierced the dark outside the train as it bumped across seas of points. For a moment she was startled—thinking still of the war, of the Allied armies, now in the new year of 1917 bloodily entrenched along the Western Front. Then she remembered. The source of the sounds was the explosive caps that railway companies placed on their rails as a fog warning.

A rash of such shots preceded the train's jerking to a halt. She would have liked to stay with the heroism of the troops; most especially of her valiant brother Guy, who was probably, that very January day, flying his Sopwith Camel over the mud and barbed wire which he had described in such vivid detail to her on his last leave.

But other, narrower reflections insinuated themselves under the feathered hat which she would soon exchange for a kerchief at the lab of the chemical works.

Recalling that silly rumor of the Russians with snow on their boots descending the length of England uncomfortably evoked Poppa's savage reaction on learning that she had flatly disobeyed him a second time; that after taking courses in science at Queen Mary's College in the face of his total disapproval, she had gone on to accept the research post at the West Silvertown factory of Brunner Monde's—the first woman to be so employed.

It was at the long walnut dinner table in the forbidding house in Leyton that her Momma had foolishly blurted everything out. Alice had just poured the soup while their ancient manservant, William-John, standing by the sideboard, muttered his conviction that, after five years, the girl was still an incompetent at serving. Each of the places for the two absent boys was marked, as usual, by a fresh flower—this time a carnation—placed carefully on an empty plate between the cutlery. Aunt Hetty said that it was Poppa's way of preparing for their deaths, but her sister, Aunt Lid, told her niece not to listen to such sentiments, as Aunt Hetty was dreadfully cynical because she'd lost her own son in an accident with a horse on a Dublin parade ground of the Irish Yeomanry—instead of at Passchendaele.

"...He was so very angry. He called me a disobedient hussy, little better than a street girl, for hiring myself out to a set of German Jews. Poppa reminded me I had already thwarted his will and stained my womanhood by attending Queen Mary's College and pursuing science. That night, with his soup going cold, he threatened never to address me as daughter any more. I cried and left the table. I loved Poppa. You see, Davey, he was the greatest father on earth!"

"Mama, why do you always call him your Poppa when he is our Grandpapa?"

"He was dead before you were born. He was never really your Grandpapa, except in a legalistic sense."

"It is the same when you speak of your brother, Guy. He was our uncle."

"Was. The same condition applies. He is nothing to you. He was everything to me."

"What about us? Aren't we everything?"

"Clean your teeth, Davey, and see that Sarah looks at your face and hands before helping with your pajamas. I shall come and inspect you in bed."

....She knew there were vexed words between Momma and Poppa after she had retreated from the dining room, flustered and dismayed. She could hear them through the vent—just as she could hear the servants gossiping—by crouching down where the pipe came up through the floorboards to feed the newly installed radiators.

Poppa's disapproval often flooded that huge house, which was further hushed by sausage draft-protectors at the bases of the doors, by felt hangings on the doors themselves, and dimmed by heavy velvet drapes of deep maroon screening the narrow, Gothic windows. Stuffed tropical birds perched silently on artificial branches under glass domes in the drawing room, whose doors were always kept closed. But even there, about the horsehair chaise-longue and the formally arranged highback chairs, his thin-lipped censure reigned as cold as frost.

The clock-ticking quiet was protected from the clatter of horses' hoofs in the High Street by two Landseer lions, at the top of broad stone steps, which Alice or old William-John whitened each morning in an incessant battle against the London grime.

This would have proved a more than fruitless campaign on such days as the famous one of the January peasouper, when she, after experiencing all the small explosions from the fog caps on the railway lines by way of overture, went to her lab and encountered the Great Explosion that sent fifty tons of TNT into the air, killed seventy people and injured four hundred and fifty more.

"Weren't you afraid, Mama? I would have died of fright!"

"There was no time to be afraid, Davey. My rats had to be returned to their overturned cages. They were scampering all over the laboratory—poor little things. I discovered my assistant lying unconscious with a nasty gash to her throat and glass shards deep in her skull. I had to bathe away the blood before the doctors arrived. She was better off than all those factory girls who were screaming from their wounds or silent in death."

"Were there many severed arms and legs, Mama? Uncle Harry says there were."

"My brother Harry was barking orders on some parade ground, while Guy was risking his life in the skies over France. But don't interrupt.

"When I described the carnage Momma fainted but Poppa suggested I should see it as judgment for my rebellion. I had been forbidden to answer back when he reproached me, but I was secretly glad to have been there when the Silvertown Explosion occurred, for my education proved useful.

"I reminded Poppa of how pleased he had been with my marks when I had taken First Aid as a supplementary course at the Loughton Academy for Young Ladies. He had smiled and stroked his beard, telling me that if I'd been born a boy and a foreigner, I would have made a good Jesuit!"

"What is a Jesuit, Mama?" I didn't really care, but such questions had proved a useful ruse on past occasions when Mama was prone to wax excessively on the subject of her father.

Mama gave me a quick glance over her sewing glasses—perhaps seeing through my little game. "Would you not rather know what a zeppelin was? It was through one of them that I took the first step leading to my acquaintance with your father. Now leave that yarn alone and come and sit on my lap, for I shall tell you anyway!

"They looked so beautiful when caught in the beam of a searchlight. Slender cigars like Poppa smoked—only silver, sailing between the night clouds as they vainly sought to dodge the searchlights and fighter planes of such great pilots as Captain Warburton-Lee, V.C., who specialized in their destruction.

"But before his machine-gun bullets could rip through the envelope and ignite the hydrogen so that balls of fire flared there in the sky, they would rain their bombs down at us. One such bomb hit Jubilee Road and I hurried there in the middle of the night with terrified Alice to see what we could do to help the victims."

"Captain Warburton-Lee was one of England's greatest heroes, Mama. He wore goggles and big gloves. I have a book with his picture in it."

"The greatest of our heroes went unsung, Davey. My dearest Guy was one of those. He died for his country just as much as Captain Warburton-Lee—even if he was not flying over France at the time."

"Tell me about Uncle Guy, Mama. You don't speak as much about him as your Poppa. Did he look like me?"

"You are all your father's children. None of you looks like Poppa or Guy. But what is there to say to those who never knew him? He had soft brown eyes, and dark curly hair that he always tried to flatten with water and by brushing it hard. He had the most beautiful nose—like a Roman emperor, Poppa used to say—and he and I never quarreled even once in our lives. The same could not be said for Harry, who was older and away at school when Guy and I were children together."

Mama gave a little sniff of disapproval and patted the waves of her pretty brown hair. Then she had to readjust the shoulder strap of her sleeveless green dress.

"What kind of games did you and Uncle Guy play, Mama?"

"Gentle games, for Guy was the most gentle of people. Poppa always insisted that children were meant to be seen but not heard—and that caused much of the friction between my father and his eldest son. But Guy was content to lie quietly with a book if the weather suggested we remain indoors. Outside, though, he was transformed and loved to laugh aloud and race me along the bank of the River Lea.

"Even if he was delicate and could not participate in many rough-and-tumble activities, he could dance with the grace of a faun. Oh, he was so full of fun and imagination! Once he borrowed one of my summer frocks and put it on, along with pompom slippers he found in the attic, and told me that he was a Greek soldier guarding the royal palace in Athens!

"Another time he borrowed Momma's boa and did impersonations for me of music hall turns such as Vesta Tilley and Marie Lloyd—though goodness knows where he first saw them, as we were forbidden to enter such low places! He was so well read and would have gone to Jesus College, Oxford, Poppa said, had he lived beyond the Armistice. That is where his dear friend Horace Bligh went, while Andrew Elphinstone, the son of one of Poppa's business associates in the City, went to the other Jesus in Cambridge. The place where your father wishes you to go when you grow up—after Christ's Hospital School, the Bluecoats school, if you are as attentive to your studies as my brother Guy always was."

I didn't like reminders that I was still a small boy. "Did Uncle Guy have lots of friends, Mama?"

"None as close as Horace, for they were inseparable. Andrew was close but fortunately of less influence. I did not always care for his airy gestures and silly expressions. I am sure it was he who put Guy up to doing those vaudeville impersonations. Horace, on the other hand, was always so tender with Guy when he had one of his spells. There were times when, I must admit, I felt quite jealous to see Horace cradling Guy's perspiring head when he had overexerted himself, bathing his forehead with a cool sponge and whispering words of comfort to my poor, sick brother.

"But you have got me off the zeppelins! Where was I? Oh yes, the bomb on Jubilee Road...."

She made it seem my fault but I wasn't surprised that she had come to a stop with Guy and returned to bombs. Mama would talk of her brother on occasion, but I always sensed a gathering reluctance as she continued, and a determination to leave some mystery about the person I knew only as a sepia photo in a silver frame, taking pride of place on her dressing table.

"It was near Knighton Farm, from whose dairy we obtained our milk, but unfortunately the bomb had missed the fields and had hit a brand new house. The family was all killed except their lodger, a woman about my own age who introduced herself as a Miss Loveday Bryant. She turned out to be your father's eldest sister, who later emigrated to Canada and married the owner of a vast ranch in southern Alberta, where they now live with your little cousins Leslie and Jennifer, twins whom you have never seen."

"I don't want to hear about them, Mama! Tell me about those I have seen—like Grandpa and Grandma Bryant and how you came down to Cornwall for the very first time."

Mama fingered the pretty glass beads about her neck. I knew she was debating whether to grant my request. I snuggled up even closer. Not that I had much doubt she'd give in. This was one of her favorite anecdotes and I knew it so well I could have carried on, were she to falter. Which she never did. Mama was too good a storyteller ever to tell things twice the same way.

"I arrived in Cornwall in the spring of 1920—your father coming as far as Launceston to board my train as he did not want me to enter the Duchy unescorted. At that juncture it was all pleasure."

"He took you in his arms, Mama, and kissed you!"

"He did no such thing, Davey. We were on a train. Where do you get these silly notions? I suppose it's when Sarah takes you to the pictures when she is supposed to be walking you to feed the ducks.

"I was naturally pleased to see your Daddy, as I had left Waterloo on the Atlantic Coast Express mid-morning and it was now later afternoon. I was exhausted to say the least. Besides, I was quite nervous. I had only met his sister, Loveday—the one of the Zeppelin bomb and Canada. And his older brother, Leslie, your uncle, who had arrived at our house on leave from the Front in 1916. Frankly, I was not looking forward to meeting Mrs. Bryant. My own Momma was trying enough—someone else's mother was not a pleasant prospect."

Mama always went "literary" at this point. It was the better to make the contrast with what was to follow.

"Your Daddy spoke of the beauties of a Cornish spring that April of 1920, but all I could see from the moment we left Launceston were frowning skies over desolate moors. I have hated them for their bleakness from that day to this. I was lulled by his warm voice into a false security which was dispelled within minutes of stepping down at that crude railway halt, which called itself St. Keverne Station even though there were no buildings!

"We were met by a trap but, instead of being drawn by a pony, it had a cart-horse in its shafts. It was driven by my prospective mother-in-law but your father, in subaltern's uniform (for he was only recently returned from Jerusalem, where the Corps had stayed on after the war), took the reins from her and invited me to sit alongside him. She was relegated to ensuring that the numerous pieces of my luggage did not fall off as we bumped along the rutted ground. I should point out that I came across no tarred roads in the Cornwall of that time. I do not recall seeing a car either. And how the wind blew! Then it never ceased to do that on those North Cornish uplands."

"I want to hear about Pol'garrow, Mama."

"Do not use that wretched abbreviation, darling. In any case, you must be patient, Davey. You are spoiling my story."

That meant we were to have the longer version with the bumping through the fords. I happily clenched and unclenched six-year-old toes in my sandals, breathed in the scent of her familiar lavender water and played with the gold bangle on her arm.

"Grandmother Bryant had positioned herself on the piled suitcases close to my back. She couldn't have been at all comfortable. It also meant she had to yell for me to hear. But that didn't put her off for a moment!

"'Can you milk?'

"I completely misunderstood. 'Just a small amount but I can drink tea without.'

"'Good! We are short-handed, what with Charlie down with that influenza, and a dozen cows to milk. Wesley here says you're a bravun good cook, so you can give a hand with the pasties and that.'

"'Wesley is full of nonsense! I am a dreadful cook and I have never *seen* a Cornish pasty—let alone manufactured one!'

"'Isabella is a research chemist,' her son told her quickly. 'She pretends to know nothing domestic.'

"'Then that must break her parents' hearts,' Mama Bryant informed him. 'And I can't see how researching is going to help her when the time comes for her to run Pol'garrow.'

"I was glad for the wind in the blackthorn hedges and the sound of the cart-horse clopping over the unmade lane. I lapsed into that and wished myself back in Silvertown with my lab staff, or with my dear departed brother—playing Happy Families in the old nursery.

"Mama Bryant persisted in her theme. 'There isn't a night I don't go down on my knees to thank the Good Lord I am the daughter of a farmer, and the granddaughter of one. I shudder to think what would have happened to Pol'garrow after your father was killed if I didn't have farming in my blood.'

"Her son merely laughed at that. 'Doubtless we would have got in a manager—just as I tried to persuade Father to do when he insisted on enlisting in the Duke of Cornwall's Light Infantry.'

"But the bonneted lady in widow's weeds, black gaiters and farm boots, bouncing up and down on my valises and hatboxes, was not about to be abashed by her only son.

"'Managers may be all right for the English, but they are not the Cornish way. You've been up there too long, Wesley. You're beginning to sound like—like an emmet—as the people say!'"

That was my traditional cue—devised, I suspected, to ascertain whether I was listening closely. "What's an emmet, Mama?"

"Davey! You know very well an emmet is an ant. But here in Cornwall it's come to mean the English residents in the Duchy. I must say Mama Bryant didn't mean anything nice by it. I think she might even have used it of me, before my arrival and her opportunity to get to know and befriend me. In those early days I was not a popular fiancée with her family. Oh dear no! They wanted no London stranger interfering with their weird ways."

"Go on with the story, Mama. You are still in the trap with Grandma Bryant and Daddy."

"There was little conversation after that. All three of us were too concerned with holding on to our seats as that rickety old contraption bounced wildly about in the huge ruts in the road. I must say, though, that Polengarrow looked pretty in the twilight, with the bats flying under the eaves as we emerged from the elms of the lane, and the daisy-starred lawns that lipped the great mullion windows that reached right down to the ground.

"After supper in the huge kitchen with slate flagstones, as I sat being grilled by that brutish Bryant family, you would have thought I was from

Mars rather than London as questions about myself and our family were grunted from assembled aunts, uncles and numerous cousins. In self-defense I tried desperately to recollect how attractive the *exterior* of the old farmhouse was, with its squat Tudor doorways and its mixture of dark green periwinkle and vermilion Virginia creeper festooning the stout granite walls.

"From Aunt Emily: 'You put enough saffron in your buns and yeast in your bread? They say 'tis awful baking up there.'

"From Aunt Liz: 'Can they pluck a goose without ripping the breast, then, up your way?'

"From Aunt Hettie: 'For certain, you do look too poorly for farm life! I bide you be without the strength to even put the wash up in the mowey—come a wishy day? You'm not used to the sunlight up there where 'tis all smoke and grime, is that it?'

"From Uncle Joe: 'Hettie's right for once. Her's a frail-looking maid, you! Be 'ee minded to be child-bearin', then?'

"From Uncle Jan: 'I s'pose in six months you'll be tellin' on us how to run Pol'garra. That's how always 'tis with up-country folks who come preachin' how to bide our ways.'

"From your future Daddy (just before I was about to leave that stifling kitchen with the open range, never to return!): 'Now that's enough from all of you! Isabella is a good sport, but I must remind you she is not a heifer being sold down at Wadebridge market. She neither needs nor wants your prods and goads. She is perfectly healthy, I want you to know, and has more brains than all we Bryants put together!'

"I am not disposed to blush, Davey, unlike you—that's something else you get from the Bryants—and I told your father, sharply, to stop talking as if I were not there.

"Then I addressed all of them sprawled at the huge scrubbed table in their workclothes, the men with orange binder cord instead of belts at their waists, the women with the hems of their black dresses tucked up to avoid the muddy puddles of the farmyard.

"'I think perhaps we are under a misapprehension. *You* think I am here to be scrutinized as a possible wife for your Wesley. I, on the other hand, have come to decide whether I am able to give up my London life for an existence down here.' The silence was broken only by the crackle of wood, and occasional hiss of sap, from the logs in the kitchen stove. I waited for a rejoinder but there wasn't any. I found the courage to continue. 'I love Wesley very much. I wish to be a good wife to him but I tell you here and now I will not try and live up to anyone else's expectations. I have already found that an impossible task.'"

She never said so when she came to this part of her recitation but I knew even when only five or six that she was referring to her Poppa.

"What did they say, Mama? What did they say?"

But she needed no urging at that particular point.

"I was about to add for their benefit that I was not a Cornishwoman and would never be one. Also that, if I decided to stay, they would have to be patient with me as I made adjustment to their way of life in that primitive place. But my mother-in-law-to-be forestalled me. To my surprise she got to her feet and placed her red hands about my shoulders. She must have felt my shivering.

"'Good for you, Isabella! I like to hear a woman say what's what! You stand up for who you are and what you believe and don't fret over what anyone else says. That's how my Robert was when he went off to war and that's how I was when I married him, in spite of all the Trebilcocks and Pengellys who thought us so *superior* to the Bryants down here to Pol'garrow. Again, I say, 'tis refreshing to hear a young woman speak so.'

"You can have no idea, Davey, how much those words from Grandma Isolda Bryant meant to me. She could have had no notion of London life, for she had never crossed the Tamar out of Cornwall. No gaslight, no electricity, no running water, no telephone, no car, no sewing machine, no domestic staff except a washerwoman and a village girl who was handy with a mop. She told me she had never seen a horse-bus or a private car until a few months before my arrival. And I will not dwell on the primitive sanitary arrangements that prevailed then in this rambling old house.

"And yet, from that very moment, I knew I had found a friend. Isolda Bryant, your grandmother, is an extraordinary woman and there is none in the world I admire more. She told me so much about the Bryants and the Pengellys and the Trebilcocks that I do believe I know more about them than all your aunts and uncles put together—even if they talk of nothing else!"

The story always slackened in interest for me when she got on to her praise for dear old Grandma Bryant and her battles with those Cornish relatives.

"Tell me about Daddy's Great-aunt Eliza, Mama, and your honeymoon. Tell me about Tregilders and the broody hen."

"It was your father's first car. A Clyno, I think it was. Or was it a Morris Oxford? It doesn't matter. All I can tell you is that when Daddy bought it I was quite a proud woman. Poppa always refused to purchase a motorcar. Right up to his death, three weeks before our marriage. That 'flu was a dreadful thing. Poppa and Aunt Augusta both in the space of six months. And the sound of the guns scarcely silent!

"Do you know, Davey, that as we drove in that Clyno down to Cornwall we passed cottage after cottage with the blinds down, and in some towns like Yeovil and Exeter it seemed that every man and woman on the street was wearing mourning. I have never seen so much crêpe and black patches and armbands. Wesley told me that he thought the authorities were playing it down to prevent panic and that the disease was claiming more than had died in the war. The years of shortages had weakened the whole population.

"I was so troubled by the time we reached Polengarrow that I was tempted to leave at once and sign on as a nurse. It was my mother-in-law who reminded me I had another duty, and persuaded me that in spite of my training I was now Mrs. Bryant and must help Wesley settle once more to the life of a farmer in St. Keverne. It was not easy. Then what is?"

"You'll *never* get to Great-aunt Eliza," I said bitterly.

"It was my mother-in-law who suggested we take the pony and trap to her aunt's place, as she thought a car would scare her to death. She was ancient, you see. Born in '20 or '21."

It wasn't until a year or two later that I realized Mama was referring to *1*821.

"She wasn't a Victorian, then," I commented. "Like you and Grandpapa."

Mama then did a familiar thing. She leaned back and closed her eyes. This, she had once explained, was to allow minor annoyances to pass her by.

"Great-aunt Elizabeth Pengelly was born just months after Napoleon died—in the reign of King George the Fourth. She remembered as a little girl the riots over the Reform Bill, and told me as soon as we had climbed down from the trap and were walking up her garden path, between huge fuchsia hedges, that she had lived through five reigns and seen the scourge of Methodism take the joy out of Cornwall. As a complete stranger to the place, of course, I had no answer to that!

"If anything, the façade of that house was handsomer than Polengarrow. The old lady told me her grandfather had built it—with money from the Duchy that a grateful Charles the Second had given the Pengellys for supporting him during the Civil War."

"Like the plaque the king gave in St. Keverne church, Mama? The one over the porch when you go in?" Then, lest she be sidetracked by my interruption to talk of boring things like her marriage in the parish church, I tugged fiercely at her sleeve. "But *inside*, Mama. Go on about inside Tregilders and Great-aunt Eliza."

"When Cousin Kate Bryant came over with Uncle Petherick from Philadelphia, they complained all the time about the damp and how cold it was at Polengarrow. But I tell you, Polengarrow was a furnace—compared to how Great-aunt kept Tregilders. I do believe it held the damp from the mist it knew when your ancestor built it! I have never known such a cold house—before or since. We sat at first in the drawing room, which was just about deserted of furniture, in front of an empty grate.

"She made us a tea—with the help of an old woman who I could have sworn was older than herself!"

"Was it a *Cornish* tea, Mama? Did you have jam splits and Cornish cream?"

"No, it was not! There was an orange between your father and me. Aunt Eliza peeled it and ate the skin. She did likewise with a blackened banana—retaining the peel for herself and offering us the soft part. You must remember, Davey, that such fruits were luxuries in those postwar days in places like Cornwall. She was definitely honoring her great-nephew and his bride."

"Is that why she ate the horrible skin and gave you the nice part?"

"I don't think so. She informed us that the outer casings of such things were both tastier and healthier. After that odd apportioning of the fruit, she provided us with stale—indeed, moldy-smelling—saffron cake, while she herself munched at a huge ship's biscuit. I believe they are called 'hardtack.' They reminded me of those enormous dog biscuits—which they may well have been, considering her eccentricities of taste.

"After tea Great-aunt Eliza informed us she was going to give us a tour of Tregilders, as it would eventually be ours. So, with her ashplant stick, that tiny hump-backed creature, clad from tip to toe in the jet of her widow's weeds, led us through dank hallways with peeling wallpaper to so many damp and barely furnished rooms that I soon lost track of their number and what their purpose might be.

"On the second floor, where the great slate flagstones were replaced by sagging wood floors, both four-poster and two-poster beds, situated at one end of otherwise bare rooms, alone suggested we were in bedrooms. There were canopies of sorts over these vast but shadowed edifices (for the sash windows were largely obscured by ivy). It was at the portal of one such room that she suddenly flung out a gnarled hand and indicated where we were to sleep.

"'The nuptial chamber,' she announced. 'And I reckon 'tis been waiting a long time! Mother and Father were the last to sleep in that one and I was born in it. They say Grandmother died of shock in 'un, too—when she heard Dutch William had landed up to Torbay back in 1688 and dear King James had had to flee to France. Grandma Nankivel was a true Cornish friend of the Stuarts, I'll have you know,' the old lady added fiercely—as if your father and I were her detested Methodies.

"Bedtime was early at Tregilders in Great-aunt's time. She had said goodnight and we had been given our upstairs candles before the grandfather clock had boomed nine. Fortunately we were both tired after the long ride in that cart without springs.

"Even so, I'm sure it was still the middle of the night when I woke to hear branches tossed by the Atlantic winds scratching their twiggy fingers against the window. I thought fancifully of Great-aunt's own veined hands, striving to get into Tregilders from out there on the cliffs—though I knew she was sleeping somewhere below where your father and I lay. Odd ideas came to me in the middle of that night. Perhaps old people—*very* old people like Great-aunt—practiced being ghosts before they died. Maybe that *was* her moaning softly and scratching brittle nails against the glass. I also wondered if all those ancestors of hers and your father's, who had come and gone from this earth in that very bed, left their presences, too, under the poster-supported canopy above my head.

"Then it happened. Then I knew we were not the only living creatures in that vast room. I suppose my sight had slowly become accustomed to the light of the stars outside. In any event, I could now clearly see the eyes staring at me from the foot of the bed. They were the eyes of a rat.

"Davey, I have told you many times of my rats in the laboratory and of how fond of them I was. That makes it all the harder to explain the horrible feeling that swept over me, lying there in bed, your father asleep at my side. Those hard black eyes and the quivering snout—questing, I imagined, for the softness of my face. I think I shrieked as I fought to escape the bedclothes. I had the sense of bared yellow teeth and a slithering tail before Wesley awoke with a shout and the creature was gone with a faint plop to the floor and away to its filthy hole.

"I don't think your Daddy ever understood my horror of those rats. He laughed when I explained my terror at waking to see that creature sitting there on the counterpane eyeing me. It was a subject I never cared to raise with him after that."

"Tell me about the broody hen. You and Daddy were agreed over that. You both laughed over Great-aunt's funny ways, didn't you, Mama?"

"That was the next morning. You must remember her house was only the second I had encountered which was without running water."

She always sighed extravagantly at that point in her recital. "I never thought then I would grow accustomed to such primitive life at Polengarrow. Or even less that my babies would grow up knowing nothing else!

"It was not exactly an *outhouse* Great-aunt had, but a small room made over. The walls were rough and limewashed and the lavatory bench was a hinged affair with a bucket of sorts secreted under it. Less crude in fact than what we have even now. But why she chose to have her hen sit on a clutch of eggs in there was a mystery—until, out of my presence (for these matters were not considered fit for my un-Cornish ears), your father asked her.

"'Well, my handsome,' she'd answered him. 'I likes to know what's going on with my special fowls. And that Speckly's a poor mother. So soon as I do hear her chicks cheep I'm in there awaiting. Right after they'm hatched I sweep of 'em up into me apron and put all on 'em into the warming oven. Mind you, I do see it b'aint too hot from the kitchener. One time I hadn't damped down the wood enough and had an accident with they day-olds. But I b'aint gin bother your pretty young head about that.'

"Your Daddy was always squeamish, Davey. You can be sure he never pressed his great aunt for more information, either. Did I tell you about the orange peel?"

"Yes you did, Mama."

I made no further requests. Experience had taught me that when Mama started asking *me* questions, she had temporarily run out of reminiscences.

CHAPTER TWO

When Mama bore Arthur, the third of us boys, she stopped childbearing. We were never to have a sister. My first major memory involving both her and my brothers I shall call NEW ZEALAND. That was the first time I remember her looming larger than Daddy, as having authority and the power to change the world.

It was the summer of my seventh birthday. The motorcar had come to Cornwall—but not too many of them. Ours had been the only one in St. Keverne but it disappeared one day after Daddy sadly informed us that we would all have to make what he called "economies." Eventually he bought a motorbike instead. Attached to it was a sidecar, but we three small children were its only passengers. Mama said it was a ridiculous conveyance and refused to squeeze her slightly plump self into it. She declared she would take Hambly's bus into Wadeford until Daddy could afford a new Morris with pneumatic tires.

That June when we lost our car was the same one the Nankivel children turned up for the last few weeks of school with bare feet. Rosemary Nankivel said it was healthy for her and her sisters to air their toes, but our brother Simon, who was eleven, said it was because Mr. Nankivel had been let go by Cornish Farm Industries and that they could not afford new shoes when their old ones wore out.

We used to walk to our village school through fields of wheat or barley, but that summer it was all returned to grass and Mr. Chenoweth, our neighbor, didn't have any more geese. Thomas Chenoweth, who came between Simon and me and was nine, told us that there wouldn't be any for Michaelmas or even Christmas as the folk up to London weren't buying them any more. I was glad of that as I hated their hissing when we passed them on the way to school and they darted at my bare legs. But when Thomas started explaining they'd all been sold as goslings, I saw him sniff back a wet one. He said his mother had told him the egg money she made would not be enough without the poultry to pay for *Chick's Own*, the children's magazine which came to him in the mail each week. I promised him my Children's Section of Mama's *Home Companion* but I knew it wasn't the same as having your own thing—especially one brought by Mr. Clemo, the postman.

It was Mr. Clemo (whose son, Neddy, was our village idiot) who actually started NEW ZEALAND for our family. On the Saturday in August month closest to the fifteenth—my birthday—our brother Simon crossed the farmyard waving the mail in his hand. I was excited, of course, as I had already started to receive the first of my birthday cards from remote relatives.

The mail was always opened on the kitchen table, and I could hardly contain my excitement when I saw a strange stamp on one envelope and guessed it was from our Aunty Mary, Daddy's youngest sister, who lived in Palmerston, New Zealand. It was addressed to him but that didn't matter. She knew it was my birthday and could have stuck a money order inside with a note for me as well as whatever she had written to Mama and Daddy.

I was to be disappointed. There was nothing for me—not even a mention of the exciting day coming up. Simon, who wasn't usually very friendly, said, "Well, shit on her, the old cow! Just make sure, Davey, you don't send cards to Cousin Thelma or Cousin Robert when it's *their* turn." But we both turned back in the direction of the table when Mama, who was reading the long, scrawly letter from her sister-in-law, suddenly raised her voice and pointed at us.

"Davey, Arthur, Simon, fetch your father from the granary!"

None of us moved—each waiting for the other, I suppose.

"Go at once! It's important. This letter could change our lives."

At seven I was in love with change. It was I who rushed outside to fetch our father. He was reluctant to leave the task of gluing back the third leg of his milking stool, but I tugged at his arm and said Mama was so worked up I thought she would explode. He started to hurry when I told him that.

"She angry, Davey?"

"Excited, Daddy. That's what she is. She says our lives could change because of the letter."

Daddy looked worried. Even more so than usual. "Best get inside then. Otherwise we two won't be that popular. She can be complicated, right enough. You know Mama!" He gave me that 'we're-in-this-together' look which I loved.

Mama addressed Daddy before he'd pulled back the latch to release the Dutch doors. "Mary's written. We're to leave here before things get any worse and move to Palmerston. There's a farm next to theirs going for a song. With a beautiful house. Labor's cheap, too, so you won't have to be up to your neck in muck any longer. We might also have a decent car again. You'd better come in and get washed up."

The way she spoke, it was as if we were to leave that afternoon—as soon as Daddy had put on his Sunday suit. But Mama only meant for him to sit down at the kitchen table and reply to Aunty Mary's letter right away.

Not long after that, Mama started getting cross. I knew by the way she started tossing her head (just as Violet, our black mare, did with her mane when I slipped off her halter) that Mama wasn't pleased with Daddy's response. Not that he said very much. Daddy never did have as many words to speak as Mama. But he kept going back and reading the letter carefully—spreading it out and flattening its creases. He even examined the envelope. That seemed to make Mama even madder.

"It's not about to jump up and bite you," she said. "What's the matter? Do you think your sister is lying?"

"Of course not, Isabella!"

When Daddy called Mama by her full name, I knew things were unusual. He always called her 'Mama'—at least in front of the three of us.

"We musn't rush at things, that's all."

"Wesley Bryant, your family doesn't know the meaning of the word! No one down here has *rushed* at anything for a thousand years!"

"You know what I mean, Mama. I was looking at the postmark to see when the letter was sent rather than when it was written. People sometimes change their minds, you know, after they've sealed an envelope and the weeks go by."

"You think Mary's untrustworthy? You've always told me that she was the most down-to-earth of your sisters. Much more so than that Loveday out there in Alberta. I know what strange notions can lay hold of her! I certainly would not be prepared to pull up stakes and leave Cornwall if she suggested we join them in Calgary."

"Near Cardston, Alberta, Mama. On the North Milk River. Ten thousand acres."

"Be *quiet*, Simon. This has nothing to do with you children."

"Well, we know just how rotten things are out there," Daddy commented. "Loveday said it on her last Christmas card. At least here we can grow our own food and we don't suffer from dust, drought and all those grasshoppers!"

"If you mean we can live on kale and stale bread and get pneumonia each winter from this awful damp, I suppose you're right. But that is not the way to raise children. It is hardly the way Poppa intended me to live, come to that."

There was a heavy silence. Daddy always went silent when Mama mentioned her father and her previous life in London.

I suppose he must have sat down and written his younger sister soon after, because it was still the summer of my seventh birthday when strangers came to see Polengarrow farm and Mama started to sell off bits of old furniture which she said we would not need in our life in New Zealand. I remember Daddy muttering something about valuable antiques, but Mama said we now had to think wholly in terms of the new.

By the time school started up again in September our house was much emptier than most, and when the threshers had finished with the cornrick in the mowey and sat down for supper we had to borrow extra kitchen chairs from Grandma Bryant.

The worst thing, though, involved our rocking horse. It's this I remember most. Mama said that we would get another in New Zealand as it was not worth the cost of transporting. Instead, she promised it to our Falmouth cousins, telling Aunty Pauline that her two boys could have it in time for Christmas as we were due to leave on the P. & O. liner the S.S. *Olympic* the day after Armistice Day. But six weeks before that momentous date a second letter arrived from Aunty Mary counseling us to at least postpone our departure if not abandon it altogether. Mama explained that the economic slump had reached New Zealand, too, and that farming had already suffered acutely.

When it was decided that we would remain at Polengarrow, after all, but that our cousins in Falmouth would be allowed to keep the rocking horse as it had been promised them, I went to bed crying. I woke up in the night to use the po under the bed, moving softly so as not to wake my brothers. I think it was because I was so quiet that I suddenly heard Mama, even though their bedroom was the other side of our thick-walled house. She was sobbing, too. It was the first time I remembered hearing Mama cry. I knew, though, that it was not because we had lost our rocking horse.

CHAPTER THREE

Two years after that, we did leave the farm—although not for New Zealand. We went instead, for the first time, to The Hornbeams, Grandmama Newcombe's house on the fringe of Epping Forest, which she had bought at her son's urging. Mama told us boys that her brother Harry had so bullied our grandmother in her widow's weakness that she had finally broken down and begged us to share her big house—in part, at least, as support against Uncle Harry and his high-strung wife, Dora, whom we children had never met. Simon said that wasn't the reason at all. That we were leasing Polengarrow to a tenant farmer from Pendoggett because Mama had persuaded Daddy to take a job as a traveling representative for a Scottish drapery manufacturer.

Then one day (when Mama was up in London seeing the family solicitors) Grandmama sat me down in her sitting room and told me that nobody seemed to have informed my father that people had more on their minds than buying household fabrics during an economic slump. She went on to remind me that we were lucky to have Grandpapa's carefully saved money to provide for us Bryants—what with hunger marches, the itinerant choirs of unemployed Welsh coalminers and, seemingly everywhere, boarded-up little bankrupt shops. That was but the first of many such homilies from Grandmama, designed to stimulate my notions of gratitude toward her late husband who had died before I was born and whom I'd learned secretly to despise from Mama's innocent reminiscences of his bullying arrogance and pomposity.

We had been at The Hornbeams for less than six months when a newcomer entered our lives. This stranger was a woman.

I should explain something. Now nine, nearly ten, I was still very mindful of our Cornish background of outdoor toilets down which you threw buckets of powdered lime, of oil lamps and candles for indoor illumination. Conversely, I also found a great deal of life amid the Stockbroker

Tudor of Theydon Bois decidedly exotic—even if it was hard to summon the gratitude for it that Grandmama sought. I can admit now, though, that I do believe my lifelong antipathy toward gloomy rooms and my propensity to switch on lights at every occasion date from my Cornish departure and my entry into the electrical world of Grandmama's woodland mansion. Add, then, to this strange new environment, a beautiful, divorced woman who used lipstick and nail varnish (Mama wore neither), owned a Knightsbridge flat in Central London and wore expensive perfume and you have the rarest of phenomena for a rurally raised child who had never known anyone who did not live in a farmhouse or cottage.

Natalie Lockyer-Pope arrived one day with Daddy from Scotland, where, he explained, she lived on a large estate on the moors. I had greater empathy for moors than for Epping Forest or Outer Suburbia. If I hadn't responded to her glamorous looks I would have liked her equally for her background.

Yet before the conclusion of that first afternoon when Natalie came to tea, I realized my own enthusiasm was not necessarily shared by all. Simon hated her, Arthur was too young to be interested and Grandmama was only impressed by Natalie's accent—telling me right after she and Daddy departed how nicely Mrs. Lockyer-Pope spoke and that I should try and emulate her and lose my Cornish brogue. Of all the million suggestions Grandmama ever made to me, I think this was the only one I ever consciously tried to carry out.

Mama's initial reaction, though, to Daddy's new friend with her bold makeup of bright red lips and vermilion nails was hard to decipher. One minute I thought she must like her, for she kept smiling sweetly at Mrs. Lockyer-Pope and asked friendly questions about family and the Scottish Highlands. The next minute, though, Mama would wince and say how much she pitied those women who had to compete in a man's world.

I may have been young but I wasn't stupid. "Mama, you are always saying that '*Man is a man's invention.*' You told Grandmama that a woman is the equal of any man. I heard you holler at her when she started to cry because we had no man in the house. You told her she shouldn't despise her own son, Uncle Harry, even if you did."

Mama then fingered her necklace and gave me her famous cold smile. "That was a reference to the vote for women and to female scientists. I was unaware the current conversation touched upon either. However, to please a spoiled and interrupting little boy, I will ask our guest. Are you a scientist, Mrs. Lockyer-Pope?"

"Please call me Natalie. You too, Davey."

Mama ignored the request. Prudence suggested I should stay quiet in the light of Mama's crispness. There was an uncomfortable pause in the furniture-stuffed drawing room. Grandmama's silly cuckoo popped out and chirped three times, which made me want to laugh because I remembered just then that Simon had said it made a bird-fart when it told the time.

"No I am not, Mrs. Bryant. I know nothing of science, although your husband tells me you are an explosives expert."

I think we'd almost forgotten the question; her reply came so late. I held my breath. Mama had once smacked me for calling her Mrs. Bomb.

"I was engaged as such at an earlier period in life. I am now quite simply what you see, a wife and mother. There are also times, when my husband is away in his car, that I have to play the role of *farmer*."

Mama made Daddy's traveling job sound like a joyride.

"We are not usually here in Essex," I put in by way of explanation—speaking quickly for fear that Mama would shut me up. "But in Cornwall, where we farm Pol'garrow, which our family have owned since the reign of Charles the First."

"How absolutely topping," said Natalie, teeth gleaming extra white between her blood-red lips. "Your father never mentioned Pol...Pol...?"

"Polengarrow—Pol'garrow for short," I supplied. "That's because I reckon he's a bit ashamed that we've put Mr. Hambly from Pendoggett in as a tenant while Daddy tries to make money elsewhere. We were going to New Zealand and gave away our rocking horse to our cousins in Falmouth but then the slump arrived in New Zealand, too, so we had to stay home. But we are only here to Grandmama's while we catch our breath."

"Davey, stop your silly chatter," Mama said. But without energy. "Mrs. Lockyer-Pope doesn't want to hear all your Cornish nonsense or watch us wash our family linen. And how many times do I have to tell you to stop saying "*here to Grandmama's*" when "*at*" is enough?"

"But your son speaks so *beautifully*, Mrs. Bryant. I could listen to that soft burr forever!"

"I have no such luxury. No time to either listen to his prattling or endure a dialect which he'll inevitably shed when he attends Christ's Hospital School. Frankly, that can't come soon enough. Three small boys are far more volatile than high explosives—and their upbringing much more exacting!"

The room rippled with Natalie's laughter. But I didn't mind as I knew Mama had just essayed one of her well-known jokes, and would appreciate such a response instead of our usual chorus of impolite boos.

"Can I show Natalie the garden, Mama?"

There was a fractional pause as she digested the "Natalie." I was certain she would've preferred me to use the more formal designation which she herself had. For some unfathomable reason she decided to ignore my disloyalty—for the time being, at any rate.

"Don't you think it would be fitting to first ask our *guest* whether she would enjoy such an undertaking? My mother's garden is something of a jungle, Mrs. Lockyer-Pope. I am not sure you should risk such beautiful clothes amongst her briars. Davey, on the other hand, is invariably dressed for moorland hikes. Again, the Cornish in him, I fear."

"Please put your fears at rest. I, too, am of the moors, and am devoted to gardens. If it is entirely convenient I would love to have your son escort me about his grandmother's flowers."

"Then you are most welcome. While you are *al fresco* I shall call for tea. But I must warn you, you are more likely to encounter *thorns* than *blossoms*. My mother knows nothing of husbandry and is in the horticultural hands of a man who is more *forester* than gardener!"

I had heard Mama in some fairly literary flights in my nine years, but that afternoon she surpassed herself. Daddy said she only got wordy when she was cross with him, but she was amazingly calm with Natalie and smiled all the time she addressed her in a specially lilting voice with long words that I didn't always understand, even when I pretended I did. So I was sure she couldn't be cross with our charming guest.

On the parapet before the steps down to the first lawn, Natalie reached out and took my hand. I was immediately embarrassed. I glanced back nervously, hoping the action had not been observed by either of my brothers. It hadn't. Instead it was balding Uncle Harry standing there, hands clasped loosely about his protruding belly, eyeing us from the far corner of the veranda, who saw.

"Who's your lady friend, Davey? Aren't you going to do the honors?"

I avidly shared Mama's dislike of her surviving brother; and at that particular moment I wished him dead.

"We are off to see Grandmama's garden, Uncle Harry. This is a friend of Daddy's from Scotland. They work together and her name is Natalie Lockyer-Pope." I remembered what Mama had said about Uncle Harry and the woman neighbor in Leyton before he and Grandmama moved to Theydon Bois. "She's married," I added.

Uncle Harry reached out for her gloved hand—as the ungloved one was clutching mine. "Harry Newcombe. Married too," he added, chuckling. "Only the wife is away in Biarritz. Then Dora seems to prefer France to this country for some reason or other. Fact is, she's never home."

"Uncle Harry makes poisons," I told my new friend. "We aren't allowed to go into his poison shed in case of an accident."

"How interesting. A pleasure to speak with you, Mr. Newcombe. Now show me your flowers, young man. Let's start with the roses, shall we?"

I had never known an adult's voice so happily devoid of command. No one talked to me that way save my younger brother and my few friends left behind in Cornwall. I think I loved Natalie Lockyer-Pope from the moment we stood on the limestone paving stones between the twin files of standard roses and she gravely answered my questions after pondering each of them thoughtfully.

Q. Do you live in a castle in Scotland like Daddy says?

A. Names have different meanings, Davey, from place to place. In Cornwall it might possibly be called one but *manor house* might be more accurate.

Q. Not like Balmoral, then? More like Sandringham?

A. Not at all like Balmoral.

I must have looked disappointed for she placed her gloved hand on my shoulder and squeezed ever so lightly.

"I do know a castle, though, where I sometimes stay. My aunt has a flat in Hampton Court. It's what's called a grace-and-favor residence, as the king allows her to live there."

"That's not a castle," I informed her pedantically. "It's a royal palace."

"Would you like to stay there? You could have the maze to yourself and there are delicious black grapes from the Hampton Court vine. You might even see the ghost of Cardinal Wolsey. Or is it Catherine of Aragon? I'm a duffer at history."

I searched her face for raillery.

"You really stay there often?"

"Would you like to stay there one weekend?"

"I would have to ask Mama, of course."

"And I, Aunt Beatrice. But that would be only a formality."

"I think mine would be, too."

"You are a strange boy. Not at all like your father."

"Nor are you the way I thought you'd be."

"And how was that?"

"Oh, I don't know. Plump and jolly, I think. Mama said that you cheered Daddy up a lot, and that we should be grateful for that."

"She did, did she? Does she not cheer him up, then?"

"Not really. Frankly, since the Slump hit, life has been difficult. Daddy did not like leaving Pol'garrow—although he finally agreed with Mama that it was best to come up here to Grandmama's."

"Well, those are matters into which I have no right to pry. I gather you don't know London well?"

"Not as well as Wadebridge or Bodmin, of course. That has always bothered Mama. My two brothers are more inclined to city folk like her, Daddy says. I am more the countryman like him."

"You have never eaten at Gunter's or shopped at Harrods?"

"Mama has always seen that our clothes come from Daniel Neale's. I know where *that* is. The Army and Navy Stores, too. Grandmama has her account there. I have also been taken by her to Fuller's for tea, where I had their famous walnut cake."

"You must have been to Buzzard's for cake, yes?"

"No. You must remember, Natalie, I am only a small boy from the provinces, and as Grandmama never tires of reminding us, we are far from affluent."

"I shall set about our Hampton Court project right away. Before you go back to school—which is when?"

"I don't know. Mama wishes me to go to Christ's Hospital, where her father and brothers went. I was interviewed by the Head last spring and am supposed to start next term. But I'm not keen on wearing those silly clothes they have as uniforms. It's a bone of contention between us."

"Is that what she called it, Davey?"

"It's what Uncle Harry called it. He told me that there are always bones of contention between men and women."

"Even between mothers and sons?"

"Uncle Harry says that there are natural enmities between men and women—like there is between him and Mama. He says the Salic law is the natural order of things."

"What is the Salic law?"

"I don't know, Natalie. I meant to look it up in our Pear's Cyclopaedia but I keep forgetting. It has something to do with Grandpapa's will because that is the bone of contention between Mama and Uncle Harry."

"That again is something you should keep to yourself, Davey. You must try a little harder to be reticent with strangers such as myself. Especially when others are involved who wouldn't want their secrets divulged."

"But you are not a stranger. You are Daddy's friend. Mama told us we were to be *especially* nice to you and treat you as one of the family."

"She did, did she." There was a small silence as we skirted the lily pond and came to the arbor, which was festooned with fragrant honeysuckle. I felt it incumbent on me to crank up the conversation again.

"Is your husband fond of going abroad like Uncle Harry's wife, Dora? Is that why you are divorced?"

"Abroad? My ex-husband is loath to step beyond his front door—let alone travel outside of Scotland."

"That's funny."

She looked searchingly at me. "It was more painful than comic when I wished to escape entombment."

"Mama says that long separations put marriage at risk. She told Daddy that when he first went on the road with his new job. Mama now thinks he should stay home and look after Grandpapa's estate, but Grandmama says Uncle Harry could do that if he were to mope less about Aunt Dora and the Salic law."

"Do you have fish here in your pool? Goldfish or carp, perhaps?"

"The herons take them. Mama says Uncle Harry is a lecher and that's why Grandmama moved out here to Theydon Bois, where there are no close neighbors."

"Do you have a tortoise for your pond?"

"A tortoise would drown, silly! It should be a turtle. They can swim and need water to live. It is roughly the difference between frogs and toads. Or newts and lizards. Though that is the difference between amphibians and reptiles."

"You seem *very* knowledgeable about these things."

"Oh, I am! I am! I want to be a zookeeper when I grow up. That or a veterinarian."

"That, of course, would require good schooling such as Christ's Hospital, wouldn't it?"

"There are others with less silly uniforms. There is the City of London School, Bancrofts, the Coopers' Company School, Merchant Taylors' and many more. I have made a study of them and can show you my list, if you like, of schools all near London."

"Later, perhaps. Would you like a turtle? I believe they are available from Harrods' Zoo."

"I would love a *terrapin*, that's what I'd like, Natalie."

"What exactly is that?"

"A North American turtle. They aren't too expensive. That would fit very well in the lily pool, as I've told both Grandmama and Uncle Harry. But they are not interested in the garden, as you heard Mama say before we came out."

"Then if we secure permission from your mother and her family, we will have two things to look forward to. A trip to Harrods together and a visit to Gunter's for tea. And then that weekend at Hampton Court." She seemed almost to be planning a trip for herself.

I pondered her statement. "I think Mama would want my brother Simon to join me on such an outing. She is against favoritism and I am far from her favorite!"

"She might well enjoy your absence, Davey. Actually, I don't think Aunt could manage more than one at a time. Let me discuss things with your mother when we go in."

That is what she must have done, because when I was in bed and prayers were over, Mama closed the door between my room and Arthur's and sat down at the bottom of the counterpane.

"I understand Mrs. Lockyer-Pope has invited you to her aunt's place at Hampton Court and offered you a turtle?"

I nodded. "Her ex-husband is loath to step beyond his front door. Would you call him a hermit, Mama?"

"Probably. Do you wish to visit Hampton Court? It would be a very grand affair, you know that?"

"Yes, Mama. I have never stayed in a palace."

"None of us has, Davey. It should prove a great adventure, if you behave and learn to curb that little tongue of yours. As for the terrapin she mentioned, I would be personally happier if you could seek to persuade her to buy you a white rat. That would remind me of those I had in the lab before you were born. I would then purchase a female companion and we could breed them. You would learn some practical biology in your summer holidays. Of course, we would hold off their mating until your return from Horsham for the vac."

Crafty Mama! I had traveled to Horsham for the interview with the headmaster of Christ's Hospital School with its bizarre clothes.

"I would prefer a turtle, Mama. It would require less attention, and *wherever* I attend school there will surely be lots of studying to do in the summer."

Mama got up from the bed. "We shall think about it," she said. "It will largely end up in your grandmother's hands. Like so much around here," she sighed. Her mouth was so tight, her lips were as dry and compressed as Natalie's had been moist-red.

CHAPTER FOUR

When Mama announced it had been arranged for her to accompany Natalie and me to Hampton Court for the weekend I flew into a temper, threw a glass paperweight from Grandpapa's desk in Grandmama's sitting room at her and ran screaming upstairs to my bedroom. If I had been able to move any of the heavy Victorian furniture to the door I would have barricaded myself in. I did not want her to enter for I did not want to reveal the source of my upset. I loved Mama, but Natalie was my new friend and I didn't want to share her with anyone. Certainly not with Mama and certainly not in a magical place like a royal palace.

For a long time I lay huddled on my bed and refused to respond to her knocking. There was no lock on the bedroom door but Mama, I knew, would act as if there were an imaginary one there. She only entered when I called out her name—when I thought that perhaps she had returned downstairs. She came right to me and clasped me tight while I snuggled to her warmth and tried to think of what to say. I didn't have to worry. Mama did all the talking.

"I think it was very nice of Mrs. Lockyer-Pope to ask me along with you, don't you, Davey?"

I made no answer.

"You know that I too have never stayed overnight in a palace."

"*Two* nights," I mumbled from somewhere in her cleavage.

"Her aunt is Lady Beatrice Spicer-Hewitt. She is the daughter of the Marquis of Leddingham. I looked them up in Papa's *Debrett*."

"What's that?"

"A book with the names of great families in it."

"Are we in there?"

"Don't be silly, darling."

"I don't see why not. Our family goes back to Charles the Second. You told me so yourself."

"The Bryants are not in there, I assure you. Even my family is absent—although I suspect that would have all changed had Guy survived the war and eventually carried on where Papa left off."

I wasn't interested in hearing more about her brother or her father—at least, not then. Natalie and her aristocratic lineage concerned me much more.

"Why does the new king let Natalie's aunt live there? Won't she have to give it up now that King George the Fifth is dead?"

"*Some* sons honor their father's wishes.... In any case, she is a widow and her husband was an important commander during the Great War. I wonder if he ever met Guy," Mama mused. "It is quite probable, as he was also on the Western Front and must have known all about my brother's bravery in the skies when he was spotting for our guns."

"Was he a field marshal, Mama?"

"He was a general, according to the book. Brigadier General Sir Arthur Spicer-Hewitt, Bart."

"What a mouthful, Mama! Why do Natalie and her relatives have names so much longer than ours?"

"You must not be disrespectful, Davey. Many of the best families have hyphenated surnames. They are sometimes referred to as 'double-barreled.' It is a way of preserving the fact that two great bloodlines have come together."

"Simon says that Natalie's name is Lockyer-Pope because there are too many Popes around. He says that people called Smith or Jones often put another name in front for the same reason."

"Simon is happiest when he is tearing people down. He will be a much better boy when he learns to build things *up*."

"But he is usually right, isn't he, Mama? Simon is very clever."

"I can't see why you ask me about hyphenated names when it is obvious you've already discussed it with him. No one loved a brother more than I did mine, but I would not have dreamed of going to him for information and then trying to trip up Papa with it!"

"I am sorry, Mama. I do these things without thinking. They just pop into my little head and make me wicked."

"You are more thoughtless than wicked, darling. Selfishly so. Such as not wanting me to see a wonderful place like Hampton Court with you. Or meet a famous lady."

"Has Natalie met the new king, Mama?"

"That you would have to ask her," Mama said. "Or your father," she added tartly. "I know nothing of her friends or her social circle. Indeed, she has probably told you more about herself. I suspect she is a woman who opens more easily to children than to adults."

"Simon says you don't like her very much. He says that you—"

"Davey! Please stop telling me what my twelve-year-old son thinks! I will ask him whenever I think it of the slightest importance. For your information, though, I am rather fond of your Natalie Lockyer-Pope. Do not forget that it was I, not your Grandmama, who invited her here to The Hornbeams. Nor would I be keen to be her guest and her aunt's if I entertained the slightest hostility toward her. She is good company for your father when he is away with all this traveling, and I am grateful, too, for that. You may pass *that* information on to Simon if you wish, as he seems so interested in my feelings over people!"

"Are you cross now, Mama?"

"How could I be cross when I'm holding my little boy's head in my arms and we are discussing an exciting adventure that we are going to have?"

"When are we going to Hampton Court, Mama?"

I felt her body relax all over as I conceded our trip was to be shared. "In just under two weeks' time. Grandmama will be here with Little Arthur, and Simon has somehow persuaded Uncle Harry to accompany him to North Weald aerodrome to watch the Royal Flying Corps aeroplanes take off and land."

I was about to correct her and tell her that the R.F.C. was now called the Royal Air Force, but thought it might lead to further recollections of Uncle Guy and the war. "I wonder whether Natalie will give me my terrapin when we arrive at Hampton Court or if we will make a separate visit to Harrods."

"I should think she would want that to be a special outing with you—which would only be proper."

"Do you think that one day Natalie will buy me a mongoose like Rikki-Tikki-Tavi in *The Jungle Book?*"

"You mustn't be so *mercenary*, Davey. Anyway, I'm sure your father would disapprove. He doesn't like pets as much as we do, and they're far too much like ferrets for him."

"They aren't really, Mama. Ferrets are *Mustela* and kill chickens. But the mongoose belongs to the *Viverridae* family and attacks snakes. I looked it up. You know how Daddy hates adders. Remember how he smashed in the head of the one we found in Uncle Nick's quarry? He wouldn't even let me keep a grass snake at Pol'garrow!"

"I cannot see your grandmother welcoming one here, either. You must not forget this is not our own home. We are not as free to do things as we might otherwise be."

"I know that, Mama. *She* doesn't let us forget for a single minute!"

"*She* is the cat's mother, young man. Grandmama has been kind enough to provide a roof for us during these difficult times."

"I bet Uncle Guy would have let me have a mongoose," I said slyly.

To my acute disappointment she didn't rise to the bait. "We'll take the train to Liverpool Street," she said. "Then a taxi to the Embankment and from there the river bus down to Richmond and Hampton Court. You'll like that, Davey. They say the decorations are already going up for next year's coronation in the Abbey. You will also be able to see so many famous buildings after we board at London Bridge. You might look them up in your books between now and Saturday week so you will be able to show me which is which."

I was debating ways to both demonstrate my enthusiasm over our projected expedition (thus pleasing her) and get back to the subject of a mongoose when Little Arthur called her name from his adjoining bedroom.

She rose with a start. "I promised him a bedtime story," she said, putting two cool fingers lightly to my forehead before hurrying to her youngest child.

******

It was over our joint expedition to Hampton Court that September that I first recall Mama complaining of one of her brief but raging headaches. At the last moment it was decided that we were to join Natalie on the steps of St. Paul's. She had a meeting in the City that morning, and this way, she suggested, she could give us lunch in town before escorting us upriver to Richmond.

When Mama put the phone down on hearing the new arrangements for the following day, she complained that her head was throbbing. She also made a funny face. It wasn't a look I could read easily, but when she tossed that imaginary lock away from her forehead I knew she was what she sometimes referred to as "put out." She didn't mention the headache again but I think that was because she was soon distracted by having to change her plans.

"We shall dispense with the train ride to Liverpool Street. Your uncle can drive us to The Baker's Arms in Leyton and we can take the tram to town."

"Can we sit on top in front, Mama?" I had only ridden in a tramcar once and had found it thrilling. I had loved the frequent clamor of the warning bell and the perilous swaying from side to side as it sped along the curve of its rails. I also enjoyed the reversible seats that allowed you to face in the opposite direction whenever you wanted. And the top deck had seemed much higher, offering better views, than those of the more prosaic motorbuses.

She had agreed readily. I think she was rather pleased that the first leg of our trip was going to be through the territory of her youth and thus something she and I would enjoy in a special way. Simon did not like going out with Mama or hearing her stories, while Little Arthur only fidgeted on public transport and pestered everyone to buy him a choc-ice.

The day started more happily than I had anticipated, considering Mama's initial reaction to the changes wrought by Natalie. First there was the bustling market at The Baker's Arms itself. I had to clutch Mama's arm merely not to lose her! The crowd spilled from the narrow sidewalk into the curb and over to the traffic island where the public lavatories and horse trough stood. And at every stall and open-fronted store there were shopkeepers raucously yelling their wares in cockney accents which I couldn't understand.

Nor could I always "understand" what was being sold. There were weird fruits which Mama said were pomegranates, and stalls of exotic shellfish which she explained were cockles and winkles and a great teatime favorite of these voluble East Enders. Even more fascinating were the huge tanks of what I took to be watersnakes sliding about behind the glass. To my horror, I saw a shirt-sleeved shopkeeper grab one such slimy length and, after amputating its head, slice its body into two or three parts and drop them, still squirming, into a blood-splattered enamel bowl. Mama heard my shriek of dismay. Turned quickly. She saw what I was pointing at with trembling arm—and laughed out loud.

"They're just eels, silly. They sell eels both live and fresh-killed. And the jellied ones in those jars over there—look!"

But I was not going to look at any more executions or chopping. I tugged her coat arm instead, my mood violently changed. "I don't like it here, Mama. I don't like their nasty, smelly fish—or the way they shout at you. Mr. Trebilcock down to Port Isaac doesn't shout when he comes around. And why don't they sell mackerel and crab, salmon and lobster, like he does?"

"I daresay they'd be too expensive up here," she said. "And different people have different tastes. Look at the French with their frog legs and snails!"

"I can't see any difference between snails and those winkles," I said. "Aren't winkles a snail that lives in the sea, Mama?" I asked. "And if I were forced, I'd rather eat frogs than snakes like those."

"*Eels*," she corrected. "And you're beginning to sound like Simon, Davey. Don't be so argumentative. I want you to be on your best behavior, as we're going to drop in on two old ladies who were friends of Poppa's and knew us as children."

"I thought we were going to take the Number 61 tramcar to Dalston."

"Right after we've visited the Misses Mumford. Miss Amy and Miss Lucy."

"Won't we be late for Natalie at St. Paul's Cathedral, Mama? I should not want to miss Christopher Wren's masterpiece."

"Certainly not. I deliberately arranged that we take care of a couple of items of business on our way up to town. That is why we left earlier than your uncle wanted. He didn't know that I was planning to take in the Misses Mumford and another stop too. Then I had no intention that he should."

We walked for some while longer but fortunately the sidewalk had grown wider and there were fewer people. The shops were now interspersed with private residences and set back farther from the road. It was at one little shop with a faded blind drawn across its windows that we stopped; Mama signaled me to enter.

I had never been in such a pokey place before but Mama seemed at ease from the outset. Then it was obvious she knew the inhabitants well and that the two white-haired old ladies who darted about with pince-nez spectacles on their noses held her in special esteem, too. I couldn't tell one from the other.

"Davey, come and meet the Misses Mumford—Miss Amy and Miss Lucy. They are twins—just like your Canadian cousins, Leslie and Jennifer."

Mama spoke the obvious when she remarked that they were twins. What she neglected to add was that they were also *dwarfs*. I swear that neither was taller than me!

They fluttered about my person like demented moths.

"So this is your little boy, Miss Isabella. Well, I can see Old Mr. Newcombe in him, can't you, Lucy?"

"Ain't no doubt he's a Newcombe," added the one with the gray shawl draped over her bent shoulders in spite of the warm day. It was the only distinguishing item between them. They both wore shiny black dresses and gaitered black boots with pointed toes.

"And not just your father, Miss Isabella," Lucy screeched through a mouthful of pins. "He's the spitting image of darling Master Guy, ain't he, Amy?"

"Oh, yes, he's Master Guy all right—all over again," Amy confirmed. "Don't you worry, Miss Isabella. While this boy walks God's earth your brother won't never die!"

I saw Mama's mouth tighten but the two old ladies seemed not to notice.

"I have brought Davey here for a fitting," Mama announced, quite startling me. "I would like him to have a Mumford Sunday suit."

Her statement sent Amy into even further paroxysms. "A suit! Why yes, of course! A suit for the boy! It will be like making one all over again for Master Guy or Master Harry. There ain't many children round here wanting custom tailorin' any more, Miss Isabella. For that matter, there ain't many men left over from the war needing fine tailoring. We seem to do only *mature ladies* nowadays. I say, what a treat to do what we do best, ain't it, Lucy?"

Her twin was neither to be outdone in excitement nor to be side-tracked from comparisons between current flesh and my dead ancestors. "I can't think whether he looks more like you, Miss Isabella, or your brother Guy when he was a strapping little lad. A Sunday suit, you say? Then it would be navy serge and a white collar—with extra material in the knickerbockers, I dare say!"

I was about to enquire of Mama what knickerbockers were when Miss Amy forestalled me.

"Lucy is still thinking of *our* father cutting suiting for *your* father, Miss Isabella, when *he* was a young fella. This one will be wanting flannel—not serge—Lucy. And he'll want shorts *above* the knee, I'll be bound."

Lucy was already advancing on me with a measuring tape. I had to struggle with myself not to back away in alarm as the witch-like little thing grew close. I noticed her white hair had lots of hairpins sticking halfway in—or out, perhaps, for I'd already seen several amid the scraps of cloth and strips of lining material littering the floor.

"When you was a girl, Miss Isabella, it was always sailor suits for the boys, weren't it? Master Guy looked so sweet in his nice broad collar Mr. Mumford made for him."

"Come to think of it, all three of you children had sailor outfits made on the premises, including you, dearie!"

Mama smiled sweetly if unconvincingly. "I do believe you are correct, Miss Lucy. Then Poppa went to great lengths to prevent jealousy among us children. And he liked us to look alike even if I was the only daughter—especially for our Sunday walk, when he always accompanied us. My goodness, what changes the world's seen since then! Fathers don't walk dutifully with their children on the Sabbath any more and children seem to wear whatever they please!"

"King Teddy was on the throne in them days, with that beautiful deaf Dane of a queen—not that he cared whether she was pretty!" Miss Amy somberly reflected.

"Why would he have cared?" Lucy spat through her pins before slipping the tape round my waist. "He was surrounded by all them rich Jews—not forgetting that Mrs. Keppel."

I was wearing my best flannel shorts from Daniel Neale's, which Miss Lucy now coldly eyed down her beaky nose through her pince-nez. "Hello! Hello! *H'amateurs* at work here, I'm afraid! These trousers don't hang straight. And the legs ain't the same length neither."

"Jest *measure* him, Lucy," her sister ordered, in a voice suggesting it was she who was truly in charge.

I started to look about me—to avoid embarrassment as Lucy's veined hand fluttered over my legs in quest of specific measurements. It was impossible to see the walls of the small shop since bales of cloth were piled from floor to ceiling in every direction. The main illumination was a naked lightbulb suspended from the discolored ceiling, but on the long, low table which took up at least half of the floorspace stood a desklamp with a cracked green shade.

I wondered how either of them could reach the tabletop, on which I saw two pairs of gigantic scissors and snapped-off pieces of chalk, until I noticed several footstools placed strategically about the table's length. They, of course, would allow the tiny tailors to mount higher when cutting the chalk-marked silhouettes in the unrolled cloth. The chief smell in the stuffy room was the acrid one of wool. It was so sharp my nostrils tingled. It made me think of sheep-dipping time at Polengarrow and then, nostalgically, of Cornwall and everything I had left behind.

My sadness wasn't dispelled by listening to the dwarfs remind Mama of their shared past with her; of visits to the local cricket field on long-ago summer days when she had sat in the long grass with her father, politely clapping for her brothers when they batted or bowled their way to invariable victory. Having no part in such memories, I became progressively more monosyllabic in my bored replies to occasionally interjected questions about how I was enjoying life in Theydon Bois, and my grandmother's home in particular. Their mild cockney seemed as alien as the broader accents of the street vendors earlier, and I was glad when Mama had chosen a blue velvet suit for me, arranged for a later fitting and bid farewell to the two diminutive women, and we had escaped once more to the open air.

To my surprise, though, Mama was as animated and bright-eyed as I felt listless. At great length, as we walked for what seemed to me an eternity along the dusty street to the place we could board the tram, she showered me with stories about the Misses Mumford, their tyrannical tailor father and their two tailor brothers, both of whom had been killed in the war. But I was determined to register my grumpiness as Mama had not commented on my unusual silence. "I can remember, Mama, your telling me that none of us looked a bit like Uncle Guy or Grandpapa, but those two dwarfs said the exact opposite!"

"Do not be disrespectful, Davey. They are getting old and the old forget how things really were. Besides, it was well known that the Mumford girls were inclined to be fanciful. One of them made up a ridiculous story about your Uncle Harry, I remember."

"Why did we go there, then? Why are they making my suit?"

"Because Poppa always did, young man. And that is good enough reason for me. The other things don't matter."

When the tram swung into sight I had begun to hate all the Mumfords, known and unknown. But I couldn't banish a vision of Mama in the long grass of that cricket field, all pretty in white with a floppy hat and looking like some painting I had seen on the lid of a biscuit tin. I preferred it to the other one I entertained of her before my birth. That was also of her in white, but in a blood-stained coat in her munitions lab with her scampering rats, and surrounded by her dead and wounded assistants while a coldly disapproving Poppa awaited her at home.

CHAPTER FIVE

Sitting right up front as we rocked and pitched our way ever deeper into London, I was blind to derelict lots boarded up and papered with competing posters displaying either the Communist hammer and sickle or the lightning flashes of the British Union of Fascists. I also ignored the miles of slum monotony perforated by gray washing poking through grimy windows for questionable benefit from the soot-filled air. For me there was no swarm of noisy children laughing at thin dogs pissing insouciantly against the tile of shop fronts. I saw nothing of the unemployed adults lounging aimlessly, occasionally yelling in the nasalities of cockney or Yiddish at the scurrying world of the working poor. I glimpsed no aproned vendors hawking cheap deal furniture on the sidewalks, no kerchiefed housewives with huge black bags queuing for offal, or newsboys, with white silk scarves unseasonably about their dirty necks, calling out headlines from early editions.

Instead, I was wholly absorbed in the role of captain on the bridge of the ship, my imagination riding an Atlantic swell as I navigated my noisy tram-craft. I sniffed only brine and was deaf to everything save those ocean gales which had tingled my Cornish ears since birth. No stench of carbon and electricity, no frying food from the busy stalls below or fumes from the incessant traffic entered *my* nostrils; no squeal of brakes or clop of Clydesdales tugging brewers' drays found *my* ears. I was lulled by the streetcar's rhythm and the lofty view from my slatted wood seat, my senses soothed by imaginary immensities of an empty ocean and a westerly sky. It was Mama who abruptly returned me to the *proletarian* sea that was her native East End of London by that summer of 1936.

"That took rather longer than I thought. We shall have to postpone our visit to our solicitor, Mr. Patmore, until we can make a special visit to Lincoln's Inn. We could combine that with a visit to the toy department at Gamages—and see all the old buildings in High Holborn. You'd like that, wouldn't you, Davey?"

"Yes, Mama," I said, resenting her intrusion into my fantasy. "Whatever you say."

She seemed to take my flat response as encouragement to chat. "You know that nearly all these arches beneath the railway bridges we go under were owned by Poppa and let out to ostlers and the like?"

"I don't know what an ostler is, Mama."

She waved a gloved hand vaguely. "Something to do with horses. It's a word Poppa always used."

If I had thought for a moment that by offering her "ostler" as a sop I was going to buy myself release from the present and return to my great, green Atlantic, I was mistaken. All I had done was set in motion one of those sterile catechisms to which all children are boringly subjected by adults, and which Mama could perpetrate with the best of them.

"Do you see that large sign for the Michelin man? Know what used to stand there?"

"No, Mama."

"A row of thatched cottages belonging to your great-grandfather. They were pulled down, though, when even I was a girl. We're coming to The Ring of Bells—right past there is Tetley's Infirmary. Poppa was on the hospital board in the old days."

Perhaps to generate a more emphatic response from me, Mama suddenly clutched my arm. "Oh, I know what we shall soon be passing. Remember my telling you about the zeppelins, Davey? Well, one of them dropped a bomb on Ridley Road where the dairy was."

That wasn't where I remembered Mama saying the bomb had dropped, but I didn't want a discussion of that any more than I wanted a quiz game over her London childhood. I kept quiet.

"We're heading for Stoke Newington, where Aunt Libby and Uncle Horace lived. We would go over there some Sunday afternoons and Aunt Libby would sing sacred songs and Uncle would play his harp. They were all very artistic, were the Harringtons. Young Sidney played the cello with the Stoke Newington Orpheus Players and his brother Cuthbert sang with the Royal Choral Society up west, I remember."

This was something I definitely had *not* heard about previously, and my interest stirred a tiny bit. It was certainly better than being told all the time that what I was looking at used to be something else! But at the precise moment she embarked on her recollections of that highly musical family, she was hailed by a stranger who sat down opposite us.

"It *is* Isabella Newcombe, ain't it?"

The tram had jerked to a violent halt. I stared crossly out of the window at an ugly fence of corrugated iron on which a mass meeting for pacifism in the Royal Albert Hall organized by the Peace Pledge Union was advertised. I didn't want a repeat of the Misses Mumford—whom this woman in a blue beret and belted raincoat sounded uncomfortably like.

"Mama, where is the Royal Albert Hall? And what is pacifism?"

I might have saved my breath. The woman across the aisle elicited a happy wave of recognition from my mother.

"Cissy Bateman! *What* a surprise! Davey, this is your Aunt Cissy, of all people!"

"I use me full name of Cecilia now, Isabella. And of course, you ain't Newcombe no more if this little lad's your son. What you say his name was?"

Here were the same whiny accents which the midgets had employed—indeed, which all that vulgar mob below in the street used. I suddenly detested this woman whom Mama was slobbering over.

"Be introduced to your aunt, Davey. Her father was your Grandmama's brother. We were such pals when we were youngsters, weren't we, Cissy? I suppose you still live here. It was The Laurels, Wellesley Road, wasn't it? Just off the Lea Bridge marshes?"

"*She* isn't my aunt, Mama. If she's the daughter of Grandpapa's brother, then she's your cousin and she's only my second cousin—or that *remove* thing."

I waited sullenly for another attack from Mama about my using 'she' for a human being and not confining its usage to a female cat—only it didn't come. She was distracted by her horrible relative.

The cockney-tongued woman laughed like an imbecile. "Ain't he the clever one!" she hooted. "He's quite right, of course, Izzy! Remember that was what we called you back in them days, wasn't it? He'd be me first cousin once removed, that's what the little darlin' is!"

She leaned across and for one awful moment I thought she was about to stretch over to kiss me, but Mama prevented the woman planting her horrible lips on my face by raising her arm to pat her hair nervously and fuss with her beads. In any case, I am sure Mama would not have approved of such unsolicited familiarity in the cause of kinship.

"Going down to Cornwall and marrying Davey's father I'm afraid has put me *quite* out of touch. Mother is living in Theydon Bois, right on the edge of Epping Forest. We are staying there until this young man goes away to his boarding school."

Mama rarely sat quite so stiffly. "So much for our dull news. And how are your people, Cecilia? I heard about poor Randal, of course, and you must know we lost Guy that same dreadful year."

"Didn't we thank God when that was all over—though my hubby says we could be at war all over again, what with this Hitler blighter startin' up in Germany."

"I didn't even know you were married, Cissy—sorry, Cecilia. Do you have a family?"

"We have Fred, who's nine, and Georgia is only five. To tell the truth, I'm really glad we don't have no more, Isabella, what with Ned 'aving his wages cut back by the gas board last Feb and my losing me job at Bryant & Mays."

"I'm sorry to hear that, Cecilia. Life is very hard for so many. We ourselves had to make a few adjustments."

"I'm sure you did, dear. Mind you, you Newcombes always had the edge over the rest of us. No doubt where your Dad and his lot were when the brains was distributed, Izzy! He was streets ahead of the rest of the family and it always showed. It was sad he had to die so young, but at least he left your Mum comfortable. You and yours was always toffs compared with the rest—no point in denying it, luv."

"Don't we have to change trams soon, Mama? We wouldn't want to be late, would we?"

"At Essex Road, darling. There's plenty of time. Why don't you tell Cecilia about where we are going for the weekend."

I needed no encouragement. Anything to put distance between us and this drab creature who claimed such close ties to Mama and the family! I gave my youthful snobbery full vent. "We are off to stay at Hampton Court Palace with friends of the new king," I piped. "But first we are meeting the Honorable Natalie Lockyer-Pope for luncheon. The assassination is at St. Paul's."

I couldn't understand why the two of them started laughing. Mama sounded even crueller than Cecilia. Tears started to run down her cheeks and she actually hugged me up there on the tram for all to see. I wriggled away and glowered at them both.

"It's not *funny*! You may want to be late but I know that 'punctuality is the politeness of kings.'"

They laughed even louder, if such was possible. That stupid Cecilia dabbed her eyes with a nasty little hanky. "We ain't disputin' *that*, deary. You're quite right there, my angel!"

"Dear child—the word's *assignation* not *assassination*."

"I said assignation, Mama."

"No, Davey, you did *not.*"

"I did, Mama."

"Are you implying that Cecilia and I are deaf? Or worse, that we are telling falsehoods?" The laughter had gone as quickly as she'd summoned it. I sensed danger.

"After that we are going to eat at Gunter's in Mayfair. From there we shall take the river bus to Richmond, where I expect the Honorable Beatrice Spicer-Hewitt will meet us. She, Cecilia, is the daughter of the Marquis of Leddingham, who served with such distinction in the Great War."

"No, darling. It was her *husband*, Sir Arthur Spicer-Hewitt, who was the war hero—just like our own dear Guy."

"Oh, I didn't know that, Isabella," her cousin put in quickly. "What was it your brother got decorated for? Other than risk his dear life flying over the German lines? Before the accident in Piccadilly, of course. We saw that in the newspaper. Then Fred ran into your brother Harry at The Green Man in Leytonstone and he give him all the unpleasant details."

"What accident, Mama?"

But Mama had grown pale and was staring wide-eyed at her cousin, who went on as if she were exchanging pasty recipes. "I gather he knew nothing about the *petit mal*, then? Tragic, when you think about it. Just forty seconds stuck like that and suffocated! If someone had heard his knocking they could've saved him. He what had risked his young life over and over again up there in the sky—a goner from being stuck in a public lavatory! The shame of it for your family! We always said—"

"Shame? There was no shame! Only pride in a young aviator who died for king and country. You are a fool, Cissy. Then when weren't you!" Mama turned away to grab fiercely at my arm.

"This isn't Essex Road. We haven't—"

But Mama was already on her feet, dragging me in her wake. She didn't even bother to say goodbye to my First-Cousin-Cecilia-Once-Removed but, with head erect, hastened along the deck of the tram toward its spiral staircase.

Even in the flurry of our departure, I realized her shaking had little to do with that of the vehicle as it sped clamorously past an edifice of ugly yellow clay bricks with giant blue squiggles on its façade, next to the legend TEMPLE EMMANUEL inscribed in brackets. Instinct as well as experience suggested I refrain, then, from asking Mama questions. But I determined to save up those which would illumine the mysterious death of Uncle Guy, which she had never, ever mentioned.

She was not really recovered by the time we had descended from both a second tram and an omnibus and found ourselves outside St.Paul's cathedral. I decided I liked Christopher Wren's building. For that matter, I much preferred the cramped City of London with its huddle of imposing buildings to the strung-out East End we had just bumpily traversed.

I told Natalie this as soon as she descended the broad flight of steps to greet us with outstretched arm and welcoming smile. "I much prefer this building, which was Christopher Wren's masterpiece, to the Temple Emmanuel we passed on the tram, Natalie. Then I do not care at all for the East End—or its people."

Mama may have been a little swept up in the warmth of Natalie's greeting, for she forgot, for once, to defend that part of London so wrapped up with her infancy and young womanhood. But she did not forget to have a peck at me. She looked at Natalie's jaunty pillbox hat with its tiny veil that just covered her forehead—and adjusted the pin in her own plain angora beret. "Oh Davey! There's no comparison—this is the Cathedral of London, the largest city in the world, and the capital of the empire, while that's just a poor synagogue put up by Stoke Newington's Jews. You must learn *proportion*, darling!"

"What's a synagogue? It said 'temple' on the front—next to some squiggles I couldn't make out."

"That was Hebrew. And a synagogue is a Jewish church. Temple is just a posher way of saying the same thing."

"You never told me. Then there's lots you never tell me," I added maliciously—thinking of public toilets....

"You usually ask, sweetheart. I can't think why you didn't when we passed the synagogue." She turned to Natalie and smiled helplessly. "He's usually stuffed with questions that I couldn't possibly answer!"

I burned at the injustice of that—recalling the blurting Cecilia and Mama's immense rage. I was almost tempted to bring up Uncle Guy dying in the lav—in spite of my good resolutions. But Natalie saved me by hailing a taxi and insisting Mama and I enter first.

CHAPTER SIX

When we disembarked from the riverboat I was vaguely disappointed to discover that Lady Beatrice Spicer-Hewitt was not there to meet us with a vast retinue of servants, but there was no doubting her palpable presence as she poured tea expressly for me shortly after we had been ushered into her drawing room above the Tudor courtyard of Hampton Court Palace. Mama and Natalie had been escorted by some maid to attend to female arrangements. I had pleaded to accompany them but had been told firmly by Mama (more reluctantly by Natalie) that my presence was not wanted and that I was to entertain our hostess instead. Indeed, the old lady herself made it imperiously clear that she wanted only me for tea, and wished to see neither of them again until they were formally dressed for the evening.

I was keenly aware of my name *not* being mentioned in the context of these arrangements. My consequent anxiety, as I sat facing the white-haired figure in her cashmere sweater and string of pearls, while age-blotched hands gripped the silver teapot, was that I was going to be fobbed off with tea and then sent packing—while the grown-up world enjoyed itself into the night. I balanced an embossed plate uncomfortably on my bare knees and eyed the craggy widow with mistrust. She smelled pleasant enough—of talc and lavender water, I concluded—but she distinctly lacked her niece's ineffable sweetness. This was a woman, I decided, who was far from being automatically well disposed toward children. Her next words confirmed my suspicions.

"Are you an obnoxious boy? You look as if you well might be!"

I wasn't sure what she meant. "I had a bath before we left The Hornbeams, Lady Beatrice Spicer-Hewitt."

She waved an arm dismissively. "You misunderstand. But let us start by addressing each other correctly. You should call me simply '*Lady Beatrice.*' I am the widow of the twelfth baronet as well as the daughter of a peer. I gather you are *David* something?"

Nervousness quickly receded before stung pride. "I am Master *Davey* Bryant," I said indignantly. "At least on envelopes. You can call me Davey, though. But *not* David. I hate that name and won't answer to it."

"My mistake. It is good enough for the present king. I only supposed—"

"But he isn't Cornish, is he? When he became the Prince of Wales he stopped being the Duke of Cornwall, and now that he is Edward the Eighth he isn't called anything else."

"To return to my original question. I did not ask whether you were *noxious* but *obnoxious*. The words have quite different meanings."

I was about to say that I thought she'd used the former but, recalling the embarrassing mistake on the tram over "assassination," thought better of it. I still had to swallow hard, though, before I could look her in the eye and reply. "I don't think I am obnoxious, Lady Beatrice, but that will be for you to decide. Mama and I are most grateful for your kind invitation, which we've been much looking forward to, Lady Beatrice."

"You do not have to use my name with every breath, especially when we are alone. You are a most precocious boy—do you know what that means?"

"Precocious means 'advanced for one's age.'"

"You appear to have that off pat. You have obviously been asked the question before?"

"Quite often, Lady Spicer-Hewitt. I looked it up when I was seven. I am now—well, nearly eleven. People often ask my age, too."

"What happened to *Beatrice*?"

I almost dropped my plate with its chocolate éclair (in Mama's absence I had deliberately foregone the prior discipline of bread and butter) as I intercepted a distinct wink.

"I am sorry—Lady *Beatrice*. I must say these are very good pastries. Do you get supplies from Fuller's? They do a very good walnut cake with cream icing."

"You would have to ask Sullivan."

"I don't think I've met him."

"Sullivan is my housekeeper. She and Heather—whom you *have* met—look after me. There is also Hamilton, who drives me about, but you are not likely to meet him in the apartments. He has a place of his own in the mews."

"You seem well provided for, Lady Beatrice. Poor Mama only had Sarah to help out with the Monday wash and Mrs. Harris, our weekly cleaning woman. But they had to be left behind in Cornwall."

"Did you enjoy that éclair? You may have another, you know. And I am told Sullivan prepared something special for you under that lid. You had better take a peek before deciding if you can manage another cake, too."

I did as she told me; found myself looking down at some kind of open-faced tart with a dark, sugary substance as its filling.

"I think I'll try another pastry first," I opined. "Maybe that cream-horn? They are one of my favorites."

"Natalie discussed the baked article with Sullivan. I believe it to be a Cornish treacle tart, and something of a delicacy where you come from, my niece tells me."

It didn't look like any treacle tart I had ever known—and Grandma Bryant served them up at least one Sunday teatime each month! Then I thought of Natalie and how kind it was of her to think of me when talking to Sullivan.

"I think I *will* have a piece of that first," I conceded. "I often get homesick and it will make me feel closer to those I've left behind."

"Gracious me! I had no idea things have been such a wrench for you. Natalie told me you discussed similarities between Cornwall and Scotland."

"I have looked up Scotland since I met Natalie and now I know we share more than what we talked about when she came to The Hornbeams. They are also Celts up there, and even if we don't have golden eagles or the Scottish wildcat, we do share the Atlantic salmon and wild moorland ponies."

"You have worked hard, young man, in your research. I gather your father and Natalie are colleagues in the same firm. He would appear to spend a great deal of time away from home on behalf of that company."

"That is one of the drawbacks of the job, and why he is anxious to farm again in Cornwall as soon as possible. Natalie has been a great comfort to him when he is on the road and Mama says we must be grateful to her for her companionship."

"Your mother appears an unusual woman. She is less single-minded than my niece."

"She is quite remarkable, Daddy says, though sometimes difficult. She is greatly wedded to London, where her Poppa owned property. That is currently in the courts, though, as Uncle Harry believes in the Salic law and is fighting Grandpapa's will. Mama's Patmore & Wilkes are involved in a legal wrangle with Beveridge, Beveridge, Philmore & Joyce, who represent Uncle Harry. Grandmama is the only one who doesn't have to worry, as she is living off the interest the estate brings in. She is not a happy woman, though, as she married above her station."

"Stop talking like that," Lady Beatrice said firmly. "It is disrespectful to your grandmother."

I fell silent.

"Where on earth did you learn such snobbish twaddle? It's bad enough with adults—from a child it's repulsive!"

Her reproving tone was new: its caustic disdain scared me. "I'm only telling you what Mama said." My eyes brimmed. It was anyone's guess whether that was prompted by a sense of injustice or mere self-pity.

"Do not cry—that won't help at all." Her voice was a tad kindlier. "I shouldn't blame a child for parroting other people."

I sniffed. "I'm not a parrot. I want to go to Mama."

"Because I forgave you as a child—it doesn't mean you should now be *childish.* You're having tea with me and neither of us is yet finished. What about one of those chocolate and strawberry things? I particularly recommend them."

I grudgingly took from the plate she indicated, only partly mollified.

She eyed me closely. "I hope you're not the sullen type of boy. I've already told you I do not blame you for repeating something someone else said. How many kinds of apology do you want from an old woman?"

I stared right back at her. I couldn't believe I was hearing aright. No one had ever apologized to *me*—not even Mama, who would sometimes clutch my head and rock it while she was saying that she should never really have been a mother.

"I know I can be a naughty boy. If you ask Mama she'll tell you—"

Again she interrupted me. But this time without a hint of anger. Only a brusqueness which, I was beginning to realize, was there all the time. "I would not dream of asking her any such thing! I detest telltales. I am sure you do, too."

I wanted her respect. I agreed warmly. "I certainly do! Mama told me she only decided to marry Daddy when she found the Cornish motto was 'One and All.' She says loyalty is more important than Beauty, Truth, and Goodness. But Uncle Harry told her she was being a female extremist again."

"She holds to an interesting view," Lady Beatrice said judiciously. "Perhaps we can persuade her to elaborate on it during her stay. I am inclined to agree with her. The world about me here could certainly do with a large dose of loyalty—not least toward the Person on whose grace and favor our presence here now depends. But that's not your problem,

Davey. Tell me, what do you know of our beautiful Hampton Court and what would you especially like to see?"

The opportunity to show off was too good to miss. In rapid succession I mentioned the initial building of 1514 and the famous Conference of 1604 which resulted in the King James Bible. "By odd coincidence Natalie arranged to meet us at St. Paul's Cathedral, so we have journeyed from one Christopher Wren masterpiece to another," I concluded grandly.

"I'm not sure if what Wren rebuilt here would be called a masterpiece or not. Some of us residents prefer the original Tudor court to that of William and Mary. But your history is impressive, Davey. That's to say I'm impressed. You must have done a lot of looking up. You seem a scholarly boy."

"Grandpapa left Grandmama a super library which she never uses. I use it all the time and so does my brother Simon. Mama says it is the most important thing Grandpapa can give us from beyond the grave."

"We have a library here and if you like I will see you have permission to enter. It is not open to the general public. There are many rare volumes, as you might expect."

"I should like that very much," I said earnestly. And I meant it. Anything that was not available to the general public had its own allure.

"I am also interested in your maze," I told her. "It means a labyrinth."

"So it does. And you will have free access to that. This evening would be good as the day has been dry and the gardens will shortly close. You would have the maze all to yourself, I expect. That is the library and maze accounted for. Is there anything else you would like to see?"

"I want to show Mama the paintings. There is a great big volume called *The Art of the Royal Collections* at The Hornbeams and Mama told me her brother Guy had given it to their Poppa as a birthday present on his last leave. There are several paintings from here in it, including some by Holbein and Cannelloni."

She threw me a rare smile. "You are confusing pasta with paint, child. The artist's name is *Canaletto*. In any case, they are right outside the door behind you. Tell me more about your uncle. You refer to a *last leave* so presumably this is not the uncle in litigation with your mother."

"Oh no!" I exclaimed, shocked that she could refer to hateful Uncle Harry in the same breath as Mama's beloved Guy. "Uncle Guy was a pilot in the Royal Flying Corps and one of the Knights of the Air. Natalie and Mama were wondering in the taxi whether the general ever met him on the Western Front."

"I recall no mention. Then that is not unusual. There were so many brave young men it was my husband's privilege to meet. Far too many."

"Mama's brother was the closest person in the world to her. When he died she made a vow not to speak his name for five years. My brother Simon says when I was very little I would ask her who the man on her dressing table was and she would just pick up the frame and hug it and not say anything for ages and ages."

"She mourned like a mother for her own flesh. I know how she felt."

"Did you lose loved ones in the Great War, Lady Beatrice?"

"If you have finished your tea I shall ring for Sullivan. We must make arrangements for your visit to the maze while the light is still good."

* * * * * *

It was still light when Sullivan bent her dumpy, black-clad figure over the wrought-iron gate and unlocked the padlock for me to enter. "Now don't stay in there too long," she admonished me in her thick Irish accent. "She bloody well knows I got better things to do—what with dinner for all of you lot comin' up—than hang around here. What's wrong with tomorrow, I'd like to know?"

"Don't you know that 'she' stands just for the cat's mother?" I asked her silently as I quickly slipped by her large backside into the safety of the maze, where I was confident she would not follow.

Lady Beatrice had promised it would still be daylight and it was. Yet it was a queer light, and one that made me restless. The sun was still reasonably high, away to the west, though already casting sharp shadows. The eerie atmosphere came from dark piled clouds overhead that reflected a mustard yellow. It was they that caused the dense yew hedge to loom black and menacing.

The paths I hurried down were narrow and the hedges seemed to grow higher as I sensed myself moving ever farther away from the plump, atramentous figure of grumpy Sullivan. But I thought I could still hear her muttering Irishly to herself—a practice she had sustained from the time Lady Beatrice passed me into her care and as I'd been led through one courtyard after another, until we reached the palace gardens. Without her directing a single word to me, I had learned how Natalie's visits were disliked by the staff and how burdensome were the occasions when she had guests in tow. I also gathered that if Lady Beatrice was ambivalent toward small boys, her housekeeper despised them in much the way Saint Patrick despised vipers; I also inferred that she would have liked to see both Mama and me dispatched from Hampton Court just as the patron saint had banished the serpents from Ireland!

I eventually reached a point in the maze where I was uncertain if it was Sullivan's low grumbling I was still hearing. I strained ever harder until it finally dawned on me that I was no longer listening to any human sound. Here, where the hedges were high enough to block out much of the sky, an unexpected breeze blew. It was the sound of that, funneling through the successive lines of beautifully topiaried yew hedges, that I had mistaken for a voice.

My sandaled feet made no sound on the ungraveled path and I suddenly felt engulfed by the hush of the maze. A strange bird flew low overhead and I held up my arm in alarm at the threatening span of its wide wings. Once I would have said it was some kind of seagull—but no screaming gull following the plow at Polengarrow ever looked at me with such hostility or pointed such a vicious-looking beak. I pushed myself against the hedge and, even in my fear, was surprised at the harsh resilience of the dense-growing yew. The bird flew on but left still more threats in its wake. Mere shadows, however stretched by the sun's dying, I had now left behind.

In the brooding quiet toward the maze's core, it was both gloomier and colder. The wind churned down the twilight aisles and the groaning and creaking of concealed branches threatened to become a chorus. I bit my lip to stop teeth chattering, whether from cold or fear I am unsure. I was not a particularly brave boy but I did not yield readily to panic. Indeed, I think I would have stayed there in the lee of the hedge, sorting out my feelings and quelling my unfurling anxiety, if I had not suddenly received the sensation of being in an environment so alien and bent on my destruction that I whimpered at the sheer savagery of it.

The now vigorous wind whipped up grit which stung my face. In its mournful sough I was convinced I heard my name. Not once but twice. Distinct and in Mama's voice. Only a Mama who sounded strangled in her losing struggle against those forces of massed malevolence so determined to prevent her summons reaching me.

"Here, Mama!" I shrieked in response. "Mama, it's me. I am lost in the maze."

Receiving no reply, I began to run toward where I thought her call had emanated from. But the only words came from my own dry throat as I strove to talk myself into calm.... "Don't be silly, Davey.... Slow down.... You are only inspecting Hampton Court maze.... You'll soon be sitting down to eat as it's getting close to suppertime.... You're almost at the middle.... Any second now the path will lead you outwards again.... Silly old

Sullivan with her Irish accent is waiting over there.... There, towards the hedge to the left....

"Mrs. Sullivan," I called in the direction in which I could have sworn I had left her grumbling. "It's me, Davey, Mrs. Sullivan. I've seen all I want of the maze and I want to come out now." But all I heard in response was the pounding of my breath as I broke from a trot into a desperate run.

There *was* no center, no final snug place which told me I had come to the heart of this horrid web. I ran down one path, then another, then another. It was all implacably similar. I was close to crying as anxiety mounted and I fought with obscuring tears as I fled, like a distraught deer, down the silent tracks between row after row of towering yew and box. When my knees began to buckle from exhaustion I turned from the path and threw myself despairingly against the impenetrable hedge, which was a good foot higher than myself. It now seemed even denser than where I had first rested against the wall of foliage. But if panic didn't provide wings, it did lend muscle—to beat and tear a jagged gap through which I could squirm my small body in the headlong flight to reach the maze's circumference.

How many times I burrowed into the jagged confusion of sharp twigs and resistant branches that lay behind the screen of minuscule leaves, how many times I emerged, scratched and bleeding, more grimy than ever, I cannot say. All I recall is the climax to my experience, as the skies turned leaden and I sobbed with relief on suddenly seeing the broad and graveled paths of the outside world in the form of fragmented patches of tawny yellow glimpsed through the final ring of sooty evergreen leaves.

Whatever joy numbed the painful lashes on my bare legs, quelled the ache in my left eye where an unseen twig had excruciatingly jabbed, was abruptly obliterated by a figure more terrifying than the amalgamated experience of being lost and deserted in that cunning labyrinth. With a thunderous voice matching the enormous height of his uniformed figure, a giant berated me as I cowered before him.

"You stupid bugger! You vicious little sod! Do you realize what you've done? You've destroyed the work of centuries, smashing through those bloody hedges. I've a team of men who do nothing but keep them as they've been for fucking year after year. Then along comes a little bastard like you and wrecks the greatest maze in England, if not in fucking Europe!"

"I was lost," I whimpered. "I didn't know how to get out."

"That's what a bloody maze is *for*, you stupid git! And all you kids were supposed to be out of the palace grounds by five o'clock. You're trespassing as well. I can hand you over to the police—do you know that? And you can get a bloody great fine. Christ! Look at the damage! You come with me and we'll see just how many hedges you've destroyed. Your parents will be billed, you little bastard, I promise you that!"

I began to shriek—hysterical in my inability to explain. It was as I screamed my frustration that I grew aware we were no longer alone. I was still there on the sandy path where I had tumbled on thrusting through the final barrier to freedom when I heard the most welcome voice in the world.

"Leave that boy alone, you unfeeling brute." Mama ducked between the giant in the peaked cap and my prostrate self. "That is my son you are abusing. We are the guests of Lady Beatrice and I shall report your behavior the minute we are back in her apartments."

I had never realized quite how petite Mama was until she stood there quivering with rage as she confronted that enormous man on my behalf. I began to feel warm again in the ardor of her protection.

"The boy's done a deal of damage," he replied gruffly, but the steam had gone from him and petulance edged his voice. Mama sensed it too. "You will provide us with an estimate through the usual channels. And now I must take this little boy in and calm him down. He is highly strung and your vicious abuse may cost you dearly."

The giant crumpled entirely. "I had no idea who he was, Madam. I am sorry if he's been upset, like. Only he was shrieking fit to be tied when he crashed through the hedge here."

"And you did everything you could to calm and reassure him? I think not! Come here, darling. Get up from the ground and we will soon have you bathed and cleaned of all that blood and dirt."

Mama wouldn't let the big lout aid her as I limped with her arm in support. Nor would she let Natalie help her later when she gave me my bath and finally tucked me up in an enormous bed.

CHAPTER SEVEN

In spite of his protestations, Mama wouldn't allow Simon to accompany me on the visit to Harrods with Natalie. When I explained my brother's absence right at the ticket barrier of Knightsbridge tube station, where she met me, Daddy's business colleague just took my hand in hers and tugged somewhat as we walked briskly through a fine rain. She explained our haste not in terms of the inclement weather but because she had reserved a table at a particularly early hour as we had a very full afternoon arranged for after we had eaten an early lunch.

She said no more until we were sitting, the only customers so far, in what seemed to me a very high-class restaurant. "I promised your father, Davey, I would have this outing for you both. I wanted Little Arthur as well, but Wesley explained that your mother would never allow that."

Grown-ups rarely referred to my father by his first name in my presence and I was once more impressed with Natalie. I wanted to soften the blow of Simon's absence—even if I was pleased by it. Besides, I suddenly had a spurt of guilt when I remembered I had a mission to dispatch.

"Mama told Simon he was to stay at home. Only she made him write a letter thanking you for the Monopoly set and the Hornby speedboat. Here it is." I extracted the stiff cream envelope with Grandmama's embossed address on the back, handed it to my hostess. To my surprise Natalie didn't open it but stuffed it immediately in her handbag. She didn't look pleased.

I strove a bit more to soften the situation. "Mama said it would only be fair on you if he saw you on his own. She believes that together we make too much of a handful."

I was quite surprised to now see a distinct scowl on Natalie's usually smiling face. "I should've thought I might be the best judge of that." She drew a deep breath and, magically, her features relaxed again. "Oh well, we shall just have to do more together—just the two of us, eh?" She reached out and patted my arm. She was silent for a moment and I waited expectantly as I scanned the incomprehensible French of the menu the waiter had brought.

"Please feel free to choose just whatever you like. This place caters specially to youthful appetites. I have a nephew who swears by it every time he comes up to London from Inverness."

I appreciated how she said that without specifically mentioning children. I decided to ignore the long list of handwritten dishes and show my gratitude by appealing directly to her. "I am very partial to sausages and chips," I informed her. "With no greens. And a Knickerbocker Glory ice cream, if there is going to be a sweet as well."

"Does your mother prepare you sausages and chips very often?"

"She used to when we were home at Pol'garrow. But Grandmama doesn't like fried stuff very much. Mama says it is because she has an elderly stomach."

"Then it might be fun if you tried something else. Something new, perhaps? Something you've never had before?"

I thought about it for a while. "What do you suggest?"

"How about a steak? Or are you sick of them? They have excellent Highland beef here. As a matter of fact, it's the specialty of the house."

"I have never had steak. But if it is Scottish like you, then it must be nice."

Natalie looked so pretty, I thought, when she dimpled, and smiled to expose those lovely white teeth.

"You are truly your father's son, Davey.... Then I shall have one too. The waiter will ask how you wish it cooked. Your father always orders it medium-to-well, if that is any help."

"We never had it at home so I wouldn't know how Daddy likes it. But I think I will have it the same way he does, thank you."

At my request, Natalie ordered everything—although she was very careful to ask me if that was what I wanted when informing the waiter of our requirements. I got my Knickerbocker Glory and could not decide, in response to Natalie's questioning, whether I preferred that to the steak, which proved delicious and immediately became my favorite main course. But the pleasures of that day had only just begun!

The crown of the next few hours was the first port of call. After our scrumptious lunch Natalie took me to the zoo at the top of Harrods, and I stopped in front of the small mammal section to stare rapturously at an Indian mongoose that glided ceaselessly to and fro behind the small meshes of its cage. Ostensibly we were en route to selecting a terrapin, but at that particular moment lowly reptiles were far from my mind.

"That is what you would *really* like, Davey, isn't it?"

Not for the first time in my as then brief life, I suppressed all potential impediments and yielded to the ache of appetite. "There is nothing I would love more. I have looked up a great deal about the *Viverridae*—especially the Indian mongoose—since reading Kipling's *Jungle Book*, and I know they make adorable pets."

"Then why are we waiting?" she said with a laugh. "Let us find someone who can help us."

The assistant who sold us Rikki (for so I had already named him) provided me with a brochure about the species and helped select a cage which he said would ideally serve as Rikki's home. My only disappointment was not being able to take my pet with me, as it needed a final clearance from the veterinarian used by Harrods. When I gave our Theydon Bois address to the uniformed employee, he told me they would deliver Rikki the next day.

That meant I had to contain my excitement for twenty-four hours, but Natalie helped immediately after Rikki's purchase by whisking me around London at a dizzying pace in a series of taxis. Before she put me on the appointed train which Uncle Harry was scheduled to meet at the other end, we had visited Hambley's huge toy shop for a giant teddy bear for Arthur, and Stanley Gibbon, the philatelist's, for a special set of Belgian Congo pictorials for Simon.

After a most creamy tea at the Ritz, we walked down the length of Piccadilly to Hatchards, the booksellers, where Natalie provided me with what she smilingly described as my "waiting present": the two volumes, in first editions of red morocco, of Kipling's *Jungle Books* which are still in my possession.

I waited until after the excitement of distributing Natalie's gifts to my two brothers before broaching the topic of Rikki. Mama was standing at the french windows (knowing she would be unseen behind the muslin) observing Uncle Harry, who, after depositing me, had returned to his favorite wicker chair on the veranda.

"I did not bring a terrapin home with me, Mama."

She did not move from her position, still eyeing her older brother. "Why was that? Did Mrs. Lockyer-Pope change her mind?"

"No, Mama. It was I who changed mine."

"Really?" She didn't sound at all interested.

"I chose something else."

That evoked no response at all.

"Natalie has bought me a mongoose from Harrods. It will be delivered tomorrow by their van."

"That is out of the question, Davey. We discussed that subject ages ago and you know I said no."

I realized I'd made a mistake. I shouldn't have taken the onus for Rikki so swiftly on my own shoulders, but blamed Natalie for the decision.

"You make me so cross with your rank disobedience. Now I must phone Harrods and cancel the whole thing."

It was time, I thought uneasily, to make amends for my initial announcement. "They won't know who you are. It was Natalie who bought him. The minute she asked me whether I liked him, when we were standing by his cage, I told her the truth. It was she who insisted on my having him. Wasn't I supposed to tell the truth, Mama? Did I do wrong?"

"What a ridiculous business this all is! You know very well your Grandmama would not allow such a creature into her house. And Daddy, too, will not hear of such a thing. He loathes ferrets—ever since he was bitten clean through the thumb as a child."

"The Indian mongoose, Mama, is of the order of *Viverridae*. I told you that before. While ferrets—"

"Davey, shut up! I will not hear another word! Your grandmother is giving me an exceptionally difficult time over your uncle and I have no one to turn to with your father away. I do not need your selfish obsessions. When it suits your purposes you can be quite the most objectionable of my three sons. I wish sometimes that you were already away at Christ's Hospital School!"

"I only told Natalie the truth and the rest was her doing. I think you should take it up with her rather than attack me." I began to warm to my topic. "And how do you *know* what Grandmama would say without asking her? If I kept Rikki's cage in the garden—on the veranda, maybe, or in Uncle Harry's shed—she would never have to see my pet. I think you are blaming her when it is you who have decided you hate Rikki. You are taking it out on me, Mama, because I do not want to go to your horrid school."

"That will do! Do not strain my temper more than you have already. And if you think I am going to be beholden to my brother, who has already caused such an intolerable strain under this roof, then you must be mad!"

"Grandmama is always saying that Uncle Harry carries on as if that garden shed were his private property. I was only thinking of a way he could show her that was not so."

I then decided to bend truth a little—especially as Mama had not responded to my unassailable position over being honest when Natalie asked me about Rikki.

"I don't know why you go on about Daddy and my mongoose. Natalie said he didn't mind at all."

"He certainly has not discussed it with me, Davey."

"It wasn't you buying me a pet, Mama. You just wanted to get another rat to mate with mine if Natalie bought me one. But she bought me Rikki instead—and these two books of Kipling as 'waiting presents.' Did you see what she purchased the other children? Will they have to return their gifts, too? *Pour la forme?*"

But she evinced interest in neither question. "I will not ask your grandmother for another favor! If you wish that animal in this house, then you must plead with her yourself. If she asks me, I shall say I am against it."

I was about to tell her that I would inform Grandmama that Natalie was obviously very much *for* it, but decided that would be tactless. I tried another route. "If Grandmama says yes, will you help me with Daddy, Mama?"

Mama stared at me. "I thought you said he was in agreement with Natalie Lockyer-Pope."

"I told you what Natalie Lockyer-Pope said, Mama. I haven't had a chance to talk to Daddy about the *Viverridae* or the Indian mongoose—which is what Rikki is."

It did not mean much to my eleven-year-old head, engaged in battling for a longed-for possession, that Mama at that moment looked drawn and haggard. But I did notice her hand go up to her head to nervously pat her curls as she complained once again of the onset of a headache.

"If the matter concerned only you, I would still say emphatically no. But too many people seem now to be involved. All right, Davey, if you manage to secure Grandmama's permission I will do my best with Daddy if he raises objections—which I know he will."

That was the best I felt I could accomplish just then, so I beat a tactful retreat. But I did not let an hour pass before I brought the matter up with my grandmother, to whom I now gave the box of Fuller's chocolate creams which I had originally intended as a gift for Mama. My stout Grandmama was a devotee of such confectionery and I knew my last-minute substitution (or change of heart, as I now had nothing for Mama) was strategically correct. Her stubby, multi-ringed fingers would soon prise the contents from that pretty red and white box.

"How nice of you to remember a poor old lady, Davey. That's more than Simon would've done. People forget that I am cooped up here and have to rely totally on others for even the smallest things."

"I remembered you like chocolate creams when Natalie and I walked past a Fuller's in Mayfair, Grandmama. She has promised me an absolutely super present but she knows it depends on your giving permission, of course, seeing as we're living here as your guests."

Grandmama munched contentedly. "You mustn't listen to your mother so much, dear. You are not guests but *family*. She seems quite unable to appreciate what flesh and blood really mean—although she is always spouting on about loyalty."

But I wasn't interested in yet another moaning session with Grandmama about her endless disputes with Mama. "Natalie Lockyer-Pope was saying more or less the same, Grandmama, when she said how fortunate we were to have you as head of the family. That's why she insisted I come straight to you and ask if I might have a little mongoose out in the garden—in Uncle Harry's shed, perhaps? She said that her relations—that's Lord Leddingham's family—always had a mongoose when they were in New Delhi and that they not only made fantastic pets and were totally tame but kept the rats and mice down. They are also known, of course, as the arch enemies of *snakes*."

"Snakes! How I hate them! Repulsive creatures!"

I sensed victory. "One of the books in Grandpapa's library says Epping Forest has lots of snakes—vipers, that is—especially at a place called Adders Common. That's right near here, isn't it, Grandmama?"

"I wouldn't doubt it, if you say so, child. I knew it wasn't a good thing to move out here to the wilds and face goodness knows what. I told Harry and wrote so to your mother. But would either of them listen? I might as well have been speaking to a stone wall as far as my children go. I hope you three never treat your parents the way my son and daughter have behaved to me!"

Again she needed steering away from overly familiar topics. "So can I telephone Mrs. Natalie Lockyer-Pope and say you will give your permission for Rikki to come here? She is anxious to let Harrods know so that they can send him right away by their van."

"Yes, I suppose. Provided your mother isn't going to throw it into my face that I interfere too much with you children. She's done that once today, already." Grandmama's ample bosom heaved in pained recollection, but I scarcely listened to her final words as I darted back downstairs toward Mother's sitting room to pass on the good news.

All Mama said when I breathlessly addressed her was, "Just remember you will have not only to feed and clean the creature but exercise it, too, if that is necessary. I am not playing surrogate keeper to a mongoose as I have to so many of your pets, Davey."

"That was only with the wounded slow-worm and the baby squirrel, which was really Simon's. Besides, I was terribly young."

She raised eyebrows. "Are you forgetting all the tadpoles that turned into frogs, and the stick-insect eggs that hatched in the airing cupboard?"

"You're talking about lowly things like amphibians and the *Phasmidae* insects, while I am referring to mammals—a member of the *carnivora* and of *Herpestes edwardsi* at that!"

"Do not try and impress me with your few minutes in Poppa's library, Davey. I was reading his books before you were born. In any case, you appear to have won your way again. Just understand that I accept the thing against my better judgment and will not look after it when you tire of it or are otherwise engaged—such as being at boarding school."

"He will be my responsibility entirely, Mama. Don't you worry."

"That is exactly what I do not intend to do. I have quite enough to worry about. But I suggest you prepare for your father's reaction. He may not be quite as easy to twist round your little finger."

I would never have described Mama as a prophet, but she scored a hundred percent success mark over the comment about Daddy. It all happened in a horrible rush. That is to say, Rikki arrived that Friday morning; restless, inquisitive and longing for freedom from the confines of his cage. Daddy arrived—unexpectedly—that same evening for the weekend. He hadn't taken off his overcoat before he informed me coldly that he had just been told by Mama about a mongoose and that the animal had to go.

My response was to break into tears. I knew words were useless with my father—whom I so rarely saw angry that it always terrified me. I fled upstairs to my room. It was from there that I listened to his harangue of Mama, in her sitting room, as he berated her for her support, however reluctant, of my recent acquisition. Later, as I lay on my bed, striving halfheartedly to pull a pillow over my head, I heard their dispute degenerate from crisp specifics over Rikki to a sore survey of his traveling career and her loathing of life at The Hornbeams. I eventually grew aware that the battle had subsided into that rasping murmur which we children had become accustomed to as a sort of perverted lullaby during our final years at Polengarrow.

If Mama came to tuck me in, I knew nothing of it. The last thing I heard was the sleepy voice of Simon calling out from the adjacent room, wishing the two of them would shut up and allow him to sleep. With a start, I remembered his shouting similarly from our shared bedroom back in Cornwall when NEW ZEALAND had been the thorn of adult contention. I suppose you could say that Mama "won" NEW ZEALAND in that we at least left Cornwall for her beloved London. There was no doubt Daddy was the victor in the case of RIKKI THE MONGOOSE.

The next morning I fled very early to my pet, to establish that he'd survived the journey and to feed him his first breakfast. To my surprise, Uncle Harry was also up. He hung around his bottling shed as I cleaned the dung from Rikki's cage, fondled and stroked my new charge and gave him his saucer of bread and milk.

"He doesn't look all that vicious," Uncle Harry commented. "Stinks a bit—but so would you if you lived in a cage."

I decided to ignore such unhelpful comments as I went about my business of tending Rikki. Then Uncle Harry changed his tack. "Can't think why your father went overboard about the little fella. God knows, if your Mama was prepared to eat humble pie for once and accept a gift from her husband's girlfriend and you managed to blarney your grandmother again into spoiling you, then what the hell does it matter? Certainly not worth the row we had to put up with last evening! I stuck it out for an hour, then went down to the pub. God, how I wish for the peace and quiet we had before you lot arrived! Sorry about that, chum. But I have to call a spade a spade when I see it."

I knew from experience that Uncle Harry liked nothing more than calling spades spades—whether he could see one or not.

"Your Dad is off his topper about lots of things these days—you and the little fella just happened to get caught up in the whole business, that's all."

"Daddy is not really an animal-hater. Farmers never are. He just doesn't like ferrets and he's got the *Viverridae* mixed up with the *Mustela*."

"He's got more than them mixed up, sonny. He's got his women mixed up—and when one of 'em is a termagant like my sister there's hell to pay and no one's safe!"

I vowed to look up *termagant* (it only led to a long-winded lecture if you asked Uncle Harry words) but in the meantime to seek further shelter for Rikki, of whose safety I now felt very chary indeed.

"Can I use your other shed at the bottom of the garden, Uncle Harry? It would only be for a little while and I would not disturb your poisons there." I was not expecting to unstopper a torrent of response, but that is precisely what happened.

"Don't see why not. Can't see why someone shouldn't make a grab for happiness in this vale of tears. God knows, what with my Dora vamoosed, Momma an hysterical wreck and now your mother sent by Satan to plague me, there's not too much to live for."

He fingered the ends of his waxed mustache, as if that guided his resolve. "But I mustn't get dragged into some great row with either of them. I've got the business of Poppa's property to take care of, and her refusal to recognize the *Lex Salica.* But it stops there. I won't come between husband and wife—like Momma came between me and Dora. The Salian Franks never for a moment suggested we do that."

I didn't wait to hear any more but quickly squeezed a squirming Rikki back into his cage and headed for the small wooden shed behind the row of poplars that screened the kitchen garden. I don't think my father had ever penetrated so far down beyond the lawns and tennis court at The Hornbeams. I was hoping he didn't even know of the hut's existence.

I was no sooner back indoors than the breakfast gong rang. We never saw Grandmama much before lunchtime and Uncle Harry took breakfast in his room. So there were just the three of us children around the table as Mama bustled to and fro through the swinging door to the kitchen as she brought us first our cereals and then our eggs—cooked according to whatever the dictates that the particular day of the week decreed. This was a Saturday and therefore our eggs were poached.

The only thing unusual was the arrival of Daddy—just as Mama sat down with her unvarying breakfast piece of unbuttered toast. Both parents were unsmiling. I trembled for the fate of Rikki and, for encouragement, touched Simon's shoe by swinging mine under the table.

We were not kept long in suspense. I have never seen Mama look so pale and I swear she refused to look me fully in the eye. "Your father has something to tell you children," she said. "So pay attention to what he says."

Daddy cleared his throat. Unlike Mama, he did stare me full in the face. He did the same with Simon. I thought he looked just as angry as when I had fled him the previous night.

"Mama and I have covered a whole lot of things since I got home yesterday and some are certainly going to affect you children. The most important decision is that we shall be going back to Cornwall. I can't tell you when exactly. But before too long."

"To live, Daddy?" Simon asked.

"To live, Simon. That means both you and Davey will be going to Probus School, down to Truro, as we'd originally planned."

I looked at Mama's face, thinking of Horsham and her Christ's Hospital School. But I was unable to read the defeat I knew must be there.

"We shall go home to Polengarrow and I shall take over the farm from the tenants. I am giving up this traveling business, which has been a strain on all of us. We shall be just one family again—living together under our own roof."

Simon cheered but no one joined him. "I shall miss London," he informed us. "But I can't say I'll miss the stinkers 'round here!"

"Simon!" Mama exclaimed, breaking her silence. "We will not lose our manners merely because we are going back down there to primitive Cornwall."

"I was referring to Theydon Bois, Mama. Neither of you can have any idea of what village rotters I have to put up with."

"Will I be able to keep my mongoose, Daddy? It will be much easier at home than here in Grandmama's house."

"The mongoose goes back to Harrods. We discussed that yesterday. I don't want to hear the subject mentioned again, Davey."

"But Mama—"

"You heard your father, Davey. That's the end of it."

"But Natalie *gave* him to me. Daddy, it would be terribly rude if I told her I didn't want her gift."

"I shall write to Mrs. Lockyer-Pope," Daddy said, "and that will be the end of that. She had no right to go behind our backs in the first place."

I began to cry, whereupon I was ordered to leave the room. I looked desperately at Mama as a last hope of support, but she kept muttering something about not contradicting Daddy and toying with the cold toast on her plate. When I got down to the little shed where Rikki scratched fiercely against the wire mesh, I told his silver-gray length that I would never trust Mama again now that she had capitulated to a mongoose's greatest enemy—Daddy.

CHAPTER EIGHT

July 26, 1939

Polengarrow Farm,
St. Keverne, Cornwall

My darling Mama:
Aunty Muriel says I must write before supper or I can't have any damson pie! I am pretty tired as we cut corn to Lanoe Meadows and I rode all day on Ruby who was very lazy and more worried by the horseflies than my willow switch. Old Beauty just plods on, ignoring both the flies and me!

We all look forward to your joining us back here in Cornwall as soon as Daddy leaves Campbell & Ingram, after three long years. It was all right when we were at school knowing we'd join you at The Hornbeams for the holidays. But coming here to Polengarrow instead of to Epping Forest, and to Uncle and Aunty instead of our parents—just because there *might* be a war and London *might* be bombed—is a *very great strain*, Mama. Indeed, I heard Aunty tell the vicar on Sunday that Uncle Leslie is also finding it a strain to manage both here and at their Pentilly home. She—sorry—Aunty Muriel has made it clear she misses her own house. So hurry on back here, Mama darling, so that we can face the future as a *united* family.

Simon enjoyed school camp and now has his Tenderfoot in the Scouts. Please give love to Daddy, Little Arthur, Grandmama and Uncle Harry. But keep most for your beloved self.

Your devoted son,
Davey

P.S. I miss you so awfully.

* * * * * *

August 1, 1939

The Hornbeams,
Theydon Bois, Essex

My dear Davey:
This will be a rushed note, darling, as I have to meet Daddy in town for lunch. The news is mostly about him. There is a strong chance he might land a very exciting job. I cannot say too much about it as it's a bit hush-hush but don't be surprised if we burst in on you with some terrific news!

You would love the great silver barrage balloons everywhere over London and even out here in Essex. Daddy says all over the Royal Parks you can see people filling sandbags. I do hope you follow the international news in the newspapers and on the wireless. It certainly takes me back to when I was still a young woman and discussing with dearest Poppa the threat of war from the kaiser. In those days it involved bullying little Belgium—this time it would seem to be poor Poland's plight.

Thank goodness you children are too young to go but your cousin Neville (whom you have never met but whose rather foolish mother you once met on top of a bus with me) is already in the uniform of the Irish Fusiliers. But then he was in the Territorial Army and they are being called up first.

Mrs. Carter's son—she does seamstress work for Grandmama—is now in the Marines and, I must say, looks very handsome. He was still in the local elementary school when you and Simon were here, and used to come over from Epping on most Saturdays to help your Uncle Harry with the kitchen garden, remember?

Now do be good children and help Uncle Leslie and Aunty Muriel in every way possible. It is so kind of them to fill the breach until we can get things settled. Little Arthur is always asking after you both and I am praying we shall all soon be together again.

With my love,
Mama

* * * * * *

September 3, 1939

Polengarrow Farm,
St. Keverne, Cornwall

Dearest Mama:

Simon and I are sitting at the dining room table where Aunty has said we must write to you and Daddy on this important day. She still has on the felt tablecloth and we have to hurry as the visiting preacher is coming to Sunday dinner and we have to take that off and lay the table before Mr. Spargo arrives.

It is hard to write because this cloth is so soft and my pen keeps pushing through the paper and makes my writing squiggly. We were in chapel at eleven o'clock and Mr. Hicks, who is in charge of Sunday school, came late because he had been listening to Mr. Chamberlain, the prime minister, on the BBC. He told us this country was now at war with Germany for the second time in a generation.

He also said that a Mr. Martin was going to be preaching in the fields up to London about it this evening but I reckon he meant St. Martin-in-the-Fields and got it all mixed up as he usually does. This is why I wished we had gone to St. Keverne Church with Father Trewin who is an educated man but Aunty says we can only go there for Evensong with her and Uncle until I am confirmed and can take Holy Communion.

I asked her why I couldn't go to church in the morning like we always did with you, as I don't care so much for Methodism. She said it was to please Uncle who doesn't like the Church of England because of its glebe policy and, in any case, he had the cowsheds to clean out properly on Sunday mornings. So I hope I can be confirmed in Truro Cathedral next term as we are offered confirmation classes at school by our chaplain.

Uncle says that there will now be general mobilization and that he will need all the help he can get to run Polengarrow. So I do hope Daddy will soon be back after fixing up the hospital system you mentioned in your last letter as he is a trained farmer and *The Daily Express* says that the British farmer will play a vital role in providing food and easing the task of the merchant navy in wartime.

Simon and I planted some of your favorite Michaelmas daisies—the very pale purple ones?—and they are already coming out this early. That means they are welcoming you home, Mama, just as we are.

See you very soon I hope as we need lots of parental advice before we go back to school for the new term. Aunty doesn't really understand what we do at Probus and has told us she thinks we should be going to Bodmin County High like Mrs. Roseveare's son, Alan. Simon told her that was foolish but then she just gave him a funny look and didn't speak to either of us for the rest of the day. Then I do not think either of them has much sense of what a good school is or the need for education. Neither of them reads anything except *The Daily Express*, *The Farmer's Weekly* and *The Home Companion*. I ask you! Did you know Aunty has never traveled farther than Plymouth? And that with the Women's Institute!

Your devoted son,
Davey

******

September 30, 1939

The Hornbeams,
Theydon Bois,
Essex

My dear Davey:
Your last letter worried me a little. It is most important you appreciate what Aunty Muriel and Uncle Leslie are sacrificing for us, now that the war has given us all our duties to accomplish for king and country and for those who are actually risking their lives as I pen this letter to my sometimes difficult son.

Your father's brother had a terrible time—far worse than your Daddy—during the Great War and he is neither a strong nor a healthy man. Aunty Muriel and he, although older than both of us, were not married until considerably later and I am sure Leslie never thought he would have to fill your father's shoes at this late date—after what he had been through. He spent so much of each year down at Tehiddy Sanatorium, when you were a baby, with his poor lungs ruined by mustard gas, that we never thought he would work again. It was even more of a miracle when he and his cousin decided to get married. She, as you know, Davey, has never been physically strong since she had infantile paralysis as a little girl and lost the strength in her left arm and leg.

I remind you of these things not only as reasons for gratitude that your parents have their full health but to understand why it is important that Muriel and Leslie do their level best to farm Polengarrow while your father and I are up here in London, where so much organization and training remains to be done before victory can be accomplished. I know it is hard for you and Simon to be patient with slightly older people who have never had children of their own. But Davey, THEY ARE DOING THEIR BEST, and as I have told you so many times, no one can be asked to do more than that. That is why I *plead* with you for patience—especially now that you are back at school again and will not have to be with them until the Christmas holidays.

I do hope you write to them regularly, though, and make it clear how grateful you are and just how much they mean to you two boys who have to be temporary orphans until this war is over, which, many people say, will be in just a matter of months—if not by Christmas itself.

Your devoted Mama

* * * * * *

October 27, 1939

Probus School,
Truro, Cornwall

Dearest Mama:
How wonderful to see you and Daddy last week! But how sad when the train disappeared from sight! I cried and cried in the dorm though I did it in the pillow and I don't think anyone heard.

My best friend, Grahame—whom you met when you took us to Silcox & Dyers for doughnuts—knew I felt pretty mis. after you left and told me he had cried when his father, who is a commander in the R.N., wrote and said he probably wouldn't be seeing him for ages and that he would have to spend his hols now with their housekeeper who is rheumatic and grumpy. (Had to look up rheumatic—hope I got it right!)

His mother died when Grahame was eight and since then he and his father have lived together at Tamarisk Lodge, their house along the Camel Estuary, near Little Petherick. It would be nice if we could go there when you decide to come home and if Daddy is sent overseas to set up more hospitals. We could leave Uncle Leslie and Aunty here to farm Polengarrow and you and we three children could join Grahame at Tamarisk Lodge for THE DURATION.

There is only Mrs. Granger there now and as she is increasingly infirm the commander would certainly appreciate you taking charge of their beautiful white house by the Camel River. Simon and I could take correspondence classes. I am sure it could be fixed up with one or two of the masters here who are always complaining they are short of cash. Two of them, though, have left Junior School this term already, and there is now talk of *women* taking their place. The school is coming apart, and boys are constantly leaving for better places.

Uncle Leslie is coming down with Aunty Muriel on the coach at our half-term but he won't enter the school, he says. He has told Aunty to bring a pasty for him to eat while she eats with us. I gather Aunty is furious but will not come without him. It is all so silly but I try and remember everything you said and take no notice. BUT IT IS NOT EASY, MAMA.

I do hope you and Daddy will be able to get down for the Christmas carol service. We shall be joining the choristers in the cathedral and everyone is very excited by it. You could stay at the Cornish Arms and I can slip in there and book a room for you.

Please let me know early as a lot of boys are having their parents down and accommodations will be at a premium our housemaster says. It would be much better than your staying at Polengarrow and then coming down here as Uncle Leslie will only find things for Daddy to do and you will again have only a few hours to spare for your *orphans* stuck down here in Truro. Last time was a torture of having so few precious hours with our darling Mama.

Because of the measles I wasn't able to start the confirmation class but will next term in time for Easter. I am looking forward to that as I am sick of Primitive Methodism and listening to *morons* when we are back at Polengarrow.

When I told Aunty Muriel I preferred attending church to chapel she said had I ever stopped to realize this way we got *two* Sunday school outings in the summer instead of one. That woman! (Even if she did marry Daddy's brother and is my second cousin once removed!)

Simon has started to shave although he doesn't need to. I hurt my knee when playing rugger last Saturday but there is now a nice scab and matron says she doesn't think I will be scarred for life. Write soon but, even better, come back more quickly and for longer than last time.

Your neglected son,
Davey

* * * * * *

January 8, 1940

T. Post, Ambulance Squad,
War Emergency Unit,
St. Aldhelm's Hospital,
London, E17

Dear Davey:
How is your Cornish weather? It is like the Arctic here! So many of the twigs and branches are sheathed in ice that the forest reminds me of Selfridges' Toy Department at Christmas! And there is a gorse bush near here which I pass each day when I walk to the ambulance depot which reminds me of old Mr. Menheniot in St. Keverne—right down to the bulbous eyes and bristly mustache!

Thank you for your birthday card which arrived on target this morning. You are a dear boy and never forget, do you? Unfortunately Daddy is unable to celebrate with me but my colleague in the unit, Miss Charlotte Churchfield, has very generously offered to take me out to dinner in the West End.

Did you get the socks I sent you? Miss Churchfield knitted the blue ones and I the gray. She was also responsible for Simon's sweater and it would be very nice if you could persuade him to write and thank her. I mentioned it in my letter to him but you know what he is like. By the time he writes he will have forgotten.

Now I must get this silly uniform off and put on civvies for the expedition to the Café Royal in Piccadilly, which is where Miss Churchfield is taking me. That should be fun and I will tell you all about it.

With my love as always,
Your devoted Mama

* * * * * *

April 21, 1940

Polengarrow,
St. Keverne, Cornwall

Dearest Mama:
I was so sure you would be here to meet us when we came from school for Easter. So was Aunty Muriel, who had prepared a huge tea for you. I wonder whether we shall ever see Daddy again as you never seem to mention him any more.

Simon is extremely upset because Daddy missed his birthday but he won't say anything to Uncle or Aunty. He doesn't like questions and tells me to shut up if I ask him if everything is all right. This is always at night as we now share the same bed over the linney. Aunty Muriel says it is easier that way as she has fewer rooms to clean, what with her leg acting up and Mrs. Trevaskis unable to come and help her since she went off her rocker over her Gerald going down on the aircraft carrier HMS *Glorious*.

Daddy hasn't replied to my questions about the farm and you never told me about your birthday dinner after you had promised. Miss Churchfield's country home near Bishop's Stortford sounds very interesting and I am glad her parents have been so kind to you and Daddy. You didn't say anything about Grandmama in your last three letters. Does that mean you are now going to Bishop's Stortford when you are off duty and not to The Hornbeams? I am sure Grandmama must miss you almost as much as I do.

Your loving but lonely number two son,
Davey

******

June 12, 1940

Chesney Court,
Great Walmsey,
nr Bishop's Stortford,
Herts

My dearest Davey:
I have some wonderful news for you. Miss Churchfield and I have some time off and have decided to use our leave to come down and

see you and Simon. You have made it quite clear how you have fretted at my absence and perhaps this time I can explain properly how important it is for you to remain in Cornwall and continue your education at Probus.

I do know how difficult it can be on the farm, but there are also things up here which I don't like to bother you with. Your Daddy has not been in the best of spirits these past months and you two boys must not blame him for not writing. *When I write it is from both of us*.

But I will try and explain all that when Charlotte and I arrive, which should be about five p.m. on Friday. I can't say just how much she is looking forward to meeting you both. I have told her about you and Simon. Little Arthur calls her "aunty" already and is very fond of her and her parents, who often have him over to Chesney Court, in the library of which I sit.

Charlotte is so excited about our visit she is constantly poring over maps and asking me questions. You would think Cornwall is a remote *country* rather than just a particularly distant *county* that is especially hard to reach with petrol rationing and the blackout. Some of Daddy's medical staff have been most generous with their petrol coupons and Charlotte has been granted extra on special compassionate grounds—just to drive me to visit you both.

I know you will treat Miss Churchfield nicely as you were always the little gentleman with your father's friends. Let us hope Simon takes a leaf out of your book.

Your devoted Mama

* * * * * *

August 17, 1940

Polengarrow,
St. Keverne, Cornwall

Darling Mama:
If only you and Miss Churchfield had stayed at Probus until we had broken up at school for the summer holidays and thus seen the true picture! Uncle Leslie is being horrible and I don't know what to do. If you were here, Mama, I know everything would be all right. Aunty Muriel wanted either Simon or me to go into Wadebridge for

her and get her some wool as she is knitting furiously for the Forces. Simon told her he was busy with his summer essay paper and was going up into the granary where he did not wish to be disturbed.

I said I would go as it was market day and my friend Grahame goes into Wadebridge then for shopping. I was dying to see him as it is very lonely here without anyone to speak to. I know there is Simon but he doesn't share my interests the way Grahame does.

Anyway, I took the Southern National bus in and saw Grahame—we had an ice cream cornet at Jago's—and I got Aunty her skeins of navy blue wool. When I got home, though, Uncle Leslie flew into a towering rage because I hadn't ridden the milk bike but taken the bus. He called me lazy and said that no boy of his would have been pansy enough to go on the bus with a bunch of old women. As he has never had a son I told him that there was no way he could really know. Then he screamed and roared at me and made to hit me. I dodged under his arm and ran down the farmyard to the lower orchard. I did not go indoors again until it was very dark outside. I could see Aunty Muriel had been crying and there was a bruise on her cheek which made me think he must have hit her.

In bed Simon told me he too had been ranted and raved at by this man who hates our presence here on the farm, which is in fact ours, not his. If only you and Daddy were here you would see immediately what I am saying and I would not have to write letters like this or have to listen to that man swearing and cussing at us as if we were some kind of oaf which is what he is!

Please come down before we leave for school. Or have us up there with you where we will be saved from all this nightmare misery.

From your UNHAPPIEST son,
Davey

******

September 14, 1940

The Unit,
London, E17

My darling son:
Never have I been more glad to realize that you are safely in Cornwall than during these most horrible of nights. In fact because I

have been reassured that my two boys are safe—and Arthur is mercifully out at Chesney Court with Charlotte's parents—I have been able to do my duty so much better than if I'd been burdened by a mother's worry.

It has been so much worse than the zeppelin raids I told you about when you were little. The damage has been grotesque and the thunder of our guns and their bombs unbelievable. You know how you hate loud noises and start when you hear them? Well, some of these bangs would make you jump out of your skin!

On the other hand, when Charlotte and I were driving through the forest, our vehicle broke down and we had to walk for help to the anti-aircraft battery near the ~~XXXXXXXXXXXXXXX~~ (I had better blot that out for security purposes).

It was just that moment that Jerry chose to drop masses of these firebombs—incendiaries, they call them—simply wasted on the forest and nowhere near houses, thank God. They are magnesium and have a fierce, coldish light. It was like *fairyland*, Davey, walking through that glade with these fiery bombs burning all about us, turning night into day. Charlotte looked at me and I at her but neither of us spoke.

Funny things often occur in the most horrifying moments. The sort of thing I think your father was trying to tell me after the Great War and which I refused to listen to because I didn't want to hear of humor in the context of all that carnage. Charlotte and I were waiting for our stretcher-bearers to bring a casualty out of a bombed home when another bomb went off farther down the street. The ambulance rocked from the blast and we saw an A.R.P. warden who was directing things hurled to the ground. We rushed to give first aid and saw it was Reg Purkis from our unit. He is a pompous little chap with long waxed mustaches—rather like those silly things your Uncle Harry used to sport. It was obvious to Charlotte and me that he was not badly wounded save for a long sliver of glass which had penetrated his "b.t.m." It had entered his backside so violently it hadn't even caused blood. He was *so* embarrassed as we two women examined him!

We couldn't dig deep enough to extract the glass—besides, we had to fight back our laughter. We took him to our unit, though (with the poor old lady from the other incident, who kept screaming for her daughter), where they got the glass out in a jiffy when he was on the ops table.

There are several landmarks from my childhood now blown to smithereens and the church in which I was christened no longer exists. People are terribly brave, though, and I have never been prouder to call myself a Londoner. Both Daddy and Miss Churchfield send their love.

Your loving Mama

******

December 14th, 1940

Polengarrow,
St. Keverne, Cornwall

Dearest Mama:
Today is my friend Grahame's birthday and I am going to have supper with him and stay overnight even though Uncle Leslie has forbidden it and Aunty Muriel has accused me of shirking work. That is an awful fib as I got three huge sacks of twigs for the copper fire and her Monday wash as well as my usual chores.

Your news of the Blitz is most interesting and the incendiaries sounded beautiful in the forest. Simon says how fortunate it is the slums Hitler is bombing most and not the nicer parts farther out from the East End. Then he calls himself a Fascist and says the mob is always crueller than its leaders.

I did not like that story about the sack of heads arriving at the hospital and needing identification. I can understand Daddy vomiting. I don't think his older brother would have reacted so sensitively—then take it from me, he is not a sensitive man.

THIS place and its occupants could do with a bomb! I hate it more as day follows day. School is not much better and I pray for three years to roll by so that I can join up as a seaman in the Royal Navy, which is what I intend to do. Simon has written away for information about the Fleet Air Arm.

Your still unhappy son, Davey

******

January 26, 1941

The Unit,
London, E17

Dear Davey:
Forgive the long delay but part of the trouble, I think, was caused by the mails having been blitzed. I do know that Mrs. Churchfield's other daughter, who is a Wren lieutenant based in Bath, did not hear from her during the same period of time, and we strongly suspect a mail train due for the westcountry got bombed somewhere.

In any case, darling, life has not been too easy here. The bombing never lets up for very long and poor Daddy has been under a terrible strain. In fact he has been made to take sick leave and will be staying at a hospital in Wiltshire which has been commandeered for those worn out temporarily from the bombing. I know he would love to have letters from you and Simon. I will write Leslie and Muriel so you needn't bother about telling them about Daddy.

I cannot go into your domestic difficulties now but hope we can discuss them if Charlotte and I manage to get away later this year. Keep your fingers crossed!

You do seem to be seeing a lot of this Grahame boy, darling. I do hope you are not proving an imposition on his family, which must be as short of help in wartime as the rest of us. Daddy says you never seem to mention sports in your letters and is wondering whether you are keeping up your cricket.

Your Grandmama is now failing rapidly and doesn't seem to know who I am or, worse, confuses me with Harry. I often think her mind has never been quite right since Poppa died. I know she would like a letter—from you especially.

You do not mention your other grandmother or any of the relatives in Callington or St. Agnes. Do they keep in touch and did you see at least some of them and your cousins over the recent holidays?

Your devoted Mama

* * * * * *

March 15, 1941
(The Ides of March)

Probus School,
Truro, Cornwall

My dear Mama:
Sometimes I think you don't read my letters at all! Either that or half of them are not arriving! You don't answer my questions and there are times when I don't think you love me any more. What else am I to think when I tell you that instead of looking forward to the holidays I now just dread them and the people who lie in wait at the other end.

I have to take your word for it that they are our blood relatives but they do not act like any other Bryant I have ever met. They *hate* children, do you realize that? And Simon and I realize that we are just a nuisance that has to be put up with and nothing more. The word EVACUEE is the most hated in the rural vocabulary nowadays, Mr. Beasley, our English master, said last term. AND THAT IS PRECISELY HOW WE ARE REGARDED BY CERTAIN PEOPLE.

We could survive all that if there were any sense of being wanted by our parents, who stay away from us and just tell us to do our duty and keep smiling. I don't ever want to smile again. And I think duty is the most horrible word I can think of.

You keep on about Miss Churchfield as if she were a relative but she is a complete stranger to me and I should not visit her mother in Chesney Court if I were ever allowed to come home to you but I would go to poor Grandmama at The Hornbeams and kind Uncle Harry who let me look after Rikki in his garden shed when no one else showed my little mongoose any kindness during the pitifully few hours I was allowed to keep him.

I did not think I would live to see the day when I could say that I feel my parents have rejected us for some stupid war which they say they hate but I think they really enjoy. You obviously have great times with your dear Charlotte, and you can't deny the war has given you her!

Yours in sad disillusionment,
Davey

* * * * * *

March 20, 1941

T. Post,
London, E17

My dearest upset little boy:
Your last letter was very painful indeed. I dare not let Daddy see what you have written for he is still suffering from Acute Depressive Reaction in that special place outside Devizes.

When your parents agreed that it was best for you two boys to stay in Cornwall with the war coming, it was our *joint* decision and one made out of *love* and the desire to have you safe and sound and not out of selfish abandonment. There was no way you could have stayed at The Hornbeams, my darling child. Your grandmother could not have coped and your Uncle Harry ignored her and became a Local Defence Volunteer as soon as possible and followed that up by selfishly becoming an officer in the Home Guard as soon as that was formed. He is *never* home and your poor grandmother is on her own for most of the time.

We have tried to get her to come to Chesney permanently, where there are so many rooms, but she refuses to budge even though the glass of the veranda all came down one night in the Blitz and the top part of the house has been declared unsafe. You would have had a screaming fit had you been there when that happened, young man.

I am sorry to *finally* hear that you did not like Miss Churchfield when you met her last year, for she took so emphatically to you. It also makes things somewhat difficult as I could not possibly get away from here without her active help—I am thinking of both the driving and the petrol coupons—and frankly I would not care to come all that way by train, what with the delays and rerouting that take place all the time nowadays.

I tell you this as you are now nearly sixteen and have to realize that there are *consequences* to our statements and actions in life. Do let me know therefore whether you wish me to try and persuade Charlotte to give up her valuable days of leave to visit a young man who has made it quite clear he has no wish to see her.

Your loving Mama

* * * * * *

April 1, 1941

Polengarrow,
St. Keverne, Cornwall

Dearest Mama:
Please thank Miss Churchfield for her letter which I will answer from school as soon as the Easter hols are over. Her mother has invited Simon and me to visit and I gather that you have given permission. Looking forward to that and hoping that you will have time off to see your sons at the same time.

I am just here for the weekend and have helped Uncle Leslie with some fencing up by Botawn Woods. I am still keeping up my piano lessons—this is the fourth year, you realize! I have made a new friend who is also interested in music. His name is George Pengelly and his family farm outside Liskeard and know our Callington cousins. He is very nice. Much taller than me and with dark wavy hair. He is also a French enthusiast and was a co-founder with Grahame and me of The Fleur de Lys Club, which shows French films whenever we can get them and is planning to do a play by Molière in French one of these days. George played Antonio in last term's *Merchant of Venice* when I had the role of Portia and Grahame was Shylock. This term we are to do *Hamlet* and it looks as if George will play the gloomy Dane.

Don't laugh, but Mr. Beasely wants me to play his mother, Gertrude, and Grahame has been suggested for Claudius. Some wags in our House are already saying it will be the Froggy Hamlet as so many principals are Fleur de Lysers—then ours is a *philistine* House and our bloods tend to snicker at everything we do because we despise their stupid rugger and cricket.

Simon is now quite an expert in Cornish wrestling and Little Arthur has had a watercolor chosen for display in the Junior School exhibition for visitors weekend—so the Bryants are well represented at Probus this year for E.S.A.—extra-school activities.

Your dutiful & devoted son,
Davey

* * * * * *

April 26, 1941

T. Post,
London, E17

Dearest Davey:
What a disappointment that we had to say no. But the bombing is now worse than ever and all day-leave has been cancelled for the foreseeable future. I know that Mrs. Churchfield is heartbroken that she could not have all three young Bryants under her roof at the same time this Easter but she says she would never be able to forgive herself if there had been a disaster.

Obviously security doesn't allow me to paint you a specific picture, but I can tell you that I haven't been able to get through to your grandmother in the past twenty-four hours and that even Chesney Court is currently without electricity, although it has been promised before tonight.

It is so reassuring to hear of your school affairs and I am glad that you have many nice friends for me to meet some day. Do please continue to keep a special eye on Little Arthur. Don't forget that this is his first school year away from home, and I suspect that, like you, he may be terribly homesick from time to time. I am so glad that he has you and Simon to rely on. I must say Charlotte's companionship—what with your father away in St. Lawrence's—makes the kind of days we are currently experiencing almost bearable. Without her I sometimes think I could easily go under.

With much love,
Mama

CHAPTER NINE

January 12, 1944

Chesney Court,
Great Walmsey,
nr Bishop's Stortford,
Herts

My dear Simon:
I still have difficulty in realizing my eldest son is no longer a schoolboy. I am sure all mothers of sons have comparable feelings but I am convinced war somehow *accelerates* these things. Now on to the specific point of this letter.

I have no way of knowing either where or when you will be reading this but I want you to know as soon as possible in the new year that your father is very much better and able to leave the hospital for good. However, what with one thing and another at this time, it was thought inadvisable for him to return to London and therefore he has gone to a small village in Essex—not too far from Saffron Walden—and taken over the management of the village inn.

The idea is for me to join him there, and Charlotte and I are working on just such a plan as I pen this letter. Neither of us, of course, has ever had any experience of that kind of thing, and I'm still far from sure it is a wise move. Your father can be very romantic in these matters—especially on behalf of others. I think he sees a sleepy inn serving rustic characters, rather as if he were back in St. Keverne as landlord of the Cornish Arms. I, on the other hand, see a wartime pub full of thirsty troops (both ours and American airmen) in a time of shortage. Nor am I too confident that those Essex villagers will take kindly to someone parachuted into their midst.

Charlotte takes a more optimistic view and keeps stressing it will provide a home for Davey and Little Arthur and give you a nice quiet base when you come on leave. You may be assured that Davey has already written to me twice this week saying it is a marvelous idea!

In my reply I emphasized that my brother Guy was most abstemious and that Poppa himself was almost a teetotaler. There is something about selling alcoholic beverages which I find distasteful. Not that I am 'Temperance' of course, like so many of your Cornish relatives.

From your proud Mama

* * * * * *

July 1, 1944

2516 Granleigh Avenue,
Victoria, B.C.
Canada

Dear Davey Bryant:
You will have probably forgotten that I ever existed as we have not met since eight years ago! But I am the Natalie whom you met at The Hornbeams, Theydon Bois, and perhaps you recall the Hampton Court weekend with my late aunt and then our exciting day together in London when you acquired your mongoose? Shortly after that time I remarried—a Canadian from British Columbia—and subsequently joined him here in Victoria.

What prompts me to write now is that my husband's niece has been posted to somewhere in southwest England and I have a suspicion it may well be Cornwall. I have no evidence, of course, that you are in your native Duchy, but I calculate you are now seventeen or thereabouts and that you may well be on your farm—the address of which you gave me in your grandmother's garden! It being summertime, I thought you might well be on your school holidays from that Bluecoat's school which you were loath to attend but at which you may have subsequently settled satisfactorily. In any case, I have given Amy your address so IF you are in residence and IF she turns up, you will not be startled out of your wits.

Before concluding this rather odd letter I must tell you how enchanting a place this coastal British Columbia is and if you ever get *wanderlust* when this ghastly war is over, you could do far worse than make tracks over the North American landmass to this magical island along the Pacific coast.

With fond remembrances of a remarkable little boy who I am confident is now an equally remarkable young man. Please give my respects to your parents if such is possible. I found your mother a most singular woman and only wish there had been time to get to know her better.

Affectionately,
Natalie Lockyer-Pope McGregor

******

August 12, 1944

The Hornbeams,
Theydon Bois, Essex

Dearest Wesley:
I am sorry that I could not get back to Saffron Walden yesterday but Momma has taken a turn for the worse and, frankly, I am needed here. Harry is more stupid than ever and is a tremendous nuisance. To such an extent that I have called several of his Home Guard cronies and pleaded with them to come up with pretexts to keep him OUT of the house for once!

This is the situation. Momma's diabetes has deteriorated to the point where she is only out of coma when Nurse Halliwell or I give her an insulin injection. This has been her condition for over a month, Nurse informs me, and it only worsens day by day. Momma has not really recognized anybody since she spoke a few words to Davey when he came in July for cherries from the garden. She would be eighty-four next birthday.

This is what I propose—and I tell you because there is simply no one else in the family I would trust to understand. I have told Nurse she can have twenty-four hours off (which she sorely needs, poor dear) and I shall simply see that my mother is not disturbed from her next coma and so passes from sleep into death.

I know I could not think—let alone write down—these thoughts had I not endured these past years and my ambulance service. But I have no reservations over what I intend to do. I am aware of the law and how public opinion may interpret my act. I have even read about *euthanasia* here in Poppa's library, and his old and sadly mildewed books are far from liberal in their interpretation! But the price of being accused of murder—of matricide, to boot!—is far less onerous than watching a desperately tired old woman being prodded into daily wakening by an injected chemical.

I hope you do not mind, Wesley, when I tell you all this. However, you cannot be called an accessory before the fact as I shall not put this in the post until I have released Momma. I realize that you are still recovering and that, in some respects, we seem to have drifted rather apart. But I never for one moment forget that you are the father of our boys and thus the head of our little family.

I shall not wish to stay under this roof too long with Harry—especially after Mother is gone—when I know he will surrender to years of guilty conscience for his abrasive tongue and for when she begged him not to leave her alone here at night when the bombs were dropping. Night after night he ignored her and went down there to the pub and bragged about his stupid Home Guard duties, while bribing his listeners with free pints of beer. All the time he blamed me, of course, for not returning here to tend her as a dutiful daughter. He once told me he held me wholly responsible for her condition, as it was my duty to be there in the house while it was equally his to be out with the Home Guard. When I referred to my work with the ambulance unit, he laughed in my face.

He would never even begin to understand how, in the light of my ambulance duty, it was hard enough to turn a deaf ear to the pleas of my little boys away in Cornwall. Then he has always resented our family, just as, earlier, he resented my relationship with Poppa. You must know, of course, how he maliciously encouraged Momma *not* to accept Mrs. Churchfield's kind offer to stay at Chesney Court for the Duration—where she would have had her own roomy accommodations and privacy, as well as all the amenities of a well-run house in the safety of the country.

I cannot return home before the doctor has been, certificates signed and the proper authorities informed. I expect no problems in that quarter as both Nurse and Dr. Quinn know she has been a diabetic for years, and that she has lately been in accelerated decline.

I think I shall try and persuade Charlotte to come over after I have done my duty to Momma. She can help me cope with Harry and also aid me in cleaning up the house, which is in a perfectly dreadful state.

I shall try and phone you in Saffron Walden—some time before opening hour. In any case, this letter should reach you on Wednesday by latest. Thank you, my dear, for all the support which I know will be forthcoming from a very dear man.

Your loving wife, Isabella

******

September 3, 1944

Chesney Court,
Great Walmsey,
nr Bishop's Stortford,
Herts

Dear Davey:
Until I wrote the date above I had not realized today was the anniversary of the outbreak of this ghastly war.

Thank you for sending on the letter from Natalie Lockyer-Pope—as was. Or did I already acknowledge that? I have been so preoccupied lately, chiefly, of course, with the funeral of your grandmother last Tuesday.

There were not many present at Christchurch or at the City of London Cemetery where she was interred. It being wartime and with such as yourself in the services, the attendance consisted mainly of elderly civilians who remembered her from earlier and calmer times. However, your brother Simon was luckily on leave, and resplendent he looked in his sub-lieutenant's uniform! He provided a wreath on behalf of you three boys and I gave flowers on behalf of your Daddy and me. He was not able to be there as he was feeling slightly under the weather.

Predictably, your Uncle Harry made a spectacle of himself, with hysterical tears and even throwing himself toward the coffin until restrained by Mr. Patmore, who put in a surprising appearance.

I am sorry you were unable to be there, Davey, but at least you were able to attend Grandma Bryant's funeral last spring, and that, in many respects, was the more important. At least for you, darling, who got on so much better with her than Grandmama Newcombe when you were living at The Hornbeams.

As I was telling Charlotte just before I came into the library to write this letter, it is still difficult for me to reconcile myself to the fact that two of my babies are now in the Navy. I hope and pray that it will all be over before you finish your training and then both you and Simon will have to think about the university and your careers.

Little Arthur is already writing from Probus saying he wishes to be an architect when he grows up. When one looks at the devastation around here it makes one think there will be no profession more in demand when the Peace finally arrives.

These doodlebugs and V2s keep us on our toes. It is rather like the Blitz all over again. But this time we know we have Hitler and his beastly armies on the run in Europe. So the morale of the East Enders—and they have surely taken the brunt of the civilian bombardment over the past five years—is much higher and we know that it is only a race for time and that we will be the winners.

I do hope you will arrange to spend your leave here when your basic training is completed. It is so crowded and rushed at the inn at Saffron Walden, I know I shall not have a minute of you to myself. Even Daddy thinks that the best plan. He comes over here whenever he gets a free moment and enjoys a game of billiards with Mr. Churchfield and even a round of golf when the weather permits.

Your devoted Mama

* * * * * *

December 8, 1944

Ord. Seaman D. Bryant,
DJX/732-367,
c/o Admiralty P.O.

Dearest brother Simon:
I hope you do get that Christmas leave and are here to see the extraordinary setup. Mama and Daddy are really treated as part of the Churchfield family and actually take part in their discussions. It works the other way too. Last night both Charlotte and Mrs. C. offered their opinions over Little Arthur's problems with Uncle Leslie and Aunt Muriel.

Mama hinted that if Uncle Harry keeps his word and never enters The Hornbeams again she and Daddy might live there. At the back of her mind I think she wants to have a home for us if and when we are at university. One less remote than Polengarrow, that is. Although I would be much happier if they were back there.

There is lots of talk now about peace and postwar—although I'll only believe it when I see it. For instance, I can't see Japan giving up in a hurry while Toothy Tojo (as Mama calls him) remains in power.

Mama and Charlotte are still as thick as thieves and I neither like it nor understand it. You are so much better than me at dealing with these matters that I hope you can get home for Christmas—I mean HERE for Xmas. You see how easy it is to be *brainwashed*, as they say!

This isn't easy to say but I ran into a spot of bother at the Portsmouth base after basic training. To do with another chap and me. Not to put too fine a point on it—I got arrested! Spent some weeks in civilian detention because of what a detective exaggerated about this other seaman and me in Victoria Park and got me charged with importuning and soliciting. I was eventually put on probation but the bloody Navy arrested me again for being AWOL and I was back in cells for another three weeks! For God's sake don't tell Mama or Daddy about this as it would probably break her heart and give him another breakdown. Naturally, it has left me in a bit of a frazzle, though I know I will eventually cope. The experience has certainly taught me a lot about myself which I would like to tell you about some day. It has also left me with an abiding hate of the Navy—then you always told me I would loathe it.

With love from your kid brother,
Davey

* * * * * *

August 27, 1945

Chesney Court,
Great Walmsey,
nr Bishop's Stortford,
Herts

Dear Davey:
Well, it is now all over and you won't have to go to Ceylon or Australia after all. Simon expects to go up to Cambridge this autumn as soon as he is demobbed and says he will read Chemistry—which naturally pleases me as I see it as him taking up where I had to leave off.

And what does my middle child have in mind for his future? I do hope it is something solid and healthy like one of the professions, and not that theater stuff which so preoccupied you at school. Little Arthur writes to say he is still determined to read Architecture when he arrives at the Varsity. Then he has always seemed to be firmly in *control* of his life. I hope it is likewise for you, dearest.

Charlotte and I are going down to Cornwall to see how things are at Polengarrow before your father leaves Saffron Walden for good and returns to the farm. Since Leslie left after Muriel's death, it has fallen somewhat into disrepair—and that means the house as well as the land.

By the time you boys want a home for your vacations it should be in some kind of shape. I had hoped that The Hornbeams would have served as a base for the three of you but Uncle Harry has seen fit to put the kibosh on that plan by playing his silly legal games.

However, I refuse to sell out to him as he desires and I slip over there from here just whenever I please. Perhaps one of you boys should talk to him about your occupancy out of term and when you aren't in Cornwall. He certainly refuses to listen to me about any kind of postwar plans. Then the whole of his life has been an attempt to put the clock back, while I have always sought to embrace the future. You wouldn't think we were from the same family, would you?

Are we likely to see you here at Chesney Court while you are waiting to see when the Navy intends to release you? You were always so keen to be with me when it was impracticable but now I hear of you visiting Falmouth with your schoolfriend Charles. Why does he take precedence over your family who miss you so much?

As always, my darling,
Your devoted Mama

CHAPTER TEN

The fall of 1945 saw me at King's College, London, struggling with uncongenial Philosophy; Simon up at Cambridge, reading Science, and Little Arthur in his final year at boarding school in Truro. During our subsequent vacation times and school holidays, Mama informed me, she intended to realize her longtime resolve to have us all living again at The Hornbeams as a united family under a common roof. She had abruptly gone back on her earlier decision to return with Daddy to Cornwall. I think she imagined that her painful decision to negotiate once more with her brother, Harry, in order to buy out his portion of their mother's home, and then the way in which she threw herself into the renovation of that bomb-damaged structure with its wretched memories for her, was a sufficient sacrifice to satisfy us all.

In the manner of families, Mama's actions were perceived differently by her children and her husband. Simon wrote to me suggesting that Mama was merely rationalizing her own desire to remain within hailing distance of her beloved Churchfields outside of Bishop's Stortford. Little Arthur complained we had been promised a return to Polengarrow after the war.

As for myself, after only a month of demobilization from the detested Navy and with the burgeoning sense of my difference from other men, I already resented the hours absorbed by commuting to the domestic situation in Theydon Bois, and was secretly resolved to find student digs closer to King's College. My brief if traumatic months in the Navy had weaned me of any tolerance of parental supervision and I was counting the time to when I could take whomsoever I wished to bed—with no one to ask embarrassing questions. I was enviously aware that my brother Simon had shed all such fetters to his own sex life by serving so long as a naval officer before slipping off to Cambridge for the freedom of undergraduate life in that most tolerant of places. Nor did many weekends pass before I realized how much Daddy still hankered after the life of a Cornish farmer—even after what was now nearly ten years' absence. It was through him, rather than his sons, that events climaxed.

He rarely spoke directly of Polengarrow. Nor did he speak negatively of his position as a senior hospital administrator in Chelmsford, where he was busy with the implementation of the Labour government's new National Health Service. After supper one October day, though, he suggested a drive over to Saffron Walden for a drink at the pub he had managed following his nervous breakdown during the war.

It was a still evening, awash with sunlight, and alive with intimations of the long hot summer recently departed. But already the trees of the forest reflected their seasonal tones. Hornbeam, oak and smooth-boled beech afforded a variety of tentative shades, while the final frieze of silver birch was now a rutilant clothing to the forest slopes as we drove the woodland lanes. Before we broke entirely free of these roan and ochre woodlands and entered the grass and plowed-earth richness of Essex, Mama's name had surfaced.

"Mama likes this kind of countryside," Daddy said slowly. "But for me it's too tame."

"Why didn't you ask her along with us?" I enquired. "Especially if, as you say, she loves it so much?"

"She's arranged to join Charlotte over there at Chesney Court. They play a lot of bridge, you know—the Churchfields, and Charlotte with Mama as partners."

"Why don't *you* partner Mama? You like cards." I was astonished to hear the petulance in my voice. "Why is it always *Charlotte* this and *Charlotte* that?"

It was a full minute before Daddy replied. I stared at his ungloved hands on the steering wheel; stared at their bumpy veins and wrinkled skin. He was wearing a reddish topcoat with upturned collar and his spectacled face, now pale and lined by wartime experience, almost disappeared as it peered beneath his peaked cap. He spoke in unusually muffled tones.

"I don't think Mama cares too much about some things any more."

"Meaning *you?*"

Daddy hated frontal attacks. "Meaning a whole lot of things. After all, you boys are now grown up. You don't need her the same way any more."

I shrugged. "Well, the war and our evacuation took care of that, didn't it?"

"The war took care of a whole lot of things, Davey. Nothing will ever be quite the same again."

"Including Mama, of course."

He took the approaching curve with particular care before replying. "Including Mama. But she needs you boys. I can't tell you how much she's looking forward to Christmas—even if it is still months away."

The moment talk turned to Mama, I felt the intimacy slipping from us, an intimacy I craved enough to risk it singeing me. "But it isn't Christmas you wanted to talk about, is it? I mean, that's not why we're driving along here—just the two of us."

"I suppose I wanted a bit of time alone with you. There never seems much opportunity in the house. Or rather—"

"Rather what?" I interrupted.

"You don't seem much in the mood for a chat these days. Of course, I realize you must have a lot of studying to do after all those lectures. But somehow you seem always to be kind of *bristling*. Know what I mean? Likely to go off at half cock if someone asks you the slightest question? Mama's noticed it too. In fact, she wondered whether I might bring it up."

I would never accuse Daddy of lying but that didn't exactly ring true. "Mama's never needed anyone to do her dirty work. Are you trying to tell me this was all carefully planned between the two of you? I've been tricked into coming out and leaving my books, is that it?"

"In the first place, I'm not just *anyone*, Davey. I am your father."

I had the strong feeling he was about to add that he was also Mama's husband but decided against it. That made me feel terribly sad for him and my spark of anger disappeared immediately. Besides, I knew he was right. At home, night after night, I had felt thin-skinned and irritable. Sexual frustration does that to you.

"It's the commute," I ventured. "It takes too much out of me. I'm thinking of finding cheap digs in town like most of my friends. Coming out all that way is okay for bankers. Unfortunately I can't keep bankers' hours."

He didn't speak for a while, once more concentrating excessively on the winding lane before us. I wasn't sure whether he was merely mulling over my announcement or striving to accommodate himself to the hurt of it. I knew very well that he liked having me there at The Hornbeams—even if he rarely expressed it.

"It's not as if I knew people there in Theydon Bois since I joined the Service. In fact, I never did feel I belonged, come to that."

"You mean Epping Forest's not like Cornwall?"

"Exactly. I've never felt I really fit in anywhere else. I know that's how Little Arthur feels, too. Simon I'm not so sure of. Then I don't think he likes calling anywhere home."

"Simon is hard to fathom," Daddy pronounced, just as the thatched roofs of Saffron Walden hove into sight. "Even as a little lad he held his cards close to his chest. A bit like Mama in that way."

Then I knew, as we drove into the car park of the Maypole Inn, of whom it was that Daddy really wished to talk. When we had ordered our beers at the counter and taken them to a chintz-padded window seat in the almost deserted "snug," my father glanced around before remarking that, even though subsequent landlords had refurbished the pub substantially, he was sure Mama would have still disliked it as much as ever.

I decided to let him chat on until he could he deliver himself of what was hardest to say. God knows he took a roundabout way!

"Mama thinks Simon has a girlfriend—a young Wren he met just before he left the Navy."

"Is that so?"

"To think that Little Arthur is in his last year at Probus! I suppose *he'll* be bringing a young lady home next!"

"I don't think we need start planning *right* away for that, Daddy," I said, smiling.

Not rebuffed, he plodded on. "I'm not going to hold my breath over you, Davey, for the sound of wedding bells. You're far too canny to bog yourself down with a wife before your education's completed."

I was certain he knew bloody well I was unlikely to bring a daughter-in-law into his life, but I again held my silence. Although he and Mama knew of my arrest, neither had ever made even an oblique reference to it. No, it wasn't the knowledge of my being queer he was about to bring up over a beer in the Maypole! Daddy was quite capable of nursing suspicions without alluding to them—let alone wanting them confirmed—for year after year. It was only with his wife that there was a compulsion before which he seemed powerless.

"Your Aunt Charlotte doesn't look as if she's the marrying type either. She's nigh on forty, you know."

"Uncle Leslie was older than that before he wed that unfortunate Muriel I had to suffer during the war," I told him crisply. "Then he was such a terrible grouch himself that he should certainly have remained a bachelor!"

"You're forgetting the gassing, Davey. He was never the same man after that. But he was a good brother to me when I was a kid. I've got plenty of reasons to be grateful."

"You're the loyal type. That's something that you and Mama share, you know."

"Perhaps that's all we share."

I was silent. I knew the hard things had finally arrived at their point of articulation.

"I've always had difficulty in understanding Mama—I think you know that. But Davey, it's getting worse. I *try* so very hard, son, to put myself in her place, to see what she means when she tries to explain something. But there are times I think I'm listening to a complete stranger. And this is a woman I've lived with for twenty-five years!"

I drank through the foam of my half-pint of bitter—more for the respite than for the influence of the stuff. "What do you mean, exactly?" I felt a total hypocrite, as I knew only too precisely what he was alluding to. Wasn't I the one who raised it more often and more loudly than anyone else?

"I suppose it's all to do with the Churchfields. They seem to have almost taken over her life."

"All of them—or just *one* of them?"

He didn't hesitate for a moment. "It's the *idea* of them, I think, she's in love with. Not Charlotte, not her mother or father—but the whole household. Come to that, even the *house*! She is just that much happier when she's there at Great Walmsey than anywhere else."

"I can understand why her memories of The Hornbeams can't be all that rosy. And she was always determined to leave Cornwall."

"It's not a matter of place any more than individuals. It's a whole *idea* which has cast a spell on her. That's it. A *spell*, Davey. Does that make sense to you?"

"This isn't Cornwall, Daddy, you can forget all about four-legged emmets and other magic. Why not try hypnotism?"

But he was not to be deflected by my fumbling attempts at humor. This was obviously something he'd been saving up to say to me and I doubt if there was anything capable of stopping him.

"She talks incessantly of that family, from breakfast-time onwards, and sometimes I think that life at Chesney Court is the only basis of comparison she'll accept any more. It's getting me down. She won't listen to a word I say on the subject. Just accuses me of jealousy and wanting to keep her tied up with useless housework there at The Hornbeams.

"I don't have to tell you that's ridiculous. For one thing, I'm quite happy to warm up a pasty or the like if she'll make me one. I've done that for years. For another, she's hardly ever there anyway. If I telephone during the day she's never in, and I'd say she's over there at least four nights a week. What's worse, she's taken to staying overnight. And if I as much as hint at inconvenience—especially since I've taken over this new job in Chelmsford—she just flies into a rage and attacks me."

"Rage? Attack? Doesn't sound like Mama to me." An idea occurred to me. "You don't think it's the menopause, do you? That's what Simon suggested."

Daddy shook his head. In doing so he caused me to notice how his Cornishly swart hair was graying at the temples. "This is nothing to do with anything closing *down*. If you ask me, Mama is opening up! Only the world she's entering has no room for me. I want no part of it, either."

He sounded so hurt that I immediately sought to mollify his feelings. "It's the same for us boys, Daddy. We all have a sense of being excluded. It's as if we are part of some rejected past. It's not very pleasant to feel like someone else's outworn experience, is it?"

"She could be going through what Grandma Bryant would have called 'a phase.' Oh God, I hope that's what it is! I don't think I can go on much longer playing second fiddle to her friends."

My father was no griper, but from time to time a little bleat of self-pity would enter his voice, and I hated it. Hated it not just because it demeaned him but because I knew it was a sound not always absent from my own throat. I heard it coloring his words there in the Maypole Inn and I reacted instantly—with a youthful cruelty which, like that shared impulse to whine and complain, has never really gone away.

"We mustn't forget when she was secondary to you. I can still remember Natalie Lockyer-Pope and all that."

Daddy eyed me uncertainly. He never could keep up with the velocity of his sons' thoughts. All three of us were quicker than he.

"What's she got to do with it? I never saw Natalie as more important than Mama. Your mother was never banished from my life—not for a single second."

But I already regretted the allusion to something which had taken place ten years earlier and which, in any case, as a small child at the time I could hardly know much about. I decided to make light of it.

"There was a time when I preferred Natalie to you! She bought me my mongoose and it was you who made me send him back. Though it was Mama who backed you up—it was she who was the real traitor, I suppose."

Daddy thought awhile. "At least she was involved with us all then. Now she couldn't care less. That's what I find so hard to take."

"What does she say when you bring it up? I presume you have told her that—"

"She laughs in my face and says it's all my imagination."

"Mama is a genius at that."

"At blaming me for making things up?"

I widened my eyes slightly. Daddy was rarely possessed of humor. That is, I presumed he was trying to be mildly funny. He wouldn't have known how to be *faux naïf*.

"No, Daddy dear—at ducking reality and living by her own rules."

He breathed heavily. "Of all the boys, I don't think I have to spend long explaining to you, particularly, how much I love Mama. But I have to add *she is an extraordinarily complicated woman*."

I sat back and eyed our two drinks on the bare table.

"Funny you should say that again. It's the second time. Remember the first?"

He glanced at me—quite uncomprehending. I was still only learning how relative shared memories could be for people. Even people who were reasonably close, like Daddy and me.

"When New Zealand first came up and Mama was so keen to go. You called her complicated to me then."

"My! You *do* go back! I'd forgotten all that business."

"It changed our lives, though. Nothing was the same afterwards."

"You always overdramatize. In any case, bigger things have happened since."

"Meaning the war and Mama getting her independence?"

"Meaning—oh, a thousand and one things." He suddenly look flustered and tired. He spoke in a yet lower register. "Do you know what she asked me the other day? Whether we should have another baby."

"That's ridiculous! Sounds like the menopause. She's too old!"

"That's what I told her. But she said that she'd looked it up and that it would only be highly unusual at her age—not impossible."

"Not impossible, but highly dangerous."

"She said we could always adopt. There were so many unwanted babies. She knows a woman who runs an excellent adoption agency."

"I hope you said that it was the craziest idea you'd ever heard and that it was about time, as a now middle-aged woman, she started to think about settling down and accepting the fact the war's over."

"I didn't have to. She said as much herself. She said that if I didn't want to have a new family in Cornwall, then we must stay at The Hornbeams and provide you boys with a home until your education was completed. Then we could return to Cornwall and I could retire."

"And what did you say to all this postwar planning?"

"I said I felt a bit young to talk about retiring and so she told me I could probably get a job running Bodmin Lunatic Asylum if I wanted. I said I'd already seen enough mental illness for one lifetime and I thought she was being a bit insensitive. We've hardly talked since. She rang Charlotte to tell her that, as I wasn't keen about a baby, she would put her second plan into place."

"Which was?"

"I don't know. She never said. I don't think she is ever likely to say—to me at least."

"You want me to ask her, is that it?"

"You must think me very weak, Davey. No, I don't want my *son* to ask my *wife* about what she proposes to do. To tell you the truth, I don't think I was much good the first time I was a father—I'm pretty sure I'd be worse now."

This time I knew he wasn't fishing for paternal compliments. My hand went out and daringly found his across the beer-wet tabletop. "Don't be an idiot!" I squeezed his index finger. "Just like you said, *Mama is an extraordinarily complicated woman*!"

We began to laugh. First him and then me. First raggedly and then in unison. Louder and louder. Until a concerned landlord came over and asked us if everything was all right.

CHAPTER ELEVEN

I moved out from The Hornbeams two weekends later—delaying the event because Daddy's birthday intervened and Mama besought us all to attend the celebration, which was held on the nearest Saturday. Simon came down from Cambridge and it was then that we met for the first time the woman who was eventually to become his wife.

I liked Joan right away and so, I knew, did Daddy. But the same can hardly be said for Mama, who from the very start treated the ex-Wren from the Wirral, across the Mersey from Liverpool, as an utter stranger and never once suggested that her eventual daughter-in-law refer to her as other than Mrs. Bryant. Not that the frost on our family assembly that Saturday afternoon could be wholly ascribed to Mama's patent enmity toward the sole other woman. Simon characteristically got things off to a poor start with our parents.

"The fucking train from Cambridge to Liverpool Street was an hour late! Christ Almighty, has anyone told these socialist bastards that the war's over and these delays are inexcusable?"

"I think the fuel shortage, son, is proving worse than Hitler's bombers. Though who would've believed it two years ago?" Daddy said.

I knew he was trying to be pacific in that he didn't remark Simon's cussing. Mama did, though!

"That may be how they speak in *your* circle, darling," pausing ever so lightly to include Joan sitting next to her son on the chesterfield, "but not even the inconvenience of train delays warrants barrack-room language. Not here at The Hornbeams, anyway."

I looked glumly at Little Arthur, who was standing by the open fire with me as we sipped our sherry. This was meat and drink to our older brother. It always had been.

"Oh really?" Simon drawled, "How interesting, Mama. You know, I really learned to cuss before I went into the Navy. It was your own brother who taught me the basics when we first moved in here to live off Grandmama."

Mama stiffened. "I cannot believe that for a single moment, Simon. No brother of mine—"

Simon deliberately chose to misunderstand her. "I don't mean *The Saint*. Don't forget we never met him, so he couldn't corrupt us. I'm referring, of course, to Uncle Harry."

"Where *is* Uncle Harry?" I blurted. "He seems to have vanished off the face of the earth!"

"Only to Guernsey," Daddy said, cluing in immediately to my strategy. "The income tax is less there. Anyway, it's the only place his wife will meet him."

"Where do you hear all this nonsense, Wesley. How would you know where my brother and his dollied-up little wife are possibly lurking?"

"He writes to me from time to time," Daddy said, albeit reluctantly. "He always has when he's been away. He started doing it during the Great War when I was in Egypt. Naturally he wrote me now for my birthday."

"You mean you've heard from him recently and never even informed his sister?" Mama stared at him and I'm sure she wasn't faking her incredulity.

Daddy obviously thought that too good an opportunity to miss. "You're here so rarely, my dear. In the few moments when we have time to talk, more important things usually come up, or I've forgotten poor old Harry's scribbled notes. This time there was a proper card, though, and sent to my office in Chelmsford. I didn't even realize he knew the address."

Mama rose. I thought for a moment she was about to stalk from the room, her small figure ramrod stiff in outrage. But Simon's fiancée addressed her. "If you're going to the kitchen to serve up lunch, Mrs. Bryant, perhaps I could help?"

Mama evidently found it easier to vent her anger on a stranger rather than a devious husband or insolent son. "Thank you very much, Miss Hewett, but I have managed to accommodate this all-male family on my own to now and I *think* I may well be able to do so for the foreseeable future. But how kind of you to ask."

She then turned with a flourish to face her spouse. "Wesley, you might ask our guest whether she needs yet another sherry. The boys will surely get their own drinks. Lunch, I might add, will be served at one-fifteen."

Crossing to the chintz-covered window seat in the alcove, she spread her gray flannel skirt, sat, patted the neighboring cushion and addressed

Joan again—but this time as if there were only the two of them in the living room. "Come and sit next to me. I suppose your people are wrestling with the servant problem like everyone else? Here, near London, industry wages are so astronomical that domestics have gone the way of the dinosaur. The situation is quite dreadful."

When Joan flashed Simon a glance, I supposed she was seeking guidance as to whether she should go and join his mother—but Simon was already busy pouring himself a second stiff gin and tonic. The young woman joined her hostess and while we watched—a rather self-conscious horseshoe of observers—Joan Hewett did her best to identify with Mama's conversation.

"I'm one of three girls so Mummy and Daddy have been rather insulated from the need for domestic help. Even when I was away in the Navy there was still Jacqueline and Eleanor at home."

"I cannot imagine what it must be like to raise three girls," Mama said. "A most peculiar experience."

"Why?" said Joan. "In what way *peculiar?*" She was smiling—but not amiably.

Mama eyed her in astonishment. "For a woman to raise more of the *same*.... The task, the challenge, I would've thought, was to cope with something *other*—children on whom life was going to lay quite *different* expectations. For little boys one has to constantly turn outward—to others for good example—a father or brother, perhaps. I—I cannot explain further as I do not have the vocabulary. Then like so much in life, Miss Hewett, the subject is either self-evident or indescribable."

While Joan pondered that, Simon spoke up. "It's all a bit academic, anyhow, as we were left in the hands of a child-loathing, sterile aunt in Cornwall for most of our growing-up, weren't we, Davey?"

Little Arthur intervened before I could get a word out—even though, ironically, I suppose he had been less in Mama's company as a child than either Simon or myself. "That's tripe, Simon, after all, you had years at home before the war. And when you were at Probus, you always wanted to go off at the vacs and stay with chums—even if Mama and Daddy were planning to visit us if they could get away from the Blitz."

Simon shrugged, swirled the liquid in his cut-glass tumbler. "We all invent our versions of history. You have yours and I have mine. Let's leave it at that, Little Arthur, shall we?"

With such uneasy banter did we pass Daddy's forty-seventh birthday party. I loathed every minute of it; even volunteered to accompany Mama to the Churchfields' later that afternoon. That was an excuse not only to get out of the house and away from the bickering of my siblings but to flee embarrassment over Daddy, who, being slightly sloshed, turned to his future daughter-in-law and tried vainly to amuse her with mildly off-color stories. She appreciated his fumbling efforts, though. At least the two of them forged bonds on that day, I believe, which lasted until Daddy's death—by which time there were no longer any family reunions to exacerbate wounds or stimulate hate.

The sting of that birthday memory was enough in itself to keep me away from The Hornbeams until the Christmas vacation, but stronger, more positive magnets kept me in London. I fell in love, or at least in lust.

Patrick Moreton was the son of a Church of Ireland priest and, quite by chance, had the room on the same landing as mine in the house on Clerkenwell Green where we had our digs. For my first full two weeks in London I had scarcely noticed the rather stooped young man with a widow's peak of auburn hair over a receding forehead. In fact, it wasn't until my second London Sunday that I recognized him sitting farther along the row of chairs in the gloom of the priory church of St. Bartholomew-the-Great.

Instead of leaving the medieval building immediately after mass was over, I noticed, he sauntered across the broad uneven flagstones, past the massive stone pillars toward the Lady chapel. On impulse I decided to join him as he stood there staring up at the lofty triforium, lost in wonder at the unornamented Norman arches and pillars. His head jerked down to eye-level long before I reached his side. I didn't have to introduce myself as he spoke at once, expressing delight at meeting someone from the same set of digs. Neither of us wasted any time in indicating our mutual attraction. We hadn't reached the lavish tomb of Rahere, the twelfth-century founder of the priory church, before it was decided we would spend the rest of that blue-skied if chill December sabbath exploring.

After visiting seven city churches—in various states of disrepair from the bombing—we extended our tour to include the cockney tumult of the open-air market at Petticoat Lane. There, under the concealment of the crowds milling between the stalls, we daringly traced excited fingers across each other's trousers—with such erotic effect that, without utterance from either of us, we abruptly fled the market for the privacy of Patrick's room. He first suggested a cup of tea, but on seeing his neatly made bed with its brightly checkered counterpane I rejected the brew and suggested we immediately respond to that stiff urge which—for me, at least—was in rapid danger of becoming an ache.

Thus began a series of sex-ridden days in his bed or next door in mine, during which I abandoned all pretense of attending lectures and he didn't once darken the precincts of the Law Courts where he was articled. I forget the precise number of days we explored and re-explored our sarcological secrets, panted and slurped our desire as our mouths competed with other organs for the total union of our writhing bodies. But I do remember with stark clarity the first hiatus in this sustained sexual frenzy. Mama telephoned to say that she was in town to visit her family solicitors with Charlotte and that they wanted to take me out to dinner before returning to The Hornbeams. I knew I couldn't get out of it without Herculean lying, so suggested my new friend, Patrick, be invited as well.

Mama took that equitably enough, although when she and Charlotte arrived at our digs she initially spoke as if a nervous Patrick dithering next to me, putting his weight first on one foot and then the other, were invisible.

"So how is the little boy who was so keen to leave the nest?" she asked.

Patrick addressed Charlotte. "It's a pleasure to meet you, Mrs. Bryant. Davey has spoken so much of you, I feel we already know one another."

Mama only smiled sweetly. "Davey, if you only began with introductions this young man would be spared foolish errors. I am Davey's mother and this is Miss Churchfield. Her only acquaintance with young men is from involvement with the Scout Movement. She once ran a Cub pack. But that was before I knew you, wasn't it, Charlotte?"

Charlotte was infrequently embarrassed because she was usually unaware of the kind of situation that caused the emotion. She was so sunnily good-natured that she rarely sensed irritation in another. That was particularly true in terms of my mother, I had observed, and when it did dawn on her that Mama was put out it was generally too late to salvage matters. Instead, being stoic as well as sensible, she smilingly endured the storm, knowing from experience that Mama's moods, though turbulent, were also transitory. To my relief this initial meeting gave rise to no such ire on Mama's part. The mistake was quickly sorted out, laughed off, and talk turned to the arrangements Mama had made for our joint evening.

As we left my bedsitter I was happy to see Patrick pairing off with Charlotte. It allowed me to hear Mama's news from The Hornbeams. About my brothers she was brief. In the most deadpan of voices she informed me that Simon was to marry "his lass from Liverpool" early in the New Year and that it was to be a stark town-hall affair with none of the family present. Without waiting for comment she went on to express hope that I would see as much of Little Arthur as possible. She feared he might be rather lonely in London as he pursued his architectural studies. That brought her for the first time to the subject which I had been waiting for with mounting nervousness—namely Patrick.

"Your baby brother is not gregarious like you, dear. He wouldn't know how to make friends with someone like your tall friend. Where was it you said you met him? I must say I am tickled by that Irish lilt."

I decided instantly that the complications of truth must be simplified. "I never did say where we met, Mama. But it happened to be at St. Bartholomew's in Canonbury one Sunday morning. We discovered that, by the oddest coincidence, we had digs in the same house."

"And on the same landing! What an *extraordinary* coincidence, as you rightly say. Then coincidence runs in our family. It is what the scientists call *genetic*. Poppa was always running into people he hadn't seen for years—right after their names had come up over dinner the previous evening."

I thought I was about to be treated to a flood of reminiscence, as in childhood, but I was in error.

"I cannot understand what this new man Attlee is up to. Bringing in thugs like that Aneurin Bevan to run his wretched health scheme. You'd have thought the country had learned its lesson from that last Welsh rotter, Lloyd George."

"Mama, that was *years* ago!"

"Nonsense, darling! He was in Parliament right up to last year and, if you ask me, was a Nazi sympathizer. And as Minister of Health, I can tell you, that Bevan is driving your father toward another breakdown. Quite frankly, Davey, I don't think he'll ever be really happy until he's finally back in Cornwall."

I pondered that piece of information as I hailed a taxi and the four of us clambered in. Mama told me to tell the driver the address of the Connaught. As I sat on the jump seat next to Patrick, facing her, I asked a question which had been spinning in my head at least since Daddy and I had taken the evening spin for a drink at the Maypole.

"Do you think he's really fit enough to farm?"

But Mama darted a glance at my lover and changed the subject. I knew that nothing would induce her to talk of the family in front of him. It was her way of telling me that my friend Patrick might be an intimate—but to her he was still a stranger.

"You must tell these boys, Charlotte, what we propose to do next summer."

"You mean go to Falmouth to see Wesley's cousins?"

Mama closed her eyes. "That is for a weekend and is so ordinary as to be of no interest whatever to these young men."

Charlotte smiled dreamily and thought again. "Oh, you mean the thing Daddy was talking about—if Uncle Hubert can pull strings with the British-Army-on-the-Rhine people?"

"Of *course* I mean that, darling. What on earth else could I mean?"

"It's all so vague, isn't it? I mean, we can only go to Munich if Uncle Hubert can persuade his American counterpart to agree. And he might be moved to Supreme HQ Allied Expeditionary Force next month, Daddy said."

"What your father said was that he anticipated no problems for us—given our background in ambulance work. I heard him myself on the phone last night, making the initial enquiries."

"What's all this?" I asked in unfeigned interest. "Going abroad so soon after the war? Isn't everything devastated still?"

"You place too much credence in what you read in the newspapers. There may be a little inconvenience—no one expects a total return to normality yet. But if one is prepared to rough it a bit and take one's own soap and toilet paper, there are many places dying to have tourists back."

"I can't see Daddy putting up with very much like that."

"He won't have to, darling. Charlotte and I are traveling alone."

I leaped away from that like a frog with a straw poked up it. "Didn't you mention Munich? I understand that's nothing but rubble and an army of occupation. For two women traveling on their own...."

"We were going to Switzerland in any case. Then Mr. Churchfield suggested his brother could no doubt arrange something in Bavaria. Things aren't quite as bad there as in northern Germany. We should be staying outside Munich—the guests of the American Army people. It will all be properly arranged before we leave home. You know how thorough Mr. Churchfield is."

"My parents have been to Paris recently," Patrick announced suddenly. "They said if you can afford the black market, and accept the ethics of it, things are certainly better there than here."

"What do you expect?" Mama said savagely. "We only *won* the war, after all. I gather food is more plentiful in Dublin, too. The ethics would seem relative."

That brought us to the Connaught—to my immense relief and also to that of Patrick, who, long before the cab had stopped, had let his jump seat spring up and, crouching and swaying over us like a vast bird, flailed his arms and shouted unnecessarily that he could see the restaurant ahead.

Entering the place, he pulled me aside and whispered quickly. "Your mother doesn't like me. What on earth can I do?"

I told him that he was talking balls and that Mama's fleeting acerbity wasn't to be taken personally but seen, rather, as a small cloud hurrying across an otherwise friendly sky. I also told him to watch and learn how Charlotte reacted. That didn't go down very well. He looked at me darkly and said that as *he* wasn't Mama's lover, observing Charlotte was of no use to him whatever.

I think we would have had a flaming row ourselves if the ladies had not then returned from the cloakrooms. As we followed the *maître d'* across the vast room, Mama announced in an uncharacteristically loud voice that she had first eaten in that very room when a little girl as the guest of her Poppa, and that she hoped that neither food nor service had deteriorated in the interim. As I counted up thirty years I wanted to sink through the floorboards in embarrassment.

"Do tell us all about your work," Mama said to Patrick when the waiter had left us. "I suppose the law doesn't change that much year after year. I had a cousin who was hoping to end up in the Inns of Court but that was eons ago."

I couldn't think to whom she referred but I was saved any speculation as Patrick—totally ignoring her question—immediately launched into a paean for the senior partner in his firm and started a long anecdote as confirmation of his boss's wisdom and wit. It was to do with the buggery trial of an airman, which was going badly for the defendant, when his barrister deliberately misquoted the Royal Air Force motto—*Per Ardua ad Astra* as *Per Anus ad Astra*, so breaking up the court in mirth that the airman got off with a remarkably light sentence from a usually severe judge.

The chill with which this anecdote was greeted did not fully disperse throughout the unconscionably long meal. True, Charlotte tried on several occasions to turn our talk to such matters as the fate of the red squirrel in Epping Forest after the invasion of the gray species from North America. But Mama was having none of it. Deliberately misinterpreting Patrick's court story, she twice told him how much she deplored verbal cruelty to one's social inferiors. And then, just when her expressly ordered ice-cream-and-banana dessert arrived, she took an even more hostile tack.

"I suppose it is rather silly to ask what you did in the war—what with your background. Although we did have an Irish friend from Glenariff who went down on the battlecruiser HMS *Hood.* And dear Terry O'Connor from Dublin served with my eldest son, Simon, on a corvette."

"I was in school in Tipperary, Mrs. Bryant," Patrick told her with a smile. "I am sorry I was too young for anything so serious."

"How odd," Mama said, smiling as extravagantly as my lover. "I would have thought you quite old enough to have known at least *four* years of war. Then appearances can be so terribly deceptive. Angel-faced Davey here, on the other hand, is always finding it hard to explain that he did manage to find fifteen months to fight against those revolting Nazis."

That was the first time I actually observed Mama as capable of concentrated bitchery. It was not to be the last.

CHAPTER TWELVE

I did not do well that term and its successor was, if anything, even worse for me. I seemed quite unable to concentrate on anything vaguely academic and many were the philosophy textbooks purchased never to be opened. I avoided The Hornbeams as much as possible and had difficulty summoning even the energy to telephone—which I did when I realized that more than two weeks had elapsed and I hadn't made any contact with my parents. This was not pure dilatoriness nor mere difficulty in concentrating on books after my turbulent time in the Navy. I felt guilty, given the resources of concentration and energy I was able to accord the handsome body of Patrick Moreton.

I could not get enough of him nor—this was the blinding bliss—he of me. Everything seemed conducive to our passion and the purely fortuitous circumstance of adjacent rooms in the lodging house made sexual congress such an easy matter. There isn't a boy who likes other boys, I guess, who has not asked: *Do you have a place we can go to?* It must be the most-put question among gay cruisers in the cities of the world. Patrick and I did not have to ask it.

Nor did we have any difficulty with sexual compromise. We discovered on that first afternoon after meeting in church that we were both cocksuckers, and from there on *fellatio* (as Patrick with his legal enthusiasm preferred to call it, while I stuck with sixty-nining) largely satisfied our sexual purposes. Occasionally pure fatigue would demand some simple mutual masturbation after hour upon hour, night after night given over to more antic sexual play.

The overriding recollection, which can still evoke my tumescence, is of Patrick's balls swinging over my face, or my sightlines determined by the huge silhouette of his cock as I gazed supplicating up his shaft to the reddish gold of his bush, and the lick-cleaned navel beyond that. He seemed equally happy hanging on my curved length, nuzzling my crotch or thrusting moist lips up and down until he had summoned and drunk all that could be drawn from my sexual well.

There was no serpent in our erotic Eden and, perhaps even more surprising, little to jar or mar our emotional relationship. True, there were differences between us. I was two years older than Patrick, even if I looked his junior (as Mama had cruelly pointed out), and I was more compulsive and more submissive than he. We were ignorant of such terms as "S&M" and certainly no roles or hints of master and slave were ever fashioned between us. But I still begged his flesh and his time; pleaded with him for his cock when he claimed his law books. But in minutes the tomes lay covered with our underpants and he was as noisily lapping up me as I returned to the prepucial joys of him.

Where the maggot entered our juice-filled apple was in the subsequent impact of the theft of all those nocturnal and weekend hours—the lifeblood of students—upon our academic standards. By early spring I suspected I might be flunking my first year; Patrick's barrister had intimated that the term might prove his articled last. By June things had attained a critical stage. Seeing disaster looming, I obscurantistically stopped attending even a minimum of lectures. When I was not lying with my head in the pseudo-safety of Patrick's loins, I was attending tennis at Wimbledon and watching the Frenchman Yvon Petra dominate the men's singles in the first postwar championships.

A week later, on learning that I had failed three out of five examinations and that my lover was now on probation with his law firm, Patrick and I left via the New Haven–Dieppe ferry for M. Petra's homeland. It was Patrick's idea and a last-minute one at that. Before leaving, I had to pay a flying visit down to The Hornbeams, both to prevaricate about my exam results and also to wheedle some extra cash above my allowance from Mama—preferably without letting Daddy know.

I expected no opposition from Mama, who was invariably generous with her sons in financial matters. I cannot recall a time when I was refused at least some money when it was solicited, though it was not always the amount requested. Nor were these mildly embarrassing transactions ever accompanied by a sermon from her on prudence or restraint. I believe she secretly liked extravagance in us although she spent very little upon herself. Her reaction that June of 1946 was typical.

"Mama, do you think you could give me an advance on my allowance? This marvelous opportunity has just sprung up, you see, to go to Paris, where all expenses will be paid by Patrick's uncle, who lives there and wants someone to house-sit while he is away in North Africa on business. It will be a super chance to improve my French. Besides, do you realize I have never been out of this country in all my life?"

"And Charlotte and I could meet with you there on our way to Munich. That would be nice, dear. How much do you want and what are the dates?"

"Sixty pounds for at least one whole month? Paris is *very* expensive—you remember the conversation with Patrick about his parents when they were visiting there. It would cover the end of June and all of July. Patrick's uncle didn't mention a precise date for his return as I gather it's rather dependent on how his business turns out."

"Mr. Churchfield says there are some silly Treasury regulations about how much you can take abroad. But if I give you forty now, I can bring extra with me if you need it when we arrive. Charlotte has made all the arrangements and I gather that thanks to her Army relatives we shall be staying at the George V, as Mr. Churchfield says it's the only one of the better hotels that is halfway back to normal. We'll be there over Bastille Day. But get the details from her at dinner this evening."

"I rather wanted to get it all out of the way now, Mama. That's why I was so glad I caught you alone. You know what a fuss Daddy makes about money and that. I'm certainly not looking forward to a meal where the chief topic is either my extravagance or my exam results."

"*What* exam results, Davey? I was unaware you knew them yet."

"I didn't do too well in ethics or Greek philosophy. But I can make it up next term. In fact, my tutor thought the Paris expedition an excellent thing for study. I was going to take some books for vacation reading in any case."

"I presume you know what you are doing. I am not altogether happy about that Patrick, to be quite honest. He didn't seem altogether *reliable*—though that is possibly a prejudice on my part about the feckless side of all the Celts—including the Irish."

I felt on safer ground after the mishmash of truth and falsehood with which I had just presented her. "That's another subject I think we should avoid at dinner. You know Daddy will just see it as an attack on the Bryants and all things Cornish."

Mama gave me an odd look. "Your father is taken up enough about my own trip to Paris and Munich without wanting to get involved in the affairs of you three boys. He insists I cook enough pasties before I go and he will heat them up, day after day."

"That's crazy, Mama."

"That is your father. And if that is what he wishes, then that is what he'll get."

I returned to Clerkenwell the next day, the richer not only by forty pounds from Mama but by a further ten-pound note that Charlotte squeezed into my hand just before I entered the railroad station to which she had kindly driven me. It was to her that I confessed that, because of my marks, my consequent college career was somewhat more dubious than I had let appear to Mama. But Charlotte was never trammeled by such matters and kissed me with a bright smile and said all would turn out for the best. I at once suppressed misgivings, and returned to Patrick not only bubbling with happiness at the success of the mission but with an erotic urgency that took us long hours of the night to assuage.

By the time, three days later, that we pulled into the Gare St. Lazare (to a flaming sunset and an onslaught of Gallic scents and sounds), my euphoria had evaporated and I knew a conflict of moods. I was fascinated by the black berets, baggy blue pants, and the smell of Gauloise cigarettes in the Paris air plus the blare of horns and the screech of brakes. I also felt apprehensive and alien. I looked at my auburn-haired companion for comfort but none was forthcoming. I felt a stranger, even toward this young man whose every arcane corner of flesh I knew better than my own.

It had not been until we were riding the swells of the English Channel that Patrick had deigned to reveal that his "uncle" was, in fact, someone he had encountered but two years earlier—and that in rather *louche* circumstances: the man had cruised him in the zoo of Dublin's Phoenix Park. To my alarmed response and slew of questions Patrick had insisted that "Uncle" George was a wealthy bachelor who had a country estate in County Cork as well as the sumptuous *appartement* in the sixteenth *arrondissement* where we were headed. He repeatedly strove to quell my incipient panic by insisting that, in letter after letter, Uncle George had stressed that Patrick was to bring a friend if he wished and that we were to stay as long as we liked. Patrick also informed me, while on the high seas, that this providential character was the senior Irish delegate with the fledgling U.N. organization called UNESCO—which was just coming into being in the old Hotel Majestic.

As the taxi drew up at a rather modern-looking façade on the Rue Berlioz I decided to be totally passive and leave everything to Patrick. He had gotten me into this highly vulnerable situation and it was thus up to him to ensure that I was safe and secure. I thanked the taxi driver profusely in unrepentant English and allowed my lover to settle the fare.

The building had a between-wars flavor and was more squat and less grim than most we had passed since leaving the Champs Elysées. In the pale stone porch there were tubs of white petunias and scarlet salvia. Like the little street it bordered, the tiled porch bore a quiet and calm that *oozed* opulence. I could feel my pulse race as we awaited a response to the bell Patrick pushed. When I heard a sound within, nervousness mingled with renewed irritation with Patrick. It had occurred to me that I didn't even know our host's surname—and I was damned if I was going to address him as "Uncle" George.

When the door opened it proved to be the concierge standing there—although at the time, unused to the French custom, I mistakenly took the middle-aged woman for the maid.

"Is M. Cronyn home, madame? We are his guests." I thirstily took in the detail of nomenclature as Patrick announced our arrival.

We were ushered across a spacious vestibule to a small elevator in which we jammed ourselves and our suitcases. "Did you gather from that woman," I asked Patrick, "that Mr. Cronyn was expecting us? Didn't sound much like it to me."

"Of course he is," my friend said airily. "The evening of the twenty-seventh—it was all made *very* clear. I'm sure he is up there on the *troisième étage* waiting for us."

"I bloody well hope so. There seemed to be no hotels at all in this exclusive neighborhood, and at this time of night they're probably all full up anyway."

Patrick prodded my private parts. "Don't *fret* so, me darlin'!" he announced in stage Irish. "Everything's going to turn out all right, you wicked old disbeliever!"

In less than an hour I was prepared to grudgingly concede that maybe he was right. George Cronyn, who met us at the elevator entrance, a drink in his hand, proved to be a most affable man of impeccable manners, with a courteous approach that immediately won me over. He didn't drag us to bedrooms straightaway but insisted we sit and have a drink and regain our composure before allowing mundane matters to intrude.

That in itself I thought most civilized, but he soon surpassed his opening gambit in a number of ways. The first was his insistence that he take us out to dinner at his favorite neighborhood restaurant. It was a meal superior to any I had ever eaten—washed down with prodigious quantities of wine, including a magnum of Mumm's champagne which George donated as a special celebration of our arrival and a precursor, he promised with a grin, of pleasurable things to come.

Afterwards, he drove us in his new Ford Mercury convertible to a discreetly concealed bar off the Champs Elysées, where the clientele consisted mainly of young men like Patrick and myself.... At George's coaxing (we had established a first-name basis before even leaving the apartment, in spite of my feeble attempts to call him Mr. Cronyn), I ordered an *Izarra*, which he explained was a Basque liqueur derived from wildflowers picked in the Pyrenees. He went on to explain that, because it was decently dry, with the possible exception of some bottles of Calvados it was the only French liqueur worth drinking. However, I noticed he ordered a brandy for himself.

There was a slight altercation when Patrick's and my drinks arrived, as the silver-haired and hunched waiter brought a less potent *yellow* version which George peremptorily refused on our behalf as being distinctly inferior to the *green* variety which he claimed vehemently he had initially ordered. I had not heard him make the color qualification and it immediately transpired that Patrick hadn't either.

"Don't *natter* at the old fart, George. He may be deaf but I am not. You didn't specify any color when you ordered."

Not to be outdone by my friend, and a little alarmed at the glower of animosity on the menial's face, I hastened to offer my portion of oil for these mildly agitated waters.

"I'm quite happy to keep this yellow, George, and save his legs. As I have never had either kind I can graduate to green the next time I have it."

It was then that I learned that compromise and amelioration were rare visitors to our host's style of confronting the world and its human inhabitants.

To Patrick he said curtly, "Your French isn't good enough to understand what I said to this imbecile." On me he rounded with the observation: "You're not in England now, my boy, and you don't have to apologize for every fucking mistake that someone else makes." To the hovering white-coated waiter he gave instructions in loud French to take away the piss he had brought and bring back the real McCoy if he ever wanted to see a tip. The green Izarra duly arrived and the aging retainer disappeared. George's mood instantly transformed, he sat back on the *banc*, beamed at both of us and asked what plans, if any, we had for the morrow.

For the remaining couple of hours of that evening—before we reeled in an amalgam of drunkenness and fatigue to the silk sheets of our bed—George regaled us with funny stories about personalities at unofficial UNESCO meetings since he'd arrived with the Preparatory Commission in the previous September. He insisted that when he had to deal trenchantly with the French themselves, he would remind them of their ignominious defeat in June 1940 at the hands of Hitler. He also described in great detail the expeditions within and around Paris that he had been planning for us. At no point, not even when the astronomical *addition* was finally brought to our table, did he reveal the slightest anger or sign of ruffled feelings. But in my cautious Cornish way I strove to store in my memory that image of George which we'd glimpsed over our introduction to Izarra.

However, all that was relegated to a faraway file in my head as I proceeded to fall in love with Paris—and to be excitingly tutored in all things Gallic by this handsome and courteous Irishman who was so patiently persuasive in opening new vistas before my adolescent eyes.

One immediate impact of this basking in the full-blooded attentiveness of our host was its effect upon Patrick and myself. Perhaps the intensity of our romance had attained its zenith before we left London. All I know is that our sexual play perceptibly slackened during that first event-crammed week in the French capital. At the most basic level, by the time we found ourselves jointly between the sheets, which was rarely before one or even two in the morning, we were both dog-tired and, more often than not, quite sloshed from the variety of aperitifs, wines and liqueurs we'd consumed. The embargo on other than Izarra lasted only that first night and the plethora of other alcoholic subtleties to which George introduced us made even the rare occasions when we were able to climb upon one another with our pricks reasonably stiff degenerate rapidly into snoring somnolence.

Once or twice it had been far worse. Either Patrick or I had had to abruptly abandon all thought of sharing lubricious liquids in order to reel into the adjacent bathroom—driven by a dreadful booming in an aching head—to await gut-wrenching upheavals and a dire legacy of clammy perspiration. By morning, though, the fact of unexplored Paris, the ebullience of youth and the vigorous encouragement of George soon combined to banish all sordid recollection, remorse and vain resolution. In those days I was a stranger to hangovers, and needed but a modicum of sleep.

Whatever the reasons for conjugal slackening between Patrick and me, it was indubitably not the erotic closedown of my genitalia. It was my own theory—though one I elected not to discuss with either Patrick or George—that the prodigious amount of red wine we were consuming at lunch and dinner, day by day, was having a distinctly stimulating impact upon my sexual longings. I found myself staring hungrily at the area halfway down every pretty waiter we encountered at the myriad restaurants visited, lingering longingly inside *vespasiennes* (those long-vanished popular *pissoir* haunts of gay men) and stiffened with arousal simply when milling with the strollers, and making eye contact with the cute ones, up and down both sides of the Champs Elysées.

For the first four days that was wholly the way of it: a thousand intriguing sights but nary a follow-up with a single one. If I found myself next to a hose-like length of penis in a pissoir, it was only to be frustratingly aware that Patrick and George stood awaiting me outside. Every bright hope raised by an amply endowed *garçon* whose cock-contours I could hungrily make out behind the black pants below the white bum jacket was an expectation doomed with the arrival of the bill for George to pay.

It was not until the conclusion of our first week that this increasingly tense pattern of arousal and frustration was broken. George had to visit his office that morning—a practice he had obviously neglected since we had rarely been out of his sight, save to sleep, since our arrival. He was to take us to lunch at noon. Patrick, far more the dutiful son, was to spend the earliest part of his morning purchasing a silk scarf for his mother and, after visiting some recently opened boutique which George had insisted was the only proper place to buy gifts for mothers, was to meet me at a *tabac* near the Etoile where we would write postcards until George collected us in the Mercury.

That gave me my first couple of hours entirely on my own since we had arrived in Paris. It was something I had been looking forward to with growing anticipation from the moment our plans had been formed but I was careful not to tell myself why. Neither did I compose a deliberate itinerary in my mind when I left the apartment on the Rue Berlioz. I told myself my purpose was simply to enjoy the sunny pleasures of the morning and to skirt the bushy fringes of the Bois before stopping perhaps for a coffee at one of the numerous cafés at the end of several thoroughfares emanating from the Etoile.

Upon reaching the Avenue Foch I elected to walk down it, and headed toward the Jardin d'acclimatation. I used the time, as I sauntered passed hissing hoses and trim displays of the ubiquitous salvia and scarlet geraniums such as graced our apartment-building porch, to reflect on the person of our host. Patrick had made little reference to either the age or the looks of the man he had originally passed off as his uncle, but in fact George had turned out to be thirty-eight, and with the slightest graying at the temples the six-foot-one Irishman proved to be both handsome and distinguished-looking. He fitted my visual notions of a diplomat and in his demeanor and deportment satisfied my stern requirements of how a mature and successful gay should behave.

But these were only the superficial constituents of his public persona. He had impressed me and evoked my admiration at far profounder levels. We had spent barely a week in his presence yet we had already attended an afternoon concert by the Pasdeloup symphony orchestra (music being an area in which I was an utter ignoramus); been shown George's favorite Fragonard in an easily overlookable small salon in the vast Louvre and been taken by him to the medieval church of St-Julien-le-Pauvre where he introduced us to the bearded Catholic Uniate priest, who happily revealed some of its grime-obscured treasures often overlooked in the dim and dusty little sanctuary hard by the Seine.

Nor had our hectic education stopped there. He had again proved an erudite companion as we covered the standard attractions of Notre Dame and the Hôtel Dieu on the Ile de la Cité—as well as the Musée de Cluny and the other Rive Gauche sites. We still had Les Invalides and Sacré Coeur at Montmartre on our lists, as well as a trip to Versailles scheduled the following week, but George always saw to it that these expeditions were carefully spaced to allow our continuing gastronomic exposure to proceed without rush or compromise.

That day we were scheduled to visit the classic seafood restaurant of Prunier's for luncheon. Our well-organized host had already conferred with the management over the specifics of our meal, at which we were to be introduced to our benefactor's favorite Belon oysters before we jointly penetrated the piscine mysteries of a specially ordered Provençal *bouillabaisse*.

My attention turned away from George Cronyn as I reached and walked past a man wearing the traditional French workman's blue blouse and pants. He threw me a glance—held long enough for me to absorb the facts that he had not shaved for a couple of days and that his hair, which peeked out from under his Basque beret, was somewhat unkempt. He was patently not an entirely wholesome-looking character. That in itself made him thus perversely attractive to me. I was aware, of course, that in my bright green English Aertex shirt, with orange wool tie and worsted pants—I was dressed for that luncheon at Prunier's—I must look every bit the British tourist. That didn't faze me. Indeed, I hoped immediately that it would sustain his attention more than had I been a fellow-native.

I wasn't disappointed. When I deliberately faltered in my step he did likewise, and when I crossed the road toward an invitingly thick clump of bushes he followed in hot pursuit. In seconds we were standing facing each other, concealed by a screen of beech leaves, as we took out our tools and began to masturbate each other.

It was all over in a few moments and I have to confess I had hardly ejaculated before I was making plans to flee him and the possibility of his importuning me for money.

The successful escape and continuation of my walk as if nothing had happened left me with a distinct sense of dejection. I felt soiled by the sheer brevity of the experience and not a little ashamed at my niggardly refusal to pay a poor man for the privilege of handling his impressively large cock and for allowing me to cup his spurting sperm in my welcoming hand. After all those months of enjoying a full measure of erotic abandonment with Patrick, this *al fresco* dalliance was rather like taking a bath with one's clothes on. But in the accountancy of the promiscuous (among which I distinctly numbered since my sexual activities and sordid public exposure in the navy), even this fleeting erotic collusion was a relief from the thrall of what had already become an overly familiar body.

Even so, when I sat down with Patrick it was guilt I concealed in my breast. He looked at me suspiciously. "What have you been up to while I was shopping for Mother?"

"Shopping for you," I replied, withdrawing from my pocket a postcard of a blond Jean Marais, the French movie actor and Cocteau's boyfriend, which I happened to have seen in a rack outside the café at which I'd stopped for a coffee after leaving the Bois. I had bought it for myself but was more than prepared to hand it over if by so doing I could deflect him from further interrogation about my morning's activity. The ruse worked and I was mildly startled to observe that Patrick was quite touched by my gesture. It certainly didn't make me feel any better when he apologized for not getting me anything when he had been shopping.

"I suppose it is George we should be getting something for," I said in response. "After all, it is he who's doing all the spending and he won't let us pick up the tab for even the smallest thing."

"That's because he's so bloody pleased to have us stay," Patrick said with a grin. "After all, he's been rewarded enough to have two such handsome boyos under his roof!"

"What a mercenary creature you're turning into," I remonstrated. "I'm sure he doesn't think like that at all. He's just lonely for a bit of company and—well, he obviously likes introducing us to new things."

"Notice it's *things*—not *people*. He hasn't introduced us to a single one of his friends."

"It's summertime—they're probably all away on holiday."

"Why are you so anxious to provide him with excuses? You keen on him?"

In spite of the preposterousness of the suggestion, I blushed. "Don't be ridiculous! Don't you know what simple gratitude is?"

Patrick gave me a sharp look. "Davey, I don't know what *anything* simple is. That's what comes of being a lawyer. For all I know, old George hasn't worked out his own motives in having us here, but I never for a moment thought it was pure altruism."

"Does shopping for your mother always bring the cynic out in you?"

But Patrick only grinned and did his irritating Irish act on me yet again. "You'll be after learning, boyo, that while George is indeed a *gentleman*, he's still a man. If Oi was you, me lad, I'd enjoy Mr. Cronyn for what he is, but don't confuse him with Santa Claus just because he carries a sackful of toys."

Further defense of our generous host proved impossible as his Mercury pulled up to the curb at that very moment and he yelled for us to jump in next to him. The lunch proved a great success, although of such gargantuan proportions that when George suggested a postprandial nap we agreed with alacrity.

As if he had overheard our conversation at the café, he also suggested we eat at the apartment that evening—to rest our digestive apparatus, as he put it, from excessive culinary assault. To abet this, he told us, he had spent the morning at Hédiard's, a famous food store near the Madeleine, and at an adjacent store where he had augmented the special cheese selection he had bought for us. This with fresh fruit and an assortment of pastries—all washed down with a smooth Beaune—he offered as a light collation before taking us on an evening drive to the palace of Fontainebleau, which was then still the Supreme Headquarters Allied Powers, Europe, where we were to meet officer friends of his for a late drink.

I will never forget that "light collation," for its progress contained an indelible moment when I didn't know whether to applaud or shudder with disgust. Having watched George cut a portion of a highly smelly and sooty-crusted cheese from the half-dozen or so he had assembled on the wooden board, I myself cut a V of a more innocuous, honey-colored one he informed me was Port Salut. To my horror, a small white object emerged—to march slowly toward the circumference of my plate. Before I had time to flick it away from my sliced but as yet uneaten apple, with the speed and precision of a serpent's tongue the prongs of George's fork impaled the creature and, with a gracious excuse-me, he lifted the instrument to his mouth.

"I didn't think you'd want it, but that chap has been eating the best of that cheese for a couple of days and might now be described as the *essence* of Port Salut." He smacked his lips appreciatively. "My, that was good! An opportunity that doesn't come too often."

Patrick eyed him from the opposite end of the table (I had been placed between them). "How revolting! George! Is that how you represent Ireland to these frogs?"

"It is obvious frogs have better judgment over what goes into their mouths than you, young man. Don't ever forget where we met in Dublin and what you were doing."

George's consumption of a cheese maggot was suddenly afforded second place at this prospect of a revelation about Patrick which my devious lover had carefully concealed from me.

"I understand you met in the Phoenix Park zoo, George—at least, that's what our mutual friend told me."

"I encountered him with a hotel porter in a clump of rhododendrons, where he was so busy placing his mouth where he shouldn't on the young man's anatomy that I had to kick him to secure his attention."

Suddenly, my morning's encounter with the scruffy workman fell into tolerable prospective. I actually enjoyed the recollection and knew I would hoard it up in my masturbatory repository for "rainy days"....

It could've been George's frank disclosure of how he and Patrick really met; whatever the reason, my friend suddenly decided to indulge in an uncharacteristic bout of taciturnity which lasted for the remainder of the evening—he neither joshed me nor made quick repartee with his fellow-countryman. Not once, for example, did his stage Irishman put in an appearance, and he chose to sit in the back of the car rather than squeeze up front with George and me as was his usual custom.

Perhaps because of Patrick's mood, our driver suggested a shorter expedition around the perimeters of the Bois and a postponement of the Fontainebleau trip to daylight on another day. I was not displeased with the change in plans as I once or twice felt that George's hand was unnecessarily brushing my thigh when he changed gear. I moved as close to the passenger door as seemed polite and decided I'd make sure that bloody Patrick was subsequently inserted between me and my host when we were next out in the car.

However, when we got back to the apartment things evolved quite differently from what I might have expected from Patrick's silence and George's questing hand. After goodnights had been said—Patrick and I had firmly eschewed nightcaps in the living room—we all went down the long parquet corridor to the adjacent bedrooms. Trailing the other two, I saw George take Patrick aside at the entrance to our host's room, speak quickly into his ear and then give his waist a squeeze.

Embarrassed, I slipped quickly into our room and awaited my lover and his explanation for the odd behavior. But no Patrick materialized. Puzzled, I went back to the door as soon as I was in my pajamas and dressing gown, and peeked down the hallway toward George's room. No sign of either of them. And the bathroom across the way was also empty. There was a second bathroom—George's—which he said either of us could use if ours was occupied, so I grabbed my toilet bag and walked toward that. Now I at least had an excuse, however weak, if George should appear and ask what I was about.

At his bedroom door I paused. It was ajar and I could hear them speaking, although, frustratingly, I couldn't make out distinct words. I peered through the crack below the door's upper hinges. Just as I squinted the talking stopped. I was in time to see Patrick tight in the older man's arms and his face lifted to receive George's implanted kiss. I didn't wait for more but tiptoed quickly back to my room and the snug security of our bed.

It was as well I did so, for I barely had time to let my bathrobe slip to the ground as I slid between those cool silk sheets, before Patrick appeared in the doorway. Whatever had transpired between him and George had certainly not taken long. Even in the throes of my mounting jealousy I could hardly believe they had had time to engage in sex!

My initial instinct was to feign sleep but Patrick wasn't having any of that. "Sorry about that, boyo," he said in his normal, plangent voice. "But George just wanted a quick word with me about you. He was afraid that he'd upset you or something in the car. Or that you were still troubled about the maggot in the cheese."

"Wrong on both counts," I informed him briskly. "Then he must've got his wires crossed. It was you, Patrick, who seemed to have the blues after dinner. You hardly opened your mouth for the rest of the evening." I was tempted to add "until George wanted to poke his tongue down it," but prudence triumphed.

As Patrick got into bed I grudgingly let him put his arm under my shoulders as he leaned over me to speak. "You know George likes you a lot."

"I gather he's rather fond of you too." I stopped. Reluctant to elaborate. I need not have worried. Patrick was quite disposed to agree.

"He really is a generous man. He's promised to put in a good word with old J. Darken-Lang, my boss, and get things straightened out in chambers. You know how much that's been worrying me. I simply don't dare bugger things up after all the money my parents have put out."

Patrick withdrew his crooked arm which was supporting his head, flopped back alongside me in the bed. When he next spoke he was addressing the ceiling. "What would you say, Davey, if I said I think I ought to go back to London and see J. Darken-Lang?"

I was silent for a moment. His words alarmed me. "You mean leave me here? Or am I supposed to move on too?"

"Of course not. I'd probably only be gone for a few days. George has kindly offered to lend me the return airfare. That will make my stay even shorter."

I played for time. "And all this was decided just now—while you were with him for those few minutes in his bedroom?"

"I'd already told him I was worried about the threat to my career from rushing off like we did. It was the air ticket he offered just now. As a matter of fact, I'll be going tomorrow."

"Thanks for the advance warning!" I felt very bitter, even angry. "I shall leave at the same time, then. So that's the end of our holiday. Thanks a lot for torpedoing it."

I suddenly felt too despondent to continue the discussion—though not upset enough not to want the last word. I turned over on my pillow away from him. "Thanks for nothing, you selfish bastard!" I switched my bedlight out.

"Why?" said Patrick suddenly, into the darkness.

"Why what?" I said grumpily—in reluctant continuation.

"Why do you have to leave tomorrow when I do? It doesn't make sense."

"So you should go back and rescue *your* career but mine doesn't count? It's that that doesn't make sense to me, Patrick. Or do you think I should stay here and become a bloody waiter or something? Perhaps your friend could get me a job as commissionaire at the Irish embassy—is that what you had in mind?"

"What I had in mind was your telling me before we left that your Dean said he'd do something for you if you promised to shape up next term."

It was true I'd told Patrick that the Dean had said he was prepared to put me on probation for the Michaelmas term if I made up my marks. He'd even agreed to ascribe my poor exam showing to a mild nervous breakdown as a result of my bumpy naval service (to which I had cautiously alluded in our intial interview, lest the naval authorities had gotten there first). But as I lay there, it progressively dawned on me that my displeasure with the youth at my side was not over his selfish decision to abandon me, or his scheming with George behind my back. It was my pride that was hurt. I was also busy digesting the fact that I didn't really care if Patrick forsook me there in Paris or anywhere else. I was finally admitting that my infatuation for him was over. The confluence of all this self-knowledge was too much. I wasn't that far from tears. I stuffed my face into my pillow, shouted a muffled goodnight and refused further speech.

I awoke in the morning with my resolve to leave when Patrick did as firm as ever. But I would return to London by myself, using the remaining portion of my Newhaven-Dieppe ticket. We woke and performed our ablutions in grim-lipped silence. While cleaning my teeth I decided to make an announcement before both of them at breakfast.

That this did not happen was entirely due to the blue envelope which George had kindly placed by the napkin ring at my place at the table. I had just slit it open with an adjacent knife when Patrick spoke up.

"Davey has decided to leave with me, George—in spite of my trying to convince him that it was quite unnecessary."

"Of course it's unnecessary. In fact I would be quite hurt to think his presence here is contingent upon you, my boy."

I was only half-listening to them. My major attention was accorded to my letter from Mama.

* * * * * *

July 3, 1946

The Hornbeams,
Theydon Bois, Essex

My dearest Davey:
In just over a week Charlotte and I will be descending upon you and I cannot overemphasize with what pleasure we anticipate July 12th. Daddy and I thank you for the postcards and were overjoyed to hear what a splendid time you are having with your two Irish friends.

Your father has not been in the brightest of moods of late, and those views of the Arc de Triomphe and of Notre Dame really cheered him up. In fact it brought back memories of Paris leaves when he was on the Western Front before going to Egypt, and one night at the Churchfields he had us all in stitches at some of the antics he described and the fractured French the Tommies invariably used.

We must have a serious talk about him when I arrive and we get a moment alone. It's these moods again. We must also speak about your brother Simon and his forthcoming marriage, from which we have all been banned. However, I don't want our stay to be just a family powwow and I look forward immensely to being shown the delights of the City of Light by my darling son.

It will be the first time that we will stand on foreign soil together and, being in Paris, where I have not been since a girl with Poppa, the occasion will be of enormous significance to me. In fact I can hardly await our arrival. Charlotte says I have become quite impossible these past days as my anticipation has grown and grown!

With Mama's special love for her little boy,
Mama

******

I looked up at the two faces awaiting my response to both Patrick's announcement of my departure and George's plea for me to stay on. Strong in the knowledge that in the light of dear Mama's letter I now had no choice, I smiled first at my ex-lover and then at my host.

"As usual, Patrick has it all wrong," I said. "We were just discussing the pros and cons in bed before sleep. I should love to take you up on your offer, George, and stay on a little while more. This letter is from my mother and she and my aunt expect to be in Paris next week, when they will be staying at the George V, I think it is."

Patrick glowered at me. "Your *aunt*? Miss Charlotte Churchfield?"

I didn't bat an eyelid. "A courtesy title," I said. "As a very old friend of the family I can't recall her being known as anything else."

Then I turned back to the handsome Irishman who sat there *à la* Noel Coward, in silk dressing-gown and cravat, as he buttered his croissant. "As long as I shan't be putting you out," I said. "I should hate to inconvenience you in any way. Nor do I wish to impose on your having previously known Patrick—that wouldn't be fair either."

The manicured hand that held the butter knife dropped it with a clatter. It now stretched out instantly to mine, placed itself over it and squeezed protectively. "*Nonsense*, dear boy. I would be heartbroken if you thought of staying elsewhere. This apartment is yours for just as long as you wish—and everything in it."

Embarrassed, I sought gently to remove that warm hand, but George's pressure was too firm. I gave in and smiled even more broadly at my host. "Maybe I can help a little about the place. Tidy things up when your maid isn't here. I'm afraid I can't cook but I'd love to help with the shopping if we were to eat in at all."

Patrick, who had pulled the top off his brioche but eaten none of it, got abruptly to his feet. "While you two plan your domestic lives, I'd better phone for a taxi."

George looked at him with an almost bored expression. "Oh, for Christ's sake, sit down and finish your breakfast. Davey and I will drive you out to the airport and sortie into the countryside from there for lunch." It wasn't until he had concluded this announcement that he deigned to remove his hand from on top of mine.

CHAPTER THIRTEEN

From the very moment we left Patrick in the hands of Air France, George's attitude toward me changed. It was rather as if some moderating factor engendered by my lawyer-lover's presence was now removed. While George still announced plans, meals and joint activities in a fashion that brooked no argument, they were now preceded by formal little "discussions" on what we might do, and (ostensibly at least) we shared counsel over the pattern of the days—though my suggestions were somehow never adopted. Nevertheless, even the hint of equity was an advance. Considerably more irksome was his new inclination toward a crisp surveillance of those remarkably few hours when we were not sharing activity and I was supposedly left to my own devices.

Example: The day after Patrick's departure, George announced that he'd be walking the couple of blocks that afternoon to the Majestic Hotel, where he'd be working for a few hours, but that he would be happy for me to walk over with him—and use his office—while he attended to the claims of his job. When I demurred, pleading the need for time to catch up on a neglected correspondence, he was quite snappish and I was uncomfortably reminded of the Izarra incident the night we'd first met. I refused to budge. I recalled something Mama used to say about starting off with people as you intended carrying on.

A similar incident occurred when I refused to attend a movie with him. I said getting to know Paris better was a more important experience than burying myself in the darkness of a cinema—something I could have done just as easily in London. George grew immediately petulant. He claimed that I had to banish all notions of being a tourist as I was now living in Paris and that attending a new film was just part of normal existence as it would be for any other Parisian. He developed his homily as I fidgeted on his sofa. When he concluded, I made no reply. Silence hung heavily between us and I could even hear the hum of the refrigerator from the far end of the spacious kitchen down the corridor. From the knitting of his extravagantly bushy eyebrows I knew he was struggling to avoid open warfare, and I felt afraid of what might surface later.

As I lay in bed that night—for a rare occasion in my young life, sleep did not come easily—I brooded over my situation and puzzled fruitlessly about how much I was precisely *living in* as opposed to *visiting* Paris. That led to considerations of how much my future would be shaped by a personal involvement with the city rather than one chained by the claims George would make on me. Not for the first time in the past few weeks, my final thoughts before slumber were troubled ones concerning my precise status in that lavish apartment on the Rue Berlioz.

With my innate tendency to prevaricate and to dodge harsh issues, by morning I was only too happy to let such nocturnally inspired dilemmas slide. George helped. Other than on those two points of disagreement where he had readily shown his disapproval, he could not have made life more pleasant for me. His kindness was immense and it seemed there was nothing he was not prepared to do in unstinting service to my well-being and even whims. How could I sustain a sense of being torn between the rival claims of George and Paris when, at every impulse I displayed, it seemed he was prepared to buy the place for me?

Walking through Au Printemps department store, I happened to comment on a handsome LP record player which was new on the market and could serve the purposes of both 33 rpm and 45 rpm discs. My protestations notwithstanding—and I have to admit they were not very strenuous—the phonograph returned with us to the spacious room which George had accorded me as my study. Nor did the instrument arrive alone. It was accompanied by albums of the leading pop vocalists of the period: Tino Rossi, Jean Sablon, Piaf and Charles Trenet. All were names George had suggested, to help me assimilate the culture of the country in which, he insisted, I had come permanently to live.

His largesse knew no bounds. One day he offered to whisk me off to the Costa Brava when I casually mentioned that someone had told me it compared favorably with my beloved North Cornish coast. I would have accepted the invitation, too, had I not the very next day received a further scrawled note from Mama reminding me that I was to meet them later that same week at the Gare des Invalides and escort them from the airport bus to the George V. I mentioned this to George at breakfast as the reason for turning down his offer to take me to Spain that week and he at once insisted on meeting them at the airport in the Mercury and driving them to their hotel.

With plans thus formalized I had a fleeting moment of unease over Mama's reaction to my substitute for the departed Patrick—but once more apprehension was drowned out by an energetic George involving me in complicated and detailed plans for Mama's and Charlotte's pleasure during their Parisian stay. He would occasionally look up from the map which he had placed over the plates, cups and saucers each breakfast time and ask me if my mother liked this food or that, this entertainment or that, even this architecture or that.

It occurred to me that I knew little about Mama's tastes or predilections: the parameters of a son's vision of his mother were a restriction I was still in the process of accepting at the age of twenty. In spite of my sense that I was woefully ignorant of her likes and dislikes, I still felt it incumbent on me to provide some sort of maternal portrait before George met her. I couldn't free myself of the feeling that Mama would likely be as prickly with him as she had been with his fellow-countryman in the restaurant of the Connaught Hotel. Irishmen seemed to bring out the worst in her.

But as I delicately suggested that my mother was in certain respects a difficult woman with some peculiar prejudices—feeling terribly disloyal as I did so—George seemed to strain equally in his efforts to plan an ambitious campaign to earn her approbation. When I hinted that she was a somewhat excessive patriot, he immediately proposed taking her to an event organized by the Royal Air Force Benevolent Association in St. George's Anglican Church at which His Excellency the British ambassador would be present.

He also proposed an informal tour of the Hotel Majestic, where the neophyte UNESCO organization was still in shambles, he said gleefully. He was careful to suggest that he would see if the visit could be hosted by the director-general-elect, Julian Huxley. As a *bonne bouche* he threw in a formal visit to the embassy so that Mama might sign the VIP visitors' book, and not just the register available for *hoi polloi*. Another idea he came up with was a trip to the zoo at Vincennes, and this I agreed to enthusiastically—not because I had ever heard Mama wax favorably about such places but because they appealed greatly to me.

In point of fact the initial encounter proved more satisfactory than I had dared hope. We spotted them without delay coming in from the plane and there was no difficulty in diverting them from the airport bus and escorting them to the waiting Mr. Cronyn and his conspicuous convertible. Mama was never inimical to the attractions of private over public transport. As she stood there, diminutive on the sidewalk, covertly summing George up as he discreetly fussed over her, and I sought to effect introductions, she turned to Charlotte and spoke as if the two of them were quite alone.

"Paris must be most enervating nowadays if this is the man we took to the Connaught Rooms last month, Charlotte. He looks twice as old, wouldn't you say? Though admittedly far more distinguished."

Charlotte smiled the especially patient smile she always reserved for Mama. "It is not the same man," she observed amiably. "This one is not auburn-haired and he is even taller."

"As I just got through saying," I interjected fiercely, "this is my friend George Cronyn, of whom I wrote, Mama. He is an old family friend of Patrick's, who, incidentally, has had to return temporarily to London. Perhaps I should start all over again. This is my mother, George. And this is her friend Miss Charlotte Churchfield."

George's hand passed firmly in outstretched greeting from one lady to the other. "What an enormous pleasure to finally meet you both. You have been graced with a loving son, Mrs. Bryant—and to hear Davey speak of you, Miss Churchfield, you have in him a most loyal friend."

Mama evidently liked George's florid approach for, in contrast to her prior confrontation with Patrick, she did not immediately embark on a series of highly personal questions but was content to listen to him describe both his official activities as Irish delegate with the new United Nations Educational, Scientific, and Cultural Organization (he carefully articulated every word) and the extensive Georgian mansion, forty miles south of Dublin, which eventually awaited him as scion of the Cronyn family.

Not that I was awash with complacency. I knew that while George's indubitable charm, social assurance and air of prosperity were not lost on Mama, there would eventually be a determination of his marital status and a probing of me as to the precise implications of what it meant to become his permanent guest in Paris.

There was no intimation of such screening, though, while they were being installed in the George V, or on arrival at George's apartment for aperitifs. I should add that Mama had only consented to *that* maneuver after insisting she would be taking all of us to Maxim's for dinner. She had used the occasion of her dinner invitation to inform us in some detail, rather in the vein of her earlier proprietary approach to the Connaught Rooms, that she had first visited Maxim's as a young girl in the company of her beloved Poppa, on one of his frequent business trips to the French capital in the halcyon days before the Great War.

The fact was, she was granted no opportunity to interrogate George as to his private life, for as he poured the ladies sherry and me a Pernod, he equally poured forth a plethora of intimate details of his current domestic circumstances and the events leading up to them. For the first time I heard of an engagement leading to a young woman's tragic suicide; of yet another subsequent betrothal sundered by a fiancée's severe fall from a horse during the Hunt. I now learned of subsequent years when his social life—let alone marital possibilities—was wholly subservient to the claims of ailing parents who seemed almost to compete with one another in the severity and expedition of their decline.

To say that George laid it on thick would be a gross understatement. No Hollywood melodrama ever surpassed his account in its welter of tragic detail. Yet Mama and her friend listened enraptured—which increased my incredulity. Nor did my amazement diminish when, turning to his drinks wagon for possible refills, he had the audacity to throw me an emphatic wink.

Late that evening, after we had finally deposited Mama and Charlotte at the George V, after a most successful meal amid the red velvet and crystal of Maxim's, George proposed a nightcap at La Reine Blanche, a gay café on the Left Bank. I might have refused at that hour, as I needed my sleep, but the strain of acting as go-between twixt Mama and George had gotten through to me. I was quite prepared to relax in an all-male milieu of chattering young men with a few slightly more sinister and older types interspersed about the flaking metal tables. What I had not anticipated was that this was the moment George would elect to make a confession of love and say all sorts of embarrassing things as I toyed with the *café fine* which he had insisted on buying me.

"You have an extraordinary mother, Davey, a truly remarkable woman. I could see right away where you get such things as your charm and your candor. Your wit, too, stems from her. You have the same kind of brilliant imagination."

The candor reference was too much. "Oh come on, George! You're talking balls. I probably do share a few things with Mama but it's going to take you more than three or four hours of lying and flattery to discover them. In fact, most people think I'm far more like my father."

George was unfazed. "Well, I haven't met him yet, of course. And as far as speed in finding out the shared traits between mother and son goes—most people don't have my advantage. Most people aren't in love with you, my dear fellow."

This time I was silent.

George took that as encouragement. "It's been growing nonstop over the past three weeks, but from the moment you arrived at the vestibule and Patrick introduced you I knew something enormous was happening to me."

George's gray eyes shone—but that could've been the cognac. His suntanned face was now close enough to mine across the table for me to notice tiny lines and a prominent white hair in his otherwise black and bushy eyebrows. I looked quickly about us. A crewcut blond in an Oxford blue shirt with button-down collar and sleeves rolled up to just below the elbows, in American, not British, fashion, was smiling in my direction. I had the traitorous wish that it were he and not George saying the extravagant things which were rushing now from my companion's cognac-moist lips.

I made an effort. "George—please don't say all that. You're embarrassing me and, God knows, I don't want to hurt your feelings. You're a dear man and I want you—need you—as a friend. Can't we leave it at that?"

Instinct told me he was about to reach out and grab my hand again so I was able to forestall him and whip it down to my lap. He looked hurt. From the corner of my eye I could see the American student-type smiling even more broadly. I poured my brandy into my coffee, which in turn made it unpleasantly tepid. I decided not to drink it.

"I want you to know I seek only your happiness, my darling. I would never do anything to embarrass you. Nor would I ever trespass upon the sanctity of your person."

I grinned in spite of myself. George could always be relied on to come up with a courtly turn of phrase. "I'm glad to hear that, George. I'd depart in a swirl of dust if you did."

His features relaxed somewhat. "Now *that* sounds like your dear mother talking!"

"I think if you attempted to trespass upon *her* person you'd get more than a swirl of dust. In spite of her size she once pushed an oversexed airman hitchhiker out of the car Charlotte was driving."

"Ah yes, your mother's boon companion. Patrick wrote to me about her. They're *innocent* Sapphists, I understand. Do everything together except the bed thing? You've no idea how much I admire that civilized sense of restraint. Just as I get tired of all these people nowadays who want to fornicate like monkeys. Like the bestial oafs seated around us here," he added, glowering and with no diminution of voice.

Mama's precise relationship with Charlotte was a topic as distasteful to me as George's protestations of romantic ardor or his audible rudeness to our neighbors. "I wouldn't know," I said crisply. "Aunt Charlotte has been part of my life as long as I can remember. It has always seemed a bit creepy to me to contemplate one's parents' sex life."

"I have upset you! I'm so sorry, my angel. Your aunt seems most benign. She doesn't come across as one of those single women who are excessively judgmental, of which my Ireland is so full! I have a spinster aunt of that malicious nature. In fact it's her presence at Cronyn Court which keeps me firmly across the Irish Sea."

He smiled drunkenly at me. "Looking at it in another way, though, if it were not for Aunt Eily I might still be in Eire, and if not here in Paris I wouldn't have met you, my darling. So she becomes an asset in spite of herself. Like the Orthodox Church making a saint of Judas Iscariot as a crucial preliminary to the Resurrection."

I hadn't heard George evoke theology before—save in his erudite explanations of the churches Patrick and I had visited in his company. I knew, though, that he was a regular Anglican communicant, because Patrick had told me. The subject of religion was infinitely preferable to talk of me as the object of his affections. I strove to stay with it.

"By extension, that would include Pontius Pilate and even Caesar Augustus, wouldn't it?"

He was not to be so facilely deflected. "Probably. Has anyone ever told you what a marvelously sculpted throat you have, precious Davey? I specialize in throats and the shape of backs of heads. You win there, too."

I sighed. "I wish you wouldn't stare at me quite so hard, George. Half the terrace is watching us, you know."

"Half the bloody terrace is madly jealous," he said. "Of me! These prissy little queens can't understand how I can merit sitting opposite such dazzling beauty." He dropped his glance to the tabletop. "For that matter," he murmured happily, "nor can I."

I bit my lip. "Mama is an early riser," I said obdurately. "And what I have inherited from her is an obsession with punctuality. She won't want to be late starting her first full day in Paris in—what did she say? Over thirty-five years? And I am now dead tired."

I knew a peculiar spurt of power when he immediately lifted his arm for the bill and, amid a welter of rambling apology, promised to drive me straight home.

When I rubbed my eyes sleepily the next morning as I lay sprawled in the huge bed—at least, it seemed huge since Patrick had departed it—and looked at the cream-colored radio alarm clock (another gift from my benefactor), I was startled to see it was almost ten a.m. Over at the window, lace curtains were billowing, and every now and then I saw a shaft of blue sky and a gleam of sun. I thought I could hear sounds from the floor below. Hesitant noises, they suggested Suzanne the maid at work, rather than the brisk movements of my landlord.

I ran one hand through my curls and with the other traced the erection with which I'd awakened. But erotic hankering immediately gave way to thoughts of Mama, whom I was supposed to phone at the George V right after breakfast. Knowing her, that meal would already be several hours in the past. As I guiltily clambered out of bed and headed for the bathroom I wondered why, if she herself had called me, George had not come and wakened me. The answer to that waited downstairs, where I found I was alone with Suzanne, who was busy with dusting.

There was a note at the breakfast table.

Davey Dearest:
I have gone out shopping. This will give you an excellent time to meet your mother and Charlotte and plan your morning together. I have booked luncheon for four at Chez Maurice on the Rue de Courcelles (it's not too far from the George V) and expect to meet up with the three of you at one p.m. Don't get too excited but I think you will be rather pleased with the fruits of my matinée expedition. I hope it will atone for my boorish behavior last night. I also hope you have forgiven me, my darling, and are no longer upset.

With adoring love, George

My only upset, I told myself as I scanned his lines, was at his extravagant language. I was not his lover and I hated the fronds of affection he insisted on throwing over me. They reminded me of the soft but insistent feel to the face when one unwittingly brushes against a cobweb. However, such is avarice that, as I gobbled down the arrangement of succulent green figs, Cape gooseberries, sweet kumquat rind and fresh pineapple which had been carefully prepared for my breakfast, before turning to the telephone and calling Mama, I couldn't help wondering what it was that George was out buying me....

From the moment I met Mama at the George V, I sensed that she had undergone a change from the previous evening. She was not in a jovial mood and her displeasure was generalized. When Charlotte joined us in the ornate marble foyer, which was bustling with high-ranking

American officers, Mama at once berated her for her choice of outfit—a plum-colored tweed costume.

"You'll be far too warm in all that stuff when we start walking. It's mid-July, for goodness' sake! Why on earth didn't you ask my advice over what to wear?"

Charlotte smiled her welcome to me. "I thought it a little chilly first thing this morning. But I agree, Isabella, it has rather abruptly warmed up. How nice to see you, Davey. I trust you are rested and dinner did not disagree with you?"

"To the contrary," I insisted. "It was superb. My kidneys were done to perfection."

"He should be rested—considering the current hour. And what was so peculiar about dinner, Charlotte, that should cause you to mention it the following day? I recall you all expressing your delight in it—when it was still the appropriate moment."

I knew very well what Mama was referring to. She had lectured her three sons on it frequently enough! In her arcane but obdurate code, doubtless inherited from her father, food—other than its necessary acquisition for one's kitchen—was not a proper subject for discussion. In fact, she viewed such talk as a significant social transgression. She would certainly have had no time for the plethora of publications on cooking and eating that abound nowadays. Not that for a moment she believed her friend guilty of such impropriety or even of a deliberate lapse in taste. It was simply a convenient cudgel at hand to belabor the two of us as witness to her being out of spirits.

"I know we are in a country where food and sex are conversational staples, but I do not think we have to leave our standards the other side of the English Channel."

I looked at Charlotte and Charlotte looked at me. It was a familiar exchange of loving exasperation over Mama's perversity of mood.

"Well, Mama, let's keep our standards intact, for heaven's sake. But let's also concentrate on this lovely sunny morning. Do you ladies have any particular ideas as to what you'd like to do? I'm totally in your hands."

Mama was not letting us off so lightly. "Mind you, one might be forgiven for wondering which country one was in if staying in this particular hotel."

I glanced about me, noted the elegant damask chairs, the thick pile carpet with its brownish specks from a succession of *Wehrmacht* and Allied cigarette burns. The matching green walls were blemished in places by the stains of dried-out damp, but the 1930s crystal and gilt ornamentation of pillars and cornices still donated a transcendent Gallic elegance in spite of those unbanished wounds of war and Occupation.

I was impressed and stirred by nostalgia for a Continental world I'd never known, and said so. "It all looks very deluxe to me. This is one of the finest hotels in the world, I understand. And it has only recently been derequisitioned by the Allies."

"Perhaps," Mama said shortly. "But the current atmosphere is still redolent of an army barracks. I feel quite out of place in civilian clothing!"

"Mama! How can you say such a thing? Oh, sure there's lots of military brass around. But it's all so palatial. It's so much *ritzier* than the London Ritz!" Then I broke off as I once more surveyed the busy, bustling scene.

"I say, isn't that General Eisenhower over there?" I pointed to a burly back of drab olive-green over paler, cream-colored pants. The figure was surrounded by a knot of other officers.

Mama's curiosity was piqued in spite of herself, but she still managed to begin with a rebuke of my gesture. "I could have seen whom you were indicating by a nod of your head rather than a rude pointing of fingers." Then curiosity took over. "Are you really sure? I thought the general was taller than that."

The Supreme Commander turned and, seeing we were civilians, offered his famous expansive smile. Mama was entranced, her mood now utterly changed. "What a courteous man," she murmured. "You can see why the king and queen like him so much."

I had the feeling she might have drifted discreetly in Ike's direction in the hope he would address her. To forestall her, I suggested that, as I had arrived later than expected, we might step out and at least see the Champs Elysées. There was no opposition. It transpired that the ladies had themselves thought a stroll up and down the famous thoroughfare would be a congenial inauguration of their stay in Paris. I deemed it an excellent way of filling in the couple of hours before our assignation with George, when I would learn what my new gift was.

We walked up to the Étoile, crossed the fairly empty expanse of pavement to the traffic-free island of the Arc de Triomphe and then slowly made our way back down the broad sidewalk on the right-hand side of the avenue. Our destination was Fouquet's, where we had decided to take a coffee before continuing to saunter in the direction of the *rond-point*, where the buildings gave out and the gravel and bushes took over as prelude to the final expanse of the Place de la Concorde.

We were not destined to reach our destination, however. We had no sooner found ourselves chairs on the crowded sidewalk and ordered pineapple fruit juice in tiny bottles than a man entered the central aisle our table bordered. Fouquet's was so busy that July midmorning, the waiters rushing from table to table with perspiring faces and short tempers, that the newcomer didn't impinge until he was virtually at my side. I think it was his smell which first claimed my attention. The aroma was an unsavory blend of dried sweat, yesterday's garlic and, so my fastidious imagination told me, unwashed orifices....

But the olfactory awareness was immediately supplanted when the man began to shout. That was when I looked up and saw this skinny male in his thirties, with a suffused rubicund complexion such as a drunkard might possess, and vinaceous-colored skin around his throat and neck which was interrupted by several suppurating sores. His clothes were greasy and ragged and I thought it was from those that there emanated at least some of the unpleasant stench that preceded him. Across the aisle from me the other customers didn't just look up; they physically recoiled as he screamed at them.

"Scum!" he hollered in French. "Parisian scum who sit here complacent while France starves!" I saw a white-coated waiter slip inside, presumably to call the police. The man also saw but ignored him.

"Tomorrow we celebrate the Revolution, only we, the people, will do it on stale *pain maïs* while you bastards will live off the fat of the *marché noir*!"

Mama clutched at my arm. "What is he saying, Davey? He speaks so fast."

"I'm here to say it's all over for you fat swine. The workers of France are sick of you. You'll be overthrown and destroyed!"

"I think he is a Communist, Isabella. He claims the masses are hungry and he condemns all of us sitting here when life is so hard for him and his friends."

I stared at Charlotte. Her French was much better than I'd given her credit for. Certainly better than mine. "I think he's a bit drunk, too," I added, "but I think he is genuinely hungry."

By now the man had turned his attention to our side of the terrace. "We want work but have none. There is a shortage of food and we scour the neighborhoods searching for crusts and bourgeois refuse. Yet you fat pigs don't need to work. You can sit idly here and play with croissants and brioches while you bask like ugly lizards in the sun! In the purged France of tomorrow there will be no room for such capitalist nonsense. You'll all be gone! Just as your type are already gone from Russia. In this postwar world it is we, not you, who'll share the fruits of that liberty, equality and fraternity which are supposed to have been the rights of all Frenchmen since 1789!"

"I got that!" Mama said excitedly. "He is reminding us of the storming of the Bastille, is he not? He is thrilled about the holiday coming up. It is very important to the French, you know. I admire a patriot, I really do!"

The man heard her but with as much misunderstanding as she brought to his shouted words. "What are you doing in our country, American cow! Go home to your gangsters and black marketeers. Who needs you tourists living off the fat of our land while my children starve!"

"He called you an American, Isabella. He was far from polite in other ways, too!" her friend informed her.

"We are not all your enemies," I shouted back at him, angry at his unwarranted attack on Mama. Then I lapsed into English, afraid my French would let me down. "You know nothing of my mother. She gave up a lot to be an ambulance worker during the war. I don't know what the hell you were doing."

Wholly unaware of my remarks, he moved down the line of tables, still yelling his imprecations at Fouquet's customers. Mama looked straight at me. "That was very nice of you, Davey. I—I didn't think you were so aware of things. It wasn't always easy and perhaps I was wrong. But I had to put my children's lives first, even if it meant breaking their hearts." She physically rocked with the anguish of recollection. "Ah well, that's all over now." Very deliberately she looked up and away from us. "I'd say that man is truly starving, wouldn't you, Charlotte?"

"Well, he's certainly angry," I commented, eager to center on him rather than on Mama and me. "It wouldn't take many like him to start a genuine revolution, I'm sure of that."

Charlotte was in a better position to follow his progress and this she did intently. "Yes, my dear. I'd say he was *very* hungry. I thought I smelled drink on his person, too, but that could be a way of blunting the hunger pains. Remember old Mr. Brockington we picked up after the Lewison Road land mine? Poor old thing had taken spirits meant for his primus stove because he was too ill to get to the shops for food. It was Lewison Road where that other poor old soul lived—the one who'd lost all her hair from the blast?"

The threat of revolution appealed infinitely more to me than Charlotte's well-intentioned reminiscences of the Second World War. But I had no need to interrupt. The man did it for me. I couldn't see precisely what happened next but there was a sudden flurry of raised voices from those closest to where he stood. I heard someone shout, Communist bastard! And a woman screaming that he should go back to the Soviet Union. There was then the resounding crash of a table being overturned and the tinkle of glass as its bottles and glasses tumbled to the sidewalk and shattered.

Charlotte became our eyewitness. "Oh, they are beating him, the cowards! That beastly man is hitting him from behind with a flask!"

To the general din there was suddenly added the raucous hee-haw sound of a police car as it drove down the stretch of the broad sidewalk. As the vehicle stopped and its doors were flung open, there came the more familiar blowing of whistles and yet more shouting as uniformed men came flying up the aisles with white truncheons drawn. I grabbed the arm of a gawking *garçon* and thrust the bill and money into his reluctant hand. I had been to enough of these classy establishments with George to realize that their waiters engaged in their own brand of war with their opulent customers by keeping them eternally waiting.

As I escorted the women from Fouquet's the talk persisted, not unnaturally, over the unkempt man who had so passionately addressed those resting their feet on that dazzlingly sunny morning. Charlotte flattered me by assuming that my brief stay in Paris had made me something of an authority on social disturbance of this nature. "He seemed so sincere," she commented. "Do you think anything bad will happen to him? Those sores on his neck looked very nasty. I wonder whether there is anything like the Women's Voluntary Service to look into his family circumstances. What do you think, Davey?"

Mama was on a quite different course. She gave me no time to reply to her friend. "Your father didn't agree with me about leaving you boys in Cornwall. Then he was always more heart than head. I think that man just now was like him. He would never be separated from that wife and children he kept talking about. I think you too are more of that nature, Charlotte. I fear I am very much in a minority."

I took her elbow as we traversed cobblestones. "Where would you put me, Mama?" My voice was light. I had no doubt whatever she would include me with Daddy and Charlotte, along with the ranting fellow we had just heard.

"You? Why you are like me, of course, Davey. We may like to think we will always put noble sentiment first. But it simply isn't so. We cannot escape clear thinking because deep down we have scientific temperaments—as I tried to explain to dear Poppa so long ago. We fare better with duty than with emotional love, if you want my honest opinion."

I refused to believe her; indeed, was hurt at the implications of her remarks. "If only that were so, Mama, I wouldn't have half the problems that plague me!"

"Is that so, dear?" Mama was walking between the two of us. I was quick to note that although she was addressing me, she had turned immediately at my words to face her other companion. "You mean over your stay here in Paris?"

I knew damn well where that was headed and straightaway changed the subject. Or rather took a less than honest alternative to what I had been actually thinking, which was about the moral ambiguities of living under George's roof.

"More about my career in general."

"I thought we had agreed back at The Hornbeams, darling, that you must *first* get your degree from King's and then discuss where you might go from there. I know that is the impression you left with your Daddy."

"You misunderstand. It is about the degree itself. I have been debating whether I might do it here at the Sorbonne, for instance."

"Had we not better turn around if we are to meet Mr. Cronyn in time for lunch? I had the distinct notion he was as keen on punctuality as we are," Mama said.

I had the marked impression she had deliberately brought up George's name in conjunction with my reference to staying in Paris and attending its university. My hunch was to be vindicated.

She did not, however, use the occasion for direct attack. After an elaborate description of the Fouquet incident—where once more she and Charlotte demonstrated their sympathy for the voluble leftist—she wanted to know about George's current domestic (read romantic) life. Only with much delicacy and avoidance of specifics, an approach at which she had possibly learned to excel in her spats with her eldest son, Simon, and his lewd references.

Unlike on the previous evening, Mr. Cronyn made little attempt to conceal his bachelor status or the *modus vivendi* that stemmed from it. In fact there were moments when I thought that he was deliberating rejecting Mama's circumspect approach. When she, for example, alluded obliquely to the fact that, when he eventually settled down and had children, he would be somewhat older than most fathers, he informed her that he was already settled and that children were neither then nor in the future regarded as part of his plans. He went even further and smilingly informed her that in fact he detested children and would go to great lengths to avoid meeting them. Oddly enough, far from being upset, Mama laughed at his upbraiding of infants and said she had every reason for understanding those who put their careers before such domestic considerations. She glanced across the table at me when making that statement and I wondered whether she was referring to that now remote time of her own when she had been torn between daughterly duty and her desire for emancipation through a professional career.

The rest of our lunch passed amiably enough and proved a happy augury of the few days Charlotte and Mama spent with us amid the polarizing tensions of both recovering and still down-at-heel postwar Paris. I was hardly to know, as final touches to Mama and Charlotte's fleeting visit were suggested, that I would be seeing them again before their return home. Then it was not until George and I were alone much later that afternoon, and the ladies duly deposited at the British embassy, that I learned the nature of George's latest munificence.

He had spent a busy morning procuring first-class train bookings for us to ride the intercontinental *wagons-lits*, which, after taking us through unscathed Switzerland, would puff down the Danube to Vienna and the hospitality of the Irish Legation. We were eventually to arrive in the Free Territory of Trieste, at the top of the Adriatic, where he promised to show me both the nearby castle where Rilke wrote his elegies, and the temporary homes of Stendhal and James Joyce. It was in fact to be an elaborate literary progress, carefully planned by George, as a formal introduction to my Continental heritage—as he so grandiosely put it.

In 1946 such an expedition would have been impossible for the average Briton, but George knew not only how to play his status with UNESCO to the full, but how to utilize his Irish nationality and the benefits neutrality bestowed. He was also independently wealthy, I realized, and was equally adept at making money talk. I was enraptured at the magnificent detail of the plan—which included not only Trieste as literary climax, but dinners with Allied bigwigs from the occupying zones in Vienna, and side visits, too, he promised, to Zagreb and Ljubljana in Marshal Tito's new Yugoslavia. I was to be accorded special diplomatic status, George assured me, and went on to suggest I might write a book out of the experience—in which case he knew just the publisher....

All this was kept a deliberate secret from Mama right up to the moment we bid them goodbye at the Gare de Lyon and they began their own complicated route to Munich—and the hospitality of those high-ranking officer friends of Charlotte's uncle who were running the place.

I felt as we made our loving farewells that, what with Mama and Charlotte's grand contacts and the "open sesame" powers of my new friend, I was beginning to rub shoulders with the power brokers of the Western world. I swelled in pride as I stood by my little mother and looked over her head at the vulgar crowds lolling about the platform. My true destiny, it seemed, was at last unfurling....

CHAPTER FOURTEEN

A prewar postcard of the Rococo Cuvillierstheater in Munich arrived from Mama the very morning that George and I took the Vienna express. I didn't read it properly until I was waiting in the living room for George to make a final check of the apartment before we descended to the awaiting taxi.

August 1, 1946

This theater was apparently dismantled piece by piece by the authorities and hidden during the war. It has yet to be reconstructed. Then the scene here is one of total devastation. The people live in rubble. If it were not for our American friends we could not stay. They drive us everywhere. We eat from their PX system. They are kindness incarnate. However, they are as incapable of making tea as during the war. *I hope you have decided to return to King's College when your vacation is over.* We shall have so much to talk about when reunited at The Hornbeams.

Your devoted Mama

I slipped the postcard into the pocket of the blue corduroy jacket which George had insisted belonged to my travel package when presenting it to me. He had also bought me chocolate-colored suede sandals through which yellow socks peeped. I stood before the hall mirror as I heard George descending the flight of stairs from the dining room.

Patrick and I had both purchased modish hessian shirts from Austin Reid for our Paris holiday. Mine was a canary yellow and with it, this day of our setting off, instead of a tie, I wore a pale blue cravat which George protested he'd bought for himself but which I was convinced was the result of a quick trip to exclusive Hermès after I had admired a green one he'd been wearing. Looking into the tall glass, I touched the wave of hair that fell to my forehead with the fork of two quickly licked fingers. I smiled—showing regular teeth, slightly tea-stained, like those of most of my fellow-countrymen. All in all, I was quite satisfied with what I saw, and once again I experienced the charge of euphoria which had coursed through me when saying goodbye to Mama and Charlotte at the railroad station. I told my reflection under my breath, but in the playful idiom of my friend Patrick Moreton, "*Davey Bryant, you're a fuckin' lucky boyo.*"

I thought so even more as we sped through eastern France and I idly turned the pages of maps and magazines about places featured on our tour. I have no idea where George found all our reading matter—especially as most of it was prewar stuff yet in pristine condition. He muttered something vague about the UNESCO geographic library collection utilizing travel brochures as a kicking-off point for its archives but would add little more.

Of greater interest to my benefactor, I sensed, was his duty to give his protégé (I was to appreciate how much he liked the term by the frequency with which he insisted on using it later on the trip) a thorough history lesson of places to be visited on our itinerary and, as it turned out in hindsight, some often prescient remarks about those immediate postwar years.

There on the train, I decided the man sitting opposite me in the velvet upholstered compartment was a would-be historian. It was his sense of the past, I concluded, which underlay this ambitious progress through Eastern and Southern Europe on which we'd embarked. It was George Cronyn, historian *manqué*, who had so generously taken on the continuing education of a young man whose opportunity to embrace that richly diverse heritage had been crudely and cruelly impeded by the war waged by his elders.

I sprawled there opposite him, legs apart, eyelids half closed, as I yielded to the beguiling hypnotism of the speeding train's motion and rhythmic chatter. I sighed drowsily in pleasurable anticipation of the excitement of unknown cities; relaxed in the comforting independence afforded by the sizable sum of money Mama had generously provided before leaving Paris; and glowed with content for my general lot. At that moment I was incapable of giving credence to the possibility of a single cloud drifting menacingly across my immediate future.

Oh, simplistic youth! Callow optimist! Sad sample of the adage that wishing does not make it so! I had barely had time to let my attention lapse from the glossy brochures of Dubrovnik and the Dalmatian Coast to the delights that Imperial Vienna might have to offer when my companion leaned across the space between our seats and informed me huskily, and no doubt hungrily, that he could make out every contour of my *glans penis*.

It was to go from bad to worse. Vienna, in its crazy silhouettes of isolated walls and shattered towers, the mountains of rubble and desolate expanses, was thrilling in the brutality of its pulverization. I stood with George, right after our arrival, in the middle of the vast *Heldenplatz* as a hot wind in the summer heat wave (George said straight from the plains of Hungary) stung the skin of our sweating foreheads and pricked my bare arms. My guide, who had not stood on that particular site since the time of Hitler's *Anschluss* in 1938, pointed out the wrecked but still standing Burgtheater, the badly damaged city hall and the rubble of the opera house off in the heat-shimmering distance.

There were not many people. Civilians, that is. There seemed a disproportionate number of sullen Soviet soldiers who were supposed to represent only one of the four occupying powers. I pointed this out to George who started to instruct me in the significance of *realpolitik*. I quickly changed the subject.

That first day in Vienna was the first time I met anyone George had ever introduced to me as a friend. It was also the first of those many occasions when the word "protégé" was overworked.

In a bullet-pitted building redolent of hasty patching by the occupying military powers who had requisitioned it, and situated halfway down a narrow street just a stone's throw from St. Stephen's Cathedral, I met George's pal, Major Brian Wilson-Duff. The major turned out to be a giant of a man with a surprisingly soft voice, sporting a handlebar mustache. He was dapper in the uniform of the Brigade of Guards. I liked him on sight.

In spite of a perpetually anxious expression on his tanned features, Brian proved amiability itself. He strove from the outset to put me at ease amid the briskly military atmosphere of charts on walls, folding webbed chairs and constant interruptions by orderlies saluting before asking questions and seeking permission as they entered and left his cramped and poorly lit office. In a jovial attempt to answer my rather awkward attempt to make polite conversation, he allowed that he had been born in Connemara, and that he and George had attended Trinity College, Dublin, at the same time.

During my catechism of his friend, George affected to closely examine the beflagged map of the city of Vienna on the wall behind Brian's untidy desk, and I knew only too well that my companion was being rather stupidly jealous. I breathed heavily, tried to ignore him, and hoped it would not prove an augury for the days to come.

It wasn't long before Patrick's name came up. His surname, that is. And in terms of his parents. It transpired that the Reverend Moreton had been chaplain to the boarding school the major had attended. His memories of my erstwhile lover were of a snotty kid hanging about the place and he seemed rather uncomfortable at the implication (by his association with me) that Patrick had turned out homosexual.

"Desmond Moreton was a splendid fellow. He helped me through a very difficult time. He and Mary Moreton were just like parents to me when my mother was dying. Are you absolutely sure young Patrick is—*that way*?"

George didn't give me a chance to reply. In one way I didn't mind that, as, already at the tender age of twenty, I was reluctant to state publicly, particularly to a stranger, that someone I knew was gay.

"That *way*, you say, Brian? You don't have to listen to Davey. Just hear me! I was having sex with our Patrick before he ever met up with this one. You should ask them along O'Connell Street—or more particularly at the Gresham Hotel. I'm sure he's slept in more of their rooms than I can count! He was almost a fixture in Phoenix Park, too, before he crossed the Irish Sea and twiddled his bum for England!"

I was aware that George's chronology was totally false and that he was cruelly exaggerating Patrick's promiscuity. But I kept quiet. I had no taste for an argument with him, or a demonstration of his apoplexy before this soft-voiced man who had kindly volunteered to act as our host in the faceless tracts of war-ravaged Vienna. Fortunately, before anything like that could happen, the subject of Patrick's profligacy was dropped. We were joined by a freckle-nosed Austrian youth named Horst who turned out to be Brian's boyfriend.

In a wholly unselfconscious way, before even noticing George and me sitting there, he exuberantly vaulted the desk, with its stacks of papers and metal ashtrays brimming with butts, to hug and kiss his British benefactor. Eighteen-year-old Horst, we were informed, had just finished his studies at his *Gymnasium* and was shortly to attend the London School of Economics—thanks to the patient string-pulling of the doting major. While there he would study Political Science under the famous Professor Harold Laski. His English, I might add, was already near-perfect.

Dinner had been arranged for the four of us at one of the requisitioned hotels in the British zone. Before then, though, it was decided by the two senior men that Horst would take me to a café where we would await their arrival. In the meantime Brian would introduce George to the colonel of his regiment and, if possible, the G.O.C. This was all part of an elaborate campaign devised by the two old friends to see that we visitors got the most lavish hospitality possible during our stay in the city, and saw as much of Vienna and its environs as the restrictive circumstances of occupation allowed.

At the café I quickly learned of the grim life the young man had undergone in the latter part of the war. He cheerfully responded to my relentless questioning, for after my own experience—which had spelled mainly the misery of parental absence and the brief sojourn in the Royal Navy where the only enemy I encountered was my own countrymen—I was implacable in my hunger for first-hand knowledge of actual war. Military violence for me had lived only in the wings—with the occasional burst of V2 rockets and the eerie silence when the mutter of V1 "doodlebug" engines suddenly cut off. And even those ancillary factors had obtruded only in the closing months before Germany's defeat.

How different it had all been for Horst! I learned of the deafening clatter of tanks as they thundered down cobblestone streets, the hurling of grenades, the huddling in cellars as water dripped, the ferocious pursuit of minimal food; the dust and the darkness; the deafening noise of retreating *Wehrmacht* and approaching Red Army. Horst spoke rapidly, excitedly, as if he were providing a commentary to something that was happening before his eyes. His tense reliving his past made me feel wan and feeble in comparison. It also made me feel at least a decade his junior. That was a sensation that was not to go away at any time during my stay.

I liked Horst, too, from the start. For one thing he was totally honest. He told me that his father was a Nazi and a violent anti-Semite but that his devoutly Catholic mother made her four children pray for "the Jews in the concentration camps" each night when they knelt by their beds and made their intercessions. He also had much to say about primitive Soviet soldiers who couldn't understand the Roman numerals on a wristwatch and who raped every Austrian girl they encountered, including children barely in their teens. He was very anti-Russian.

His frankness pulled a corresponding candor from me. I told him that I would like to see the HQ of the Austrian Gestapo so that I could spit on it. I also told him that I was still grateful for our Russian allies, who had taken the brunt of the Germanic hordes. I made quite a speech over that and afterwards gulped at the cheap white wine Horst had ordered to wash my words throatily down. But he didn't seem affronted by my abrupt aggression—indeed, he retracted some of his Red Army criticism and agreed that—all other things being equal—Hitler was perhaps more evil than Stalin.

Having extracted that confession, I felt guilty for flaming at him. I had the uneasy feeling that my sense of inferiority over wartime experience had fueled my disagreement. I was even more perturbed over whether I had picked up some of George's capricious behavior in the short time I had known him. It was another thread, however fine and ultimately unjustifiable, in the warp and woof of our relationship. In my youth I was always worrying whether I was too impressionable when around my elders.

That was something George didn't help mitigate. Nor did his friend Brian. When they eventually joined up with us, Horst and I were brimming with political and philosophical agreement and full of the fellowship of youth. Right away I sensed George's jealousy of Horst. I shrugged off my irritation when he insisted on placing himself between us on the rough wooden bench at the trestle table. I do not think that Brian had a jealous bone in his body and I think he would've been wholly surprised if stupid George had suggested Horst and I were attracted to each other. But it was the jovial Guards Officer who next succeeded in mildly vexing me.

"So how have our two handsome lads been entertaining themselves?" he asked. "I'm sure Horst would love a delicious yellow shirt like yours, Davey. And what have you set your own heart on? A pair of lederhosen to show off what I'm sure are beautifully tanned legs?"

I was about to say sharply that I was neither a clothes horse nor a fashion model when Horst anticipated me. "Davey was asking me of what it was like living under the Nazis. And then of the battle of Vienna and the Russian victory and again, what life was like for us civilians. I have promised him to show the Gestapo Headquarters. Perhaps tomorrow?"

I flashed him a grateful smile and then turned not to Brian and his patronizing chatter but to green-eyed George. "We also got to talking about the future. Isn't it fun but it looks as if we shall be in London together for at least two years or more. L.S.E. is only just down the street from King's, you know, George."

Mr. Cronyn looked black. "I thought you were to take up your studies at the Sorbonne. At least, that's what you gave me to understand. Of course, if you change your mind every time you see a pretty face...."

I glowered right back. "I think I might even change subjects and study English instead of Philosophy. Probably easier to get a teaching job afterwards."

"I wouldn't bother your pretty little head about it here in Vienna, Davey," interjected Brian. "Our experience was that it didn't matter a tinker's cuss what you did as an undergraduate, don't you agree, George? It hasn't affected my army career and I'm sure it hasn't made the slightest difference to old George as a diplomat. Enjoy being young while you've got the chance, that's my advice to your generation. You've escaped the bloody war and you should make the most of it. That's what my fair-haired darlin' here is going to do, I can tell you that!"

Horst smiled thinly at me. Again I sensed a chord of shared discomfort struck over the excessive language of our elders. But he said nothing. Then he was wholly dependent on the supportive efforts of Major Brian Wilson-Duff, I ruefully reflected. I suspected George would have liked me in a comparable position, but I patted the wallet in my inside pocket which contained the money Mama had handed me. I certainly needed my own Irishman at that juncture in my life, but he was a long way from owning me.

I didn't really get an opportunity for any substantial talk with Horst until the brief stay in his native city was nearly over. We had done all the famous if wrecked buildings, and while George was reluctantly being the major's guest at a formal reception in the French zone, Horst and I took off for a return visit to the *Gänsehäufe*, where he promised to show me where one could sunbathe in the nude. It wasn't until we were lying there on our backs, on khaki military towels Horst had procured, that we started to talk of our two middle-aged men in highly personal terms.

"I am very fond of Brian, please understand that," Horst began. "But he talks to me in front of people as if I were just a pretty face. It is not nice and I know his fellow officers snigger behind his back. I am for the moment being a kept boy, but that will not always be so, Davey. You understand, *ja*?"

I rolled on my side to face him. I couldn't help being aware of his exposed genitals—just as I knew he was evaluating mine. By some miracle I avoided a hard-on. Probably by swearing to myself that I would never give George the satisfaction of evidence for his perpetual jealousy if I was within three feet of any other male. Then the earnestness of our talk pushed sexual awareness aside. This was the very first chance I had had to release my thoughts about certain matters and I intended to make the most of it.

"Being treated like a cute date, as the Yanks say, isn't the worst of it—at least with George. What I really hate is when he doesn't listen to a thing I say because I'm too young or haven't had his bloody experience.

Well, I may be pretty unsophisticated compared with Mr. Cronyn but I'm not a complete nincompoop."

"What is a nincompoop, Davey? That word has not come my way."

"George prefers the word 'oaf' to describe his inferiors—which, incidentally, he considers most people. They're all totally stupid and dense according to him."

"That is something I hear always from Brian and his friends. There are times when I wish I was a little bit ugly. And not like a seventeen-year-old schoolboy, always with the big smile? Then perhaps I would be allowed to have a mind as well as a body. But here in Vienna it is only the good looks and the big cock they want."

He scowled, paused for breath and then looked away toward the slow-moving waters of the Danube. "In the London School of Economics it will be otherwise, no? At your King's College it is the brains that count?"

I reached out for his hand, took it and gave it a squeeze. It was surprisingly rough to my touch. "Exactly," I said. "That is just how it is at King's."

I exaggerated and generalized with the ardor of someone who had just found a co-believer in the exalted Life-of-the-Mind. "The University has professors like Harold Laski and J. B. S. Haldane, who are not even aware whether their students are male or female! Our friends Mr. Cronyn and Major Duff-Wilson think only in terms of the flesh and which boy can be bought and which cannot."

I half expected Horst to disagree. To at least defend his Brian. But it was not so. When he turned back from eyeing the brown Danube, the scowl and clenched jaw still distorted his remarkably handsome features—making him look more like the age he probably wished to appear.

"I tell my mother I work for the British Army but she knows nothing of the major. And when I go to England I shall not tell her. And when I come back home I will not have to, for he will be gone."

He was not prepared to elaborate further. Instead he counselled me to turn on my belly so that my pale back and shoulders might receive the benisons of a warm but no longer fierce afternoon sun.

I brought up this conversation with George, albeit in a carefully laundered version, when we were on our way by train to Prague. But that destination needs some explanation, as it was not part of our original itinerary. In fact our heading toward the Czech capital also had something to do with Horst. I had asked him one day, when he and I had fallen behind our "benefactors"—as we had come to call them behind their backs—and were staring over a mound of rubble at the shambles of the *Rathaus*, if he ever got depressed with acre after acre of ruins. He had shrugged and shaken his blond curls. "You get used to them. Like you get used to most things." It was then he mentioned Prague as the only city in Eastern Europe which had not been devastated by the war.

I had asked him if he'd been there lately but he had shaken his head again. "We Viennese do not get out of the city easily in these days. Only if the occupying powers provide us with papers. That is how I go to London this autumn. If I went to Prague, even with Brian, I would not be feeling too safe. We sometimes go to the country beyond the Vienna Woods to the east. That he likes better than any city as we have more chances to fuck in the fields or vineyards and he loves to do that in the open airs."

I was about to genially correct his idiom when George turned around, saw us close in conversation and immediately proposed that Brian drive us in his jeep out to the Benedictine monastery at Klosterneuburg, where Horst had an uncle who was a monk.

"It'll be nice to be somewhere which isn't bombed out," I said to George as the ancient train swayed violently while it chugged over an ill-kept permanent way. "Horst mentioned it although he's never been there. I guess Brian told you all about it. He's been there several times since the Liberation."

"What that old goat told me," George said, staring expressionless out of the grimy window at the forlorn countryside of Slovakia, "is that virtually every Czech under the age of ninety was available to him!"

"I didn't know he was into sex with old men," I commented with a smirk. "You'd hardly know it to listen to him!"

"Vocal appearances can be the most deceptive of all," said my self-appointed mentor. "To listen to you one could be forgiven for thinking you've lived the life of a nun."

I crossed my legs and folded my arms about myself. I smiled at him but didn't open my mouth. At that precise moment I was promising myself some Prague duplication of my very last sexual experience, which had been with the man in the *pissoir* back in Paris. It wasn't the life of a nun that appealed. I was at that moment fully determined to be an international whore.

Prague. Melancholy city sprawled across the snaking Moldau River. The huddled charm of the Old Town Square; the exhilarating expanse of the sloping Wenceslausplatz. The medieval Jewish cemetery with its ghostly golem a palpable presence. But above all, at least for my twenty-year-old self, was the sheer romanticism that these entities created in combination. From the moment we boarded an ancient prewar cab to the Hotel Bristol (which prudent George had already notified from Vienna) I sighed with great gulps of unfathomable yearning at every historic vista we passed or could see in the mist-wreathed distance.

George, too, was affected by the gentle melancholy of the place. I felt it made him softer with me. Until the second evening, that is, when I met Sacha, via his reflection in a shop window, at the foot of the Wenceslausplatz. I make no defense of my behavior because I can think of none. I lied to George by stating I was slipping downstairs to buy more postcards in the vast vestibule of that mausoleum of a hotel. Instead I made quickly for the square, where the pulse of the city beat more strenuously than on the quiet sidestreet our hotel inhabited.

In less than five minutes I spotted my goal: a skinny young man with hair not quite as straw-blond as that of Horst back in Vienna. From the outset there was a radical language barrier. I had already been warned that to speak in German to a Czech was to invite at least a spit in the face. But as my German consisted only of old Herr Gotlieb's feeble attempts to instill his native language into our recalcitrant class at Probus School at the height of the war, the risk was academic. It rapidly emerged that Sacha knew neither English nor French. Only later was I to learn that he didn't speak Czech either, as he was an uneducated Slovak from a village outside of Bratislava.

He smiled when I smiled, stood silent with head slightly drooping when I addressed him in English. His rather large hands stayed suspiciously close to his private parts as he stood there, immobile on the sidewalk next to me, using the shopfront as a mirror for both of us.

What to do with him? Without consulting me, George had reserved a double room with two beds for us in Prague, so a return to our hotel was out of the question.

Sacha himself solved the problem. With a sudden nod of that wheaten hair he indicated for me to follow and took off down a passage at the side of the store which led to a maze of further narrow streets, until we arrived (I was almost running to keep up with him) at a plain wooden door set into a damp-stained wall bordering a cat-piss-smelling alley. He knocked twice, with bare knuckles. So hard it made me wince. There must've been someone standing right inside because it opened immediately. With a quick nod for me to follow he disappeared into the windowless building. For one moment I hesitated—every internal alarm jangling and screaming for caution—then I followed my quarry out of the warm light of late afternoon into a darker world of uncertainty and possible danger.

Beyond the door, though, proved a good deal brighter than I'd anticipated. Illuminating a room full of small tables and folding chairs were a series of lightbulbs with only minimal shades, suspended from the ceiling and spilling harsh light over the scene below. The place reminded me of a cafeteria in a YMCA. However, the patrons of this place were not at all like the folk I'd seen in a Y. By their excessive makeup and frilly clothes I surmised that most of the women sitting at the tables were prostitutes. And the men, nearly all in cheap and ill-fitting double-breasted suits and a majority sporting plastered-down brilliantined hair, I supposed were either pimps or male hustlers. Of my blond quarry there was at first no sign.

As in Paris and Vienna my own clothes were obviously a giveaway. Indeed, a man detached himself from behind the makeshift bar, this one dressed nominally as a waiter by his far-from-clean white jacket, slouched over to the corner where I had sat down and addressed me in English.

"Welcome to Globus. You want drink?"

I smiled a smile I didn't feel. "I'm looking for my friend? He came in just before me?"

"Sacha? He go bathroom. Be right back. You like Sacha, huh?"

I was a little put out by the bluntness of that. "We have only just met—on the Wenceslausplatz. He seems very nice."

"You need Carl for English talk. Wait here. I get him."

With that laconic utterance he left my table—without even bothering to take an order. Then, as I surveyed those about me, I noticed that some had drinks on their tables but many didn't. If the Globus was a bar it didn't seem to depend entirely on the plying of drinks for its existence. The waiter soon returned, with both a smiling Sacha and a man in his late twenties with prominent teeth and balding head who was introduced by the waiter as Carl.

Carl didn't talk so much as gabble. He provided myriad details concerning Sacha—they were obviously good friends—told me of himself and his job as an English teacher, of the horrors of the German occupation and of his desire to quit Prague and emigrate to America. He also made a determined effort to camp things up, and explained that the Globus was some kind of semi-private club that catered to prostitutes and gay men. He didn't mention gay prostitution but I somehow had the impression he was pimping for his blond friend from Bratislava.

If I hadn't started to develop the hots for Sacha, I think I would have enjoyed Carl's offbeat flavor rather more than I did. But we hadn't gone beyond ordering a flask of wine (which it was quite obvious I was supposed to pay for) before Sacha and I were playing "kneesies" under the table. It was when I was about to move from knee pressure to manual groping that I happened to look at my watch and see that nearly an hour and a half had passed since I'd left George in our hotel room. It was not difficult to summon up a disturbing vision of a livid Irish face and a coldly crisp voice to accompany it. I got to my feet.

"I am late for another appointment," I said lamely. "I'm afraid I have to go."

Carl spoke rapidly to Sacha before the two of them rose too. "That is all right. Sacha come with you. Sacha likes you very much."

Often Carl spoke on Sacha's behalf, as if he himself were not there. Out on the street again I began to panic. What the hell was I going to do with the two of them? We more or less retraced the route Sacha and I had previously taken. As I vainly struggled for an excuse to shed the pair, I found we were once more in the broad vicinity of Prague's main square. Only we were somehow behind the main façade of the shops and still in the world of narrow streets and tall buildings which allowed the sunset sky above to appear only as slivers of sickly yellow light between rooftops.

I knew I must do something very soon. I stopped. I don't think it was just my imagination, but the spot I'd chosen was not only quite devoid of people but seemed even darker than elsewhere.

"My father is awaiting me at the hotel. It is only a few yards from here." I looked at Carl, awaiting his translation. It took more words than I would have imagined, but it immediately galvanized his companion. With one leap Sacha had his arms about my neck and was kissing me hungrily on the mouth. Carl had somehow come behind me and thus effected a minimal screen should a passerby materialize.

I felt it incumbent on me to respond to my passionate Slovak and eagerly held him tight to me. "I'm so sorry it has to end up like this," I panted. "Perhaps tomorrow at the big restaurant on the Platz. Could you explain that, Carl?"

But neither of them had anything like a future rendezvous in mind. Their concerns were very much with the present. As Sacha's hand went down to my already bulging front (it appeared to be an automatic response with me, *whatever* the circumstances!) I felt buck-toothed Carl come up from the back and push powerfully, meaningfully, against my buttocks. I did indeed feel the international whore at that moment. But at the same time I knew this abrupt erotic moment doomed to failure.

Early evening on the streets of downtown Prague was hardly an appropriate occasion for three-way sex—or any other kind, come to that.

With a sharp effort I broke from them and moved so fast down the alley that I was almost trotting. I didn't look back, didn't lessen my pace until I was on a broader, bustling street and saw a building I recognized as one George and I had passed on several of our forays. Within two minutes I was bounding up the steps of the Hotel Bristol with its cavernous rooms, armies of silver-haired servants and so singularly few guests. My mind was concerned with none of these matters. My one and only thought, of course, was of George and the reception I was about to receive.

With Celtic fatalism I elected the gloomiest of constructs. He would yell and scream—even assault me physically. I would seek to explain my absence in an already rehearsed fabrication involving my falling down, spraining an ankle, fainting and recovering in a restaurant from which a kindly waiter escorted me to the foyer of the hotel. As I entered that foyer I had more than half persuaded myself that such was precisely what had happened. That left half a conviction clinging uncomfortably to the far less palatable truth. I had nearly reached the rickety elevator when the more dismal but honest construction of recent events led me to fall back on the armor of my financial independence as a last resort.

As the bent old man used gnarled fingers to pull the elevator folding door open for me, I felt for my wallet—and found it missing. Despair enveloped me. While we slowly trundled up to the third floor I felt steadily more and more vulnerable. I was now not just to face my benefactor, but to face him penniless.

I had a key to Room 304 but I didn't even use it. I knocked instead. At first there was no answer. At least, I could hear nothing. I turned the handle and walked slowly in. George was standing by the tall windows. They were open and a small amount of street traffic sound came in at the narrow balcony.

"Where the hell have you been? I've been worried out of my skull!" He didn't sound cross. In fact he spoke rather quietly for him; plaintively. So geared was I to his expected wrath that I was taken totally aback.

My carefully detailed explanation of my extensive absence slipped quietly out of mind. "I'm sorry, George. I've been a complete fool. There are times when I don't think I'm quite sane."

He looked not so much at me as through me as he continued to talk in that unnaturally quiet voice. "I thought you'd gone. Left Prague... Czechoslovakia." His arms rose in a funny little gesture—dropped helplessly back to his sides. "Gone back to England, perhaps. Anything to escape me and my temper." He took an audible breath. "I can't say I'd have blamed you."

"I left here like a bitch in heat. There are times when my loins rule my head. That was one of them."

"You don't have to tell me everything. You are under no obligation to account for your actions. Don't think I don't know how I've been behaving.... No one in his right mind would blame you for leaving me. Brian even warned me back there in Vienna."

I was unused to seeing a proud man crumble. It fueled the mounting sense of my trashiness more than ever. Suddenly I gave way. With tears flooding down my face I rushed across to him and buried my weeping self in his protection. Loud and long I cried—with every convulsive shudder accompanied by a stronger tightening of his arms about me.

Eventually he got me to the bed. Sat me down and took a chair close by. "Feeling better, boyo?"

I smiled but it wasn't easy. Between sniffs I also tried to talk. "It was probably some kind of setup. Anyway, when the younger one embraced me and the other concealed him from behind, he must've taken my wallet. It had everything in it. Photos...addresses...everything. He didn't leave a penny!" I started to cry again.

George crossed to me but didn't cuddle me again. Instead he offered me an enormous white handkerchief. "Here, use this. A good blow and you'll feel better."

I did as I was told. I put *everything* into that blow. I re-experienced the violation of being robbed, I thought of how ungrateful I had been to George, I guiltily remembered being disloyal to Mama in what I'd said about her in Paris, I thought of Daddy and how lonely he must be in his mental depressions.... When I finally took the handkerchief down from my nose it was because I had not a vestige of breath left in my lungs.

From then on there was a gentler, warmer feeling between the two of us. It continued throughout our trip, which proved to be one of the richest and most informing experiences of my life. I don't mean to say that George was never again testy—especially with the behavior of his fellow men who served him in restaurants or impinged upon him from an inefficient bureaucracy such as a post office. Nor can I say that I was never tempted again by the sight of some comely youth. There was a particularly good-looking Italian sailor in the international port of Trieste.... But we accommodated ourselves to such traits in each other. The rest of the trip, though hardly a matter of dramatic reportage, was a delight for an avid student of art and architecture being tutored by someone who was steeped in European history and had traveled that imperial Hapsburg route before, acquiring much fascinating knowledge in the passing.

Back in Paris a further card awaited me from Mama, saying that she and Charlotte had decided to stay overnight at the George V and then travel by Golden Arrow train back to London the next day. She did not explain why this change of plans had been effected—but I had an uneasy feeling it was somehow to do with me and my plans to stay on in Paris.

George and I had discussed that subject many times since the Prague episode and I was now quite amenable to his pleading that I attend the Sorbonne with the advent of autumn. Indeed, I was eager to do so, and right away began to investigate what possibilities lay in store and what George would be able to do for me, if anything, from his UNESCO diplomatic vantage-point.

My premonitions of Mama proved only too true and the evening I spent with her—she persuaded George and Charlotte to dine by themselves, stating that an important family council was in order between mother and son—was a protracted and bitter one. Put simply, Mama argued fiercely for my return home, ostensibly because I had already begun my university career at King's. She did not hesitate to invoke the plight of my father and her own maternal need for my presence. Implicitly I knew that beyond those constituents was that of my relationship to George Cronyn and my living indefinitely in his apartment.

I do not think that even under torture Mama would have succumbed to dotting "i"s and crossing "t"s. She was far too Anglo-Saxon for that. There was no reference to my being "kept" nor hint at an unnatural relationship. Nevertheless she knew and I knew that we both knew that such were the implications.

In vain did I hint that there was no romantic link between George and me; that I would in fact pay him rent from my Armed Forces Postwar Educational Grant and whatever she was disposed to give me. I suggested with equal delicacy that if I were in London there was always Patrick, whom she hadn't much liked, to divert me—and added, for extra ballast, that a charming Viennese named Horst would be a further "close friend" for me if I were to return to her native city.

But beyond all of that was something of even greater significance. I had only been sensible of it in the most shadowy way before our bleak dinner, which Mama once more provided me at Maxim's. But before we'd gone very far I knew with increasing clarity that what I had now to do was related to that hard moral choice she herself had had to face over separation from her children at the outbreak of war. It was the identical topic which had briefly surfaced when we had listened to the irate man at Fouquet's, shortly before Bastille Day. But I was no more able to articulate these things succinctly than she was able to provide details of her misgivings over my proposed life with George on the Rue Berlioz.

However, she experienced no difficulty in urging me to make The Hornbeams my base. "You need your family about you, Davey. You are too pliant, too weak with strangers. Besides, your academic record isn't so strong that you can afford to interrupt it. Let alone in another country where you are surely not fluent in the language."

"I can get by, Mama. My French isn't that bad."

"I expect more than just a 'get by' from my sons. And with Simon now completely involved with that woman, I need your support more than ever."

I toyed sullenly with my Coquilles St. Jacques. "What about Little Arthur? You'll have him at home now that he's finished at Probus, won't you?"

Mama glanced sharply at me. I had the sudden notion that she and George had a common ability to explode with no apparent time fuse. Perhaps it was that shared propensity which drew me to him.

"There are times, Davey, when you can be just ridiculous. Little Arthur is a *baby*. He knows nothing about these things."

"Mama, Little Arthur is *eighteen*. I was in the Navy by then and Simon had spent three years dodging torpedoes at sea."

"That has nothing to do with it! He is not equipped to do the things for the family—especially with the strain your father is under—that I expect from you. And would have expected from Simon if he hadn't decided to marry that woman."

"My sister-in-law's name is Joan, I believe."

Mama leaned back, her fish soup untouched. She signaled discreetly to the waiter to remove it. "Don't be pedantic, darling. It doesn't suit you."

"Going back to England doesn't suit me. I wish you would accept the basic truth of that, Mama."

It was then that I decided to go as close to the bone with her as I dared. "There are times when we all have to make decisions without knowing the ultimate consequences. But at the moment of making them we have to believe in our judgment and do it in good faith." I paused momentarily. "I am sure there must've been a time when you faced your own hard decision—and had the courage to act on it when you decided it was the right one."

For a split second I thought she was going to take my bait. But instead she looked coldly about the crowded tables. "This place isn't a patch on what it was in Poppa's time. I shall not come here again."

CHAPTER FIFTEEN

Feast of St. Michael the Archangel...Michaelmas Day...September 29, 1947...Paris...George and I attending Solemn High Mass in the presence of H. H. Princess Marie-Louise, Queen Victoria's granddaughter, in St. George's Anglican Church. Only she was unaware we were there....

George had decreed that the day was to celebrate my first full year as a Parisian resident. Then he always held to his own peculiar way of reckoning, and airily stated that the July and August of my first year were to be dismissed as apprenticeship or tourist time and thus of no real significance. However, we had already celebrated four separate anniversaries of the birthday of our "relationship"—as he still persisted in calling it, in spite of my frowns when he did so. The first of these was of the day I'd arrived at his front door with Patrick; the second when Patrick left, leaving me alone at 33 Rue Berlioz; the third when Mama departed and I had sadly made it clear I would not be returning to England; and the fourth observance our initial appearance together at his regular place of worship. That practice was something I'd resisted until I had begun studies at the Sorbonne and become duly homesick for a few English-speaking voices.

After the first Anglican Mass George had persuaded me to attend since my regular church-going in London, he had taken me to a slap-up luncheon in the Ile de France, where we feasted on traditional Michaelmas goose. We were scheduled to do so again now that a full year had elapsed. Before that characteristically culinary gesture of thanksgiving by George for our shared life on the Rue Berlioz, I had consented to this *spiritual* acknowledgment of mutual good fortune.

I looked about me at all those Anglophone worshippers drawn from those places around the globe where the English language had rooted over the past few hundred years, and I did most truly feel gratitude for the past year's experience.

The Sorbonne—more especially the set of courses an unusually sensitive Dean had arranged for me—had proved just what I had needed, and my marks for the endless tests and essays integral to the French university system of that time were uniformly gratifying. I had made several good friends among my French classmates, one of them being gay and someone with whom I was able to have a warm if wholly platonic relationship.

What was true in the academic context proved equally so at home in the sixteenth *arrondissement*. I would be lying if I were to say that, from the day I crossed the Seine to register at the Sorbonne, I never cruised another *pissoir* or had sex save with myself. But it was infrequent and kept well away from George's sharp and jealous eyes.

More crucial than any sexual vagaries, I slowly discovered as the year gathered momentum, was the fact that, while George could still occasionally embarrass me in his ardent protestations of affection, he never once confronted me sexually or even entered my bedroom or study unbidden. Put positively, we did in fact grow closer and learned to be much gentler with each other. If I did not tell him every time lust nudged my groin or which male had recently caught my eye, I did talk freely with him of many problems and seek his counsel when I was distressed or depressed.

What helped, I think, was a streak of prudery in George which matched a comparable element of reticence in me. It was several months, for instance, before I even hinted at a spasmodic propensity for tall black men, such as the superb Sudanese mechanic at George's local garage. It was even later that he offered an account of the time he and his buddy Brian had combined an extensive pilgrimage to Saharan cities associated with St. Augustine of Hippo with an even more vigorous pursuit of young male Bedouin across the concealing folds of the desert.

The truth of the matter, I suppose, was that—in the fashion of the times—we were something of closet queens. And in a perverse but quite real way, this provided a substantive part of the glue that bonded us. Indeed, in his franker or drunker moments, George would asseverate that an excess of *confessionalism*, as he called it, could sunder ties between people.

As we moved swiftly from the "Nine-fold Kyries" (Madame Dreyfus conducting the choir; gay Kim Oldroyd, student of the great Nadia Boulanger, thundering away at the organ) to the "Gloria in Excelsis" and on to the "Credo," such were the vaguely thankful thoughts ambling through my head.

I opened my mouth wide and let my praise stream forth: "Therefore with Angels and Archangels, and with all the company of heaven we laud and magnify thy glorious name, evermore praising thee and saying: Holy Holy Holy, Lord God of Sabaoth. Heaven and earth are full of thy glory...."

I looked across the aisle toward the Lady chapel, where I had become progressively aware of a row of young people accumulating as the Liturgy progressed. They were definitely newcomers to our congregation. I scanned their faces—which was no easy task. One or two held hymnals or missals close to their noses, while scanning unfamiliar words. Others looked downwards, as if awkward and out of place amid all that ardent nineteenth-century Gothic, which was by now quite misty with incense and brilliantly aglow from a profusion of candles.

Their general age group suggested students. By such factors as the casual way they stood, the women's spectacles and the men's haircuts, they appeared to be Americans. For me there was an indefinable glamor about them. I felt a strangely powerful innocence in the air. It seemed to emanate from one in particular.

As the "Sanctus" evolved into the "Benedictus" I involuntarily secularized the triumphant words: Blessed is he that cometh in the name of the Lord.

I looked hard at him. He was the tallest of the young men in the group. He was also fair-haired, crewcut and by far the most handsome. He caught my eye and smiled. I felt something course through me with the velocity and impact of a lightning bolt.

With the sixth sense of an alarmed mate, George suddenly swiveled ninety degrees to face me. He had been straining in the opposite direction to catch a better glimpse of the princess amid her bunched retinue. He looked straight over my head at the tall youth in tweed jacket and gray slacks. "What's he staring at?" he growled—loud enough for me to be glad the choir was still hanging onto the final notes of the "Benedictus."

"Hosannah in the highest...."

"I think *he* is blessed," I replied, a strange happiness quivering in my throat. "Blessed in the name of the Lord."

"Jesus Christ! Don't be blasphemous," George said inconsistently. The music stopped. Mercifully he did too.

After the Mass, the congregation had to wait for the departure of Her Highness. Then, as was customary, we wandered outside and hung about in small groups. The sun shone strong and warm on the penultimate morning in September. The redolence of expensive perfume replaced that of incense on the air. St. George's was a wealthy congregation—a fact signified not only by the costly scents but by the fashionable clothes and chic millinery. In that era hats for women were *de rigueur* in Anglican and Roman churches.

When I say "we" hung about, I should stress that it was very much at my instigation rather than George's. He was anxious to be off to the country and the goose luncheon he had ordered. In any case, although an enthusiastic worshipper there at St. George's, George always insisted on keeping his profile low with the rest of the congregation. But I was determined to see the young man who had affected me so powerfully in church. I won. I *had* to! I would have killed to make social contact with him of the marvelous smile, commanding height and light brown hair!

I licked dry lips and launched my ploy. "Are you people new to St. George's? I don't think we've seen you around before."

"Hi, I'm Ken Bradley. You're dead on! I only got off the boat at Le Havre last Wednesday. We're part of a group of students taking a special course on French Civ. We met up at our embassy yesterday and Nancy suggested, since we were the only High Episcopalians on board ship, we should all come here to St. George's for the Feast of St. Michael. We didn't know there'd be royalty present. That was a bonus."

I stared at him, fascinated. Unused to such a generous offering of detail from a complete stranger.

"My name is Davey Bryant," I replied in a daze. "And this is my friend George Cronyn." I tried to comply with his free flow of information. "He's Irish and I'm a Cornishman—if you know what *that* is."

Meticulous George's hand shot out where Ken's and mine had stayed at our respective sides. As I looked into Ken's eyes his sheer beauty rocked my senses for a second time. I was made mute and prayed George would take over socially.

As the two of them began to chat, enabling George to build on the knowledge Ken had vouchsafed me and discover that Ken had been born in San Francisco twenty-one years earlier, was attending Stanford and visiting Paris for the first time, I did something of which I would never have imagined myself capable. I interrupted them to ask George if Ken might accompany us to the Ile de France if he was free. I could no more believe my ears than my sudden access of courage when George readily agreed and Ken quickly added he would like nothing more. I felt I would burst with bliss and must have shown it.

"What's happened to you?" George asked amiably. "It's only goose—plus their special *foie gras* as starters if you behave."

My spurt of audacity had already died down. I was quite incapable of telling dear, generous George—and he possessed doubly those qualities as my happiness expanded—that I had abruptly and overwhelmingly fallen in love, that the conviction now burned in me that the young man beside us was to change my life totally. Instead I said that goose was quite my favorite dish and that the Michaelmas meal last year was the one I cherished most of any he had ever provided.

That night, after a most buoyant lunch with George playing every Irish card of charm known to man, I told him the simple truth. I could contain my excitement no longer. He immediately counseled caution—his word was *prudence*—but he was not for a moment hostile; nor did he reveal even a gleam of the anticipated jealousy which I was convinced must be present.

His acceptance of Ken and me went even further. Incredible though it may appear in the light of previous events (when his notorious *green eye* had so often gotten on top of him), it was my "benefactor" who solemnly provided the two of us with the wherewithal to get to know one another better. He gave us specific funds which he insisted must be used to escape Paris during the Armistice weekend of 1947 and spend a time of mutual discovery. After poring over maps, with George volubly in attendance to instruct and guide, we chose the small cathedral city of Senlis, where we spent a series of rain-filled days primarily in bed....

When we returned, momentous decisions had been made—though we were wholly unaware of how we could ever realize them. After Senlis we knew we wished to live together. But even more significant implications were confronted. We decided that when Ken went back to Stanford to pursue a PhD, I would either accompany him or follow as soon as humanly possible.

George won over our protestations when he insisted Ken move in and share the accommodation he had provided me. We stayed there together until we left France for an eventual sailing on the *Liberté* for New York the following August. After then, though—after we had left France—George proffered mainly silence. He had mumbled something toward the end about being a poor correspondent but that was only an excuse. I knew he was hiding feelings which I had forfeited any right to probe.

There remained a major task. The one to which I was least looking forward. I dithered several weeks before a terse note from Mama enquired as to my health, my academic career and my domestic life—in that order.

(Letter written but never mailed)

July 31, 1948

Paris

Dearest Mama:

Thank you for your note enquiring about your second son. Please do not be anxious on my behalf as I am in good physical shape and have put most of the problems you know about well behind me.

Life has been truly hectic in recent weeks and when I explain why you will certainly see why I've been so slack in writing to you. Remember my mentioning I'd met this young American student at church who is here at the Sorbonne studying? Well, we have become great friends. Oh, Mama, who am I kidding? I have fallen desperately and eternally in love with Ken and he with me.

George has been terribly sweet and not at all jealous. If this is going to be a totally honest letter, let me modify that just a little bit and say he has hardly been at all jealous. Our landlord has certainly been most generous, and after encouraging us to go to Senlis last year took us to the Costa Brava over Christmas. That is when I suggested to you, Mama, that I was going with Fiona Neville from St. George's to her people at Montreux. A bit of a white lie, I'm afraid, as Ken and I did go to Montreux to stay with the Nevilles—but that was over Easter.

Since then, as soon as exams were over—in which I did very well, Mama—Ken and I went off on a long hitchhiking tour which took us to Lyon, and then down the Rhône Valley to Nîmes and Arles and finally to the Mediterranean and Villefranche, where we put up at the Welcome—which is where you and your Poppa stayed once, I remember you telling me when I was a little boy.

Now the hardest part, dearest Mama. I am going with Ken on the SS *Liberté* to New York the day before my birthday! I have applied to Stanford University and will complete my degree work there in California. The Sorbonne people were most cooperative and there is a famous Frenchman at Stanford to whom I have been given a letter of introduction, so I am sure there will be no problem.

What all this means, of course, is that I cannot see you and Daddy before I go. That almost breaks my heart but please believe me when I say there is no real alternative. I would not come without Ken and how would I explain him to you both? Daddy is under enough pressure, I gather from your previous letters, without wanting the sexual nature of his son paraded about his own home. And I simply couldn't stand to see either of you show even the slightest hostility to the person I love most in all the world.

So I am taking the coward's way out. By the time you receive this letter your homosexual son and his lover will be on the high seas, bound for the New World. And if that sounds romantic and dramatic it is, because I *am* romantic and my life is *hugely* dramatic at the present time.

The funny thing is, Mama, that I know that under less stressful circumstances—I mean with a longer period of time for acceptance—you would come to appreciate Ken's qualities, just as he would love yours. Perhaps all this awaits us in the future. Dear God, I do hope so!

Dearest little Mama, I know if I came home first you would help me financially and give me good commonsensical advice and buy me underwear. But this I have to do on my own. True, I have had to borrow my fare and a little more from George, but I will pay him back in fairly short order. Students in the U.S. pay their way through college and Ken says he knows I will have no difficulty in getting a job with the Stanford University Library. Incidentally, it is a cousin of George's who is acting as my sponsor for my American visa. He certainly knows how to pull strings, does that one!

Can you ever imagine, can anyone really know, how thrilled I feel to go halfway around the world for someone I truly love! Oh Mama, I am humbled it should happen to me!

With hugs to you and Daddy as well as Simon and Little Arthur,
Your devoted son,
Davey

(Letter mailed)

August 8, 1948

33 Rue Berlioz,
Paris, 16ème

My dear Mama:
Thank you for your letter. No, all is well with me and my exam results were all tops. The exciting news—and I have been waiting

all this time to get it before writing to you—is that I have been accepted as a student at Stanford University in California, where I shall finish off my BA and probably go on to do an MA. I won't bother you with the details, which are complicated. Because I really must be independent I have only borrowed the money from George Cronyn, who, incidentally, thinks this transferring from the Sorbonne to Stanford is an excellent idea that will help my career prospects enormously.

I also have had the singular good fortune of meeting a brilliant Stanford graduate student at St. George's Church, which I regularly attend each Sunday and Feast Day. His name is Ken Bradley and he is a fellow Anglo-Catholic. I cannot tell you how helpful he has been over this business of getting into Stanford, which is his alma mater.

Now to the hard part. To take this scholarship I have to be there in early September—American universities begin much earlier than ours. So this means I am unable to get home and see you, Daddy and the family before I depart. I know that is absolutely terrible but there is really no way around it.

Believe me, I have racked my brains trying to work things out differently! It is just one of those things that has to be, so please do not make it any more difficult.

I will write, of course, immediately on arrival. There is a four-day transcontinental train trip before I arrive in San Francisco. From there, the end of my long journey, I will send a telegram. AMERICA, HERE I COME!

Please give special greetings and love to Charlotte and tell her I will write to her as soon as I am settled in on the Stanford *campus*, as Americans say.

Also give my love to dearest Daddy and tell him that I hope he is feeling chipper and that the job in Chelmsford isn't getting him down. You had better send me Simon's new Cambridge address. I've not written him since he got married. Give him and Joan my love—as please make sure you do to Little Arthur. But over and above everything and everyone I send my love to yourself. Please forgive.

Always your devoted second son,
Davey

******

August 15, 1948

The Hornbeams,

My dearest Davey:
I am writing on my little boy's birthday as he sails away from this island across the Atlantic to the New York address of Mr. Cronyn's cousin, which you at least included in your devastating letter.

This will not be very long as my heart is too full and my eyes too moist to follow the pen across the paper. You have made this *huge* decision quite on your own and I do hope you never have cause to regret it.

You cannot imagine the gaping wound you have left and it is pointless for me to dwell on that—besides being of no value to you in your radical new life. I do hope your meeting your friend in church isn't a bad omen. Wasn't it a church where you met that earlier young man, Patrick? You do not mention him any more.

I do not want to fill you with sadness or reproach as you start out on an existence so remote from us and so completely unimaginable. The little advice I have stems from things Poppa told me.

Make sure you put iodine in American drinking water as it is somehow deficient in minerals and will cause goiters if drunk raw. Also beware of mosquitoes, which are malaria-carrying—especially in New York and New Jersey. Avoid lounging under tall buildings and standing by windows in California because of earthquakes. That is all I can tell you of a practical nature.

I have not told your Daddy everything you are up to as he is still far from well and if he were to know that you had fled to America and that he most probably will never see you again, it might easily summon up a heart attack or the mental thing.

Partly for his welfare, I have decided to sell The Hornbeams so that we can finally go back to his beloved Cornwall. In fact we return to Polengarrow at the beginning of next month. I shall sell the farmland as Daddy can no longer possibly work all those acres—and I wouldn't want him to. He will look for part-time supervisory work with the Cornwall Agricultural Executive. Nothing to do with hospitals or medical organizations, which, I am sure you remember, he so hated!

Mr. and Mrs. Churchfield have also decided to retire to Cornwall and have bought that lovely house where Daddy's Great-aunt Eliza lived and where we spent our honeymoon. It will cost a fortune to modernize it, of course, and have running water and electricity installed. But it means I will have Charlotte in the next village, and with your Daddy's health what it is, that is an enormous boon. Indeed, I don't think I could have contemplated the move back had the Churchfields not made their decision first.

But all of that will seem pretty remote, not to say *parochial*, to you, my darling. What more is there for a mother to say? Be a good boy, remember your family's name and honor. And try and not yield to every whim that courses through that wilful head of yours. Write regularly but please NOT to Uncle Harry as he is so inclined to gossip. I will inform my brother of your nomadic activities in my own good time.

One other thing—if you are ever desperate for money you know you have only to ask.

With all my love and prayers,
Your devoted Mama

BOOK TWO: VOYAGES

CHAPTER SIXTEEN

San Francisco, 1960: For years there had been muffled moans brought to these safer Pacific shores from the pain of my beautiful Cornwall by blithe blue British airletter forms. There had been familial tragedy, as in the death of a teenage cousin thrown from her shying horse on the moors, and the pain of arthritic old women holed up in damp granite redoubts, seeing no one but equally pursed-lipped siblings and cousins and writing scrawled notes on foxed Christmas cards (bought God knows when!) to the fading image of an elusive great-nephew as they keened for a Cornwall dying about them.

In the ten years of our separation Mama never mentioned such things. Her pen invariably affirmed a positive past and a stoically neutral attitude to the present. She dutifully recorded the uneven graph of my father's health and the salient activities of my two brothers, particularly, for example, when Little Arthur fathered her only grandchildren.

Her letters suggested she genuinely loved her two little granddaughters—though not as much as Daddy did. The role of grandmother did not prevent her making incessant war on her son's wife, or insisting, even after the birth of my nieces, that her daughter-in-law refer to her simply as "Mrs. Bryant." Simon's wife, of course, had never been allowed to call Mama anything else, and the feud between them had not faltered since the day in 1945 when Simon had brought Joan home to meet us all at The Hornbeams.

Mama's Cornwall was very remote from that of my father's extant family. It was not the Duchy of his many relatives—my two morose great aunts up on the moorland, *their* daughters or the daughters' restless offspring. My cousins Loveday, Deborah and Jan—having no time for Celtic obduracy—had fled upcountry to London as soon as dependency on kith and kin was outgrown. Instead, her correspondence suggested she had come to see her grudgingly adopted Cornwall as a kind of springboard jutting out intrepidly into the Atlantic and suggesting the lure of the eternal voyage.

She wrote more and more frequently of an impatience to travel and of a frustration with the stay-at-home attitudes of my contented Daddy, happily returned to the ghosts of his ancestors, his sulky relatives and the house of his birth. It was this persistent friction between them, I think, which made her so opposed to nostalgic sentiment for a native Cornwall from an exiled me. If I expressed even a hint of homesickness she immediately reminded me of my decision to leave Europe with Ken, without seeing either of them.

She never relented. Indeed, she wrote to me shortly after a brief and ill-fated return to my birthplace in 1950 with my lover (during which she had wholly ignored Ken and thus relegated him to the status of a *third* daughter-in-law!) to tell me of her decision to emulate my action and, as soon as feasible—by which I understood her to mean after Daddy's demise—to escape her surroundings. Her burning desire, she wrote, was to see more foreign places, as she had begun to do with her beloved Poppa on her visits to France before the First War, and which she had tasted subsequently in the company of her friend Charlotte on their excursions to Scandinavia and Bavaria in the late 1940s. She had to nurse this ambition for ten years before finally realizing it in the company of my "aunt" Charlotte in the spring of 1960. By then Daddy was dead of a heart attack and Mama's mobility was thus restored.

It is a time I am unlikely to forget. The day in May they intended to sail from Amsterdam in a freighter, I was at San Quentin prison observing the execution of Caryl Chessman, the kidnapper, robber and rapist who had found defenders in the likes of Schweitzer, Casals and Aldous Huxley, and who had been on death row for the same twelve-year stretch I had been a resident of the United States. This was just one more example of the kind of ironic coincidence that has peppered (I was about to write *savaged*) my adult life, or at least a goodly part of it. As I stood before the warm plate glass with my fellow journalists, watching in the shadowless light the valiant little smart-ass twist and jerk from the devouring cyanide, I was bizarrely conscious that on the very same day Mama was setting out with her boon companion on the first oceanic voyage of her life—which, after three continents, would lead her finally to California and perplexing me.

When I recrossed the Golden Gate Bridge, feeling spiritually unclean in the moral desolation of witnessing the choreography of a state execution of someone who had never murdered—I chivvied myself into thinking about, alternately, Mama's proposed visit and what plans Ken and I should make about receiving her and Charlotte.

At the time we were renting a small two-bedroom apartment in the Marina, which overlooked the Bay and afforded us spectacular views of the Golden Gate Bridge, the precipitous slopes of Alcatraz and the leafy escarpment of opulent Belvedere. Just out of sight was the sullen yellow of the prison I had left, nestled amid the mild undulations of southern Marin County.

Chestnut Street had convenient bus lines for both of us, and was generally considered an attractive section of the city. But as I skirted the Presidio on the way home on that grim second day of May, I wondered whether the apartment would be large enough for four and if the neighborhood would not prove too noisy for a couple of elderly English ladies. Somewhat more dubiously, I also wondered whether the presence of two major prisons (both painted in obscene yellow variants of the Schöbrunn palace on the outskirts of Vienna) would prove too oppressive for them.

Ken disabused me of these several worries as soon as he returned home from Stanford that afternoon.

"At this point we have no idea whether they intend staying a week or a month, Davey. If we find ourselves too cramped we'll just suggest that motel farther up Chestnut toward Van Ness. It's in walking distance and not all that expensive. Anyway, between the two of them, they are obviously feeling no financial pain. They'd hardly be taking a world trip if they were. As for the noise—this is quieter than the London your mother and Charlotte grew up in, and down there in Cornwall I can remember nothing but cattle bawling, pigs squealing and endless hissing, quacking and clucking from all those bloody birds! I've never heard such a din anywhere else!"

Ken had grown up in Los Angeles, where the only sounds are police sirens and raucous coughs from smog-choked seagulls—or so I was tempted to remind him. In fact I remained silent. The Chessman vision still held me in a vice and the proposed arrival of Mama was just the added weight of trepidation. Looking across at me from the other end of the love-seat which we had placed facing the view of the bridge and the choppy waters of the bay, and picking up on my discomfort, Ken suddenly reached over and hugged me.

"It's that fucking business this morning, isn't it? You should never have gone. But for Christ's sake don't worry about your mother yet. They've hardly left Europe and it is *months* before they're due."

That evening I poured out my heart to Ken to a degree I had not used before him for a very long time. At my request we had gone out to dinner but, following our usual *course of conciliation*, as we rather sententiously called it, since I'd suggested eating out, my partner had first choice of where it was to be. We ended up at the Copper Lantern, a gay restaurant in North Beach which we knew well and where we were in turn well known. It was not the wisest choice of places for a *tête-à-tête* meal. I saw a closety colleague from the *San Francisco Tribune* whom I didn't particularly like and who I suspected didn't like me. Fortunately, he was so busy covertly ogling his swish young waiter—the staff were chosen very much with their looks in mind at the Lantern—that he had no time for us and pretended he hadn't noticed our fast retreat to our preferred corner table.

Joe Meserole was not the only hazard we encountered. There was worse in store. We had just given our order and I had begun to formulate my anxieties about Mama's impending visit when a familiar voice boomed from the direction of the bar.

"My! If it's not San Francisco's favorite lovebirds, Davey and Ken!"

I didn't bother to look around but spoke quickly to my lover. "Jesus, that's Delilah! She's not about to leave us alone."

"Yes she will," said Ken firmly. Then, smiling, "If I ask her nicely."

When Delilah sauntered over to us, as I had prophesied, I could see he was quickly searching for a third chair on which to park his fanny. Eric, our waiter, had cleverly seen to it that there were only two. Not that it would have mattered. If Delilah had determined on a chair he would scream and act up until he got a chair.

Ken forestalled him. "Hi, Delilah. Nice to see you. Would you mind terribly if you came back later? Davey has some rather worrying news from his folks back in England and we really have to do some quick planning. O.K?"

Delilah, a.k.a. Dick Carlsberg, raised his eyebrows—only to drop them just as quickly back into place. "Sure. My Mom is due for an operation any day now back in Cleveland. These things happen."

With that he turned full circle on his heel and glided back whence he had come. I wasn't sure whether I was more surprised by his response or by the invention of my lover which had obviously sparked it.

"That was quick of you," I said. "You don't usually come up with a story so right off the bat."

"It was the truth, wasn't it? You *are* worried about your Mama's arrival and what she'll make of things."

"Only that she'll hate being in an apartment and take some wild dislike to San Francisco. You know what she is."

"Not really. I didn't see all *that* much of her, remember. And that was over ten years ago. Was she really given to violent hates over different places? And I sure don't recall those English rooms being especially big."

"You're missing the point. You don't talk generalities when discussing Mama. She doesn't fit neatly into stereotypes or national patterns."

"That's for sure. The one thing I enjoyed about your mother was her disregard of consistency. I distinctly remember her saying the Champs Elysées was too big for a short race like the French."

"She always qualified that by saying the reserved and lanky English went on far too much about the virtues of intimate buildings and pretending Britain was Lilliput. When she finally went to Dublin with Daddy to see the old barracks and parade ground from his Great War days, she said that Dublin was the most English-looking city in the British Isles."

"It's not really her architectural opinions you're worried about, is it?"

"I suppose not. I don't really know what's eating me. I guess I don't know her well enough any more to second guess what she'll like and what she'll hate."

"She's your *mother*, Davey, for goodness' sake! You can't expect to know her in the same way you know other people. She knows you, though. At least she thinks she does. Only as her little boy, don't forget. If you're the arrested adolescent kind of gay, then you should have no difficulty in *getting on with Mom*. It's only those who have grown up and grown away whom mothers find hard to handle."

"Which am I? I don't think you've ever told me."

"That's because you're hard to pinpoint. It really depends with you on the time of day and the day of the week. I don't think your mother would have any difficulty in recognizing her child either at breakfast, taking your dog for a walk or dodging hard decisions."

I decided to skip the last as too close to home. "We don't *have* a dog—even though you know I'd love one."

"We have Maria."

"She's a cat."

"Your mother would recognize your comparable reluctance to do all the basic things like cleaning her out and coaxing her from under the refrigerator at three a.m.—even if you do like the idea of her presence in the apartment."

"This is becoming an inquisition. I don't think I'm going to enjoy my meal—that is, if it ever arrives. We seem to have driven off the waiter as well as Delilah!"

"Don't be silly, Davey. You asked my opinion about you and your mother and you're getting it. For *kitty maintenance* read *dog care*, if you like. I've always thought you would be one of those dog owners who would really like to fall back on—what's that charming British term?—a *kennel maid*. To handle the routine stuff. That would be me, of course."

"I thought we would be getting to you, sooner or later."

My lover smiled, albeit faintly. "I wasn't expecting a skirmish—just some easy talk between the two of us. But perhaps you have a right to bitch. You've been through a lousy experience this morning and here I am handing out home truths. Stupid me!"

Ken's blue eyes bored softly into mine and I knew if I held his gaze I would dissolve. It was somehow important I resist the teacher in him who sometimes threatened to come between us. "It's your approach that bugs me. I'm never sure whether the beginning is just the Freud bit and you'll move on to Jung and Adler later. As a matter of fact, I don't want to talk about me at all. It's Mama who's coming and her I want to discuss in terms of us."

"But I really know nothing about Isabella Bryant, widow of Wesley. It's her son Davey I've known for twelve years. I'm only qualified to talk about him."

I relaxed immediately, wondering for the umpteenth time what mysterious dew had kept his love so fresh for me for a dozen years in spite of all the quarrels, disagreements and vagaries of mood which had crossed our joint path since that magic Michaelmas in Paris.

The food came, and with it the danger of rift further departed. Pink-cooked liver and crisp-fried onions always comfort me, and Ken's spirits invariably soar when his Caesar salad actually contains the salty anchovies the dish is too often denied.

"I suppose deep down I still feel guilt in the way I did when we left to come over here without seeing her. I really was a heel, Ken, leaving her with Daddy when he was sick, and her having to handle the selling of The Hornbeams and returning to Cornwall and Polengarrow."

"We *did* go back, remember, and had a ghastly time on the farm. No one had said your father was that sick. And don't for a moment forget those two brothers. It was hardly your fault if Simon proved drunkenly vicious and that pompous Little Arthur remote. Along with her deliberately confusing me with that Irish number you picked up in church and took to France, those are *facts*, my boy. They must all be taken into account before we embark on any guilt trip."

I reached out and squeezed Ken's hand. That was an advantage of dining in a gay restaurant, even if the potential presence of acquaintances threatened in other ways.

"I'm glad you weren't there this morning," I said suddenly. "Ken, it was so *defiling*. I've always felt smirched enough—something to do with that business in the Navy, probably—but you're so American clean. One of your greatest attractions! That's why I'm so glad you were too young for World War Two."

"I managed Korea."

"But you were stationed for those months in *France*. Not the same thing. And thank God I wasn't left here alone too long. I still thank God every day for when you returned."

"Poor Davey, you were never good at being alone. I guess you made a smooth transition from Mama to me."

I admitted my good fortune by grinning. "You mustn't forget George Cronyn in Paris."

"I was thinking more of mothers than thwarted lovers."

I searched Ken's eyes. "Let's go home after we've eaten and not to a bar. I think I'm more in need of a lover than a mother tonight."

CHAPTER SEVENTEEN

Rotterdam: May 2nd, 1960

I haven't kept a diary since I was a girl and I don't want to even think how long ago that was! All I know is that my brother was alive and the Great War was still raging. Guy almost came down in his Sopwith Camel over Holland, which was neutral in that war, and I remember him saying he would hate being interned there, where the Dutch were all sympathizers with the German kaiser. Nor do I care too much for the place nowadays, what with all those bicycles jingling their nasty little bells so early in the morning. I think even Charlotte—who loves *everything*—was relieved when we sailed out of Rotterdam harbor this afternoon.

She is on deck now, ignoring a *very* fresh breeze while she catches what she calls "a spot of sun." I told her there would be more than enough of that when we got to the Med and Africa but she just smiled sweetly as always and said she wanted to get acclimatized slowly.

I am here in our cabin making a cup of tea, even though the steward offered to bring me one and was quite shocked when I turned him down. We shall see later what he is capable of but in the meantime I am enjoying being out of the wind, away from the smell of raw herring and the horrid mess everywhere from seagulls ejecting *lime*, which is so difficult to get off. I do hope that we meet up with more constipated ones before we get too far, and that these Dutch gulls will eventually give up and return to their home port.

I am enjoying unlocking and opening this handsome leather ledger and writing my initial entry. It somehow makes this *circumnavigation* of the globe a more profound adventure. Really, Simon could not have given me a nicer going-away gift, even if he did feel it incumbent on him to add that he was convinced I would give it up long before we reached Charlotte's relatives in South Africa.

I shall confound him! I will make regular entries, even though this diary is not destined for anyone's eyes but mine. It may contain some quite odd information—particularly when we reach Davey and his peculiar friends in California.

I mustn't forget I promised Charlotte's mother we would telephone when we reached Marseilles as first port of call. It is so much better to *talk* to the old lady than send her some postcard which she has to get her "daily," Kate Trewethern, to read aloud to her, now she can hardly see. Those Trewetherns were always gossips and I do not want my business spread indiscriminately over North Cornwall. It was bad enough when her policeman brother-in-law brought the news to us on the farm about that nasty business over Davey in the Navy all those years ago. I know very well she sells her homemade pasties to enough malicious creatures scattered about the parish who resent the fact that I am not taking this voyage with one of Wesley's old and decrepit aunts, but the woman of my choice.

But I must not make this a *bitter* journal. After all, I am stepping out on the adventure of a lifetime! Even the trips to France with darling Poppa pale in comparison, while those Charlotte and I took on behalf of her Girl Guides to Scandinavia and elsewhere proved quite boring. Thank goodness we will have no truck with bossy Girl Guide Commissioners on this expedition. I can certainly do without that awful Miss Croager, the one from Exeter who liked to call herself "Devonshire" at those insufferable international jamborees.

P.S. Must remember they are called Girl Scouts, not Guides, when we get to America.

Later: I had to interrupt this to talk with our steward, who informs me his name is Paul. He says tea will be served daily at this hour on our passenger deck. I told him in turn that I would be most likely brewing my own here in the cabin but that Miss Churchfield was a free woman and he had better enquire of her what her choice might be.

If we have been advised correctly, there are six other passengers, and I think the major meals will be time enough to socialize with them. Charlotte probably knows their family histories already!

A funny thing happened when we stayed overnight at the Majestic Hotel in The Hague before driving to Rotterdam and coming on board the S.S. *Ijmuiden.* We had just finished dinner and were passing through the foyer on the way to the lift to our room when I saw someone I thought I knew. I was about to turn to Charlotte and ask her if she, too, recognized George Cronyn, the Irish diplomat we met years ago in Paris who befriended my son when he was a student there. But she had wandered off to a boutique in the lobby. I don't know why, as we had both agreed the English china they were displaying—mostly commonplace Royal Doulton and Wedgwood—was at prices astronomically higher than at Tremain & Pendennis in Truro, or even in London when we had last gone to the West End to visit Lillywhites for our tropical clothes for this trip.

There is nothing whatever wrong with my sight. Nor my memory, for that matter! But the silly man refused to budge when I addressed him—persisting in a blank stare when I mentioned our time with him in Paris and all his kindness to Davey, who actually stayed under his roof as a student for a considerable period of time. In the end he just backed away, still smiling like a Cheshire cat. I was quite furious with Charlotte for not being there to help me identify him, but she had been buying me a paper-knife souvenir of Rotterdam with views in the handle, so I couldn't say too much.

Oddly enough, it is usually the other way round. I suddenly want to tell my beloved friend how much I appreciate her—yet, when the words start to flow, they too often turn critical and make me seem ungrateful. I am afraid I suffer from the same tendency as my middle son: an inability to keep quiet and not spurt out inadvertent things. Or so I used to say. He may well be quite the stranger now after—what is it?—a whole ten years since we last saw each other?

Our captain appears to be a very nice man. I hope that proves so as we are bound to see a great deal of him in the coming months. Paul seems a pleasant lad and will hopefully turn out a good steward—though I wish he wouldn't flutter his eyelashes so. There was a schoolfriend of Guy's from Christ's Hospital School who used to do it and I do not think coyness an agreeable feature in a man.

I think I had better go up and see how Charley—that's my secret nickname for my friend—is faring with our fellow-passengers. Her extraordinary good nature makes her so easily put upon.

Before I do that I want to make an entry about our plans. If I do this at the outset I can always turn to the front to make sure I am not getting off the track and failing to accomplish the things we originally set out to do. I regard this as enormously important.

Of course we are embarking upon a glorious adventure and a holiday. But in my son and those various old friends we haven't set eyes on for years whom we intend to meet as we traverse the oceans and visit three continents, there will also be something of a mission. There will be Charlotte's Uncle Cyril and his wife, Gerta, when we arrive in Port Elizabeth, and then the Boskellys in Calcutta—or is it Bombay? (I must look their address up before we dock in India!) In New Zealand, of course, there are Wesley's first cousins in Christchurch. And last but not least there will be my son on the American west coast, and whatever surprises that situation may bring.

I think I will send postcards *en route*. That will forewarn them all of our arrival and allow them in each case to make adequate preparations for our visit. There should be no slip-ups, as this enterprise has been in the planning stages for nearly eighteen months from the first day we walked into Thomas Cook's to make enquiries. Now up on deck to Charlotte!

CHAPTER EIGHTEEN

It was Ken's idea for us to visit Reeves Fawcett. Nothing was said specifically at the time, but because he was a good twenty years older than most of our circle (the more bitchy among us would have put that at thirty) his advice was often solicited when matters of social expertise were involved. I wondered whether Ken had Mama in mind but I said nothing. Reeves, who was distinctly short in stature, lived on Nob Hill, a stone's throw from Grace Cathedral, and when Ken called to say there was something we would like to discuss with him, we were immediately asked to dinner.

I especially liked the small white house, which was sandwiched between two apartment blocks, because—a rarity in that part of San Francisco—it boasted its own back garden, where a combination of giant ferns, aromatic shrubs, madrone and eucalyptus cleverly created an impenetrable screen of privacy from the bordering buildings.

Mr. Fawcett had a distinct fondness for my lover so I was not surprised at the alacrity of his invitation. I was, however, rather taken aback by the lavishness of the retired lawyer's hospitality for the occasion. The little man had a reputation, if not for downright stinginess, at least for economic prudence.

We dined with him perhaps eight or nine times a year and Reeves invariably provided interesting visiting firemen such as movie stars (we had met both the reclusive Jean Arthur and the gauche Rock Hudson at his table) or public figures such as the predatory poet Stephen Spender or his equally persistent fellow-countryman, the actor John Gielgud. But only rarely did we eat off the best of his three china settings. He was also quite conscious of the price of his victualing, and it had become apparent to Ken and me over the years that Reeves' board was strictly regulated by his snobbish evaluation of the importance of his guests.

That this wasn't invariably the case when we ate *à quatre* (for Reeves had a permanent companion, of whom more in a moment) I put down to the tender esteem in which Ken was held by the diminutive Texan. Even so, on the evening in question, I was surprised to see the rarely used *Florentine* Wedgwood brought out, and even more to note first the appearance of expensive Alaska king crab, followed by wild boar from the Santa Lucia mountains south of Big Sur.

I was quite relieved and reassured as to my belief in the parsimony of the rich on learning later from Arnold Decker, the fourth party at table, that Reeves had been originally expecting the distinguished actor and author Emlyn Williams. The Welshman, famous for both his Dylan Thomas and Charles Dickens impersonations, had unexpectedly, and to Reeves' chagrin, backed off at the very last moment. Arnold suggested maliciously that Mr. Williams' absence was the result of a *subsequent* dinner engagement with an even more renowned personage with a mansion down the Peninsula.

Arnold claimed encyclopedic knowledge of Bay Area hostesses for, when a young man in the prosperous twenties, he had enjoyed some reputation as a lieder singer from Mexico (Reeves cattily told us that Arnold in fact was Jewish from Montreal) when musical soirées of varying kinds had been popular in the more sumptuous homes, and he had been much in demand.

Naturally, Reeves was far too much of a gentleman to inform us then and there that the generous spread, so ornately presented at the long rosewood table, had been intended for more famous eyes and stomachs than ours.

Ken seized the opportunity, through the halo of candlelight from intricate candelabra reflecting on sentineled cutlery guarding the purity of the bone china in front of each of us, to remark on the civilized prospect. He also informed our somewhat dejected host that someone who would readily appreciate such a scene was at that moment on her way to San Francisco via Africa, New Zealand and the Pacific Ocean.

Reeves' innate curiosity over people was fortified by a zest stemming from his pique at Emlyn Williams' defection. I decided that was the precise moment to add my contribution to that of my diplomatic lover.

"My mother would adore your *présentation*," I said—giving the word its French pronunciation and falling into the extravagance of language which both Reeves and Arnold considered normative; indeed, less hyperbole was positively uncouth. "She inherited her Wedgwood from her grandfather and I understand it's original Josiah stuff. Mind you, there's no way she could compete with your silverware. She'd swoon over that," I added artfully, salting praise with challenge.

"I never knew you had a mother," Reeves said.

"Most people do," Arnold said, helping himself once more from the wine decanter.

I presumed it was familiarity and long practice that enabled Reeves to ignore him. Even we knew that Arnold preferred interruptions to speeches—and his partner the opposite.

"So Mrs. Bryant is a collector of fine china, is she? And a world traveler according to Ken. Tell me more, Davey. Is she really interesting—or just a possessive mother feeding off her gay son, like Arnold's was for so dreadfully long."

I could cope with that—though only too often Reeves intimidated me, and I have never been particularly good at explaining my family to outsiders.

"She would have died of emotional starvation a long time ago," I retorted. "I haven't seen her in years. And even for a large chunk of my childhood I lived apart. She drove an ambulance during the London Blitz and I was a schoolboy away in Cornwall. By the time peace came we were more or less strangers. It wasn't too long after that that I went to Paris to live and met Ken. Then you know all about that."

"Yes," said Arnold, "we know *all* about that."

"You must have met her then, Ken," Reeves reflected. "You tell me what she's like. Is she amusing? Do you think she'd fit into one of our little dinner parties, for instance?"

"Let me see," said Ken. "I gather she charmed Eisenhower in Paris when he was still Allied Commander or whatever. And *he* was always considered difficult. I found her delightful—but that was on her own turf in Cornwall." He drew breath to swallow that falsehood. "But I ought to add I don't think she suffers fools gladly. She was a scientist before she got married, wasn't she, Davey?"

I would have loved to expatiate on Mama's experiences in the laboratory of an armaments factory during World War One—but Arnold was looking balefully at me from the gloom across the table. Besides, I had got the impression from my first attempt that our host was not in the mood for *extensive* explanations.

"She was involved in the Silvertown Explosion in 1915, when many lives were lost," I informed the company. "Odd, it was the same year as the Pacific Exposition here, wasn't it?"

"The Lord giveth—the Lord taketh away. Only it should have been the other way around," said Arnold. "What should have been blown up is that ghastly Palace of Fine Arts." I could sense the argumentation lurking around his words but wasn't at all disposed to take him up on his challenge.

Reeves was. "I'm sure there are those who'd say it should have been the opera house that was blown up. It probably depends where you want to vent your sexual frustration."

Having felt he'd settled Arnold's hash, our host turned again to me. "Is your mother sexually frustrated, dear? If so, perhaps she should have a chat with Arnold."

Ken came to my rescue. "Isabella Bryant is the widowed mother of three grown sons. She will be accompanied on her trip by Davey's aunt, who's quite a remarkable woman in her own right."

I scented danger now from another quarter and scurried to avert it. "She's not my aunt by blood or marriage. She's been a friend of the family since my childhood and mother's closest friend. They call them *courtesy* aunts—at least, they do where I come from."

Reeves eyed me steadily. "Fascinating. Do I detect Sapphic tendencies on the part of someone? Your *aunt* is unmarried?"

As Ken had often argued that Mama and Charlotte had at least an implicit lesbian relationship, I was both surprised and grateful at his instant pouncing on Reeves' innuendo. "I think we have to be very careful about handing out labels in these situations. Don't forget we're talking about two Englishwomen. And also ones of a certain generation."

It occurred to me that both Reeves and Arnold were at least as old as Charlotte, and probably closer in years to my mother—but even if I had been tempted to comment so, I was abruptly preempted.

By Arnold. "I can't see what *that* has to do with anything. Is there some special problem for British dykes being honest with one another? Or can't lezzie love over there dare to speak its name even now?"

Reeves donated him a smile that had nothing to do with humor. "My dear, what brave words! Only I can't remember you ever screaming from the rooftops that you're a giddy belle. Half the time you're terrified to let it be known we share this address! The other half you're simpering at middle-aged women—as if for one moment you were able to fool them!"

"I'd suggest the furor over *The Well of Loneliness*," Ken said, "may still have some relevance."

"Oh how much I agree!" said Reeves with dainty vehemence. "Isabella Bryant seems a woman after my own heart. You must bring them here to dinner, Davey," he added. "We so rarely get to meet the family of our friends and I'm sure it will add enormously to our knowledge of you."

It wasn't only that our goal was obtained and an invitation secured, but I was also feeling irked by the subject being so protracted. And perhaps the notion of Mama being a conduit to further knowledge of me just to pander to the ferrety instincts of my host was also quite uncongenial. Anyway, I changed the subject.

"Did I hear you use the term *belle* just now?" I asked our host (quite disingenuously, in fact, as I had heard him deploy it several times before). "Forgive my ignorance, but what does it mean exactly?"

"It's an antiquated Southern word for faggot," said Arnold. "He likes to use it to remind us of his magnolia-and-mint-julep background—only he was raised on a Texas pig farm before Pappy bought himself a judgeship and they moved to sophisticated Fort Worth."

Reeves toyed with his cheese knife—looking at me all the time, as if the interjection were not occurring. When Arnold was through, the little man drew breath, smiled sweetly at me and began to discourse evenly.

"*Belle* was the term used in educated circles instead of the revoltingly coarse *queers*—at least through my graduation from the Sewanee Law School. I have no idea what language was used by the class of people he calls *faggots*—a term I had never heard in that particular context until I met him and his circle. Of course, all one now hears is *gay*, but that is a term I personally find impossible to employ when sharing a home with such a morose old queen as Arnold."

Arnold promptly left the table, spilling claret from his tightly clasped wineglass as he did so. Both Ken and I stared in pursuit of his somewhat hunched and wispy figure as he pushed violently through the green baize doors into the adjacent library. Seconds later we heard his feet stomping on stairs in some dim recess of the house.

Only then did Reeves deign to pick up the thread of his discourse. "I think we shall not be seeing Mr. Decker again this evening. He is suffering from his usual amalgam of booze, Jewish guilt and Canadian cultural insecurity, which I'm convinced has something to do with their climate. How about some good French coffee and liqueurs in the living room?"

There was no further reference to Arnold that evening but a great deal of talk—all of it originating from Reeves—about the social abomination of people who, having accepted one dinner invitation, shed it later for another that looked more prestigious or congenial. As our little host fulminated I ardently concurred, proudly asserting how I had never in my life committed this heinous sin. I fiercely, if superfluously, repeated the fact to Ken as we walked a trifle unsteadily home.

I was feeling too benign from the drink and the food to be unduly upset when my lover reminded me that although I might well be a *paragon* in the matter, I had confessed more than once that I had frequently, in the heat of sexual dalliance, made promises of subsequent assignation which I had broken when more alluring erotic prospects intervened. As usual, I had sought quickly for some chink in Ken's ethical armor with which to counter-attack. But Reeves' drinks had slurred my wits and I was forced to resort to the tired old charge that he too often failed to back me up in public over matters on which he would normally agree when we were on our own. But I went too far and finally accused him of disloyalty, adding that such was even worse than breaking social contracts in my book. Loyalty, I declared, surpassed even love.

His quiet response, as we walked down the steep and deserted hill behind the looming bulk of the Flood Mansion, was that when I talked like that he grew as apprehensive over Mama's forthcoming visit as I did. He knew only too well the source of that particular creed....

CHAPTER NINETEEN

At sea/Bay of Biscay: May 7th, 1960

In spite of my good resolutions, I could not make an entry here yesterday because the ship was rolling so—the Bay of Biscay living up to its reputation! But I seem to have found my sea *hand* as well as my sea *legs*! At any rate, I am able to write quite legibly and Charlotte and I walked almost the length of the cargo deck before breakfast this morning. We were the sole bodies bent against the gale and the driving rain. I can confess here I didn't care to look overboard more than was necessary. I have never seen waves as tall as buildings, and all that gray-green sweep of water with incongruous little swirls climbing about in it was very daunting.

I had the weirdest thought. It looked safe enough to drown in. Wesley always used to say when we sat in the car on a stormy day, looking down at the surf at Boscastle or Trebarwith, that he thought drowning the most Cornish way to go. Perhaps I have picked up more of that place over the years than I ever suspected.

Charlotte took it all in her stride. Then I do not think that woman has ever known a moment's fear! It was so when the bombs rained down and is likewise now when we are tossed about like a cork here at the mouth of the English Channel. She is more concerned with her fellow-passengers than with the elements. Especially the Wilkinsons. Especially Frank Wilkinson.

But here is where a little fear—or at least caution—would serve her in good stead. The man is a rotter. I was convinced of that before we had concluded our first dinner in his company and that of his neglected little wife. Everything since has convinced me the less we see of him on this voyage the better for all of us.

The food, of course, is not what we are used to. And I am not speaking of all those special Cornish things, the saffron bread, the bacon and egg pie, the ubiquitous pastry in pasties and pies. It is not English either but very, very Dutch. I mentioned this to Captain Schaepmann (very delicately, of course) and he said that part of the attraction of this particular trip is that the food will change from port to port as we circumnavigate the globe. Most of these freighters have a cook who serves the nationals of the ship with their own cuisine. Not the S.S. *Ijmuiden*. Our Dirk van Dorp claims he will serve at least one dish from the country or continent visited throughout the voyage. But that still means lots of cheese and pickled herring before we reach the Mediterranean and the south of France!

The passenger list has not turned out as we were originally led to believe. There are *not* six other guests but only four at present. Twelve, the captain has now explained, is the maximum the *Ijmuiden* can accommodate.

We shall pick up an extra couple in Italy, I understand. It is possible, however, that we will lose our Mrs. Brierly and her son, Nick, in Marseilles—if the news from Edinburgh arrives for her son, who may be about to make a major move up the hierarchy of the BBC in Scotland. Those two are very close with one another and keep very much to themselves. I'm afraid I have never been that thick with any of my three boys. It must be rather nice for a mother. I thought at one time Davey and I might be a little like that but it somehow didn't quite turn out that way. Oh well....

I do wish it could be the Wilkinsons we were going to shed on our first leg, but Frank was announcing in that loud and common voice of his that they would be on board all the way to New Zealand, where they also have relatives to visit. Charlotte has suggested I not react too strongly to the man, as we are going to have to put up with them for such a long while. She has a point, of course, but it would be much easier if I were as phlegmatic as she. As it is, I shall strive to concentrate on nervous Thelma Wilkinson and do my best to ignore him and all his socialist blather.

Fancy running down Winston Churchill in front of all these foreigners! Then the man was apparently a headmaster before retirement, and I have always mistrusted such people as pedants and as too fond of the sound of their own voices. After a lifetime of talking down to helpless children they are incapable of seeing fellow-adults as equals.

Davey's headmaster at Probus, Dr. Walford, was a similar type and resented my offering ideas and advice over my son. He may have understood "education" in the abstract but certainly had no idea what kind of boy he was dealing with when it came to Davey with his sensitive ways. Then that was the cost of Davey not attending Christ's Hospital School, where headmasters were used to such imaginative boys as my brother Guy and Poppa before him.

The reality is that such men as Wilkinson resent a woman standing up to them. I could tell right off the bat the fellow was contemptuous of my opinions. Then to see him squash his wife whenever the poor shivering thing opened her mouth told me all I wished to know about his uncouth background as well as his bullying nature. Even so, like most men, he is wholly susceptible to flattery. That is why he got on so with Charlotte, who will tell just about anyone whatever he wishes to hear! But he had better beware. Our Miss Churchfield is a worm who can not only turn—but even back during the war, when we shared our ambulance work, could turn into a veritable serpent if she felt someone was being a bully. And he is the sort of man who *never* knows when to stop.

His wife told me that his only son was not on speaking terms with him because Frank had interfered between him and his wife over how the young couple should bring up their children. That is why, Charlotte inferred, they are going to New Zealand to visit their grandchildren by their daughter. Distance has intervened to prevent him interfering in *that* marriage and Thelma is obviously anxious he not be the cause of marital dissension as soon as they reach Wellington.

It is on hearing cases like that that I feel less envious of Mrs. Brierly and her Nick, and grateful for our own family. True, I know Simon can be difficult, and he did not get on too well with his father in the last years before Wesley's death. And Davey has caused us a fair share of anxiety with his unorthodox ways. But Simon did give me this splendid book in which to record such thoughts as these. And I have to admit that Little Arthur and the children were politeness itself when Charlotte and I visited them in that cold and drafty house just prior to sailing.

Then there is Davey, of course, and his California friend. He has made it quite clear over the months since I notified him of our trip that he is dying to see us and would never forgive me if we returned to Cornwall without stopping off in San Francisco. In his first response to the news he said he was counting the days, and in his most recent letter he said he hoped we would stay a really long time.

We will have to see about that, of course. In some respects we are in the hands of these freighter people as to where we pick up the *Ijmuiden* again. Perhaps that is not a bad thing. I do not like to be *beholden* to people for it can make for difficulties on both sides. I have a lively fear of being under excessive obligation.

Charlotte knows no such qualms. Then her family were always such magnificent entertainers and hosts, I think that at the back of her mind is always the idea she can repay whatever kindness she receives. I, on the other hand, was raised by Poppa, who did not enjoy much social life beyond the immediate family—though I was dying to meet new faces, especially those of my brother Guy's friends. Of course, when I married into Wesley's Cornish lot it was to find dinner parties and house guests not just a rarity but completely unheard of. Nor was much love lost between relatives in that family either! So it is only now, in widowhood, that this denied side of my nature is surfacing, and I hope this voyage will allow it to meet and overcome my natural shyness.

I think Simon is very much his father's son in this respect and prefers to meet strangers in pubs and places rather than at home. Which also suits his wife, who thus avoids the work that such entertaining inevitably involves. Davey takes more after me. At least, his letters suggest they always seem to be attending parties. From what I recollect, Davey's problem was rather one of too great an appetite to meet new people, so that he spread himself too thin—with often dire emotional consequences. Little Arthur, on the other hand, is a closed book. I have no idea whether he shares the social proclivities of one brother or the prickliness of the other. Of course, he has the responsibility of a growing family and the onerous complication of a slovenly wife who, frankly, is neither his intellectual nor social equal.

I wish I knew more about that biblical "Benjamin" son. I ought to have more conscience over my youngest as he provided less trouble to us as parents and now has *her* to put up with. I'm afraid we always took Little Arthur for granted. How unfair life is!

We shall be docking tomorrow afternoon in Marseilles, Captain Schaepmann says. Unloading electrical appliances and some lumber. We will be going ashore and have until the following day to do as we please. Charlotte wants to take me to dinner to a restaurant she knew as a girl—if it's still there!

It will be nice to be on shore again and have a change of pace and food. It will also be pleasant to be free of our shipmates for a few hours. I do hope Charlotte doesn't suggest that any of them come along with us. That would quite spoil France for me.

RESOLUTION: I must make a big effort not to be a typical British grumbler—something Charlotte insists I am inclined to do in foreign parts. Perhaps I have a slight tendency in that direction. At any rate, she keeps harping back to our time, particularly in France and Austria, right after the war. But there were so many restrictions then and there was that dreadful black market to contend with.

Later in Scandinavia it was all the bureaucracy of those socialist countries. Nor could I abide those snobby Girl Guide Commissioners and their slobbering over Charlotte as soon as they discovered her parents had money. I really cannot understand why people get so stirred up about wealth. That is something I have at least taught my sons to behave naturally about.

P.S. I remember now I have already mentioned the Girl Guides in this journal. I must not repeat myself!

CHAPTER TWENTY

Janet Lipton and her friend Doria Lehman, who worked a ranch just outside Santa Cruz, lived quite openly as lesbians before it was even remotely acceptable beyond literary and artistic circles. Maybe they paid a painful price for their behavior (which some of our gay friends, disturbingly hostile to their female counterparts, called "brazen") and it was perhaps true it had made them rather professional Sapphists.

Maybe this. Maybe that. All I know is, whenever Ken and I dropped even a hint, they would immediately invite us down to the stout wooden house they had sawn, nailed and erected with their own rough-skinned hands. There we would find prodigious quantities of plain food at the kitchen table—to be washed down with their homemade wine—all to the vigorous tune of lots of loud, authoritative talk.

Not that we always agreed with them. (Though the keener disagreements were usually saved until we were on our way home, or at least safely out of earshot!) But it was still a relaxation for over-scrupulous us, with our ingrained tendency to dance and dither around a problem or decision, to hear trenchant opinions untrammeled by the trappings of our bourgeois caution.

In fact, Janet and Doria were at least as middle class as we were, and, from family inheritances, distinctly richer. Janet's parents were Oklahoma oil people who had gravitated to Kaula, Hawaii, where they lived like hermits, refusing to return to the mainland even to visit their only child. Plump Doria's father was a highly successful Wall Street broker who had probably never seen a California ranch house, let alone the intricate and expensive tools his daughter and her lover had purchased in order to build one. But if our dykes were ostracized by their parents, that was not to suggest they lived a lonely life or experienced pangs of isolation. They were in fact highly popular with both gay men and lesbians, and when Ken and I descended upon them it was rarely to have them exclusively to ourselves.

Sometimes this was a frustration. The nuances of female cohabitation were subtly different from ours; the relationships between women partners (the stronger need for hierarchy perhaps?), and a kind of "masculine" strength that our own kind rarely exhibited, all meshed into a compound that I found both refreshing and challenging, and I wanted to know more.

I have never wanted to be a straight man. I have often wondered what it must be like to be a dyke. I invariably left the ranch outside Santa Cruz with genuine regret that conversation hadn't become more intimate. Then perhaps there were barriers which, in the nature of things, could not be transgressed.

Transcending these somewhat baffling attractions was the indubitable fact that our two women had not only an extensive circle of acquaintances but a remarkably interesting one at that. We had met so many people *chez elles*—of all persuasions—who had become part of our own "extended family," as the subsequent generation would be prone to say.

When Ken proposed visiting them one weekend in July I was at first lukewarm. I was quite busy at the *Tribune* and he was teaching some special summer session at Stanford. I also fancied that most of those we had come to enjoy as fellow-guests at Janet and Doria's place would be off somewhere on vacation. Besides, that time of year could be obscenely hot away from the ocean—and, as I chain-smoked in those days, I did not look forward to Ken, as a native Californian, being absurdly cautious and eternally tut-tutting about matches and warning me about where I jettisoned my cigarette stubs over the dry hillsides among the mesquite and sun-bleached grass.

All that was blown from my mind by the public events that began to unfurl—at least to our ears and experience—on the Tuesday before we were due to take the Greyhound south.

Ken returned home to the Marina looking just as I must've appeared to him after witnessing Caryl Chessman's execution. He almost stumbled in at the front door, his face quite ashen and his clothes disheveled. He ignored me, went straight to the love-seat in the window, slumped down heavily and stared silently out at the bay, where a huge aircraft carrier had just come under the Golden Gate Bridge.

"What the hell's happened?" I asked, convinced that he'd been in some kind of accident and was suffering from shock.

In a way he was in shock. But what had buffeted him so harshly was nothing physical. It was the news he had received that afternoon as he was about to leave his office. A group of men—many of them known to us, indeed three of them friends—had been involved in an elaborate police trap in the men's room of the same Southern Pacific Depot in Palo Alto where Ken arrived and departed each day. Fourteen people had been booked over the space of a single week and the ages of those arrested extended from a Palo Alto high school student of seventeen to a retired Episcopalian priest from Redwood City who was nearly eighty.

Ken's informant was Keith McMasters, a friend of my roommate's from high-school days and currently a budding virologist at the Stanford Medical Center. It was he who had burst into Ken's office as he was packing to leave and, between gulps and sobs, and shaking with fear, told how he had been arrested the previous evening, insisting that when it all came out at trial his career would be in ruins.

Keith had been incapable of attending the hospital that morning and, after a night of wide-awake nightmares fueled by dread, he had paced his apartment, wondering what to do. In the course of his anxiety he had twice been phoned by others who had been similar victims of the extended police surveillance and subsequent bookings. One call was from Jimmy Fields, who worked for the advertising department of the local Palo Alto newspaper and had been found in one of the toilets with a black sailor from Moffatt Field. The other was from a Maurice Stern, who had been an undergraduate with Ken and was now working as a junior partner with a prestigious San Francisco law firm. He had been caught red-handed with the high-school twelfth-grader and had been told he was to be charged not only for gross indecency but for contributing to the delinquency of a minor, and possibly for sodomy. He could conceivably be imprisoned for ten years or more.

But Maurice Stern's news contained even worse tidings than his own possible fate. He told also of Gordon Passmore, a recently appointed Special Collections librarian at Stanford with whom Ken often lunched on campus. He had gone home after being charged and had blown his brains out.

"There's more," Ken croaked rather than spoke. "It doesn't end there. Some other poor bastard has a high security job with the Stanford Research Institute, working on top-level government contracts—imagine what'll happen to him!"

I rushed over and clasped him. "I don't want to," I said, my voice muffled in his shoulder. "I can't take any more."

That evening, as we went lifelessly about our business, Janet phoned again. To remind us that the dog show at Pebble Beach was coming up and that, as she was interested in acquiring a bull mastiff bitch as a guard dog, they would gladly drive us over to Carmel if we were interested.

Ken didn't even answer her query—just told her what had happened and how it looked as if the police were determined to make an example of the local gays. (There was some town-and-gown tension between Stanford and Palo Alto, with the latter often seeking redress on university students who were purportedly getting too uppity.) She at once reinforced the invitation for us to go down for that weekend; almost ordered us to do so. With the proviso that we first check if there was anything we could do for those arrested which would necessitate our staying in town. We gratefully accepted.

Three anxiety-racked days later, when Doria turned in off the snaking road and began the even steeper ascent of the dirt track that wound up the hill to the ranch perched on its peak, she suddenly spoke. "I think you'll know the other guests. And guess why they're here."

The bumps and lurches as we churned up thick clouds of dust and traversed deep gullies and clefts in the dry earth must've absorbed her attention, for she made no effort to elaborate. Ken and I exchanged glances as we were squeezed by the spread of her ample buttocks on the bench-seat of the pickup, but said nothing. The quiet between the three of us came easily. It had prevailed ever since she had collected us at the Greyhound depot and, as she was usually far from taciturn, I surmised it was the news we had conveyed on the phone that accounted for her grim expression.

We eased stiff joints out of the dusty truck, and walked down to the rocky dip between the toolshed and the galvanized steel watertank—amid the kind of agricultural debris and domestic litter which is endemic to the California rural landscape. Looking up at the ranch house, I saw good reason for our driver's demeanor. And an explanation of her cryptic comment. Keith McMasters, a slight figure in jeans and white shirt, stood on the back porch. He had obviously already seen us and was about to dart inside. But when we waved he faltered and waved back. By the time we had reached him he was smiling sheepishly, nervously brushing his thinning blond hair back off his forehead and talking a mile a minute.

"Gee, it's good to see you two. The gals said you were coming when they called. In fact that's *why* they called. It was good of you, Ken. I think I'd have gone mad cooped up in the apartment all by myself—not knowing who was going to phone next and tell me they'd been caught, too."

"I made an asshole of myself," panted Doria, rolling up from the truck. "I started talking to Ken about the dog show. Jesus!—with all that goddamn police ensnarement going on—and me talking about fucking bull mastiffs! Why didn't you interrupt me earlier, big boy?"

"Ken wasn't feeling at all like doing much interrupting that night," I put in, more defensively than the occasion warranted. Keith's nervousness was contagious.

"You don't often get so much bad news about your friends at one and the same time," Ken added.

Keith bit his lip. He was very pale, especially in the brilliant afternoon sunlight flooding the western porch. I noticed his slim shoulders were hunched and he seemed incapable of standing still. "Jesus-Mary, you can say *that* again! It's bad enough to know—bingo—you're finished professionally. But then to hear that a friend's shoved a revolver up the roof of his mouth...."

Doria shoved past us. "Let's go inside," she snapped. "No good yakking about things out here."

Inside Janet took over. Towering over all but Ken, she shepherded us into the kitchen, with its enormous plate-glass window overlooking the eucalyptus grove bordering their twenty-acre spread; sat us down at the familiar trestle table.

In spite of their alfresco lifestyle, our hosts favored a mid-afternoon "tea time" in the British fashion—at least at weekends, when guests were most likely to be present. Janet had already put out ceramic crocks containing butter and jam. While we chose chairs she added scones straight from the oven and placed three piled plates of them before us. There were also English digestive biscuits and a stolid-looking fruitcake which, Doria proudly informed us from her end of the table, constituted the first one she had ever baked.

There was tea (which only Doria and I drank) and coffee. After over half an hour had elapsed I noticed that the bulk of the food was still untouched, and that what had been eaten was only by the women themselves.

So much for the appetites of distraught queens.... By contrast, our jaws worked hard and endlessly at discussion. This was especially the case after the arrival of yet another of those arrested. Maurice Stern, the young lawyer, drove up in his MG sportscar shortly after the five of us had sat down. After detailed accounts from both Keith and Maurice of their harrowing experiences with police *agents provocateurs*, and sad allusions to poor Gordon's suicide, the talk turned to the future of those now awaiting trial and what kind of sentencing might be the outcome.

We had drifted imperceptibly from tea and coffee to the coarse red wine that Doria bottled. We drank this homemade concoction from thick ceramic mugs fired in Janet's busy kiln. By now Maurice had the floor as the one most qualified to hazard the outcome of the eventual court proceedings, even though he was professionally involved with corporate law. He put us in an even darker mood than we had conveyed at the outset by suggesting the trials could quite easily be postponed until as late as early fall—citing crowded schedules, court backlogs and the like.

"There is that old priest from Redwood City. And another guy—some of you may know him? He's a teller at the Bank of California in Menlo Park—who I gather has a heart condition and is already in hospital. I tell you, it may not be only Gordon who goes before this is all over."

"It's the waiting," Keith said tightly. "The trying to carry on at the hospital as if nothing's happened. Forever wondering if any of them knows what happened to you, if anybody has already read something in the papers."

"Oh God, I'd spend every dollar I've got if it could prevent my name being mentioned," added Maurice. "Without that I'm lost. There'd be nothing—absolutely *nothing*."

It was obvious Janet considered this thinking excessively negative. "It's far too early to give up," she said crisply. "Let's not play dead until we have to."

Her lover patently was of like mind. "Christ! There hasn't even been a remand to stand trial yet. We don't even know if bail is to be set. All we know are the original bookings when they loaded you in the paddy wagon and took you to the precinct."

"I hadn't even thought of the bail business," Ken said. "That could be pretty tough for some, couldn't it? I mean, that seventeen-year-old kid—we don't know his parents' financial situation. Not even if they'll support him."

"If it's any of *our* crowd," Janet announced, standing up and crossing to fetch another bottle of wine, "then of course we'll help out. That goes without saying. Right, Doria?"

Doria nodded. "If someone's broke, it's a gift. If not, then an interest-free loan until the whole thing is way behind us." She looked enquiringly from one to the other. "You understand what we're saying, guys? I know what it's like when you're just starting out as a lawyer or doctor. None of you is exactly flush."

"That's terribly sweet of you," Keith said, blushing, I thought. "But I can't even think about the money angle yet. It's not just the probability of my career going up in smoke—there's the little matter of my parents, too. My Dad will probably have a heart attack like that bank teller. Come to think of it, they're about the same age! As for my Mom. She...she...." He broke off, tears welling. Then he seemed to pull himself together, the old, cool and collected Keith resurfacing. "I'm sorry," he said quietly, in a firmer voice. "I'm just not myself."

There was an embarrassed silence around the table before it was quickly broken by Maurice.

"My parents haven't a clue, either," he said. "The proud Sterns just don't go in for being queer. As for cruising a public john—well, I'm sure they'd be happier with a son who forged wills or was a rapist!" His bitterness made me wince.

"*Lawyers!*" said Janet. (I was going to say "thundered" for it was indeed in her loudest voice.) "We have to arrange lawyers for you. And then you'll need witnesses. Character witnesses. That's something *we* can get to work on."

"I can just see it," said Maurice. "'Maurice Stern? Oh yes, I've always regarded him as one of the promising younger men in the firm. Of course, none of us was aware that he liked cock—and favored sucking those of strangers in public places.'"

"You are not being helpful," Doria said reprovingly. "I can smell self-pity in this room and that's no good to anyone! Now just listen to Janet and her suggestions. We have given this a *lot* of thought. It's not something we dreamed up just before you guys arrived."

I could not rid myself of the notion that, somehow, tall Janet with her boyish fringe, her press-stud checkered shirt, stained jeans and cowboy boots, was rather enjoying this mapping of strategy. She even had a notepad and pencil laid out on the table. It wasn't exactly maps and calipers and a general's paraphernalia for planning a battle, but I suspected it was for her the next-best thing.

The trouble for a carping me was that they *had* done their homework. They *did* have the names and addresses of lawyers written down and they *did* have a series of questions and proposed actions which made me immediately aware of what cool reasoning and sound common sense lay behind them.

Janet commenced to adumbrate their general approach. It fell into two major lines of attack. The first was behind-the-scenes activity when as much pressure as possible would be applied to settle out of court and to restrain the press from providing names—even if we proved unable to prevent accounts of the police action and the subsequent arrest of fourteen men.

If all failed and the accused came to trial, Janet suggested the best defense lawyers available be employed to defend such as Maurice and Keith—and our absent friend, Jimmy Fields. It was also her conviction that once there was no longer a chance of anonymity being preserved, every stop in the repertory of power should be pulled to get the indictments thrown out of court. She spoke of politicians known to her: of a congressman, of a gay county supervisor whom she and Doria wouldn't hesitate to blackmail! And last but not least, the wife of the governor, whose own close friend was both a lesbian and a mutual friend of theirs, and a regular visitor to the ranch.

At which point Janet sat down again. She had been standing, her back to the view, and facing us at the table. If the window had been a blackboard, then she might well have been briefing her crew at operations center....

Her speech had emptied us. We were all silent. "Well," she said eventually. "It's you men who have to make some hard decisions—especially if we have to fall back on plan two. What do you have to say?"

"What Janet means," Doria elaborated, "is, are you prepared to really go public—knowing it will destroy your careers—even if it does keep you out of jail?"

Janet seemed oddly hostile to assistance at this stage. "They understand, darling. They aren't idiots."

That could have been interpreted as if she were defending Keith and Maurice from the insinuation that they were being obtuse. But I thought otherwise. The brusqueness of voice and the frost to her eyes spelled, "Doria—bug out!" There was, I felt, a controlled tension between the two that was rarely observable. Then the four of us men, with our sense of fatalism as we contemplated the uncertain future, were not generating the kind of mood that Janet and Doria found at all conducive to solving dilemmas or even seeking solutions.

Doria, though, was not to be put down quite so peremptorily. She eased her large bottom on the hard kitchen chair and drew on her cigarette with a force that turned its tip to a fierce glow.

"What do *you* think, Ken? If these guys feel too depressed to react properly—and who can blame them?—what do you think they should do? After all, you and Davey sort of stand halfway between Keith and Maurice on the one hand, and the two of us. You're always good at planning campaigns."

I quickly recalled my lover's prowess in such realms, but did not expect a major contribution from him at that juncture. Indeed, I rather hoped none would materialize. The girls were quintessentially planners and campaigners. For them it was meat and drink.

Ken's thoughts, as so eerily often, were totally in tune with mine. He sought to stave off potential conflagration between our hosts rather than to come up with an alternative blueprint to what we were subsequently to dub *the Depot Affair*. "I think the two of you have done a remarkable job in covering the alternatives, and we should follow the behind-the-scenes tactic and then turn to the defense ploy if that doesn't work."

"The only thing," I added slowly, "is that we should leave at least a couple of eggs out of the first basket, just in case we have an initial failure. Big-shot lawyers and high-profile character witnesses tend to have busy schedules. We can't start sounding them out too soon."

Janet sniffed. I knew it was at the word "failure," which they were so reluctant to include in their vocabulary. "You obviously didn't hear me the first time around. I think you can leave that in *our* hands, Davey. We may be lazing away in the boonies with our cattle and goats but we haven't entirely forgotten how city folk hoard their time."

I would have sworn she bestowed her sarcasm with a semi-Southern accent derived from her Oklahoma upbringing.

In any case, I bridled immediately. "Well, at least that's reassuring," I said. "I know just what it is for the average Joe who doesn't have to use an agenda every day."

Ken scented my antagonism and moved in swiftly.

"I think we're all talked out—and probably *thought* out, for the moment. Let's say we give it a rest, huh, folks? Shall we make a real effort to put it aside—at least until tomorrow, after a night's sleep?"

Keith gave him a grateful look before drinking deep of his mug of wine.

Maurice got to his feet and joined Janet. "I'd love to see the livestock. I don't think I've ever seen a goat!"

She put an arm protectively around his shoulder and looked over hers at Doria, who was helping herself to a final slice of the fruitcake she had baked.

"Then you are in the same position as Doria when we started up here. But it wasn't only goats that were new to her. I don't believe she had ever seen hay, either!"

On that uncertain note we two remaining men scraped back our chairs and got to our feet to join Maurice, Janet and Keith in the early evening air, as a glorious sunset ruddied the scattered clouds and gilded the Pacific sky. Doria, though, insisted on staying indoors—explaining loudly, without looking up at our retreating backs, that *someone* had to prepare the table for supper and put away the uneaten buns and biscuits.

* * * * * *

In the event, the trial, which was subject to two lengthy delays, proved less draconian than we had feared. There were no more suicides and the heart-attack victim recovered. The octogenarian priest was found unfit for trial and two teachers lost their jobs on being given suspended sentences. We were told that another man began to drink heavily on being found guilty (but put on probation) but this information never really rose above the status of rumor.

Our friend Keith, mercifully recovering something of that personal detachment which had hitherto characterized him, found it expedient to leave his hospital post after an unpleasant talk with the dean. He was young enough, he decided, to return to medical school and acquire a different specialization. He told us he chose tropical medicine purely as a means of working outside the country. The following spring he would take a position with the World Health Organization—ending up in Madagascar, where he was to research a local species of mosquito and the particularly virulent form of malaria which it carried.

Maurice, who was also put on probation and fined, but kept on (he felt reluctantly) by his senior partners, eventually moved south, practising civil law on his own with a largely Spanish-speaking clientele in East Los Angeles. At first there was a flurry of letters and postcards but he gradually lost touch with us. Janet and Doria maintained contact, however, visiting him and his subsequent Mexican lover, when they went south each January to visit two women friends with a desert place outside Palm Springs. On returning, they always reported having had a congenial time and pleasant dinner with Maurice and José in their little stucco home in the *barrio*.

Finally, Jimmy Fields, on being conditionally discharged, was rudely fired from his newspaper the day the news of the raid on the depot was carried in its pages. He subsequently left Palo Alto for Fresno, where in a matter of weeks he had married the daughter of a wealthy Armenian farmer. He returned with Mary to the city and a job with a local TV station. In a surprisingly short time the Fields had acquired a little daughter and, concomitantly, it seemed, Jimmy had gone from being almost a teetotaler to developing a drinking problem. Though whether his alcoholism was directly connected to the S.P. Depot scandal we shall never know.

CHAPTER TWENTY-ONE

Marseilles: May 11th, 1960

The French spell it without a final "s" just as they do "Lyons." I am all for *vive la différence* in these matters except with such things as we witnessed last night. Neither Charlotte nor I brought it up at the time. We were both too embarrassed. But if I do not enter such experiences in this journal then I fear they will get no mention at all! Even so, this is not the easiest entry to make by any means!

We found Charlotte's restaurant all right—though it proved to be situated in a rather odd part of the town and not one where I thought the Churchfields would have taken their young daughters all those years ago. It seemed more like a native quarter by the number of men with turbans and fezzes on their heads. But Charlotte says that the place has naturally changed over thirty years and that Marseilles has become very cosmopolitan since the end of the war and with all the immigration from those impoverished French colonies across in North Africa.

I must say the *bouillabaisse* seemed very authentic and was delicious. The dessert—some dry pastry thing smothered in honey and nuts—was unmemorable, but my companion reminded me that one does not go to France for stewed apples and custard!

Afterwards we decided to take a stroll as it was a little early to return to the *Ijmuiden* and retire for the night. Besides, it was a delightfully warm evening with a strange but entrancing scent of spices on the air. There was nothing of that incessant breeze we had known while at sea and I think we both wished we had left our evening shawls behind.

There were a few Arabs sauntering aimlessly but they ignored us entirely. I did not for a moment have apprehension for two English ladies walking those narrow alleys under connecting arches which only found their proper purpose in daylight and the presence of the sun.

Less than a hundred yards from the broad square in which we had dined, we came across a smaller one with a corner café where they were still serving outside. It was a bustling place and I suppose we chose it because it stood in contrast to the lonely streets and their poor lighting. However, other than the suggestion that it was a popular establishment (at least for the late-night crowd), it seemed indistinguishable from the scores of others we had passed since leaving our ship at its berth in the old port.

We chose a table where we could eye the scene without ourselves being a cynosure for others. How fortunate we did! I must say that Charlotte has an extraordinary ability to see and recognize both people and things from afar. When we are driving about Plymouth, for example, having gone there to shop, and are in need of petrol, she will see a Shell station from miles away. And I am supposed to be on the lookout while she is doing the driving!

But I stray from last night. We had just ordered coffee in tiny cups and decided against anything stronger with it (we had consumed a whole flask of *vin rosé* with our meal) when she nudged me.

"Isn't that Paul?" she asked.

I had no idea, of course, to whom she was referring, and crossly told her so. Once in Harrods, some three years ago, she asked me if someone wasn't "Alec." On asking Alec *who*, she merely smiled and said, "Alec Guinness, of course!" I told her that, living in Cornwall, I was hardly in a position to recognize those in the world of entertainment. I added that Guinness was an actor who looked different to me in every film he made. It was at that juncture that we overheard the saleswoman complimenting him about some picture he'd been in—*The Bridge on the River Kwai*, I think—and Charlotte was insufferable for the rest of that day.

This time, though, even as I answered her, I saw who it was she had spotted—and recognized him also. It was young Paul Leiden, our steward. He was not alone. He was with someone who obviously didn't belong to the ship. I placed him in the same age bracket as Paul, though it is sometimes hard to tell with those of other races—which this one indubitably was, with his dark skin and hooked nose. They sat at a table at the opposite end of the café but far enough forward toward the curb for us to see them clearly. It was apparent they were acquainted. Very well indeed, I should say. They were not only laughing and joking but acting in such a way as was sure to attract attention.

Or so I first thought. Whenever a newcomer appeared across the small square we faced, they would burst into giggles, tug each other's sleeves excitedly and make what I can only call ribald comments. For I could hear surprisingly well against the low hum of the other patrons and they were speaking loudly in English. But no one else took the slightest notice. It was then Charlotte pointed out that we seemed to be the only women on the crowded terrace.

What she *didn't* point out—but only a fool would not have noticed—was that these men, most of them in couples but others in groups of three or four at a table, afforded no impression of awaiting their *wives*. The ugly truth was that they did not look as if they had wives. They were all creatures of *a certain kind* and as they smoked and murmured, smiled soppily at each other, they evinced no shame for it.

Even as I was absorbing this unpalatable fact, I grew uncomfortably aware that Paul and his friend were holding hands. Nor was that the end of it. I almost fell off my rickety chair when the Arab, or whatever he was, leaned over and kissed the steward of the S.S. *Ijmuiden*!

Naturally, as soon as we could catch our waiter's eye, we quickly paid and vacated the place—taking the street farthest from Paul and his *companion* so that we could escape undetected.

We soon hailed a taxi, and on returning on board ran full tilt into dear Captain Schaepmann, who prevailed upon us to take a nightcap with him. Normally I think we would have both refused but it was a heaven-sent opportunity of washing the taste of that place from our minds and removing the necessity for us to discuss it. This did not mean I wasn't determined to bring the matter up with Paul—though I decided to do it when Charlotte was absent from our cabin and so would not suffer any embarrassment.

Strange, that. I had no qualms about alluding to his behavior with Paul but with my dear friend I would have found it difficult if not impossible. Then he is young enough to be my son—and my boys have been an education for me in themselves. That is something I feel a spinster like Charlotte could never understand. It is not a role I have always relished, but being a mother has its consolations when it comes to learning about and understanding this wicked old world!

I chose the time after breakfast when Charlotte likes to take her constitutional—if we are in port she strolls around the quay rather than around the deck of the *Ijmuiden*. It is also the occasion when young Paul comes down to tidy up and ask if we have any special wishes for that particular day.

Before I go further I should explain that Paul and I had already had some chats. I knew, for example, that his father had died when he was quite small and that his mother had married again—to a customs clerk in Rotterdam whom the boy heartily disliked. I had also learned that Paul adored his paternal grandfather, who had also been a mariner and had thus implanted the notion that the sea was for his grandson, too. He had spoken as well of a sibling, a much older sister.

But as he entered our cabin this morning I was strongly aware that in all our little talks since leaving Holland, although he had succeeded in drawing me out on the subject of my three sons, getting me to show their photos, he had discreetly avoided mention of his own private life. I was determined, in the light of last night's unsavory incident, to balance matters.

I started by asking whether he had family in Marseilles. He looked as nonplussed as I expected. When he denied it he added that he had no relatives outside the Netherlands. Then he asked me the inevitable: Why do you ask?

(I must try and get this as verbatim as memory allows, although I shall not make excessive attempts to reproduce his charming Dutch accent.)

"Because I thought I saw you with your brother last night."

"Where, Mrs. Bryant?"

"I do not know the name of the establishment but it is not far from a restaurant called La Pieuvre where Miss Churchfields and I dined. That is on the Place de l'Armée, I believe."

There was a distinct pause before he next spoke. "You mean Le Lutin? That is just for—for—"

"Men?" I supplied.

He gave a ghost of a smile. "Outside. Inside it is mainly women. *Couples*, you understand?"

I stared at him. "*We* sat outside," I told him.

His shrug would have done any Frenchman proud. "You are visitors. English. You would not be expected to understand."

I was not for one moment going to let him get away with that! "I think we understood only too well, young man. You and your *friend*"—I stressed *that* for all it was worth—"were doing your best to tell the world what kind of place we had come upon. Your hands were entwined, I believe? And at one point he leaned over...."

He at least had the grace now to look decidedly fidgety but I, too, was running out of steam.

"He certainly didn't act as I would have expected a brother to act. Not, in fact, as I would expect any *man* to act, if I may be brutally frank. The point I am making, Paul, is that you did no credit in that—that *backstreet* café to Captain Schaepmann, your shipmates, or, indeed, any of us currently associated with the S.S. *Ijmuiden*! That is all I have to say, and even that, I can assure you, is most painful to utter."

I don't know what I really expected in response. I certainly was not prepared for his falling before my chair and burying his curly head in my lap. Of course, I could not be cross with him from that moment on. It was a child I held, and I must note in these pages a great warmth welling in me as I rocked him in his grief.

I also bought a dress from a boutique run by an Algerian merchant in Marseilles but that is too prosaic for elaboration here—especially after that tormented boy poured out his soul over his confusion and loneliness.

CHAPTER TWENTY-TWO

I went to a priest for counseling because I didn't like psychiatrists—not since one in London had suggested electric shock treatment to rid me of my "sexual inversion" when I was still a guilt-ridden student. The room in which I sat nervously awaiting Father Knowles held only a wooden table and two kitchen chairs. These cheap pieces of furniture, mottled in their flaking white paint, conveyed an institutional flavor—but it was the sparse green walls that disturbingly evoked San Quentin. The reminder increased my already growing tension, which I strove to alleviate by recalling the fact that dithery Delilah regularly sought this man's advice and praised him to the skies for the effectiveness of it.

Some days earlier I had stopped off at the Paper Doll after working late at the *Tribune* and run into our willowy friend. "She" was still brimming with elation over her recent session with Father Knowles, who had quickly quelled her agitation and provided advice as to how she should handle her latest emotional crisis. Delilah was once more suffering a characteristically febrile love affair. This time with an eighteen-year-old Oriental whose alternately mercenary and coy antics were abetted by parents who were decidedly cool to having a thirty-year-old Caucasian invading the privacy of their Chinese home—let alone as courtier of their teenage son!

I had little time to dwell on racial or sexual prejudices: instead licked lips nervously as I heard footsteps on the slate flagstones of the cloister beyond the door. I told myself fiercely I must remember to refer to Delilah by his real name of Richard and skip the camp pronouns, before concentrating on the purpose of my own visit, which certainly had nothing to do with a sulky Chinese boy and his protective Mom and Pop. There was just time to establish how I would voice my worries over an increasing friction between Ken and me, before a biretta-headed figure entered in a swirl of cassock, hands outstretched, and a flurry of apologies on his lips for the few minutes' delay. This was no formal confession, of course, as I was there for advice, not sacramental absolution—so there was no "*Bless me, Father, for I have sinned, etc.*" but rather a prompt question from Father Knowles as to the reason for my presence there.

I responded without difficulty. I had, after all, been a regular attender of the confessional since childhood, and, even before my enforced and public coming out in the Navy, had confessed to desiring sex with other men as readily as I would refer to lying or losing my temper. This easy unburdening was the result of confessing masturbatory images to our young school chaplain, who arrived in my final year, and whom I much admired for his modernistic approach to life. He had told me through the grille that, while being homosexual was a perfectly honorable state for the likes of both of us, the Catholic Church was necessarily conservative and thus a trifle slow to adapt to God's revelation of certain truths through twentieth-century psychology.

Better then, Father Monk had advised, to err on the side of scrupulosity in confession than to take upon oneself a censoring role as to what should be mentioned and what omitted. That was spiritual counsel which I had ardently and permanently taken to heart! In fact, it enabled me to continue as a penitent after I started to attend church with Ken—first in Paris and then in San Francisco. (Though up to the mid-1960s and the Vatican Council, which re-examined the whole practice of sacramental confession, I entertained a substantial list of reservations about what was properly sinful and what was not, and sought only formal absolution and penance—skipping the corollary of priestly advice.)

It was soon apparent that Father Knowles owned to a wholly different brand of moral theology from that embraced by my contemporary-minded school chaplain of some twenty years earlier. In response to his asking why I was seeking his advice, I told him candidly that I was worried over my increasing quarrels with Ken (largely inspired by me), which were taking on a progressively ugly hue. I was careful to point out that they had not degenerated into the physical but I truly feared they could become violent. It was that notion which horrified me. I also said how I loved Ken desperately and that I would do anything to keep our relationship intact. I told the priest how ashamed I was of the promiscuity which led to such risky venues as the park on Filmore with its specific clientele of blacks, or the busy toilets of the public library along Chestnut near the Marina.

When he finally stemmed my flow it was with a brisk interjection that almost congealed my blood. "Forget all that for the moment. What I want to know is whether you have ever had a physical relationship with this other young man."

I was totally bewildered. "Of course! I thought I made it clear. We are lovers."

"That you love him, and he you, I understand. That is not my question. The Church has no problem with that."

My fuse is so lamentably short! It was briefer than ever that afternoon. "I came here for help with *my* problems—not the Church's."

Skilled at least in pastoral lore, the silver-haired cleric did not respond angrily in kind but persisted in soft, even tones of a kind with which years of churchgoing had made me all too familiar. Even so, I could detect an underlying steeliness.

"There is no love greater than Holy Mother Church bears the *sinner* for it is, of course, the Love of Our Blessed Lord Himself. But such is certainly not accorded the *sin*. You have come to the right place as a troubled soul trapped in the homosexual condition—but not, young man, for the whitewashing of perverted acts. As a priest of God, that would be more than I dare do."

I could hardly believe my ears. And Delilah had come away comforted by this asshole? I launched into attack.

"My pagan friend who recommended I come to you has been itching to climb into the pants of his teenage boyfriend over the objection of the kid's parents. And what did you advise? You told *her* to be firm with her bum-twitching, gold digger of a lover, and be patient with the parents because they're another generation!

"Now you tell me to be frigid with my lover of twelve years! What is this, Father? One law for the faithful and another for the secularists?"

The priest sighed—long and irritatingly. "As a good Catholic I would have expected you at least to respect the law of the confessional, both for your friend *and* for yourself. You know I can't possibly discuss another's confession with you. Nor am I prepared to argue over what constitutes evil. You must also know very well that what you do with your sexual partner is a mortal sin and will lead to eternal damnation."

"All I know is, I love Ken, and he me—and nothing you say can change that in the slightest. I'm talking about *love*, Father. That's what has brought me here. I came for your advice because I wish to keep my love as strong as it has been since the day Ken and I first met."

"I would be the last person in the world to besmirch true love. It is you who do that when you speak in the same breath of your mutual lust—leading to all those carnal perversions. God has given you a remarkable relationship—but he has also given you specific laws to abide by. You may not like these words, my son. You may think them cruel. But I must obey St. Paul and '*speak the truth in love.*' As a priest I am offered no alternative."

"That's the point," I persisted. "You are a priest, and presumably a celibate one. So God has called you to the sexually inactive state. But He didn't give me a vocation to be gay—any more than He calls people to be male or female. A vocation can't be automatic—or it wouldn't be one!

"Know what I think? Because you're obviously a gay priest, you're jealous of the likes of Ken and me and our freedom to share our bodies."

The words were no sooner blurted than I knew I'd gone too far. He didn't answer immediately, though. Not until he had gotten to his feet and, with hands loosely clasped, his back to me, stood facing the bare wall.

"You had better leave," he said quietly. "Come back when you're feeling less rebellious toward the teachings of Our Lord and His Church."

Years of dutiful obedience since I was a tender little altar boy struggled for possession of me in that oppressive room. But the image of Ken won out.

"I'm sorry for being rude, Father," I managed. "And I respect what you're saying. But when it comes to love—because of Ken—I'm the expert, not you. Don't think I'm unaware of how arrogant that sounds, but I sincerely believe God gave me him to *learn* love. I knew it within seconds of seeing him for the first time, standing there in the Lady chapel of St. George's, Paris, as the choir sang the 'Benedictus.' Nothing in the past twelve years has altered my conviction that Ken—the total sexual, emotional and spiritual aspects of him—was my truly appointed vocation. I know I have acted against that and—when my temper has gotten the better of me—even blasphemed against it. But nothing can persuade me our union isn't a gift of God. In fact it's the most precious thing that's ever happened to me."

I was almost in tears but fought them back. With draining relief I watched his black back as he shrugged off what I'd just said—and then, mutely, left the room. I gave him a minute or so before I followed. I didn't want to bump into him before I quit the church property and fled home. When I got there Ken was scrubbing the kitchen floor and the scent of ammonia pervaded the apartment.

"I don't know how you can stand that smell. It must be terrible for your lungs."

Ken shrugged from the linoleum—as broadly as Father Knowles had thirty minutes earlier. "*Someone* has got to do it, sweetheart. If both of us were allergic to fresh paint, used kitty litter boxes *and* this disinfectant, the place would not only be a mess but we'd have the Health Department in!"

In the light of what I had been through, I was not about to argue. To the contrary, I never felt more keenly the need to be at one with him.

"I'll do that if you like."

He dropped the floor cloth. "You feeling all right?"

"I'm just *offering* for a change. It isn't good for you to do all the nasty stuff. You make me lazier than I ought to be."

Ken smiled ruefully. "One of our friends been bitching? Why do people always want to protect me against your exploiting me? They never stop to think what a spineless jerk it makes me look."

"You know I think you're the opposite of spineless, Ken. Even so, that's exactly what I'm talking about. I've just had a lousy experience with an idiot of a priest. And you're right as usual. It *did* begin with one of our friends who is always trying to 'help' our relationship—one who can't manage to sustain a relationship himself!"

"Meaning dear Delilah, I suppose."

"How did you guess! I can't blame Delilah, though, for what that reactionary old fart was trying to put over me this afternoon."

He searched my face closely. "What the devil were you doing talking to a priest on a Wednesday afternoon? It isn't even Lent yet. Besides, today's your busy one on the *Tribune*."

"I was feeling depressed and just snuck off. I know it's stupid but I went to the Church of the Advent—to the man Delilah sees when she fucks up one of her love affairs. What I wasn't expecting was a dose of medieval theology about sex. Especially from a man who calmly sees Delilah at least once a month, screaming and carrying on about one of her underage tricks!"

"My!" Ken exclaimed. "He sure did get under your skin!"

"He made me feel dirty—or tried to. He tried to put dirt on us—on our relationship. Only I wasn't having any."

"Bully for you then, darling. So we've lost a priest I've never met. Then there are plenty more where he came from."

Although I tried to make his words comfort and restore me, they did not do so. The old priest had prodded and probed around areas I had skated over and prevaricated about for a long time. The exposure was now a very sore affair.

"The point is that if Father Knowles was right, then I'm dead wrong. Which means I am no longer in any sense a Christian. Which also means, why do I bother to go to Mass on Sundays any more?"

"I thought you'd already worked that particular one out. We just have to be existential about everything until the moral dust about being gay finally settles and proper patterns emerge."

"Listening to *that* creep, I'd say Catholics need another two centuries!"

"All the more reason for our holding in there, then. What do we have to lose by being patient until the Church once more yields to its Galileos and concedes the earth isn't flat, and circles the sun? After all, Holy Mother has finally admitted that witches and heretics are not for burning, that indulgences can't be bought and sold, and that heaven and hell are less well mapped than previously supposed."

"We can lose our immortal souls—according to that shit. He was making no concessions over that!"

"So who's infallible? Vatican Two has put a colossal dent in all that line of thinking. In any case, Davey, who are you kidding? You never did subscribe to *everything* uttered by the *Teaching Church*, as you used to call it. There was one rule for the peasant faithful, you used to argue, and quite another for the educated."

I was disconcerted. "Did I really say that?" I asked. "What snobbery!"

"You were an *awful* little snob in those Paris days. I don't know how I put up with you! You've no idea how boring it was for me as a Californian to listen to all that nonsense about schools, the job one's *Daddy* had and whether it was all right to say *lavatory* or *bathroom*."

"Now you're mixing me up with those others. That ghastly Desmond Skeffington, who smelled, and that Cheltenham Ladies College cunt, Imogene Hewlett-Whyte, who was always correcting you."

"In some ways you were worse, my pet. You not only offered the *hundreds-of-ancient-Cornish-acres* bit in response to their schools and *Daddy's-in-the-Life-Guards* routine, but you insisted, too, on all that endless churchy talk about dear Father Scrotum at St. Buggery's, Leeds, or Rosary & Benediction with the holy Sisters of the Blessed Urine at St. Sodomy-in-the-Wold. God, you and your fellow Anglo-Catholics could go on! You were worse than baseball fans. Give me: 'I knew Eddie Collins when he was still with the Phillies—before he became vice-president of the Boston Red Sox' any day, over 'They have a proper tabernacle at St. Pubic's, Paddington, while Father Foreskin has to put up with a hanging Pyx at All Testicles, Holland Park Road.'"

I was torn between laughing at Ken's inventiveness and being aghast at how much he had suppressed for so many years. The giggles won out.

CHAPTER TWENTY-THREE

Genoa: May 17th, 1960

I was hardly expecting to stop so soon after Marseilles at Genoa but I am rather glad we did. For one thing it enabled us to have a brief look at the Riviera di Levante (after having seen the Riviera di Ponente only from the sea) but far more important, it provided the opportunity to take fragile Thelma Wilkinson ashore with us for dinner and give her a rest from her dreadful husband.

The only bonus to that indifferent meal on the smelly quay (I have told Charlotte we *must* learn to penetrate further inland at subsequent ports!) was Thelma's unwitting warning of a danger brewing for young Paul. That repulsive Wilkinson had already informed her that our ship's steward was light-fingered and that he suspected the dear lad of thieving Thelma's gold vanity case—evilly insinuating that it was probably for his own use. Thelma only alluded to all this in the vaguest of terms, as she was obviously in a highly agitated state and no doubt scared of the reprisals should her husband ever suspect her of confiding to others on board.

It is obvious Wilkinson is unused to servants for he has no sense of the *vulnerability* of the likes of young Paul in glibly accusing him of dishonesty. Although in his life as a *pedagogue* he must have had employees, the man is quite ignorant of that *noblesse oblige* by which I set such store. My reason for comforting the boy after his tearful breakdown in the cabin was precisely because I could see how exposed he might be to the likes of Wilkinson, should someone blab as to his antics ashore. Even blackmail was possible! I think I not only reassured Paul as to our total discretion but also convinced him we would not let him down if he ever needed our protection. I like to think those anguished moments in the cabin marked the birth of true friendship.

Needless to say, I am certainly not prepared to let this retired schoolteacher do a job of character assassination—after the boy has swallowed his pride, and perhaps some shame, to inform me of his unfortunate propensity for those of his own gender. It is hardly difficult to visualize what a man who is already prepared to throw wild accusations of larceny would do with *that* information!

As we sat at dusk at Il Ristorante degli Appennini Liguri eating plates of heaped pasta and *vitello parmigiano* (which disconcertingly smelled more like fish than veal), I made it quite clear to Thelma that I knew Paul to be totally honest and that I was prepared to defend him strenuously if need be. I did not accuse her husband of barefaced lying, but after expressing formal condolences for his stomach upset (of which he had been complaining in unseemly detail all day, and which had sparked my decision to invite his wife ashore for a meal), I did suggest it would perhaps be prudent on this voyage—when the ubiquity of fellow-passengers was a consistently onerous problem—that he strive to lower his voice, even if he was incapable of completely bridling his tongue!

Thelma did not take this piece of advice as I had hoped and muttered something about her husband's poor digestion and the richness of Mediterranean food. I looked across the soiled tablecloth at my companion for support. Unfortunately I did not have the degree of Charlotte's attention I would have wished. The reason was clear enough, and I had every intention of recording it earlier in this journal as a separate item. However, I have been preoccupied since leaving Marseilles with darning a small tear in Paul's white jacket, which he ripped while adjusting the shower nozzle in our cramped little bathroom. The entry which fell victim to that deprivation of time relates to the phone call she made to Cornwall from Marseilles to Mrs. Churchfield—when she learned her father's shingles were acting up again.

This is an ailment from which I have not yet suffered and by all reports it is among the most painful. But Mr. Churchfield's debilities at eighty-five include a wobbly heart and recurrent arthritis in his right hip. He bears these burdens stoically but not always with grace. In that, he is a typical man and thus a poor patient. Yet, as I informed a despondent Charlotte one day—in a mood, I'm afraid, of extravagant bleakness—she should be glad he is alive at all. I reminded her that I lost my own Wesley long before he attained the biblical three-score and ten, and that dear Poppa left us in the promise and energy of his middle years. Indeed, I have never ceased to mourn his loss at a time when a father and daughter could have shared life uniquely together—when all the misapprehension between generations has been overcome and the very real things in common between us could have flourished without restraint.

I was never as enthusiastic as Charley about her parents coming to live in our isolated Cornish setting. They all pooh-poohed my fears. Told me to stop talking as if I were still a young bride about to be gobbled up by a moorland world of brute farm life—when the Great War was still a din in our ears, even if the guns had ceased to thud.

Subsequent events have more than vindicated my premonitions. The Cornish climate is far too damp for a man of Mr. Churchfield's infirmities and, quite apart from her fading eyesight, his wife is a townswoman born and bred and will never be capable of the radical adjustments I had to make.

It is odd...all through the war I thought how much we had in common—even though I was only a few years older than her daughter. But it wasn't really the case. True, we shared a London background, a comfortable circumstance in childhood compared to my husband's, and then motherhood, of course. The differences were all subtle and subsequent.

To have plunged into the Celtic world of Cornwall in the 1920s was not merely to exchange the modernity of petroleum-propelled London for a primitive farm where neither gas nor electricity, telephones nor running water was to be had, but to enter another country. Nor was Poppa's modest affluence a positive influence on those proud poor Bryants who, instead of servants, conscripted their even more penurious relations. I now see clearly that if it hadn't been for my darling mother-in-law with her loyalty and belief in me as a wife and mother of her three grandsons, I never could have lasted in that sea of studied insult and animosity from all those *beholden* to me as mistress of Polengarrow farm.

But I stray from my purpose. (And how easy is that to do when the blank page invites every teeming thought in my head!)

Charlotte has indeed had her parents on her mind these past days and I would be the most unfeeling of friends if I did not sympathize with her. All the same, it was "deuced inconvenient" (as Wesley would have said to our boys) sitting there amid all the shouting and yelling of the dockworkers and fishermen—my, the Italians are noisy!—as I observed Thelma growing progressively agitated while I gently suggested some rules of behavior which would be mutually advantageous as we spent more days at sea and the possibility of friction grew ever greater.

She had stooped for the second time to pick up her white kid gloves—useless articles on a warm evening at that most unpretentious of restaurants—and began to play with her cutlery like a fidgety child. I again urgently addressed Charlotte, asking whether she did not agree that Paul was honesty itself and that it would be hideously unfair to suggest otherwise. She did indeed lean over to speak to me—but it was quite obvious the subject of Paul and Wilkinson's reckless allegations was remote indeed from her concerns.

"Do you know, Isabella, I really think that man over there with the bucket of fishheads is *ogling* me," she said.

I could hardly believe my ears. But Charlotte's words were nothing to the wild accusations now spewing from Thelma's bright red mouth as she thrust her lipstick at it while twisting and turning on her rickety chair, for all the world as if she were suffering an attack of worms!

Her voice now was almost a scream. "My husband worships me, I'd have you know. He knows my every need and he is never *ever* wrong. Then what would people like you two women know about things like that. How dare you criticize Frank when you are such outsiders. I tell you, I've had enough of your patronizing. Now can we get out of this filthy place? I shall take Frank's advice after this and steer clear of *marriage busters*, as he rightly calls you."

I made one final effort to enlist the support of my companion. "Thelma is feeling and looking far from well. I think we should get her back on board without delay before she does herself harm."

My voice was as loud as that of the skinny, neurotic creature now dusting far too much powder onto her already pasty face. Miss Churchfield continued to simper in the direction of the Italian toying with his enamel fish bucket. I drew in a lot of breath and snapped my handbag open. For once it was I, and not Charlotte, who called for the bill.

CHAPTER TWENTY-FOUR

The large elevator that whisked me up the score of floors to our editorial offices was symptomatic of our newspaper. It worked smoothly. It was clean and smelled so. And the brass fixtures duly shone. But from the uniformed attendant with his peaked cap and shining shoes to the silent, belly-conscious men in their quiet suits and homburg hats there lurked intimations of a bygone era.

Yesterday's bonds might be faint, near-invisible to the alien eye, but they were impossible to dispel, and those like me, who sometimes sought to do so, were largely ignored in our efforts. Not that the corporate body of the *San Francisco Tribune* was inherently reactionary or a slave to the past. To the contrary, it was jingoistically proud of being a *newspaper* and recognized the journalistic goal of contemporaneity.

And yet.... And yet.... Television was not about to go away—in fact, had now joined the prosperous Bay Area radio stations as a steady gnawing at print media advertising revenue. In half-hearted reaction we seemed to spend an awful lot of editorial time deploring outdoor advertising as a desecration of the California countryside—concealing the fact that a dollar saved from roadside billboards was a dollar most likely to end up in newspaper coffers.

Those of us in the elevator were mainly the editors and sub-editors, the layout men, feature writers, critics and columnists, ad salesmen and clerical staff. We might have been employees of the Bank of America. But at differing times of the day could be seen the rearguard warriors, the "James Cagney" holdouts who traditionally despised the overdressed indoor types; the feisty daily reporters and press photographers, whose open shirts below rakishly tipped fedoras and corduroy jackets replaced the wool suits of those I mingled with on the Sunday Department floor or, admittedly as infrequently as possible, in the staff cafeteria on the thirtieth.

The offices for the writing staff were in reality just cramped cubicles from which, when standing, it was possible to see and talk to one's neighbor on either side. Only the section editors had less public, more spacious arrangements, and even their walls were low enough for them to yell commands over the noisy area beyond—or to hurtle material scrawled with derisive comments back to a hapless author.

My boss at the *Trib* had the twin titles of Sunday Editor and Entertainment Editor, which meant he was responsible for all the inserts, including the Religious Pages, the TV tab, and a color rotogravure supplement covering fashion, travel and gardens. My work lay primarily in the Entertainment Section, where a major job was rewriting the publicity material sent by the Hollywood studios about forthcoming movie releases and stories about their stars. I also conducted interviews with sundry artists (from painters to poets) for the section, did travel articles from time to time for the color magazine and occasionally even wrote book reviews for the daily part of the paper.

Our editor, Donald Cameron, was a tall man in his late thirties, with a laconic manner. He favored expensively cut gray flannel suits and button-down Oxford shirts with blackknit ties, and wore an expensive porkpie hat of dark green felt which he was reluctant at any time to remove from his balding head. He told me when he hired me that at least one reason for doing so was that his own half-Scots ancestry, in conjunction with his wartime service in England as an army captain, had turned him into something of an Anglophile.

Maybe. He still spent an inordinate amount of his time, I thought, proving my British background to be a liability rather than an asset when I was working on a newspaper which he was determined to make the best in the city if not in the western United States. In my never openly stated opinion (at least around him), that was hardly an extravagant goal, considering the competition.... It was from Cameron that on bad days my rejected copy came fluttering over the section wall between us like malevolent snowflakes. His annotations were diverse but unified in theme:

> This overwritten and under-edited stuff may well suit the *London Times*. It is hardly up to snuff here on the *Tribune*.... Rewrite *in toto* please. D.C.

> You may well be from a place which evolved decently written English before we Yanks did but it now appears to have regressed. May we have the *traditional* agreement between noun

and pronoun please and none of this *The cast are* British nonsense. Thank you. D.C.

This happens to be a newspaper and not a creative writing department. Will you therefore check such things as FACTS before you submit material. This piece on the Academy Awards is a case in point. Your fellow-countryman still spells his name *Laurence* (not Lawrence) Olivier in *The Entertainer*. Perhaps you were confusing him with *D.H.* Lawrence when you were carried away with unwonted personal opinions in your references to the contending movie, *Sons & Lovers*. Please ensure both Shirley M. and Fred M. get the "a"s in the Macs of their surnames—to which they are surely entitled? This item needs a total rewrite.

P.S. I have passed on your comments as to the legitimacy of Elizabeth Taylor winning Best Actress for *Butterfield* 8 to the *Trib*'s movie critic. After all, her opinions we pay for and she is accorded a column to state them. Neither you nor the Entertainment section has been asked to do her job for her. *No more* Davey-Bryant-goes-to-the-movies insertions please!

Such tart commentaries were never subsequently referred to. Even on Thursdays, when Don and his mistress, Karen Cohen, who edited the TV tab, went out to eat with perhaps two or three other scribes from the section, the talk was rarely shop and *never* recrimination. Our Thursday "staff" dinners and their attendant rituals, after the sections had been safely "put to bed" for another week, were sacrosanct in my boss's eyes and were supervised by him with the same rigor as he applied to overseeing our joint journalistic efforts.

As a junior member of the Sunday Department writing team—i.e., one of the most recently hired—I often had the duty of hurrying from the Tribune Building with its multiple frescoes and murals (the airships and ocean liners of the *streamlined* world of the 1930s) around six o'clock on Thursday evening and grabbing a cab. My destination was invariably Karen Cohen's Portero Hill apartment and her refrigerator, where my hebdomadal task was to see the martini glasses were evenly chilled, as well as make sure the gin bottle was likewise decently cold.

This accomplished, I was expected to rush back down to the waiting taxi and be again at my desk by 6:30. Two hours later—or as close to that as the exigencies of completing all the copy, captions, layout and dummying in the ads dictated—Don Cameron would boom in his baritone to the four or five of us remaining that he was finally satisfied with our product and that we would now repair to Portero Hill and the ice-cold martinis awaiting our parched throats.

The martini ritual lasted one hour. It next befell each of us (on a roster basis) to announce the restaurant we would be attending, at which we had duly made reservations. Roughly speaking, this meant the late-night dinner arrangements would fall to each of us about every five or six weeks. The only variation in any of this was the precise establishment at which we ate. We paid by dividing up the total bill and ignoring each and every discrepancy of price over either dishes or drinks. Don Cameron chose the wines, which were always Californian and always from the vineyards to the north of us.

It so happened, the day after I had experienced the dismal run-in with Father Knowles at the Church of the Advent, that it was my Thursday to select our restaurant. After being absent on Wednesday afternoon I had to put in several frenzied enquiries on Thursday morning, as not all establishments were prepared to seat a largish party that late in the evening. (It was sometimes ten o'clock before we actually sat down, and a good half-hour later before we finally finished with the cocktail routine which had begun, of course, back in Karen's apartment.) The first two choices having failed me, I ended up reserving a table at Le Gavroche, a French restaurant I knew Don approved of as it was one of the few on Portero Hill, so there would be no excessive hiatus between his last martini *chez* his mistress and the first before he ordered the wine.

That night six of us sat down. Apart from the boss and his girlfriend, there were two other section editors and the art director, Nancy Abrahenian, a vivacious Armenian girl from the Livermore Valley who made a special habit of tossing her long black hair, flashing her teeth and beaming smiles of excessive brightness at those she thought had failed to warm to her charm or just plain didn't like her.

I was not feeling in the best of spirits that evening but her tiring presence, along with that of the closet queen, Joe Meserole, who rarely addressed me but who I could swear wanted my job, depressed me yet further. But if acne-scarred Joe, with his drearily incessant sports talk, jealously resented me, it was nothing to the hate Karen Cohen lavished upon the most glamorous woman employee in the Sunday Sections. In the small-mercies department came Nancy's decision to sit between Joe and the last member of our group, George Wisdom, who, as direct assistant to Don, was responsible for putting everything finally together and seeing we came up each week with an acceptable product. George was a decent man and would do his utmost to both palliate edgy Meserole and proffer flattery to Nancy, who relished such from all comers. Unfortunately, eleemosynary motives were confined to George. Otherwise it was mainly full-blown animosity, and the queen of the team was Karen.

Karen Cohen was a woman of exquisite grooming, still possessing the form of a girl but interesting rather than comely in facial features. She was also the owner of a lively if caustic mind which she largely employed in furthering such misanthropic goals as deflation and embarrassment. My own too-familiar experience was that if she could succeed in impeding someone's conversational track—or, better still, in causing her victim to blush or stammer—the mamba-like eyes would blackly gleam in triumph, the flashing tongue desist—and play instead at remoistening her excessively sanguinary lips.

The mere fact that the stiffly upright lady sitting next to me, sheathed as usual on Thursday evenings in a tight black dress, her comparably jet hair drawn in a tight bun to the nape of her neck, was Donald Cameron's girlfriend was cause for circumspection. But it wasn't prudence that nudged me that night. It was fear. I can't say that socializing with straight people generally presented itself as a difficulty. Experience had long ago taught me that if there was no prior knowledge of Ken and our relationship, I could easily pass for straight. I was partially abetted in this by looking considerably less than my thirty-four years. Also nature had kindly withheld the stereotype attributes of a shrill voice and limp gestures, which would have raised the suspicions of at least the sexually paranoid and personally insecure.

I never attempted deliberate *butch* talk (thus trying to compete with the likes of Joe Meserole) but, with what I considered consummate cunning, I always divulged as much of my personal life as the far bounds of discretion permitted. I had a hunch both Don and Karen suspected my sexual predilections. I had told Don I had a roommate who was a grad student at Stanford—and I knew he passed on everything to his ophidian companion. But in the interest of extra insurance I had prudently added that Ken's parents and mine were friends back in England and that we boys had known each other since childhood. If it looked as if we were two young English immigrants making our way in San Francisco, then I was quite happy to leave such an impression. In any case, as all gay men out there in the jungle know, *suspicion* is one thing: *knowledge* quite another!

This was no ordinary Thursday, though. From the moment I busied myself in arranging the reservations, I knew nothing could be taken for granted. Now, as I sat between Don and Karen, I brimmed with an apprehension which had been mounting ever since I arrived at the office that noon.

"What happened to you yesterday afternoon?" Karen suddenly turned to me and said. "I looked for you all over Editorial to check a story for the TV tab but couldn't find you any place."

The question wasn't delivered with venom. Indeed, knowing Karen's usual demeanor, I found it almost friendly. Nevertheless Nancy chose to see it as an attack and imprudently leaped to my defense.

"I don't see why Davey has to be cross-examined every time he leaves his office to go to the bathroom. I seem to remember you always asking the same question of one of us. It was me just a week ago."

I saw something close to relief sweep Karen's features as she dipped happily into her ever-ready pool of verbal vitriol.

"Memory's never been your strong suit, has it, honey? Otherwise we wouldn't have had that screw-up this afternoon with the photo captions. And Davey can defend himself. He's started shaving, you know. He can survive without you playing big sister. I guess it was nothing more adventurous you had in mind. Even so, if I were you, I'd stick to your own style and be predatory rather than protective."

I closed my eyes as I awaited a further salvo from my Armenian supporter. However, it didn't come from that quarter at all, and when it did come it wasn't remotely a defense of me.

"Who the hell booked us into this joint again? The menu never goes beyond animal innards and bony fish." The speaker was Joe Meserole and I knew bloody well he was aware it was I who'd made the arrangements to eat at Le Gavroche.

"You raved about it last time you were here, Joe," I told him. "In any case, when I mentioned it to Don this afternoon, he was as keen on here as he's always been. Isn't that so, Don?"

That should have shut him up. Joe wasn't one to cross the boss. But it was Don himself who was to let me down.

"I don't have shares in the place, though I've always thought it satisfactory. But you left it so late there wasn't much choice, Davey, was there? Yesterday afternoon would've been a good time to book but, as Karen says, you seem to have done a vanishing act around the time one of us usually checks where we'll eat."

My abnormally thin skin was not so much pierced as rent. I exploded. "Christ Almighty! What is this? The fucking Inquisition?"

George Wisdom dropped his tooled leather menu so heavily that it made the cutlery about his place setting jump in all directions. Nancy's jaw dropped, and Joe looked furtively at Don—as unused as any of us to hearing someone shouting at the Sunday & Entertainment Editor. Only Karen continued to smile as she toyed with her knife.

I felt it incumbent on me to continue—in explanation of my eruption if for nothing else. "I didn't know I was really working in an industrial plant and had to clock in and out all the time. If you're suggesting I failed to pull my weight, then I wish you'd told me at the time. Up to now I've always thought how civilized it was that we left work behind when we sat down to dinner."

"Hold it, sonny," Don said quietly. "You're overreacting. *Nobody's* accusing *anyone* of goofing off. Nor are we going to have a post-mortem about what did or didn't happen over at the *Tribune*. And that applies to everyone, Nancy. Now, for Christ's sake, let's order."

I was far from mollified, and besides, I resented his omission of his girlfriend's name from the general remonstrance. "Then what's with Karen's crack about my disappearing act?"

"I said *drop* it, Davey." Don's expression resembled in its severity one of his acid little memos.

When will I ever learn?

"I still hate the idea of being spied on by the two of you. Do I really have to bring back a note from my doctor every time I visit him?"

I thought that quite clever as I had provided a reason for yesterday's absence without actually telling a lie. There was another reason for my prickly attitude, for my refusal to let things go. The visit to the priest at the Church of the Advent was by no means the only reason which might have accounted for my afternoon absence. *Any* afternoon might have witnessed my slipping out of the Tribune Building—though in all other cases I had been careful to see I was back in my cubicle within forty-five minutes or so. In fact, I never left unfinished work behind me when it came time to leave for the day, and I was invariably back typing away by the time the fog crept between Twin Peaks in the late afternoon and the foghorns started their familiar moaning.

The cause of my afternoon expeditions was not one I would ever explain to my colleagues, and if I had, I doubted whether they would have been my colleagues for much longer. What took me out of doors and down Market Street for half a block was the existence of a seedy restaurant with a highly active toilet-room scene down a steep flight of stairs. There I could enjoy promiscuous sexual release after a matter of minutes with some highly diverting strangers. Sometimes it was as frequently as thrice in one week that I would return to sit at my desk and rewrite material concerned with

Bishop Fulton Sheen or the singing career of Anna Maria Alberghetti after having my tongue probing the tonsils of a sleek young Norwegian sailor or giving head to the enormous hosepipe of a burly black janitor from one of the adjacent office buildings.

The quick transition from the delights engendered by erotic acts perpetrated under the sidewalk of the city's main thoroughfare to the respectability of the *majority world* in the *Tribune*'s Sunday Department was a pleasure all its own. But the excitement of risk-taking, the exhilaration of cocking a snoot at the heterosexual arbiters of so much of life, was forever threatened by the dire correlative of *being found out*. It was this which animated my rebellion to my boss's wishes and which sparked my hysteric response to snaky Karen—at least as much as the unhelpful priest or the truancy from my desk.

"I shall shut up because you say so, boss," I told Don, knowing full well how he hated the title, "but I still feel I should have to answer only for my work and not my personal actions."

Don grunted—which I took to be a reluctant acceptance of both my position and my puerile desire to have the last word. But it was not: I was leaving gay traitor Joe Meserole out of account.

"I know where our Davey goes when he sneaks out," he announced softly and slowly. "He goes down Market Street to Forbes' Café. I've seen him several times."

I held my breath, feeling the sweat distemper my forehead at his announcing the name of the place of my sexual assignations. I'm convinced my heart joined my stilled breathing.

"He's such a snob he goes into that sleazy dive for a coffee rather than joining us up in the cafeteria."

"One more word from you, Joe, and I'll ask you to leave," Don said.

I was about to defend myself from the unfair charge of snobbery when I thought better of it. This was far too close to exposure. A few more indiscretions and friends could become enemies and fragile alliances could be sundered.

"As no one seems keen to order," I began, "let me start. I think I'll have the scallops first, followed by the brains in black butter." Then I looked at my neighbor, Karen Cohen, who could so easily turn hostile if she ever found me out. "And what will you have, my darling? I see your favorite abalone are on the menu."

When she nodded agreement at the word *abalone* I sagged with relief. We were back on the rails of convention and thus back to gay safety again.

CHAPTER TWENTY-FIVE

Naples/Alexandria: May 20th–June 1st, 1960

Neither Charlotte nor I was swept off our feet with Naples, which we finally left early yesterday morning. Admittedly, we did quite enjoy the rickety chairlift to the crater of Vesuvius, and inspecting the Lacrima Christi vineyards on the volcano's lower slopes *en route*. Another plus, we both thought, was the ruins of Pompeii and Herculaneum. But all the poverty, like some horrible pyorrhea oozing between those tooth-like tenements sprawled around the curve of the bay, made me very angry. Perhaps I'm a bit of a reactionary in some respects but I do *not* believe such stinking squalor necessary in today's Italy. It wouldn't exist if the proper political will were there—and, as I pointed out to Charlotte, you don't have to be a dogma-ridden Communist to reach such a conclusion!

I must register here yet another reason why our protracted visit to that huge city along the edge of beautiful Naples Bay didn't come up to expectations. It had nothing to do with the noisy poor, huddled in their mishmash of sunless alleys. Rather, it was competition on board—in the persons of the Brierlys, whom Charlotte has gone out of her way to befriend since leaving Marseilles, where they did not in fact disembark as Captain Schaepmann suggested they might. It now appears they intend to remain with us for considerably longer. Ida Brierly casually mentioned Durban after dinner last night, which is a little odd if her son Nick is due back to take up a position with Scottish television.

Even if I confess to having acted like a typical ship's busybody in my efforts to extract information from Ida, I have to admit in the privacy of these pages that she is an extraordinarily *stubborn* as well as very private woman. On the other hand, I must say that

Charlotte always does better at extracting information from people than I do. It is because they blurt things out in front of her as they don't think she is really listening when she's laughing so loudly all the time!

Nick is always begging my friend to play deck quoits with him when *she has other things she should be doing*. I tried to indicate this on the funicular trip to the top of Vesuvius but she just laughed it off and told me the poor boy needed plenty of exercise as he really wasn't as healthy as he looked—in spite of his suntan and slim figure.

After she told me that, when Nick suggested accompanying us on the excursion to Pompeii and Herculaneum, I was not surprised his mother insisted he accompany her to the much closer cathedral instead. Ever since leaving Holland I have observed she rarely lets him out of sight. The odd thing is that Charlotte has learned Nick is twenty-seven and thus hardly to be treated as a child!

After we hauled anchor and were heading for Alexandria I finally got my first opportunity to have a talk with Nick along the lines Charlotte seems to enjoy on a regular basis. I was on deck to enjoy the squally weather with Charley and look out for the schools of flying fish which Frank Wilkinson boasts he has seen on several occasions since we reached the eastern Med. At first we two women had the deck to ourselves—as has so often been the case when the weather has turned inclement and the sea a trifle rough. I was, in fact, feeling a little guilty in playing truant for so long from this diary, which it has become my custom to turn to immediately after breakfast, when Charlotte has gone up for her first morning trot around the cramped deck space allotted us. But I quickly forgot this minor duty when she got me giggling over the prudish antics of our guide on the Pompeii trip.

The wretched man seemed to feel two mature Englishwomen must be sheltered at all costs from the licentious depictions of another age. I had pointed out to him, as nicely as I could, that both Miss Churchfield and I were familiar with the lewd images on those fifth-century Athenian vases housed in the British Museum. I threw in for extra ballast that I happened also to be the mother of three sons. But he still tried to prevent us from seeing the sexually explicit frescoes for which Pompeii is, of course, famous, and which we were determined to peruse, having paid a somewhat excessive number of lire in supplement to the general admission.

It was just when Charlotte finished caricaturing the poor man's frustration at our refusal to yield to prudery that Nick Brierly, crisp in a freshly laundered shirt and spotless white shorts showing rather an excess of thigh (this is 1960, *not* fifth-century Athens!), plonked himself down next to her. I suppose he might be described as attractive, in a weather-beaten sort of way. Under slightly thinning blond hair and a broad unlined forehead, he has gray-green, rather melancholy eyes. All in all, in terms of proportion, his face is somewhat longer than it should be: a *physiognomical* trait I have often found among the Scots.

His opening words went more or less as follows. "You ladies seem to be enjoying yourselves. I wish you'd have a go with Mother. She's so dreadfully down in the dumps this morning—and it's not just the weather."

Actually, even if I were an expert reporter, as I suppose Davey must be and I most certainly am not, I would have difficulty in recollecting Nick's exact conversation, for it was impossible to hear much of what he was saying from across the width of Charlotte's deckchair. Given his Scottish burr and low voice, all but drowned by the sound of the heavy waves slapping against the prow of the *Ijmuiden* as we sailed eastwards, I had to strain frightfully to get much of his drift. It became distinctly easier when Charlotte volunteered to go down to Mrs. Brierly's cabin, chat with her and seek to persuade her to join the three of us on deck.

Nick and I were thus alone together for the first time since we had shared a particularly turbulent passage in the Bay of Biscay. I started by asking him whether he had received any more news of his impending appointment with the BBC. He got up and lay down on the deckchair Charlotte had just vacated, where he flatly said no and added he didn't think he was going to.

"Oh? I understood from your mother it was all more or less settled."

He suggested that such was mere wishful thinking on her part, adding that his mother had a tendency, when it suited her purpose, to dwell only on the brighter side of things.

I smiled at him. "Perhaps that's just compensating for an unduly gloomy son."

He smiled back—though there wasn't much warmth to it. "Oh, I'm not that bad! Ask Charley. She'll tell you I've a sense of humor."

I was so astonished he should use the nickname I thought I—and I alone—had bestowed upon my friend that I was quite bereft of words. I felt I could hardly wait for her return and the opportunity to ask why she had yielded to a stranger that intimacy between us which I myself would not have ever dreamed of mentioning to another soul!

Nick plowed on, unaware of my sense of betrayal; apparently keen to unburden himself to a degree he had not evinced before. He told me the whole business of his awaiting employment with the TV in Edinburgh, though not entire fabrication, was somewhat less than the truth. He said his father, the managing director of a car-hire company, had himself written to the Scottish Service of BBC Television suggesting his son might make a worthy addition to their producing staff. Nick had subsequently attended an initial appointments board. But there the matter stood. He now awaited at least a shortlist interview before the slightest chance of him securing the position could present itself. In his opinion such chances were meager.

Recovering from the shock of Charlotte's treachery, I was about to ask him whether, under such circumstances, a long sea voyage away from the country was a prudent move. But he forestalled me.

"My coming on this trip with Mother has really nothing to do with that. In fact it is all to do with a conspiracy on the part of my parents which I'm not supposed to know anything about."

"What might that be—if I may ask?"

"I've already told Charley." He must have read the wince that crossed my features. "Miss Churchfield, that is."

"I can assure you she does not regale me with everything she is told. To the contrary!"

"I don't want to make a big thing of it. That's the trouble. That's precisely what my parents have done. It's just that I have a kidney complaint called *nephritis*. I'm not supposed to know I have it but I've been aware of it ever since I was nineteen. Nearly eight years, that is. That's why we're on this trip, you see. They thought it would do me good—lots of sunshine and rest, that kind of thing. But Mother—although she tries so hard not to—*will* treat me as some kind of invalid. That's why she didn't want me to come with the two of you to Pompeii."

"I see," I said. "It must be very hard on her. I can see that now."

And I did. I felt sympathy with Ida Brierly in a way I had not before. Again, it was something I knew Charlotte, given her spinsterhood, could never fully comprehend. But I could also see Nick's dilemma. If I had been victim of a chronic disease as a young woman I would have rather had darling Poppa ignorant of it. I know that was the situation with my brother Guy. Poppa died never knowing the son who had predeceased him as a war hero and air ace had actually been felled by his epilepsy.

Nick had looked extraordinarily desolate at that point, sitting hunched over the deckchair as he confessed his complete inability to demonstrate gratitude for his mother's solicitude over his health. I could not help feeling for him, even though it was rather a novel experience for this particular mother to hear a son confess to such a failing!

I cannot truthfully write here that my own three sons would have spoken thus to me. Simon, I fear, would've gone out of his way to revel in contempt for any worry I displayed. Then such is his attitude over anything I say. He does not take me seriously in any way. Little Arthur would have behaved in the manner he feels is the socially acceptable way a son should act toward his mother—or would have done so until he surrendered all responsibility to his wife, who now makes all decisions. That, of course, leaves Davey. He would probably speak of filial frailty and how guilty he felt over leaving me. But confessions would emerge only after he had lost his temper or was in tears. Or am I still thinking of him as the little boy he is no longer? I have to get used to the fact that he is now in his thirties and that I haven't set eyes on my wayward son for a full ten years!

Nick seemed determined to pour out his soul that morning, and as I lay there, silent, my eyes closed, he went on in that flat, unemotional way of his. I felt a bit like a psychiatrist, which made me quite uncomfortable, for I have no expertise on the distressing subject matter he was airing before me. He told me he so often felt drained of energy and these were the times when his mother's anxiety was insupportable. Then there were the other days he awoke, bright-eyed and tingling for some fresh experience: bursting to cram as much as possible into life. This was when he loved to play deck quoits with Charlotte and would have liked so much to take part in the various expeditions we passengers arranged every time we docked.

It was a little while before I grew aware that he had paused in his account and, from his throat-clearing and restarting sentences, seemed to have difficulty in finding opportune words. I opened my eyes and turned to him. "You don't *have* to tell me anything, you know. These 'high-seas' conversations are quite notorious, apparently. People have difficulty in getting back on track after them. Rather like those famous shipboard romances, I gather."

"But I want to talk," he insisted. "As for shipboard romances—well, I've never had a romance of any kind."

I state here unequivocally that, even if I have not rendered every word the boy said with total accuracy, my reaction at that point was one of complete incredulity.

"You have never been in love—not for one single moment?" I asked him. "A good-looking young man like you and now in your late twenties. I find it hard to believe."

He looked me fully in the eye. "There *was* a girl—Elfreda—whom I met one summer holiday when we were in Swanage in Dorset. I thought her very beautiful and she seemed fond of me, too. I was to take her to a dance in Wareham but my parents forbade it. They insisted it might bring on one of my attacks. The same old story, you see.

"We left Swanage much earlier than expected. I never did get to say goodbye properly to Elfreda. I am sure it was all to do with my wretched kidneys and Mother and Father's excessive sense of protection."

He also told me of Rosemary, a distant cousin who accompanied her mother from Dumfries when the Brierlys were living in Kirkcudbright. It was all perfectly innocent, Nick assured me. He was twenty-one and she eighteen and they loved to take their bikes and explore Wigtownshire. His mother grumbled that long bicycle rides were bad for him but he was convinced it was more to do with Rosemary's presence than any old bike! His father too, apparently, had been quite determined to keep Nick clear of romantic entanglements.

The boy then sighed with an extravagance which tugged at my heart. "God! It was far worse than I'm implying. I haven't been allowed any friends either. I went down to Cumberland, to St. Bees School. I first got ill in the Sixth Form and that's when I had to leave. What friends I made at St. Bees sort of evaporated.

"When it came time to go to university it was assumed I would go to St. Andrews, where my father had been. So what did they do? They sold our house and moved to St. Andrews! Dad said it was because of the golfing but I knew damn well it was to keep an eye on their one and only—sickly little me!

"So what all this means, you see, is that you're looking at a kind of ghost. I have no existence away from my parents. Mother in this instance—though I won't be surprised if my old man flies out and joins up with us, somewhere along the way.

"They actually *compete*, you understand, in protecting me from the Big Bad World that can so easily set my complaint off. I'm afraid the truth is that you are looking at a freak, a hangover from a nineteenth-century novel. The kind of consumptive heroine who must be kept in isolation for the good of both herself and anyone unfortunate to seek entanglement with her. Nick Brierly has become a set of malfunctioning kidneys! Personally, I don't think it worth it any more."

Now I could understand the fixed sadness of those eyes. "There's just one thing," I said, when he wound down. "Could you not rebel? Have you never thought of upping and departing to live your own life?"

He grimaced. "About a million times! I know it sounds as if I'm just a softie with no willpower, but it's much more than that. I'm not excusing myself entirely, but when I have an attack I become so drained of energy. It's hard to explain." He fell silent.

It was just then that I had an idea. I asked Nick how well he knew Paul Leiden—only I put it casually, as if I had embarked on a whole new topic between us.

"Not very well," he told me. "He flies around the cabin cleaning and tidying up. But he doesn't talk much. I think Mother intimidates him. She has that effect on a lot of people. She told me once I should avoid strangers as I might be susceptible to any disease they were carrying. That was before we came on board this ship, but I wouldn't be surprised if she felt the same way about the *Ijmuiden*'s crew. She's not too keen if I go up on the bridge—which is always at Captain Schaepmann's invitation, of course."

"I suppose Miss Churchfield and I are to consider ourselves lucky then."

For the first time Nick accorded me a young man's ordinary grin. "Well, she doesn't know about this chat, does she? And for some reason I cannot possibly fathom, she doesn't mind my playing just a few games of deck quoits. Then she rather approves of Charlotte. As far as she approves of anyone, that is."

"My friend has that effect on people," I murmured.

"Why do you ask about Leiden?" he queried suddenly.

I responded very carefully. "He's an interesting young man, with an unusual background. Not quite what you might expect from a ship's steward. I've had some intriguing talks with him. I thought you might do the same."

He was about to answer when he spotted his mother and Charlotte approaching from the cabin quarters. I swear he switched the substance and tone of his words. "I'll bear in mind what you say, Mrs. Bryant. Hello Mother...Miss Churchfield.... We've just been discussing life. Having a fine old time of it, too!"

The two women stood facing us as Nick scrambled to his feet. "I do hope my son hasn't been inflicting his wild theories on you, Mrs. Bryant. I warn him the day will come when someone will pluck up the courage to tell him to shut up. But as with most boys, his mother is the last person he'll listen to. He doesn't think I have a brain in my head—though where he thinks he gets *his* I can't possibly think!"

As she spoke a smile played about her mouth and her voice turned gentle. It was obvious to me—and not for the first time—she worshipped the ground he walked on.

"All right if I ask Miss Churchfield for another hand at quoits, Mother? She beat me last time and I'm thirsty for revenge."

Charlotte rippled one of her famous laughs. Actually, it was close to a snort. "What's all this 'Miss Churchfield business'? Especially since it's been 'Charlotte' and 'Nick' since long before Marseilles!"

I was tempted to say that somewhere along the way "Charley" had crept in but constrained myself. Ida Brierly stood watching her son, in his white shirt and shorts, check the net and go to the equipment bin and extract a quoit which he threw to Charlotte, who looked quite young and fetching for her age in a cream-colored frock and floppy white hat.

Only then did Ida Brierly take the deckchair her son had vacated. As I turned to begin conversation with her a daring plan was already formulating in my mind.

Alexandria & Cairo: June 2nd

Never have past and present merged more intensely than since we docked and made our way to Cairo, but the odd thing is that I am not referring to *my* past but to that of Wesley—so many years before. He flew these skies during the Great War—not as a pilot like Guy over Flanders, but when taken up by a friend in the Royal Flying Corps. It was between the Sphinx and the pyramids that he looped the loop in the open cockpit of a biplane. The poor man never recovered and could not be prevailed on to fly again until his death over thirty years later. The recollection was enough to provide the first impetus to my plan. I decided to arrange a small party from the *Ijmuiden* to visit the haunts that had remained indelible in my husband's mind to his dying day.

Let posterity record via this diary that that is how I started to plan this campaign of action, which is intended to benefit Nick Brierly through the vital aid of my friend Paul Leiden. By tomorrow we shall have succeeded or failed. If the former it is most unlikely Ida Brierly will be speaking to me, but that is something I cannot prevent. But in any case, more of all that later. It is my late husband who is such a surprisingly palpable presence.

Wesley served out here in the Imperial Camel Corps and it was his five long years of desert service which constituted our separation when we were unable to marry. Apart from my not realizing the two cities were miles apart—he never even once mentioned the journey in his frequent letters—everything else has afforded me a weird sense of *déjà vu.*

Common sense suggests such an impression owes much to the fact that little has ostensibly changed since my then fiancé, as a youth of nineteen, wandered these narrow, refuse-laden streets past filthy hovels and extravagant mosques; saw Egypt's poor in snow-white robes and her eternally beseeching beggars with fly-caked eyes, and skin leathered and cracked from the omnipotent sun—just as I do now some forty years later. (There's nothing like overwhelming poverty to preserve the past in a kind of pernicious aspic!)

Wesley always wrote vivid daily letters—a trait, I am sorry to say, which totally deserted him after our marriage bonds were forged.

Perhaps that is a trifle ungenerous. In the mid-thirties, when the economic depression threatened to bankrupt us and he had to put in a tenant farmer and start a career again as a salaried salesman, he *did* start to write me weekly again. But those letters consisted mainly of questions about how the children were doing in their

Essex exile, and what I must or must not buy them. In any event, the war put paid to that when he duly became a hospital administrator.

I stray from my duty as a diarist—which is to record the present and not bemoan the past. When I told Charlotte the ruse I intend to employ to remove the threat of Ida Brierly she accused me of acting in a reprehensible fashion and we almost came to blows. (She actually accused me of not being sporting!) For the life of me, I can see nothing dishonest in telling someone one might do one thing and then changing one's mind and doing something different. My goodness! Our whole sense of freedom is surely based upon the right to act as we please, *when* we please—provided, of course, it is not at another's expense. And I have never seen much virtue in just being consistent. Love often demands the very opposite.

The hardest thing is to be loyal, and in this instance I am confident I am giving my loyalty to him who most sorely needs it. That is Paul's opinion, too. We both have very strong views about loyalty, I am happy to say. Then I have never met a boy with such mature views and childish emotions.

Back in Alexandria: June 9th, 1960

Thank God I had the foresight to enlist the aid of Paul, for otherwise we might not have averted total disaster! I must be succinct and state exactly what happened this afternoon and early evening, after our party, consisting of Charlotte and I, Paul and Nick, arrived at the pyramids without the presence of Ida fussing oppressively over her son.

My plan worked perfectly. Ida went to the telephone to receive the announced call from Scotland, which in fact was from Amsterdam—thanks to Paul's friend who was enlisted into my scheme. We knew that the Egyptians would be blamed for the confusion and inefficiency and that by the time things were sorted out we four would be safely on our way to see the sights.

What I did *not* know, of course, was that poor Nick was destined to have one of his cruel attacks. My God, they can be so sudden! One moment Nick was struggling up the steep slope with the best of us—admittedly with perspiration falling down his face—the next he was a crumpled, doubled-up figure at our feet. For one ghastly moment I thought he was truly a goner, but Paul was able to avert that unthinkable tragedy. I should also praise Charlotte, though, for it was she who quickly summoned the ambulance by her ability to converse in French, raising her voice against the welling babble of Arabic as the crowds excitedly milled about us. She also kept them from actually stepping on us as I knelt there in the heat and dust, mopping a sweating forehead as Nick lay limp as death and white as alabaster while Paul held him gently in his arms.

How I wish Ida had been here when her son was brought back to the ship, but the headstrong woman had gone storming off in pursuit of us when Frank and Thelma Wilkinson sneakily told her they'd overheard us ordering a taxi to drive to the Sphinx.

After Paul had laid Nick gently down on his bunk in the cabin adjacent to Ida's, I moistened a facecloth from the nearby washbowl rack and attempted once more to cool the boy's forehead. But Paul was having none of it. Tenderly but firmly, he took the square of white flannel from my hand, soaked it afresh in cold water from the little basin and moved quickly from wiping the fresh bubbles of sweat from Nick's face to addressing first the neck and then the upper part of the torso. Right down the hairless chest to the stomach and navel. Only then did he look up, as I awaited orders and Charlotte hovered behind my back—equally anxious, I knew, for something positive to do.

But I think Paul's motives were more prudish than medically inspired. "Charlotte, I wonder if you'd slip down to my cabin and fetch the bottle of Dettol disinfectant from my cabinet."

The effortless way he conveyed her intimacy with his domestic quarters, and the manner in which he calmly instructed her to run his errand, evoked in me an only too familiar spurt of hostility.

"Our cabin is much closer," I said crisply, "and we also have Dettol—it is on the table where you last used it, Charlotte. And please bring the box of surgical wool, too."

She bounded away like a happy puppy. As usual, she had no idea of my displeasure—just delighted in being of service.

Paul, too, seemed oblivious to my reaction. "Thank you," he said to me. "That's an excellent idea." When he turned back to the flat stomach revealed by the unbuttoned shirt, he clearly returned to the thoughts that had been occupying him when he dispatched Charlotte for the Dettol bottle. "I think I should bathe him all the way down," he said hesitantly. "Who knows, it might help cool the fever."

I was ready for him this time. "In which case we must take his trousers off," I said in my best Florence Nightingale manner. "I'll slip them down as you lift him up."

My breath was a little faster than I had hoped. I must record my thrill of relief when Nick chose that very moment to open an eye. I was no longer faced with having to share with Paul the confrontation of another man's sexuality in that disconcerting state of potential power yet floppy vulnerability.

"Oh, look, Paul," I blurted, "our friend has returned to us! Would you believe it! Scots modesty has brought him round when all other methods failed!"

"How do you feel?" Paul asked tenderly. "You had us all much anxious. Does it always come upon you as fast as that?"

Nick tried a smile. I noticed again how dried and cracked his poor lips were. "I—I just overdid it. If I get in the sun or too worked up—then bingo!"

There was a sound at the door and I turned to tell Charlotte the welcome news. Only it wasn't Charlotte. It was an outraged mother, distraught over her frail son. "What are you people doing here? Leave my boy alone!"

She didn't so much shove us aside as fling herself between us, down by the side of her child. She grabbed his unresistant hand that hung limply over the side of the bunk and began a kind of formless chatter which I could neither hear properly nor make sense of when I did. Something about it being her fault for listening to lies and thus allowing him out of her sight. More about how close he had been to death and that he must forgive her for keeping the truth of the gravity of his illness from him for so many years. By this time she was crying, moaning and mumbling, all in one and the same breath.

In the middle of all this Nick opened his eyes much wider and, with increasing color to his voice, strove to silence her self-reproaches. That was when she abruptly returned to the subject of our presence.

"It is you interfering people I have to blame for this. And you, woman, most of all! Not the pansy steward—he does what he's told. But you and that—that *galumphing* creature who has been trying to take my son away from me ever since she cast her sluttish eyes on him."

"You are speaking of Miss Charlotte Churchfield—a woman of total rectitude and my best friend," I spat. "And you are nothing but an hysterical female who for years has been suffocating her son."

My jibe prodded her to leap to tiptoe and confront me from her commanding height. Had we been of equal stature I suspect our noses would have brushed! She ignored my words, though; concentrated on her venom toward my dearest friend.

"Twice my boy's age if she's a day. In my book the woman is a pervert, and so I shall inform Captain Schaepmann. A deviate preying on a young man who is too ill to be aware of her designs and too frail to resist them. She must be ordered off the ship!"

This was getting out of hand. Even Nick, who had closed his eyes again when his mother had newly erupted, started to protest in his weak voice.

"Don't be silly, Mother! You have it all wrong. Anyway, you *like* Charlotte—and no one is to blame."

I was not about to allow young Nick to take the burden of what had happened. I also suspected she was about to turn on the helpless Paul and make him the villain of the plot. "Before we start on useless recriminations, I will say the idea of giving Nick a few hours respite from you was mine and mine alone."

I proceeded to explain how I understood her anxiety over Nick because of experiences based on a son of mine. I didn't mention Davey by name. I also absolved both Charlotte and Paul—stressing yet again how it was my sole intention to conceive a plan whereby Nick could enjoy a break from his dismal routine.

At that point her son sprang fully to life and Paul and I became mere spectators of a mother and son's fierce exchange. He began with what was obviously a bombshell. "Mother, she knows I have *nephritis* and so do Charlotte and Paul. I make it my business to immediately tell my very few friends—mainly because you and Father make such a ridiculous secret of it."

Her silence was born not of anger but of shock. She actually rocked at the impact of his news. "You can have done no such thing," she hissed. "Because we never told you! We decided when you were still a child that nothing would be served in telling you. I defy you to tell me even now what has to be done daily for your health—to actually preserve your life. You know nothing of all this, Nick. You just think you do. Or are you telling me you have consulted a specialist without our knowledge?"

Nick sighed with a heaviness I hate to see in one so young. "In the first place, I was *not* a child, Mother. I was in my late teens. And I could read, you know. After the second or third attack I started looking things up—in medical dictionaries, the encyclopedia—anywhere I could. I can hardly remember when I didn't have the knowledge I could die at any time.

"But that was never my worry! It was always you and Daddy. I felt so guilty I was never going to ever do anything to make you proud. That I was never going to 'amount to anything,' as Grandma Brierly used to say. All those fantasies we used to play!... *Nick would one day be a doctor.... Nick was going to take up the law.... Nick was a late bloomer but would end up this or that....* I could have retched each time we went through all those stupid farces—including the latest one about the BBC and my becoming a television producer.

"And then came this trip and a chance deck conversation with Charley—I'm sorry, Miss Churchfield," he corrected, turning his head in my direction. "God, Mother, you've no idea what a marvelous woman she is. Never asked me a single personal question. Never mentioned illness. She could always see when I was getting a bit puffed at deck quoits or our little jogs so early in the morning. I was so relieved to tell her I had nephritis and how my illness was ruining the lives of the two people I loved most—you and Dad. She couldn't have been more understanding. Suggested I have a chat with Mrs. Bryant, who also had a son she found it difficult to communicate with and had problems of some kind."

I do not think I could have taken much more in that vein but, with blessed coincidence, Charlotte chose to return right then with a bottle of Dettol clutched in her hand.

"Oh I say!" my friend exclaimed. "Cat's out of the bag and all that?"

"You are all breathing up the air my son craves in this crowded cabin. I wish you'd leave us alone."

"No, Mother, I don't *want* them to go away. Please let me have my own way for once." He sounded as tired as he looked—but there was no mistaking the determination.

Ida Brierly retreated into a position I found uncomfortably familiar.... "Who am I to prevail against you and all your friends! They know what's best for you, of course. After all, you tell them *everything*. I'm only here when you have one attack after another and need nursing."

"If you wish me to leave your son's cabin, madam," Paul said, "I would not disobey you. My job is to serve you—not to defy your wishes." He gave a funny little European bow which in other circumstances I would have mimicked to pull his leg.

"Stay! Stay!" Ida Brierly said. "You have heard what Nick says. I am outnumbered four to one. Besides, I have to believe the evidence of my own eyes. When I am alone with him and one of those attacks comes on and he hovers near death—it is hours before he speaks, and he refuses to open his eyes in case he has gone blind. Someone has probably told him the end will be along those lines."

None of us spoke. None of us felt like countering the prevailing bitterness that edged her words. I for one did feel like a stranger in that cramped cabin space.

"I have seen him die—or thought I did—so many times that somewhere inside me now I am dead too. I have no feeling. Just a dry little prayer that perhaps he will open his eyes one more time—and be able to see me."

"Mother, why do you go on so? It is not only torture for you but for me too. And my friends don't want to hear all this stuff. Nor do I want them to. Christ Almighty, Mother, it's *my* illness! It's me that is—"

"I have never explained myself to anybody else. Not even to your father—let alone complete strangers. But it is as if you were a hemophiliac and the slightest prick of your skin could lead to the end. Only that would be so much more easy to explain. People understand that. They know about Queen Victoria's children. They know all about the last czars of Russia and that sick little hemophiliac heir to the Romanov throne. Everyone understood *that* mother's daily fears for the young czarevitch and her having to trust a simple sailor to keep danger at bay. But I have no one. Besides, who on earth has heard of *nephritis*—that has already ruined my son's life and made Nick a stranger to me."

"What the disease has done to me is nothing compared to the havoc it's done to the two of you. That's what I hate most, don't you see? My fucking disease has totally ruined your life and father's. I feel so guilty—even worse, I feel so powerless."

I didn't want to say anything to make my presence felt between them. But I couldn't help it. Too much of the mother in me insisted on speaking out. The pressure was almost a physical hurt.

"All this mutual recrimination," I murmured. "It's no good. It is no one's fault. That's the hardest thing I had to learn over my own boy. It took me years to accept that there was nothing his father and I could have done that would have altered things. Nothing whatever."

"What things? What kind of things?" Ida's voice was flat, colorless. I felt she was dulled by her own self-buffeting.

I was about to answer when Charlotte forestalled me. "Her son went away without saying goodbye. There were lots of things that should have been said years ago but never were. I think I could have helped more. It's not that I've got much worthwhile to say. But I try to be a good listener. Perhaps all this is a good thing after all. Get things off the old chest is what I say, isn't it, Isabella?"

I nodded. But I must confess I was afraid. I was truly scared of what Charlotte might say next.

As Nick started to vigorously agree with Charley, I nudged both her and a discomfited Paul, who felt so palpably out of place. "Come on, you two," I said, "let's leave them to have a darn good chat. That's what I'm going to do with my son when we eventually meet."

I didn't mention San Francisco and my approaching rendezvous. It is hard enough to mention here in the privacy of the page, and while there is still the luxury of many weeks to plan and prepare a strategy.

CHAPTER TWENTY-SIX

When my boss, Don Cameron, flung one of his terse little notes over the transom, I had no idea that Friday afternoon of the eventual import of his action. It simply said:

> How about a Pacific Northwest vacation? I provide transportation. You provide us with a travel story. O.K.?

I was feeling unusually ebullient that afternoon. After all, it was a Friday. More important, Ken was taking me out to a swank restaurant that evening to celebrate the June anniversary of our arrival in the apartment. I stuck a piece of copy paper into my machine and typed:

> Your proposition fascinates. But need more info before I succumb. F'rinstance—would we share the driving?

That in turn elicited a bellowed "Come on in here!" which I did at top speed. As I sat before the bald-headed figure in his immaculate white shirtsleeves and loose-knotted tie, his voice dropped several decibels.

"I don't want the whole world to hear this. Travel junkets for newspapers seem to be drying up and I've only two or three to give out. Normally I operate by seniority but your work has been tops and I think you're entitled to jump the gun. Besides, it's about time you tried your hand at some travel writing. Who knows, it may enable you to see how real red-blooded Americans live—not just a bunch of overrefined San Franciscans."

I sensed his underlying meaning to that "overrefined" but for once didn't bridle. I was far too intrigued at the thought of a free trip.

"What's the score, Don?" I asked. "I was kidding. I'd love to go somewhere new."

"It's a bus company that does tours out of the East Bay. They'll provide the transportation and hotel fares and we run your story on Seattle and Vancouver—specifically mentioning how you got there. It's just a means of subsidizing vacations for underpaid newspapermen, that's all. It's the free-enterprise system—otherwise known as wholesale bribery. It works as well as your European socialist subsidy programs for the working poor."

"Did I knock it? Are there specific dates, by the way?"

Don looked at me thoughtfully. "It's for two. Some junkets aren't. I thought you might care to take your sidekick for a look at part of what's left of your British colonies."

I was used to that kind of ribbing from Mr. Cameron. "I don't think Canadians would take kindly to your description. But I'm sure Ken would love the chance to see Vancouver and Seattle as much as I would. He has a friend in Seattle and there's a woman in Victoria I've known since I was a little boy. That's up there too, isn't it?"

Don looked down at the sheet on his desk. "Their letter says the tour includes a ferry trip to Victoria after staying overnight in Seattle and before going on to Vancouver. It's a weekly schedule so you can go when you please—provided it's within your vacation period. You're near the bottom of the totem pole so it won't be any time your elders and betters choose theirs. That list will be posted next week. Karen is working on it."

By making a superhuman effort I managed to save my good news until Ken and I were sitting down that evening in the Blue Fox and studying a tooled-leather menu. Instead of his usual prudent caution at my suggestions, my lover was delighted. He spoke enthusiastically of an old friend from undergraduate days who now lived on a houseboat there. He readily agreed about visiting Natalie McGregor (previously Natalie Lockyer-Pope) in Victoria—the childhood friend I had not seen since those distant days when my father had been a traveling salesman with her as his partner.

As Ken characteristically proceeded with the fleshing out of ideas for the trip, I reached over and clinked the tall stemmed glasses containing our brimming martinis. There were times when his planning made me almost uneasy at the inexorable dismissal of random incident from our lives, but this was a special moment between us and I welcomed his concentrated care and suggestions.

"Happy anniversary," I said. "We'll make the trip a real celebration of our first twelve years together. All sorts of things can happen on a long bus trip."

He smiled at me indulgently. "Don't raise your hopes too high. In any case, I shall take *Le Rouge et le Noir*, *Madame Bovary* and some inflated effort by Victor Hugo to read as preparation for next quarter. I was wondering when I'd find the time to get all my preparation done for my nineteenth-century French lit course."

I reminded myself that this was a festive evening and that I must be on my best behavior. I usually avoided mentioning it to Ken, for I was ashamed of it, but I nursed a quite irrational jealousy over Stanford's place in my lover's life. Later I was to settle quite happily into the role of "faculty wife" but I was far too insecure, even in my thirties, to confront his work or, even more, that of his colleagues, with equanimity. Oddly enough, his students (so many of them, he frequently informed me, amply endowed with Californian good looks) presented no such challenge. I simply willed their nonexistence—a survival technique I had begun to develop as a small boy whenever I'd felt threatened by external realities.

"I shall flirt with the other passengers if you insist on ignoring me. There's bound to be some amusing ones, don't you think?"

Ken sipped at his drink. "It's a tour, you say? From the East Bay? Probably all retired people who will have to pee every two hours. If that's the case, I'll find even Victor Hugo enthralling!"

In the event, neither of our speculations proved wholly accurate. A few weeks later, on boarding the bus across the bay in Oakland, we did in fact encounter several couples in late middle age who were obviously retired, but there were also a few single women about our age—and a pair who I quickly decided were *not* father and son. One was a bald-headed, middle-aged man dressed rather incongruously in a tan three-piece business suit. His more interesting companion was a handsome youth with stiff-looking, straight hair—a lock of which he kept brushing away from his eyes. He wore a blazer over chinos, a "rep" tie and a button-down Oxford shirt. He might have been a college librarian. I would have sworn he was gay.

They were seated as we entered and I insisted we take places across the aisle from them. I hypocritically offered the window seat to Ken with his books—so that I could better overhear their conversation.

At first I was content with that situation. We were soon out of the suburban patterning of the East Bay, and were headed north from Oakland before their prevailing interest was made clear. They were railroad enthusiasts: passionate patrons of the rail systems crisscrossing the U.S. As they chatted I wondered why they had bothered to take the bus tour, as they animatedly denounced both autos and buses and never stopped lauding the superiority of earlier transportation systems—except to express apprehension at the burgeoning airlines.

Until that time I hadn't the slightest idea of the encyclopedic knowledge owned by such vehement protagonists of *the iron way*—a term the older of the two actually employed several times. I soon perceived other aspects of this oddly intense hobby while I pretended to look at a magazine on the northwest provided in the back of the next seat, as the countryside opened up and rutted tracks appeared, leading to untidy farm buildings surrounded by shady groves of immensely tall eucalyptus trees and the occasional tacky-looking palm tree. I was intrigued by their selectivity. Everything that came into their visual orbit that was old, worn or plainly disintegrating earned their approbation; contrarily, all that was new or modern received their opprobrium. They represented an absurd degree of romanticism which was wholly novel to me, and which my straining ears found hardly credible.

We passed a derelict drive-in, forlorn in its weather-mottled cement walls, boarded windows and garish mantle of littered debris. Its curved corners and use of bottle glass as ornamentation suggested it was a distinct relic of the 1930s. It made me think of broken dreams and bankruptcy. By their heavy sighs and verbal swoons the boys obviously loved it. We slowed down where a bridge was being built. Perhaps it was across the Sacramento River—or maybe a tributary. I was immediately attracted by the nude-to-the-waist and suntanned construction workers (these were the halcyon days for gays, before such road work was usurped by women). Not so my rail-fan friends. They only recalled the narrower green-metal bridge this was replacing and regretted its passing.

The older man, whose name I had now learned was Ferris Conrad, took the opportunity of deploring the erection of the Golden Gate Bridge and the longer Bay Bridge in his youth, both of which, he declared, were hideous and had destroyed the romance of the ferries which had plied the Bay and, in those blessed days of *yore* (his word), had linked Marin County with San Francisco.

At this point I chose to introduce myself. I said something vague about Ken and me coming from the city, but it was not to the sense of my words but only to the sound that Lionel, the younger and far handsomer of the pair, responded vociferously. Before I could get to my conversational cudgels about appreciating the modern in North America—after confronting since childhood a plethora of oppressive decay—he was purring with pleasure at my accent, which he clearly rated alongside Stonehenge as a prize attraction!

I couldn't stop him. When he did pause for breath, Ferris took over. By this time personal embarrassment made me deaf to their Anglophilia, but their endless shopping lists of English delectables in no way impeded my growing sense of Lionel's physical attractiveness, which by now had extended below his handsome head and slim torso to the intriguing bulge at his crotch. As his flutey tones extolled Wells Cathedral, sausage rolls from Marks & Spencer, Marmite yeast extract and a carefully individualized roll call of the royal House of Windsor, I actually lowered my head slightly. Not in regal reverence but the better to examine that mysterious mound stretching from his zipper toward his left trouser pocket. I gave the good god Pan praise that Lionel should be sitting across from me on the aisle, and that two artful words from me immediately evoked hundreds from them—thus providing me time to eye the young man's concealed attractions at leisure and to give dalliance to my imagination as to what I would do if that tight-fitting trouser material were removed and I had free access to the warmth and touch of his skin and prominent artifacts in those nether regions.

I grew gradually aware that one or other of them had asked me a question and both were now mutely awaiting my response. I also sensed that a sizable erection had arisen in my own pants. With a spurt of alarm I felt Ken give the arm of my shirt an impatient little tug.

"Why don't you introduce your friends?" he asked briskly. "They've asked you *twice* now, Davey, whether we're together on this trip."

I swallowed hard. "I guess it's time for introductions. I'm Davey Bryant, American landed alien and European refugee. This is my native Californian roommate, Ken Bradley, who teaches French lit, met me in Paris and brought me back along with his diploma from the Sorbonne."

Everyone dutifully laughed. Correction. The rail buffs did. Ken doesn't like a whole lot of information about us offered to strangers—let alone disseminated in tour buses. He smiled thinly. "You haven't given them your mother's maiden name," he whispered savagely.

"Ken wants to know which of you introduced the other to all that railroad business," I said sweetly, as if by way of interpretation of the whisper.

Lionel of the big basket answered. "Neither of us. We met on the Skunk. Do you know the track between Fort Bragg and Willits? It's real great if you want to see snow. We've done the Great Northern since, and on this trip we'll leave the bus tour at Vancouver, take the Canadian

Pacific ferry and ride the little railroad south from Nanaimo on Vancouver Island to the capital city of Victoria. We've ridden the biggies, of course. Across Canada—the CPR and the Canadian National northern route. And stateside, both the Union Pacific and the—"

"Lionel," his companion interrupted. "You'll be giving them the names of all the *South* American railway lines that the British built next! Not everyone's a rail buff, you know."

I decided Ferris Conrad was a long-suffering man after my lover's heart. The knowledge was not pleasurable. On the other hand, so many aspects of Lionel were.... I felt it incumbent on me to defend the dear boy.

"Oh, but I find all this train stuff fascinating. I had no idea there were people who actually cared about such things. Lionel, you really must teach me heaps more."

Ferris leaned over his companion and took up the conversation with me. "We shall be delighted to tell you all we know about the older forms of transportation. We actually have a copy of your excellent British Rail guide, Bradshaw, with us on the bus. That's the same book Sherlock Holmes used, you know."

"I didn't know. But again, how absolutely fascinating. And to think I wasted a whole childhood and youth without knowing about the railway schedules you actually have in your suitcase! Then it's a small world, isn't it?"

Ken pinched me for my thick sarcasm. Ferris Conrad merely pursed his lips. When he replied he was icily polite.

"We rarely meet people on buses, as we infrequently travel on them. This time we had to make an exception. My family happens to be the major shareholders in the company and Mother insisted I check out just how well these weekly tour affairs are being run. It's something of a novel business venture for us."

"I think the idea of such young drivers a pleasant touch," I said. "And that powder-blue uniform is really cute. You didn't design it, by any chance?"

This time portly Ferris witnessed to his irritation by a loud and heavy sigh. "We have nothing whatever to do with the operation of the business. I cannot think of the last time I climbed aboard one of these vehicles."

His young companion sought to offset his friend's testiness. "What Ferris means is, his grandfather had shares in the Southern Pacific and sold them to buy the Conrad Traction Company stock after World War

One. If Ferris had his way he'd reverse the process but his aged mother won't hear of it. Actually, Ferris and I do ride the bus when we go into the city from Berkeley and use that naughty Key Authority Terminal."

"There you go again, Lionel, pouring out all kinds of useless information to people. You really are too much." Ferris turned his attention—not to me, who distinctly grated against his sensibilities, but to my silent partner. "I gather you went to Stanford? I'm a Berkeley man myself. Do you attend the big game each year? A Redskin fan and all that?"

I had to swallow hard to prevent myself from laughing out loud. I had never seen Ken evince the slightest interest in any sport—let alone football between the University of California and his alma mater. It made me wonder whether Mr. Ferris Conrad might really prove straight.

Ken, of course, was incapable of being bitchy to anyone other than me. "Afraid not. As an undergraduate I wasn't really interested and since then there never seems to be time for that kind of thing."

"I know what you mean," Ferris said warmly. "I even feel guilty about taking this tour coach up Highway 101 to Seattle when I might be at the university library. I'm contemplating doing a history of the Baltimore & Ohio Railroad—in which case I shall be spending a great deal of time on your lovely campus. Stanford has an excellent railroad collection—then you'd understand that, what with Leland Stanford being such a great and important railroader himself."

"Ferris loves scholarly things," his companion proudly volunteered. "He's much more like your roommate," he said to me. "They're both academics. I guess I don't have the right kind of concentration. You might not believe it but I also went to Cal, and European History and Civilization was my major. I don't know how I ended up at the Crocker-Anglo Bank! Dreary joint!"

"It was so much nicer when it was still just Crocker," Ferris sighed. "You were treated as a gentleman then."

I privately felt sure he would have never been treated other than as a fussy queen. But I was taking my tip from Ken now. "You two must be examples of how similar types get on. With Ken and me it's the other way around. I keep miles away from his academic world and I know he hasn't a clue as to what goes on at a daily newspaper."

Lionel was at once all excited. "A newspaper! You didn't tell us you worked for a *newspaper*. Do you hear that, Ferry, he works for a newspaper. When I was in high school in Berkeley I worked summers at the *Oakland Tribune*. Ferris' Dad knew Senator Knowland very well, didn't he, Ferry? He worked with him in that China lobby."

Ferris smiled patiently. "What Lionel means is that my Dad also had Far Eastern interests and that he and the senator were politically very close. Very close indeed." He nodded his two or three chins in emphasis.

"I'm afraid I have very little intercourse with the owners of my newspaper. Then I don't think a brace of young queens are quite their cup of tea." I strove to make my vowels and consonants as extravagantly British as if I had just had such a cup of tea with the other, more famous queen—presiding over the teapot with her pink hat and handbag, from an enormous chintz sofa in the depths of Windsor Castle. That brought as resounding a silence as I ever dared hope for. In fact, Ferris turned back to gazing out of the window. My lover stiffened, sighed with what I recognized as all too familiar exasperation and returned to his tome.

Only Lionel made any kind of response, and that was to shrug his slim shoulders in a kind of schoolboy glee, followed by a further opening of his long legs in a gesture that had nothing to do with schoolboys. Sheer physical limitation prevented me extending my own right leg across the aisle to make contact with his—although that was uppermost in my mind. But I was able to acknowledge his gesture by staring even more brazenly at where his body movement had taken place, and to lick my lips as if in encouragement of further stretching and easing.

We continued to bounce speedily along the highway as we headed north, and shortly thereafter the driver announced we would shortly arrive in Redding, where there would be a rest-stop and we could take lunch. Conrad Tours would be picking up the tab. From there on, it probably looked as if I were closely studying the highway ahead as we ate up the miles, passing slower-moving traffic as the air-conditioning hummed a lulling rhythm and the diesel engine purred. But I was actually imagining an undressed Lionel and praying fervently that he would follow me to the washroom as soon as we disembarked at the promised restaurant at the north end of the Central Valley.

My prayers were happily answered. I had no sooner stood at the urinals when the younger of the rail buffs joined me. I was more skilled in these matters than I'm sure my lover ever dreamed of. I spoke quickly in a low voice. "Show me!" And while he was fumbling with his zip, "I'll call you from the hotel in Seattle. I'll call you." I looked at what he was now toying with for my delectation. "I'll take care of that in a way you won't forget. Call me if I haven't phoned within the hour, O.K.? We'll have to get rid of our mates for a while. Persuade them to go shopping maybe?"

He looked doubtful. I suddenly felt skeptical too over such hasty arrangements—but lust gave wings to optimism. "We could bribe the desk clerk to lend us a closet. I've done it before. It couldn't be for long, of course."

"I don't think Ferry will fall for that—even if it's for ten minutes. He doesn't like me out of his sight. Especially when we're on a trip."

I reached over and gave him a hasty brush on the cheek for encouragement before returning to the restaurant and joining Ken. I found my lover smiling broadly. "Good news," he announced. "I called ahead and got Larry at home. He insists on throwing a party for us on his houseboat for our evening in Seattle. I explained we were on a bus tour and had to get up early to head for Victoria."

I suppressed disappointment at the frustration of my plans to rendezvous with Lionel. "Did you explain we were on a junket—courtesy of the paper?"

Ken looked mystified. "No. Should I have?"

"I just thought it would explain why we're on a bus tour, of all things. Why our time isn't exactly all our own as we have to cope with their bloody schedule. You could also have explained it's a working trip for me at least. He would then have understood what we're doing on a coach with a bunch of trippers."

My irritation at the frustration of the feverishly constructed plans made out there in the washroom was certainly not mollified when my roommate began to laugh.

"You're such a snob, Davey. What difference does it make how we get to Seattle? You can explain all that to Larry when we get there."

I shut up. If I got too huffy Ken would accuse me of overreacting again, and if I got rattled something about Lionel might easily slip out. As it was, he did make allusion to our traveling companions.

"Did you make any arrangements with our railroad addicts? You may have upset that nice old thing but I think you've got his young friend trotting after you like an obedient puppy."

I looked him straight in the eye. "As a matter of fact, I did suggest we might all meet in Seattle if we had the time. Of course, I didn't know then that you were attending to our social calendar."

"Well, I hardly thought you'd also be handling our schedule in the john, while I spent a couple of minutes on the phone out here. Which reminds me, sweetheart, I think I should empty my own bladder here rather than in the cramped space those buses offer. Order me a hamburger when the waitress comes, will you?"

As he left the pomegranate-pink table, I wondered once more just how much my Ken fathomed the workings in the devious darkness of my head.

Different musing occupied me as we headed north again. I could see that the opportunity of erotic dalliance with the young man now feigning sleep across the aisle had been reduced to a minimum. And in that cold realism my desire disintegrated. With it gone I was again able to reflect how much I risked each time I was disloyal to Ken. By the time the bus arrived in Seattle I had come fully, if provisionally, to my senses. That basic conflict between importunate desire and native prudence was not to achieve more permanent resolution for some considerable time.

Larry Mercier proved as mercurial as Ken had depicted him. He was a volatile imp of some five foot five, black curly hair, quick brown eyes, an incessant grin and a quickness of movement to match. Within minutes of the beginning of the party for us on the houseboat, I could see he was the venerated clown for his friends, on whom they seemed to rely for ever more frantic bursts of laughter.

It took me about the same amount of time to realize I didn't particularly like them. They seemed so covert over their gayness—shrieking when Larry made some crack but then all suddenly going quiet when one of their number made reference to the other houseboats and the chance of being overheard. One moment they reminded me of those crazy little birds that flocked on the shore near the ranch of Janet Lipton and Doria Lehman, that would suddenly take off in shrill confusion, darting in every direction and alighting and falling suddenly silent again for no perceptible reason. The next minute, though, they evoked another avian image when they began to shriek like screaming parrots.

The living room we stood in holding our drinks was cramped enough to seem crowded although I counted only nine present. It occurred to me the number didn't include Ken. I decided to combine a little exploring with a search for my roommate. If I was generally ill at ease on these social occasions among strangers, without the presence and support of my lover I roundly detested them.

The adjacent room, which was opposite where we had descended Larry's gangplank with its border of geranium-filled tubs painted a nautical blue and white, was a tiny galley. I moved swiftly beyond this toward what I saw to be the stern of the vessel. There was first a lavatory and shower stall (which I'm sure our host referred to as "the head") and beyond that a bedroom. The drape across the entrance was drawn but from beyond I could hear voices. Instead of interrupting, I took the narrow flight of scrubbed wooden stairs at its side, estimating that they could only lead to the deck and an open sky.

I wasn't disappointed. I was alone at the houseboat's stern. A rapid survey informed me that the immediate space in which I found myself was being used as an outdoor bedroom. A neatly rolled mattress was stuffed under the port gunwale with pillows and blanket stowed opposite. Where the final portion of the deck became a raised poopdeck was a small skylight, partially opened, from which I could hear the same voice I had heard below. Curiosity assailed me and I knelt to the wooden deck planks to hear better.

I was genuinely surprised I hadn't recognized Ken's voice—even if it had been previously muffled by the heavy velvet of the wine-red drape serving as a door, and he had been speaking in quiet tones. The low speech was now explicable as I observed him through the skylight sitting on Larry's bed. He was using a telephone.

I had to drape my body over the edge of the poopdeck and lower my head to the much-scrubbed wood of the deck to avoid being seen from below as I strained to listen to my roommate. I don't think I would have gotten very far had I not heard him make a laughing reference to railroads and the charm of old-fashioned houseboats and thus realized he was talking to one or other of our bus-tour companions.

Whether I could have discerned from a one-sided conversation if it was Lionel or Ferris Ken was addressing became moot. I was rudely interrupted in my eavesdropping by an unpleasant laugh. Without turning I could feel the shadow of its author blocking the warmth of the setting sun. "Can I play your Dr. Watson?" the voice said.

My mind is most fleet under the prod of embarrassment. "Hi, Ken," I called down. "Come up here when you're through and enjoy the fantastic view."

I don't think Ken heard my words for he simply lifted his head, grinned and waved. I beckoned, praying he'd come quickly. Then I turned toward the source of unpleasantness. I was looking up at a slightly overweight gent in his early thirties with thinning sandy hair, granny glasses and thick white socks below faded jeans. His arms were folded about his short-sleeved madras shirt.

"I was talking to my lover down there when you snuck up on me. Can I help you?"

I don't think he liked that "snuck." At least, he looked sour and wasted no time zeroing in. "I'm Larry's lover, and you are scuffing our bedroom-under-the-stars."

I looked down, genuinely perplexed.

"Your shoes. They make a mess of any deck. We have a house rule on board. They are forbidden. Didn't you see the sign Larry made?

With a lady's pump and stiletto heel—and a large red sign painted across it?"

"I assumed that was for your guests in drag. Or that it was only applicable when you were serving Japanese cuisine."

"You seem more imaginative than observant. If you'd looked down half as keenly as you were staring through that skylight, you'd have noticed we're all in stockinged feet."

I could hear Ken coming up the companionway and knew I must move quickly to get in an effective riposte before he arrived to spread calm and forbearance.

"I noticed. Only I thought it an old Seattle custom dating from the Depression. Or a sign Boeing was going out of business. By the way, I should congratulate you on those wonderful socks you're wearing. It's so rare one has an opportunity of complimenting people on their choice of undergarments."

His lip curled so extravagantly I was tempted to ask whether he had learned the gesture at the movies. "I'd have thought you often had the chance. That Peeping Tom routine looked so practised!"

Then Ken appeared, panting from having bounded up the short flight of stairs. Apart from a breezy "Hi" he ignored the squinty bastard who'd been criticizing me so nastily. "Larry said I could invite the rail buffs," he said. "That's what I was doing. Only apparently Ferris is weary from the journey and they've decided to stay in their room and read up on the *puff-puff* they'll board in Victoria tomorrow."

"It's probably just as well. Otherwise you'd have to warn them to wear their swishiest hose and to kick their fucking shoes off before coming on board. I've just been admonished by the Captain of Dress Code here."

Ken smiled at the oaf in the coarse white stockings. "Sorry about that," he said. "My lover's British and *very* formal." Then he addressed me again. "Come on, I think we'd better mingle with the guests."

As Ken led me back down the companionway I noticed for the first time that he, too, was minus shoes. It made me think him some kind of traitor.

"Do you mind if we keep on the upper deck a bit? I don't think I can face Larry's friends. They're so prissy. Terrified of dropping beads—even though it's obvious there isn't a straight man on board!" We had reached the area of the heads below deck when I tugged restrainingly at his sleeve.

"Not everyone has your classic education in gay emancipation by way of a prison sentence, Davey. Then not everybody is as intolerant."

In other circumstances we would have had a flaming row going in seconds after such gritty remarks, but I think we were keenly sensible of the fact we were guests. At any rate, he gave in and instead of joining the noisy throng amidships we climbed the further companionway and headed toward the prow of the boat instead.

The sunset was gathering momentum and it was the fiery drama of the skies that soon quashed our friction. Indeed, it was from those first moments of evening light in the Pacific Northwest that there developed an entrancement which was to grow into a beguilement that would never subsequently release us.

There was something mystical about those seconds we stood squeezed close together—for the space by the bowsprit was somewhat cramped—staring out at the jutting figurehead of the mermaid who shone gaudily as the dying light picked up the gloss of the innumerable coats of paint that had been lavished upon her over the years. I also knew restlessness; an unease about something as ineffably hazy as it was slightly ridiculous. It involved the weather in California. I had the oddest sense of betraying another, earlier climate: the one which had basically shaped me and which I was now experiencing again after an interval of ten years on that scintillating sheet of water in the center of Seattle.

I was about to try and put all that into words when Ken spoke up, his train of thought on comparable if more literary lines. "This is the time of evening Proust called *l'heure bleue* in Paris. Only I think it more applicable here than there."

"There's something about this light," I responded, "that makes me nostalgic. *Déjà vu* and all that? I keep remembering, as a kid, driving with my Dad along winding Cornish lanes, along the cliffs over the ocean. It always seemed to be sunset with the Atlantic glittering like the lake here. And another thing—it was always high tide, so the waves were breaking right at the top of the beach at Polzeath or Constantine Bay, or splashing the cobbles of the quay at Trebarwith or Boscastle."

I remembered red-admiral and peacock butterflies swaying up and down on the flower cones of buddleia bushes in the gardens of whitewashed fishermen's cottages. And great clumps of tamarisk and marram grass where the lane came down by the water's edge and snaked between sand dunes.

I sighed. "*L'heure bleue*, you say Proust called it? I should have said it was more cobalt blue."

"It keeps changing all the time though," Ken observed. "You can see why artists were so attracted to Paris, can't you? It's the same kind of light."

"Then there should be lots of painters here as well," I suggested—slightly sarcastically.

I was not expecting the answer I got—although I should have. It was not untypical of my academic Ken Bradley. "They can boast both Morris Graves and Mark Tobey as coming from these parts. I came across their names when I was doing some reading for the trip. Not bad for starters, I'd say—and I'm sure there're lots more we know nothing about."

"I've never heard of either of them," I confessed. "Then I'm totally ignorant about art anyway."

Something else occurred to me. "That's another thing that's always bothered me about San Francisco. It loves to talk, buy and show artwork but it has a pretty thin reputation for *creating* it, wouldn't you say?"

Ken pondered. "There's Richard Diebenkorn in the East Bay, of course, and then think of photographers like Ansel Adams and Edward Weston."

It was turning into a kind of parlor game, which I so Britishly loved. "Oh well, if we're including photographers we may as well go the whole hog and have authors and architects. I can give you Maybeck, the two Gertrudes—Atherton and Stein, and Robert Frost. Then he went to New England for a reputation, while Gertie buggered off to Paris. Maybe there isn't enough sticking power for native talent. Jack London didn't hang around Oakland or the Sonoma Valley very long. He always had itchy feet."

"Notice how late it stays light up here," Ken said, peering over the prow. "Then we're over eight hundred miles north of San Francisco."

"You've changed the subject!" I exclaimed triumphantly. "That means you've lost the argument!"

Ken turned round and faced me. He was smiling, his face soft with affection. "If there *was* an argument, Davey dear, you were having it with yourself."

At such times I longed for intimacy with him. "Let's make our excuses and go back to our hotel room," I said huskily. "But unlike those rail buffs, I've got more exciting things than trains on my mind."

CHAPTER TWENTY-SEVEN

Somewhere off the African coast, June 20th, 1960

I am unsure precisely where we are. It isn't only because the Red Sea *looks* endlessly the same; *feels* the same with these hot and gritty winds that never seem to falter; and still *smells* like Egypt—that is, of dried human waste mixed with something vaguely exotic like cinnamon or cloves. I think the real cause of my confusion stems from the extraordinary events which have made our lives a torment ever since we reached Egypt and I ran afoul of Ida Brierly and her unhappy son. Where to start?

Just as she had threatened to do, that stupid woman (my son Simon would surely have described her with a word starting with "B") went to Captain Schaepmann and complained I had risked the life of her boy with a plot to alienate her and to secure his seduction by Charlotte, of all people. Not content with that, she then claimed I had bribed poor Paul to aid me in my scheme. All this, mind you, in direct opposition to her son, who defended us all and vainly asked to be given a cabin as remote from his mother's as possible.

By the time we had docked at Port Sudan—a ghastly place where we stayed for days, although none of us alighted as there were rumors of typhus or some such plague—there were already some radical occurrences. Paul had been put on probation and told by Captain Schaepmann that this trip would be his last unless he remained aloof from the lives of us passengers. I knew this ultimatum would never have been delivered on the word of Ida Brierly alone. But she had gone at once to our inveterate troublemaker, Frank Wilkinson, secured his support and that of his terrified slave of a wife and got them to libel Paul still further over his relationship with poor Nick.

Although it was not easy for me (for I found her Teutonic arrogance hard to stomach) I went with Charlotte to call on Dr. Inge Wetzler, our new and seventh passenger, who had joined us in Alexandria. She had somewhat escaped my notice at first, as we had been preoccupied with other matters than the arrival of a new fellow-guest who was understood to be some kind of doctor. To my pleasant surprise she agreed at once to defend our steward before the captain. More than that, she proved quite willing to suggest, as a psychologist, that it was her opinion Ida was in need of professional help.

Not that, in the event, the woman's contribution proved of as much worth as we had hoped. Wilkinson somehow implied she was not fully qualified and even hinted to us that she had some kind of shady Nazi past!

Of course, I have no means of knowing how much Captain Schaepmann believed or disbelieved any of us, but it has become very clear to me that the Master of the S.S. *Ijmuiden* is of the opinion I am not a good influence on his vessel. Which leads me to Charlotte and her role in this dismal affair. I can put down in this book what I cannot possibly tell another soul. In spite of Ida's lies and the cheap leers of Frank Wilkinson—who was as free with his allusions over Charlotte as he was over Paul's designs on Nick—I have to admit to my belief that my dear friend is indeed romantically attracted to the young man.

I had noticed how defiantly she continued to play deck quoits with him and how they always managed to find some spot on board which was small enough to allow only two to stand or sit there together. At first I had seen this as a justifiable means of escape from an increasingly persistent parent who would shout at them behind their retreating backs. But it slowly dawned on me that the ill-assorted couple were not only intent on dodging Ida, but would also pick up speed and take these evasive actions if I hove into sight! The sad truth is, it was only in the confines of our cabin or at table that I was seeing anything of my friend. The penny finally dropped one morning when I was expecting Charlotte to join me for coffee and, on going to investigate her absence, found them almost cheek to cheek staring over the side of the ship in a position only attributable to lovers.

I decided the air needed clearing. That evening, as we were dressing for dinner, I confronted her with my suspicions. She just laughed it off, of course, and told me not to make mountains out of molehills. That she was indeed fond of Nick—but only as a fellow-sportsman and as someone with whom she shared the fact of living an exceedingly protected and sheltered life. But I didn't miss the initial blush and stammer of confusion. Her words sounded well but her steadfast refusal to meet my eye did not escape me. I let the matter drop when I could see she might become hysterical if I persisted. But our friendship is too deep, of too long standing, to be allowed to be torn to shreds on the spurious breeze of a shipboard romance!

On the face of it, of course, the whole thing is ridiculous. A woman of fifty-two in love with an invalid of twenty-nine or thirty. A jealous mother. A diabolical intriguer and—last night a further bombshell—the visit from Paul and *his* confession.

I have already recorded how tenderly I feel toward this young Dutchman when he comes to me as if I were his mother and reveals the most stark intimacies of his heart and mind. This is what happened last night—ironically when Charlotte and her young man were presumably on deck (this was a time when she and I usually had an aperitif in our cabin before dinner) watching a swift African sunset and blabbing the nonsense people are only too prone to make on such occasions. I would thus be dishonest if I were not to admit that Paul found me in far from an amiable mood when he knocked timidly and asked whether we might speak. When I asked him what it was about and he said Nick, my attitude changed materially. Even so, I was *not* expecting anything like what I heard.

"He is the most sensitive boy I have ever met, Tante Isabella. How can such a one have that Ida for a mother?"

I should point out that he had taken to calling me *Tante* on that hectic day when he, Charlotte and I had struggled with the prostrate Nick on the disastrous visit to the Sphinx. I wasn't particularly fond of the title but I had not the heart to deny him, knowing how he felt about me.

"He doesn't know my thoughts, but since that day we nursed him and brought him back to life I have felt stronger and stronger toward him. Of course I fought those feelings, Tante. I know the complications for a humble steward falling in love with a passenger. The company is very strict over such matters with its employees."

He gave a staccato laugh. "And the company is thinking all the time of us men and you ladies! If they thought it was with another man they'd have us shot!"

I had still hardly opened my mouth—partly through sheer astonishment at his confession of amorous feelings toward the same object as Charlotte's romantic ardor, and in part because I felt the whole of our shipboard life was getting dangerously out of hand.

Let me put Paul aside for a moment while I try and describe what I mean. Somehow it is so much easier to explain in writing. I doubt if I could make sense of my feelings in conversation.

I look at what is happening and one side of me says it is like a farce—the sort of comic nonsense you'd find in a novel. An infatuated woman of middle years...a swooning heroine as sickly as a tubercular star in a Victorian opera—only in this case it is a *young man!*...an apparently equally infatuated *male* suitor...the most frantically possessive of mothers...an evil busybody who is only happy when there is strife...and a mysterious German psychologist who strides about the deck talking to herself and offers everyone she meets counsel whether they've asked for it or not.

I am, of course, leaving myself out of this cast of a shipboard comedy of perverted romance. The reason is simple. I DO NOT SEE THIS BUSINESS AS FUNNY AT ALL! It is all too painful. Indeed, part of that hurt is my ability to see what is happening from outside myself—with another's eyes.

Perhaps it is always so. Perhaps you cannot have comedy which isn't at someone's expense. To the world at large, Charlotte must appear the most ridiculous, in her coy confusion best suited to a young girl, but she is the one who *lacerates* me. I hate to admit it, but what a serrated edge has the knife of jealousy....

Back to Paul. Thank God he seems so full of suppressed passion for the innocent Nick that he is quite unaware of a rival in the person of my closest friend!

"He lets me massage him, Tante Isabella, and I am so grateful I take a course in that activity before I joined the company. I thought it would help my advancement—not having thought of my love-life! He has told me how thankful he is for my attention and seems to especially like it when I stretch the beautiful skin of his temples and forehead."

Strange notions slithered in my mind. Oh my God! If it were not for this journal, I swear I could never express these things.

"Has he ever given you reason...reason for encouragement, Paul?"

"Oh, I do not think he knows what I am thinking. I do not think he has such thoughts about other men."

"My friend thinks he is quite impervious to women. From my own discussion with Nick about his illness and his upbringing I'm pretty sure he's a virgin as far as women are concerned."

"Impervious? That means he does not like? Why then do I see him playing with Miss Charlotte at the quoits all the time?"

"That means nothing! Absolutely nothing at all!" I did not intend to sound so vehement. "You have to understand how much that foolish mother has deprived him of true self-discovery. You will not find the true Nick unless you *push*, Paul. Not being uncouth, mind. But *aggressive*. Yes, that is the word. You must be gently but firmly aggressive with Nick—and you will be surprised what you will find in response."

Even as I spoke, striving to sound as cool as possible, I knew my appraisal was really a prayer.

"You think I have a chance, then? Oh, if that is true I have found the answer to my life! Just when I look at him when he does not know it, like when he is up there now in the moonlight counting the Arab dhows with their little lanterns with Charley—sorry, Miss Charlotte—I know I am for the first time really in love."

"Well, it's no good telling *me*, is it, when it is he who should hear your words." (I couldn't believe the cunning of my speech; the slyness of my words. I felt inhabited by a stranger.)

Before he left a few minutes later he gave me a kiss, his face all smiles. Nor could I help noticing the spring to his gait as he departed. I felt slightly flushed but was breathing easier as I reflected I now had some ammunition to deal with poor Charlotte's predicament. With a little luck I might soon be in control of it all!

Later same day:

I feel terrible. I have done the unforgiveable. I have made Charlotte break down and cry. She did her best, poor darling, to fend off my attack. Laughed and ridiculed herself as she always does. But I was relentless. I think I was demented. I did things which I never thought I was capable of doing. I lied outright. I told her Paul had told me that same evening that he and Nick were lovers. I also said Captain Schaepmann had asked me to warn her away from the Brierly boy as her conduct was becoming the talk of the S.S. *Ijmuiden* and there were oversexed crewmen who might easily get the wrong idea about her notions of propriety and morality. No matter that we kissed and hugged and were reconciled before we climbed into our bunks, my deliberate falsehoods had not been confessed and I had done nothing to make poor Charley's dilemma any easier.

I now feel a powerful urge to look at myself as unflinchingly as possible—and by peering into the mirror of this journal try and comprehend the image that stares back at me. I don't like what I see! If anyone had suggested just a week ago that I could be capable of disloyalty to my closest friend, I would have laughed in his face. I have not only deceived Charlotte but exploited Paul's trust in me in such a way it could lead to his destruction. It cannot be allowed to go on. That's to say I owe it to both Paul and Charlotte, and of course to the unsuspecting Nick, to try and set things right.

I am not sure how, as of this moment. It will not be easy. Certainly not just a matter of setting the record straight by correcting my lies and withdrawing my false insinuations. It's very odd, but I can't rid myself of the impression I have put myself into the same kind of situation that Davey might find himself in. Not that I am suggesting my son is a liar. Indeed, I pray my own dissembling was only an aberration. No, it is a kind of pride we share. Or should I call it arrogance? What I mean is the propensity to let an ability to run things (both Davey and Simon share this with me, while Charlotte, Wesley and Little Arthur do not) turn into a tendency to run people.

Oh dear! It is such a very little distance between being merely bossy with people and exploiting them for one's own purposes. I know I have done that in the past. I believe Davey was doing it with that Irishman with whom he was living during his Paris student days. But what I have just done makes all my past errors in that respect pale in comparison. And of course I have no right to blame poor Davey, who for all I know has long ago learned to treat his friends and loved ones with the respect and trust they deserve.

Interruption. Paul at door. Will continue later.

Ten p.m. Same night. Mogadishu, Somali Republic

Why Captain Schaepmann should have been bothered about the risks of illness at Port Sudan when we have docked at this festering swamp I cannot think! But I have more on my mind than fetid smells and gross poverty. What is that saying I used to hear so much on my mother-in-law's lips, which I so often repeated to my sons? *Man proposes—God disposes*. The truth of that has been vividly drawn for me by Paul arriving in distress to tell me Nick had firmly resisted his overtures and informed him that he was not a queer and that his "heart was lost" (Paul's expression) to the healthy, athletic Charlotte Churchfield! I hardly had time to digest that before further revelations tumbled out from quite another direction.

I encountered Ida Brierly outside our cabin as I was about to climb above decks for a breath of air and to search for Charlotte. Here was a chance for me to repair a tiny bit of the damage I had wrought. Before she could speak I burst forth with an apology for my interference and the promise I would do all I could to stop matters from getting more complicated than they were. To my surprise she merely nodded sadly and muttered something to the effect that there was nothing she or I could do.

She spoke that with an air of despondency but her looks were even worse. I had never seen her so haggard and worn. The hot and fetid atmosphere of Mogadishu—we are now very near the equator—had flattened her hair and her face fairly glistened from the sweat pouring down it. Only Dr. Inge on board has been comparably ravaged by the tropical heat—then she is decidedly overweight and besides, with her constant marching and unceasing chatter, she has surely invited the sea of perspiration which has enveloped her for the past few days.

Ida then told me her son had informed her of his feelings for Charlotte—indeed, had solicited his mother's aid in promoting his attention, as Charley had given him no cause for encouragement. (How different from my own lurid imaginings!) She also said Nick was convinced that Charlotte's tepid response to his overtures arose from her concern over his health. He was therefore asking his mother to talk to the woman who had come into his life and assure her that his illness was not so severe as had been suggested during the altercation in his cabin and that the kind of attack we had all witnessed was considerably more infrequent than in fact it was. In other words, for Ida Brierly to deny all she had said in the heat of anxiety.

As she concluded her startling news an idea occurred to me. It was just possible that my Charlotte was basically unaware of the depth and sincerity of Nick's feelings for her, which his mother emphasized as much as the despondent Paul had done. If that was so, then her usual blithe approach to life might the more easily be misunderstood by her youthful suitor.

When we parted I think I had given Ida at least minimal cause for optimism. I have to believe she's now convinced that Charlotte is still susceptible to persuasion, and that it is just possible my friend was speaking the truth when answering Nick and talking with me—that her response to the boy is totally consistent with her attitude to anyone less fortunate than she. It has led her into misunderstandings in the past but none of those incidents remotely involved romantic feelings such as this *imbroglio* taking place off the African coast.

The matter didn't end with that chance encounter with Ida Brierly—although I am happy to record that the tension between us was resolved then and there.

I wonder how much the weather informs our actions and thoughts—maybe shapes our dispositions, if only temporarily? I do know I feel a different woman since we left the Mediterranean and have pushed farther and farther into these clammy climes. It is not just the heat and change of climate we have experienced but also the actual quality of night and day, the ocherous moon and white sun; the brilliance of stars against a velvet darkness and, recently, the sickly smell of rotting vegetation from an invisible land. It has made me feel far more vulnerable and powerless when it has come to the Charlotte/Paul/Nick triangle. The unremitting heat removes all thought of vanity and reduces life to such basic simplicities as keeping cool, clean and conserving of energy.

Energy is what I need now, to have the frankest talk ever with Charlotte, when I must beg her forgiveness and at the same time try and improve the situation between her and Nick. I must also be there when Paul needs me as I am only too aware of how much I have been responsible for nudging him further into an impossible situation which has only brought him such distress. I shudder to think I might have also threatened his job.

Another problem arises from the seeming *ubiquity* of all of us on board—wrought by the long time at sea and the inhospitable and enervating places at which we have berthed over the past ten days. It is impossible to get away from people unless one stays in the cabin. But an inefficient fan, which does nothing to remedy the stifling atmosphere, makes that an impossibility.

HORRID HEAT! That's exactly what we have right now. I must stop writing and get on deck or I'll die!

CHAPTER TWENTY-EIGHT

Ken and I stood looking over the rail on the ferry's sundeck as we headed westward across Puget Sound toward the snow-capped range of the Olympic Peninsula. The breeze was brisk and ruffled our hair although, paradoxically, the sun was warm on the napes of our necks. Tiny, white clouds, like a child's cut-out creations, sped inland across the otherwise untrammeled blue. The air was so pure it hurt.

"I've just had an odd thought," I said. "I wonder if Mama is somewhere else on the Pacific at this very moment."

Ken shook his head. "More likely the Indian Ocean. Wasn't her last card from Dar-es-Salaam? She was certainly dying to get to Port Elizabeth—I guess the climate was getting to her."

"Mama wouldn't let a little thing like climate get her down. But I agree, she did seem a bit put out. Whatever it was, we'll never know. She doesn't believe in going too deeply into things. Certainly not to her sons. She'll be all bubbles when she gets to Port Elizabeth, though. The brother of Charlotte's father lives there. Very wealthy, very grand. Mama will lap all that up. The Churchfields can do no wrong and Charlotte's uncle and aunt enjoy the same halo in my mother's book."

Ken nudged my elbow resting on the rail. "The way you carry on! You've *invented* Mama, do you know that? You haven't a clue what she's really like any more. She's just some figment of your imagination. Then neither of you ever had much sense of the other. I thought that when I first saw you together. Just as I could see how much alike you both were!"

I was silent. I'd heard Ken on this tack before. It made me feel peculiar. I liked the notion and was disturbed by it at the same time.

There suddenly hove into view a perfect excuse to dodge the issue. Ferris and Lionel, our rail buffs, were taking a constitutional around the deck—bundled up as if they were elderly passengers aboard the *Queen Elizabeth* in mid-Atlantic! Eyeing them as they strove toward us, heads down against the breeze and with the staccato purposiveness of marabou storks, I realized that Lionel, in spite of his youth, already exuded a geriatric whiff. Maybe the slightly desiccated quality of Ferris Conrad had rubbed off on his friend-*cum*-lover. Or perhaps it was something to do with being so tightly wed to the mechanical trappings of an earlier age.

We had to holler to capture their attention. Ferris looked up, came to a halt, offered us an old-fashioned bow—and was about to continue, I suspect, when Ken beckoned them to join us at the ferry's rail. Lionel continued to avoid my eye as he had done on the bus the previous afternoon. I concluded our aborted relationship was to stay that way.

We started to chat in desultory fashion. I asked Ferris about the railroad they were about to ride and then about its history. I had no real interest in his answers—so it was hardly the journalist in me that prompted the questions. I was quite aware I all too readily fell into the role of interviewer with anyone who bored me or whom I wished to thwart as would-be interrogator of me.

I asked the questions and listlessly heard his excessive answers as I listened to a more interesting conversation between my lover and Lionel. The latter was describing the Victorian charm of Port Townsend, across the Sound, which Lionel insisted had escaped the curse of the modern world.

I would have loved to do battle on behalf of our own century but was brusquely interrupted by the appearance of half a dozen or so creatures who, in their silence, size and simplicity, suggested the primitive past when man himself, his towns, let alone his railroad systems, hadn't even begun to happen. A pod of killer whales, or orcas, were threading the lead-gray chop of Puget Sound with their huge black-and-white lengths, not thirty yards from where our stub-nosed ferry frothed the waters.

We oohed and aahed with the rest of the passengers on board and shared an inexplicable sadness when the pod suddenly veered toward the mouth of the Sound and were quickly lost to view. The four of us and a handful of others stood there straining to catch a final glimpse of a dorsal fin or gigantic tail in a dive. I think we were wondering what arcane attraction had sped them away from the orbit of our appreciation; our human hubris remained intact.

Shortly thereafter the two "rail-fans" decided they wished to renew their promenading. Ken opted for a return to *Madame Bovary* and I was left standing there gazing out to sea. The mood of yesterday's sunset still hung about the wings of my consciousness, stimulated afresh, perhaps, by the sight of the family of killer whales. I was still thinking of Mama. I felt uniquely if tentatively connected to her while sailing the ferry. The sea, the glorious sea, however much of it, however far the distances it traversed, was currently a shared property linking mother and son.

Most of the time my inclination was to thrust her impending visit to the far reaches of awareness, but there were limits to such powers of resolution. Especially when so much about this northwest region of the continent stirred memories of what I had left behind in Cornwall, including dear Mama, of course. Not just last evening's crepuscular glories seen from the houseboat or the current sensation of sharing the earth's watery surface with her, but something in me had been sparked by these external factors which simply refused to go away. I wondered if there were whales off the coast of Africa....

I stared down at the eddies and swirls our progress created and—wouldn't you know?—they suddenly composed her face! I felt the atavistic ache of a son for a mother—at once so powerful and yet so demanding of utter secrecy from even a lover.

I moved restlessly toward the bow of the ship, where a group of young people were congregated; laughing, joking and joshing one another. For once I didn't eavesdrop. I was content to have the unspoken company of their physical presence. Perhaps I needed it.

We left the rail-fans shortly after we docked at Victoria and, in addition to expressing courteous hopes for good times ahead, made vague promises of meeting up when back in the Bay Area. Ferris Conrad even handed Ken his visiting card, which my lover, with exaggerated deliberation, passed to me. As my fingers touched its surface I registered that it was duly embossed—the result, I concluded, of an authentic copper printing plate.

After the two of them had gravely pursued porter and baggage in search of times past, I set about looking up Natalie McGregor's address and telephone number. I hadn't spoken to her since I was ten so it was hardly surprising I didn't recognize her voice. She wouldn't have recalled mine either, but she did respond at once to my name with an exclamation of surprised pleasure. When I explained we were in Victoria for just a few hours, she at once asked us to lunch. At least I *think* she said "you both" but I was subsequently less sure. She gave complicated instructions—signifying her belief we would be walking—but we took a cab.

On alighting I noticed a tall, white-haired woman working in the well-cultivated garden of a mock-Tudor house overlooking the Juan de Fuca Straits. I was about to ask her which was number 159 Pacific Drive when it occurred to me I might be looking at Natalie herself.

I was. She offered her apology for not being ready to greet me but she hadn't expected me to arrive so swiftly. Nor did she leave the implication unspoken.

"I didn't know you would be so goddamn extravagant as to take a taxi."

I was not about to argue the point with an elderly friend who had been generous enough to suggest lunch at such short notice. I was more concerned with the fact that, up to that point, she had addressed me exclusively and ignored Ken, who was standing there nodding as if he strenuously agreed with her Scottish sense of economy.

"And this is my friend Ken Bradley, who is with me on this trip I'm doing for the travel pages of the paper."

"Good! Good!" Natalie exclaimed. "And how is your mother? I know your father died some years ago. She wrote and told me that."

"Mama is currently touring the world on a freighter and will eventually come to stay with us in San Francisco. When exactly is it we expect her, Ken?"

"These cargo ships don't operate on tight schedules," Ken replied, "but we hope to have them with us by the end of the year. Hopefully for Christmas."

She gave my lover the longest look before speaking. "They? Them? But Wesley.... Your father...."

"Died," I said patiently. "You read Mama's letter quite correctly. She is traveling with my courtesy aunt, Miss Charlotte Churchfield. They have been boon companions for many years."

"You have quite a literary turn of phrase," Natalie boomed. "If I remember correctly, you get that from your mother. I was impressed by her manner of speaking when I visited—no, don't tell me—it was The *Hornbeams*, wasn't it?"

I had to smile. "Your memory is impressive. After all, your visit was so fleeting. You saw more of me and Mama when you took us to your aunt's Grace & Favor residence at Hampton Court. I will always have you to thank for that. It was one of the most exciting things in my life."

"Frightening, as I recall. You got lost in the maze, remember, and were quite off your little head with fear when we found you."

I distinctly recalled it was Mama—and Mama alone—who found me, but I wasn't disposed to correct her. "I'm sorry we have interrupted your gardening," I said. "I can see you're quite busy snipping off those dead rose-blooms."

That tweaked her. "What on earth am I thinking of—nattering with you out here when I should have invited you indoors right away. Please come in. You too, young man. You really must forgive me, Davey, and remember I'm now a silly old woman. Deaf as a post, too—but I expect you've already realized that."

What I had indeed begun to realize—for it was a progressive unfurling—was the murderous impact of the years on people once familiar, whose images had been permanently congealed in the aspic of separation. The exotic Natalie of my childhood—she of the pungent perfume, bright lipstick and daring eye-pencil—now had an ugly black hair sprouting from her chin and a face that was wrinkled, leathery and pronouncedly unglamorous. I almost swooned thinking of what the intervening years might possibly have done to Mama.... By the time I had convinced myself that the two situations were not all that comparable (I had a relatively recent photo and had seen my mother only ten years earlier), Natalie was addressing Ken for the first time.

"Are you like him or are you married?" she asked.

I jumped right in. "Talking of marriage, where is Mr. McGregor? I'm dying to meet your husband. I remember you writing during the war to tell us you were remarried and that your stepdaughter was in England—in the Wrens."

"God knows! Living off his relatives—if he can find any of 'em still alive—he's not likely to come back here."

Her bitterness put a further bullet into my picture of a sweet-dispositioned aristocrat with a sense of humor and unfailing patience with little boys. Then regardless of what she'd become, I was no longer a little boy....

I recalled something else as I still smarted over her sneer at our marital status. "At least this one didn't turn out a hermit like Commander Lockyer-Pope."

"My first husband? Oh, that's all damned history. Let's leave it in the ashcan. The great news is that I am a grandmother. My stepkid just had her first child. They live outside Seattle so I get to see them fairly often. What more can an old woman ask?

"Time you were doing something for your own Mom, Davey. Got to find the right gal first, eh? That the delay? Don't forget we females live by a time clock. The old womb can't wait forever."

"No one need bother to wait for me, Natalie. I have no intention of getting married—nor have I the slightest desire to sire offspring!"

She was unabashed. "Sounds damn peculiar. Unused goods and that. Then I guess you've got your reasons."

Only she didn't sound as if she really thought they *were* reasons.

Ken stepped in. "I guess it takes all sorts. And I'm sure it would be wrong to marry just for the sake of it. My parents always insisted on leveling with each other and us kids. That's the way they were themselves—and they had a marvelous relationship."

If he thought that would pacify her and the inference his parents were deceased would give her pause, he was mistaken. I don't know whether something was bugging her or whether she had an instinctive antipathy to gays, but she wasn't about to seek fresh conversational pastures.

"Do you always back him up? Don't you have some different opinions?"

"Many," my lover told her calmly. "They haven't had time to surface. I'm sure you and I would agree on a number of things, Mrs. McGregor."

All this time she had been preparing cups of powdered coffee, and she now poured from a boiling kettle as we sat around a table in a room crammed with family photographs and memorabilia—presumably from various places and times in Natalie's life since her days in Highland Scotland. An old lady's room, I coldly decided. I also had the impression by this time that her circumstances were a good deal less flush than what they had been when she was Daddy's mistress. It wasn't often I was up to calling a spade a spade in *that* quarter—but Natalie had rarely crossed my mind until this trip had been proposed, and with my father's death I had mentally interred his past peccadilloes with him.

I still tried to be on good behavior. For Ken's sake rather than hers. "You have a beautiful view from here. We haven't seen too much of Victoria but what we have seems very attractive. I love the suspended flower baskets. Very English!"

In truth my instant reaction had been quite derisory. I thought the place ludicrous. A phony combination of immigrant recollection and North American marketing methods. It had been my first negative response since arriving in the Pacific Northwest.

"You'll find it very different from San Francisco. No bachelor boys wandering around here!"

"How extraordinary! You mean everyone is married? Is it difficult for you, Mrs. McGregor, as a divorcée or separatee—whatever the term is? I know there's still prejudice in *royal* circles, but I am amazed to think it extends this far."

I looked at Ken in astonishment. I never thought him capable of such arch sarcasm.

"It was just the *fellows* I was referring to. Most of our apples, cherries and grapes grow in a valley in the interior of British Columbia called the Okanagan—we like to think all our fruits are up there."

That was open warfare. I stood up. "Come on, Ken, it's time to leave. I can do without all that crap. Coming to Canada hasn't helped you to be tolerant. Nor, apparently, have the years!"

It was Natalie McGregor's turn to look perplexed. "But you're here for lunch. It isn't the greatest but it's the best I can do."

We looked at one another, unfathoming. There was a distinct wheedle to her voice. I could have sworn she was entreating us to stay. Again it was Ken who seized the initiative.

"I don't know whether you really meant to be so insulting. But I think we all three know what you mean when you refer to *fruits*. If we were Jewish we'd hardly feel welcome if you referred to us as *kikes*."

"I live alone. I don't see people much. I'm sorry if my tongue ran away with me. You're right—I had no right to jump to conclusions. God knows there are a thousand and one reasons people are single."

I wasn't going to let her get away as easily as that. For auld lang syne's sake, if nothing else, I would remind her that the present Davey—like the one she'd known in short pants—was disposed to frankness. I spoke loudly and it wasn't entirely to facilitate her hearing.

"We're single for only one reason, Natalie. We *are* your standard fruits. The English language in the hands of bigots is quite generous in its terms to describe us. Take your pick from *fruit*, *pansy*, *faggot*, *queer*, *poof*, *fairy*, *homo*, *nancy*—and if you want a little recondite Royal Navy terminology, I can offer *brownhatter*, *wings*, *ops*, *bash* and *ass-bandit*. The word we prefer is none of them. It's *gay*."

Natalie lowered her head. "Stop it," she said quietly. "Sit down. I'm sorry."

I did as she bid. Her tone now precluded argument, let alone hostility. "I should have told you right at the start. As soon as I talked to you on the phone and you mentioned your friend I had my suspicions, and then when you arrived I knew right away."

Ken smiled wanly. "I didn't know we were so obvious."

The new Natalie pursed her lips. "It isn't that. My husband, you see. He was like that too. He didn't leave over some woman, as I have told everyone including his daughter." She sighed from some wrenching depth. "Nor was it just for a man. Here, let me get that food on the table or we'll never eat."

Suiting action to word, she retrieved a pile of plates, followed by a handful of cutlery. She looked from me to Ken before asking one of us to lay places while she moved into the kitchen, after asking us whether we liked tomato soup and Spam slices with salad.

She offered little bursts of information every time she put in an appearance.

"It was kids. Boys. He was scoutmaster at St. Margaret's. He was always inviting them back here. The house was overrun with them. Adolescents...teenagers. Some of them were no more than fourteen or fifteen. I must have been blind!

"The penny didn't drop for years. Then I swear at first it was more or less innocent. At least nothing happened in *this* house. I'd swear to that on a stack of Bibles. Would you believe me when I say it was years before I began to suspect? It was all right between us, you see. Nothing even slightly unusual there.

"Then one Thanksgiving—that's in October up here north of the border—John was supposed to be chopping wood for that fireplace. It wasn't all that cold but I thought it'd be nice. Cosy around the hearth—that kind of thing? Well, it came dinner time and no John. My stepdaughter, Kim, and her husband from Seattle were here. I was about to ask Rick to go down to the woodshed and tell his father-in-law and a kid named Stephen, whom John had invited as his parents had recently been killed in an auto accident. At the last moment I decided to go myself. I still breathe a sigh of relief I went and not Rick. Neither Rick nor Kim knows to this day what I saw through that grimy little window."

Ken stared at his waiting soup plate. "You don't have to tell us."

"I want to. I must. He was *fondling* the kid. I crept away. Hollered his name about twenty yards. Just said dinner was on the table and he was to get the hell up to the house. Don't ask me how but I said nothing till Thanksgiving dinner was over. Not until Kim and Rick had left for the ferry, the kid gone back to his aunt's and I was alone with John in the bedroom that night."

By now we were eating. "That must've been tough," I said, spooning my soup.

"He just denied it. Said I was out of my mind. Seeing things. He never did admit it to me. But when I said I was prepared to ask Stephen what had happened out there, he begged me not to. I ordered him out of the house and he made no fuss. If I said nothing to Stephen, he said, he'd be gone the next day. That was what happened."

"Ugly," Ken commented.

"You know, Natalie, of all that shopping list of names I gave you—none of them really covers what you're talking about. Your late husband's problem."

"They call them 'chicken hawks,'" Ken added. "And we're no more like that than you are."

"After he'd gone—oh, a month or more later—the RCMP came by, making inquiries. Nothing very specific, mind. Just wanted to chat with him. I told them he had left his sister's address in Toronto for forwarding. I hadn't had a peep out of him since he walked out that door."

There was enough silence around the table to make the noise of our cutting and munching obtrusive. Natalie broke it. "Of course that's all in the past. I'm talking years ago."

"I wonder what happened to him?" I finally ventured. "He may be in jail. On the other hand, people are so unsuspecting over that kind of thing. God knows, he may have ended up a social worker with juvenile delinquents."

For the first time since before the lunch, Natalie smiled faintly. "In which case he's been long retired. He was a good deal older than me."

"I'm sorry we should have dragged all that up for you," Ken said. "Believe me, I've no patience with that kind of exploiting innocence."

"Innocence can be relative, though," I said. "Not all teenagers are sweet little darlings. They can be seducers too."

"I don't care," Ken persisted. "The human race has a right to protect its young. If pedophiles shouldn't be imprisoned, at least they should have obligatory help and be kept from temptation as far as possible."

Natalie's expression suggested she was far away from all that. Her words confirmed it. "I wasn't shocked by what he did. I didn't even feel particular sympathy for Stephen—though I guess I should've. It was his deception over all those years that got me. If he had told me what was going on with all those boys—what they meant to him. And there might even have been some real kind of love. God knows, he certainly put himself out for lots of them.

"Anyway, none of that really mattered. My life was shattered, my trust in anyone all gone. Deep down I've nursed this hate for perverted...for all that kind of mental sickness.

"There! I've told the two of you more than I've ever told anyone else. I only regret the way it came up. But I've said sorry. I hope you've forgiven me."

It was Ken who reached out and squeezed her hand.

We had to leave for Nanaimo soon after that, and the mood of thoughtfulness that characterized the end of the meal and our goodbyes persisted during the taxi journey to the bus depot. Then child-molesting wasn't exactly the kind of subject one wanted to air in front of a cab driver.... We didn't really recover our ease until the bus had taken us through the mountains and brought us to our second ferry for the day. It was to take us to Vancouver.

This time we were sailing eastward from Nanaimo, a scruffy little port on the east coast of Vancouver Island, toward a city which, somewhat confusingly, also bore the name Vancouver. I vaguely recalled learning at school a poem by John Masefield that referred to Vancouver in one of its verses. Apart from that I knew nothing until I picked up a brochure on the ferry for my eventual *Trib* article, which informed me that British Columbia consisted of two former British colonies and that Vancouver was a busy grain port and contained the biggest Chinatown in the Western Hemisphere after San Francisco. I liked that reference. My feelings for San Francisco were ambivalent at best but at least I possessed them. The port to which we were headed meant nothing to me and, what's more, now suggested a mild threat: a sense of unease.

The experience at Natalie's had started the misgivings ticking. Her belligerent behavior and later revelation had been alarming, all right, but it isn't only that to which I refer. It was rather Victoria's superficial trappings: the plethora of Union Jacks, the Walt Disney version of British parliamentary buildings, the boutiques with windows stuffed with bales of Scottish tweed and English china, the double-decker bus I glimpsed and the constant references to Olde Englande and the like on the ubiquitous travel brochures and posters.

Not that I was expecting Vancouver to be some kind of exaggerated Victoria. But of course they *were* in the same province and country. And we were scheduled to dock in a city the map of which showed schools called Prince of Wales or named after such imperial war heroes as lords Byng and Kitchener; theater complexes under the banner of Her Majesty Queen Elizabeth; streets and highways named after Nelson and King George—and finally, charter banks incorporating both "royal" and "imperial" in their titles. I had never felt part of a world which spoke of "The Mother Country" and sang "God Save the Queen." I was wholly unfamiliar with remote places with obscure initials like B.C.—and which shared the traditions that I had personally fled when leaving for California with Ken. I hadn't given it much thought but I was far from sure what my reactions would be when I set foot on the Dominion of Canada's mainland.

Then something happened which over the years has become a familiar pattern. My mind was bumped from vague political and cultural considerations to an emphatic response to an exhilarating spirit of place. As we sailed past islands wooded with arbutus or madrone, the snowcapped peaks of the Coastal Range towered in their white immensity ahead of us, and the urban spread of Vancouver hove into view.

There was no imperial nomenclature discernible from that distance. Only a huddle of highrises in the downtown area looking cowed by their mountainous backdrop. The restless sea perforated the mouth of the city—as snaking creeks and narrow waterways recalling Venice. We passed under a tall and graceful bridge and thus into a giant marine basin that separated mounds of sulfur and grain elevators and their ancillary docks and railway yards—all at the foot of the North Shore mountains—by a broad stretch of busy bay from the hotels and halls of commerce constituting the city's downtown core. As I breathed it all in I felt a deepening response. I touched Ken's arm and he turned and smiled. I knew he was experiencing similar sensations.

We had just booked into the Grosvenor Hotel when it began to rain. My mood took a nose dive. It rained for two nights and two and a half days and we did not see the mountains again until shortly before we boarded our tour bus for Seattle. We had arrived in Vancouver on a Saturday and on the next day I discovered that the dismal British Sunday of my youth was alive and well in this moist outpost of Empire. Indeed, it had thrived and swelled its puritan proportions. Not only were all bars shut tightly down but stores were closed and every movie theater darkened.

I sat morosely on an uncomfortable chair by the radiator while Ken sprawled on the bed reading his bloody *Madame Bovary*. As the fierce rain hissed and spat at the window I thumbed disconsolately through the pages of the Vancouver telephone directory.

"Who you looking up?"

"No one. We don't know anyone in this fucking place."

"What you looking for then?"

"Read your goddamn book." I relented. "I'm just noticing all the Camerons and Campbells. My God! There are pages and pages of them! I'm surprised they didn't serve haggis for breakfast. This city is obviously jam-packed with Scots. Is it just here, or is all Canada—*Ecosse Outre-Mer?*"

"You tell me, sweetheart. It's *your* history, not mine. I can give you every state capital and the principal battles of the Civil War."

"Here's something after the Camerons that looks interesting."

"The Cunts?"

I ignored his ribaldry. "I refer to the Canadian Broadcasting Corporation."

There were several numbers given, including one for Public Relations/Radio. I had an idea.

"What time do we take the bus back tomorrow?"

"Late afternoon. Why?"

"I want to call these people and perhaps go see them in the morning."

"Why?"

"For part of my *Trib* article, of course. I can say how much like the BBC it is—or how different, for that matter."

The next morning found us tramping through the sluicing rain to the stolid pile of masonry known as the Hotel Vancouver, where the CBC Radio facilities were housed. Usually on such expeditions it was Ken who did the talking, but a mark of his reluctance to be part of this one was his insistence I take that role.

We were ushered up to the seventh floor, where I asked at the counter if I could speak with someone who could tell me all about the operation, particularly in the area of talks and documentaries—these being the productions to which I felt particularly indebted to the BBC in my youth. The rather fey young man in horn-rimmed spectacles who smilingly responded to my enquiry exuded a discreetly gay flavor. Less discretion was evinced when another beautifully attired type falsetto'd the information that there was a long article on CBC Radio in that morning's newspaper and that he was cutting it out for their records. A third young man swished between the two of them, declaring he was late for the "Coming Up in the Legislature" production meeting because his hair was a mess and someone had stolen his brush from his desk drawer. I had yet to sight a woman.

"Looks like we've come to the right place," I murmured to Ken at my side.

Before he could retort, a further figure appeared before us. He thanked "Spectacles" for calling him and then beamed through his own glasses at the two of us.

"Hi, I'm Pat Roberts and I'm in charge of Public Affairs. That's our equivalent of your Talks Department. I gather you're both from the BBC? Just visiting or on assignment?"

I immediately felt embarrassed. "Neither actually. Just inquisitive. I'm sorry if I've dragged you away from something important." I explained the whole business, beginning with the newspaper junket and ending with leafing through the pages of the phone book at the Grosvenor. I also added truthfully that broadcasting fascinated me and that I had been doing some book reviewing for a radio station in Berkeley. This seemed to intrigue him and without more ado he invited us through to his office, where we might chat more relaxedly.

How to describe the events that ensued? If there is such a thing as a platonic love affair between three people, it was sparked that Monday morning. After vague generalities, Ken's position as a French lecturer at Stanford was revealed, and from there on the talk centered on books and literature. It transpired that Pat was writing the Great Canadian Novel, but we primarily discussed U.S. literature, with Ken doing me proud with his refreshing erudition outside his prescribed field. We were still heatedly giving our views on such as Paul Bowles, J.D. Salinger and my idol, Wallace Stegner, when Pat looked at his watch and asked us whether we would care to join him for lunch at the Arctic Club.

The morning had flown, as they say, and it didn't even occur to me that Mr. Roberts hadn't been interrupted once by his secretary, who sat just outside his office door. He introduced us to her—a soft-spoken Nova Scotian (from a Gaelic-speaking family, Pat informed us) with a sharp little face perched on a plump little body. She addressed him as Brother Pat and informed us that, on seeing how much we were all enjoying each other, she had fielded all calls, informing Pat he could deal with those requiring a decision later that afternoon.

As we descended in a crowded elevator I thought what a civilized institution the Canadian Broadcasting Corporation had proved to be. After we had concluded an excellent meal which served as a refutation of my erstwhile charges of provincialism, we made for the street again.

It had stopped raining. The skies had been washed clean of cloud and the towering peaks of the North Shore were once more vividly in evidence. We were all laughing and shared a mysterious ease as if old friends.

On the steaming sidewalk he took out his visiting card and handed it to us. I thought fleetingly of Ferris Conrad and his superiorly embossed card. I had a hunch that this current exchange would have far more profound implications than what had transpired in Victoria.

CHAPTER TWENTY-NINE

Madagascar: July 30th, 1960

Even Captain Schaepmann is refusing to say when we will reach Durban—let alone Port Elizabeth. Trouble is, there are all these places I'd never heard of that suddenly appeared on our itinerary. We've done Pemba, Mozambique and Beira, after simply ages docked in Dar-es-Salaam and, during last night, apparently turned eastward from the coast for a surprise visit to a small place called Faradofay at the southern tip of Madagascar.

After being kept on board so many times, Charlotte and I are determined to get ashore this time. The poor girl needs a chance to get away from Nick, who is still finding it difficult to take no for an answer. On the other hand I have to admit that things do seem to have died down—with the exception of Paul, who contrives to keep away from Nick as much as his tasks permit, but who compensates by pouring out his frustrations on me! Unlike my Charley—who locks up so much in her heart, smiles bravely at the world and quietly insists Ida Brierly join in deck quoits whenever her son seeks to play with her.

Thank goodness the conversation—and that means whispers and innuendoes on this vessel—has shifted focus. Frank Wilkinson is convinced we are involved with gunrunning in these flyblown ports we've been visiting and suggests the captain is pocketing the profits. Thelma Wilkinson thinks we are bringing supplies to Communist rebels who have fled South Africa—this from a woman who insists on confusing Madagascar with Mozambique! Then her ignorance feeds her dreadful husband's pedantry and bossiness.

That leaves our mysterious Frau Doktor—Inge Wetzler. Considering she talks all the time it's surprising how little she reveals of herself. She told me she was a psychiatrist but informed Ida she was a psychologist. That could be a faulty grasp of the English language, but she is so fluent, even if guttural, I can hardly believe she'd make mistakes over words so basic to her profession.

I know Frank Wilkinson would love to put it about that the woman is a Nazi war criminal, intent on concealing her appalling past as a concentration camp doctor. But even our retired headmaster has to admit she is at least twenty years too young for the role. Besides, I wouldn't be at all surprised if she was Jewish. When I mentioned my second son's name was Davey she immediately assumed I'd said David—and informed me it meant "beloved" in Hebrew. We'll probably never know all her secrets. And come to that, why should we?

Although the high drama has receded (no more tantrums, weeping revelations and bitter recrimination), I still have the impression things are only temporarily quiet—probably held there by the tropical heat and the sense among us that the way we were going could only lead to even more tension and culminate in God knows what kind of human wreckage.

AND WE PAID GOOD MONEY FOR THIS "VOYAGE OF A LIFETIME!"

As it is, I cannot wait to get to Madagascar and join Charlotte in a quest to see some of the lemurs that live exclusively on that island. I found a moth-eaten volume on Madagascar and discovered it has one of the most interesting fauna in the world—and unique at that.

When I started to jot down from its pages the information that the name derives from a Greek word meaning "devouring monster" and that, although related to the monkeys, lemurs belong to their own family of *Lemuridae*, I couldn't help but think of Davey as a little boy and his passion for such classifications. He got that from me, of course. That is to say, he inherited it from the young woman in a lab coat who so proudly oversaw her laboratory with its white rats—down there by the London docks, so grotesquely many years ago.

I also note the island is plagued with malaria, which literally means "bad air." Fortunately both Charley and I took all the requisite injections in London. I will write again when I have had firm land once more under my feet!

Berthed at Faradofay: August 5th, 1960

I had forgotten the date and Charley (who has her little pocket diary which would have told me) has gone with Paul to the sick bay to get me something for my headache, which I fear is presaging a cold of all things. How ridiculous! I mean, a *cold* in this oppressive heat, and almost complete lack of air!

Well, we have seen the jungle, the dripping leaves, the curious gloom, and heard the endless shriek of invisible birds. But the great thrill was indeed the lemurs, though we only glimpsed those as they fled from leafy branch to leafy branch high above our craning necks. Where we really had a chance to inspect them was in the market of Faradofay, where the poor little things—dispirited bundles of soiled fur—were awaiting their fates. Paul said they were destined for zoos but I suspect my young romantic's wishful thinking and am afraid many will end up in the natives' stewpots.

In any case, when I plied him with questions about the local wildlife and Charley wanted to know what treatment existed for the dreadful gaping sores we observed on the bodies of so many of the people, his replies were quite desultory. I knew his mind was back on board the *Ijmuiden* where he had left Nick, who claimed he was feeling too frail to tackle the heat and noise of that benighted little port. At the time I think I felt Nick might have just made the effort to accept Paul's invitation—especially as our young steward was only going to show him the local bazaar in a taxi and get him safely back aboard within the hour.

But lying here now I am inclined to sympathize with Nick's reluctance. My head aches abominably and I have the sensation my insides have dissolved into liquid. It is becoming an effort to prop these covers up and I wish they'd come back soon. My sheets are all wet again and Charlotte is the greatest puffer-up of pillows in all the world. I wish...I wish...I must stop writing so I can wish what wish...wish.... Sleepy....

Antananarivo, Madagascar: September 21st, 1960

I am starting a fresh page as virtually seven weeks of my life have just disappeared! This is the first time I have been allowed to take a pencil to this book, which has been locked (with its key in my handbag) since I got sick. I still don't feel too well and I have an idea this entry isn't going to be very long. My handwriting has become so dreadfully scrawly I fear I won't be able to decipher it in an hour or so. And if *I* can't—no one will!

I spent some minutes yesterday afternoon—or was it the morning?—reading past passages. I wonder how I ever found the nerve to state things so frankly! It all seems so remote. I have been off the *Ijmuiden* for so long that people like the Wilkinsons and the two Brierlys are like ghosts. I know Paul journeyed up here to see me but I have no idea if that was recently or at the beginning.

Dear Charlotte was here half an hour ago and will soon be back. I have so many questions for her! And my mind is so ragged and fitful in recollection. Let me try and see what I know.

I got ill on the Ijmuiden: *That was* ? (I shall fill in dates later)
I am at the World Health Organization Malaria Center
My friend Charlotte is staying near me
Dr. McMasters says I will be here for some time as there are so many tests and I am under "intensive observation"
Dr. McMasters is American and knows Davey! How well?
Will we catch up with the ship farther along its route as Charlotte believes?

If I continue to ask questions here I will never stop! In any case, I am already feeling washed out. That's the worst of all this. The total lack of energy, something foreign to me.

Later: (i.e. six p.m. and already pitch dark!)

I now know the date, including the year, month, week, day and hour! I have Charlotte's traveling clock by my bedside and she has given me her precious little pocket diary from Lett's—the one with a nice blue leather cover—so that I can distinguish between the indistinguishable days!

Name of My Form of Malaria: anophelitus? (Not sure I heard Dr. McMasters aright.)
Attempt to Recall Conversation with Dr. McMasters:
"It took me a good two days after you'd been admitted, Mrs. Bryant, before I wondered whether you could possibly be related to Davey. Then it all tumbled into place. I guess that would have happened twenty-four hours earlier if we weren't living here in Antananarivo. This town turns us all into zombies!"

"I hope not you, doctor—for my sake!"

"Sorry! How are we feeling?"

"Are we going to be friends?"

"My goodness, yes! I hope so."

"Then you'll have to promise me something. *Never* call me 'we' because I am lying in a hospital bed. Call me 'she,' the cat's mother, rather than that!"

"Sorry again! That medical cliché is now banned from my lips forever! So now how are *you*?"

"Better than I was but not as well as I might be."

"Headaches still there?"

"Why do you always harp on them when it is my bones which have ached so, and my flesh virtually melted away in a sea of perspiration."

"I can see what you mean by better than you felt before. I ask about your headaches because you have had a form of malaria with specifically cerebral implications."

"You expect me to go mad?"

"You give no indication so far! But this is going to be a long-drawn-out business. It will need lots of patience from both of us, I'm afraid."

"The odds are against me. It should be my friend Charlotte lying here. She has enough patience for both of us."

"Miss Churchfield is incredible. She has been at your side all these weeks. I envy you such a person. Most patients here are very much alone. Even husbands or wives don't always prove up to the strain of endlessly watching and waiting."

"Are you married, Dr. McMasters?"

As he stared down at me he reminded me vaguely of Paul on the ship. Only it wasn't physical. Nor was his answer anything like Paul might have said. Then this Keith is an American doctor, speaking his own idiom. The two may be of approximately the same age—but this chap has saved my life. Not only Charlotte but the nurses all testify to that.

"No. Like Davey...." There was a fractional pause. "I'm a bachelor too."

Again I thought of Paul. He has taught me so much!

"How *much* like my son? Do you have a friend like Ken?"

As I lay there feebly on the pillow, feeling the opposite of strong or resolute, I realized it was the first time I'd mentioned my son's friend by Christian name to a stranger. To anyone in fact save Charley, who herself insists on including his name whenever she mentions Davey!

"Less. I have no specific companion. Nor is Antananarivo the kind of place to change matters for me."

"Buried in your work? Or merely avoiding things?"

I caught the slight frown before he dismissed it.

"Has your diarrhea cleared up?"

Our eyes met in contest. We both broke out laughing.

"Why don't you call me Keith?" he said. "After all, you are Davey's Mom—though all their friends refer to you as Mama, as Davey always does."

That intrigued me. "He talks a lot of me then? I would've thought I was half-forgotten—considering how few are his letters and infrequent his visits."

He would have nothing of my self-pity—born, I'm sure, of my wan state.

"Shame on you for searching for compliments! Davey adores you. Maybe he's a little scared, too. He's certainly anxious over whether you and Miss Churchfield will find their hospitality up to scratch. He can be quite obsessive on the subject!"

"My son could always be obsessive. On one memorable occasion it was over mongeese. At school it was everything *French*—acting in French plays, attending French films, reading French novels. He even went about speaking with a French accent!

"There was also his Anglo-Catholicism. From his first year as an altar boy when six or seven, he filled the house with crucifixes and little statues of the Madonna and the saints. It drove his father mad!" As I used that last word my list of Davey's youthful enthusiasms gave out. "You said 'obsessive,' didn't you? Isn't that a form of instability?"

He immediately caught my train of thought. "I'm not a psychiatrist but I would've said Davey was as sane as most people. And what we are monitoring with your malaria has nothing to do with genetic inheritance—even less your son's quite natural desire to see his mother has a good time when she visits him."

He paused—but not long enough for me to interject. (I was still much exercised by this brain business.)

"It's the first time, isn't it?"

"That I've visited my son since he went to live halfway around the world?"

"That you'll be enjoying his hospitality. Sharing their social life. Meeting all their friends."

"They have a great many?"

"Lots."

I capitulated. "I've never pictured Davey in that way. That can make a mother quite nervous, you know. We're as vulnerable as our offspring. And if I'm going to arrive in a slightly dotty state from this ridiculous illness—"

"There is nothing ridiculous about what you've got. I can't say that too often. You may feel a little better but you are not yet recovered. You have had a grave bout of malaria and there are still potential complications. Please believe me—there is absolutely nothing funny about it!"

I sank a little lower under the bedsheets. "I know personally it isn't funny. But you don't want me to be frightened of it, do you? I'm convinced it is only because I want so much to live that I can beat it and things will eventually be all right. That and what miraculous things *you've* done, of course."

Keith took my wrist almost mechanically. Looked at his watch. "Without that will to fight on your part I couldn't have done much. Sure, a little biochemistry, the fact I'm fresh from the tropical disease center and recognized pretty quickly what strain of malaria was attacking you. But to be honest, there were at least a couple of times when your life was in danger.

"I do believe those crises are now over. The worst thing about malaria, though, is its complications—which can be so unpleasant. In theory you should have already recorded some symptoms of cerebral disturbance—which we'd have picked up on the scan, however mild.

"You've been very lucky. And if anyone ever tells you there is no luck in medicine, tell 'em to go jump off the dock! You have registered no abnormal activity in the brain. Come to that, you didn't even exhibit the regular malarial cycle in its early stages. Both these factors give grounds for guarded optimism. We shall only know as day follows day—over a sustained period of time."

"How long?"

He shook his head. "Ask me in a week and I may know more. If I were you I'd write to Davey and, without scaring the living daylights out of him, tell him we aren't sure yet when he may be seeing you. I will write, of course. But I think it best if he hears from you before your doctor. More reassuring."

I think I was asleep before he had finished and I may have made the last bit up!

October 5th, 1960

Another great chunk of time disappeared!!! Things don't seem to have gone quite as Dr. Keith and I planned. I woke this afternoon with Charlotte asking me whether I'd like a cup of tea and me explaining that I had only just had one. The odd look on her face made me look at once at her traveling clock but that didn't help.

With difficulty, for I was feeling extraordinarily weak, I reached over for the little blue diary. Before I looked at her again and asked the date, prior to turning the pale blue pages the requisite nine times, my heart sank to dismal depths. I felt like crying but with Charlotte there, of course, could not do that.

It wasn't until I had assured her I felt much better (I did), and she had gone reluctantly off to try and call her uncle and aunt in Port Elizabeth to tell them I had surfaced again, that Keith came into my room. Now the stupid tears did flow. Odd that I could weep before this young male doctor and not before my dearest and oldest friend. Then I suppose I am an odd woman. Correction! An odd *older* woman, getting odder and older as the blue pages of Charley's calendar turn and turn.

I couldn't raise a smile from my serious young physician however much I tried. "Mrs. Bryant. I'm worried. You have had a severe relapse which has included pulmonary damage with the return of the fever. Your red blood cell count is also in extremely poor condition."

"Am I any madder?"

"The severe delirium and memory loss you have again suffered is quite in accordance with the fever. I am not prepared to say that the sporozoan parasites have caused permanent damage. In fact I have some possibly good news in that quarter. While you were flitting in and out of consciousness I got in touch with a colleague in Mauritius who also specializes in the particular form of anopheline mosquito bite which you suffered. This colleague has had remarkable results with—well, let's just call it medication—that would be precisely in the area of my concern. I have since been in regular contact with him and the medication is on its way by air at this very moment. In a very short time we should have quite precise results. This may sound like locking the barn after the horse has bolted, but I am inclined to think you will not have a recurrence of this third bout—at least neither in severity nor in duration. As a matter of fact your blood count is up. You are a very resilient woman—do you know that?"

"I have such uncertainty. I'm no longer sure whether I may disappear for another week, month or year! Worse, I have no way of gauging if my mind is disintegrating at the same time."

It was so true. As I lie here—whether making entries in this journal or not—I have only one thing on my mind. I can only think until my head is sore whether insanity is creeping up on me.

In the end I could stand it no longer. I decided it was not worth asking Keith as he had never known me on my feet. There was only one person in probably a thousand miles who could answer my questions. The next time I opened my eyes to find Charlotte patiently sitting at my bedside, a ready smile in place for my encouragement, I begged her to hear me out and not seek to avoid serious discussion.

I spoke very carefully. "I don't know how much Keith has told you, my dear, but there is the chance this kind of malaria could permanently affect my brain."

"We have spoken a great deal, Isabella. There were long stretches when we both sat here watching you and talking at the same time. He is a marvelous doctor, dear. We are so fortunate to have him. I believe he saved your life not once but several times!"

"So you have many times told me, Charlotte. And I am grateful. But it is of my rationality I wish to speak now. You are the only person in the world who can reassure me. Please concentrate on what I say."

The words were hardly out of my mouth before the dear woman was on her feet again. "If there is anything I can get, you have only to tell me. What is it you need, Isabella? I'll have it in a jiffy!"

Beloved Charlotte has always been more Martha than Mary: all her instincts are to translate love into actions and deeds.

"I just want you to sit down again and *think*. To take your mind back over all our time together—and then to think of me since I've been in this place, lying here in this beastly bed. Now listen very carefully. In what way have my words or actions differed from the past, from back on the freighter, back in Cornwall, back at any time since we first met? *Can you think of any departures in my behavior from then to now?*"

Charlotte thought. "Well, darling, you have been very quiet. Then you haven't been conscious for much of the time."

I was disappointed. "Is that all?"

"Not exactly. You've been delirious, too. So you've been saying a lot of strange things. Things I've never heard you speak of in the past."

It wasn't what I was seeking but I was intrigued all the same. "What kind of things, Charlotte?"

"Well, most of it was all mixed up. A lot to do with Thelma Wilkinson on the *Ijmuiden*. You seemed so terribly sorry for her. Kept saying, 'poor woman, poor woman.' Then during this last spell you kept mentioning Davey and Ken. You...you...."

"What did I say, Charley?"

"It was almost as if you were quarreling. Only you said nothing really angry to either of them. It was more like—oh, dear! I am really not good at this! It was more of a self-defense. I had the impression you were trying to clear the air—although I can't think of what. I'm sorry, that's about it."

I hadn't the heart to interrogate her further. I invented a need for a packet of envelopes as sooner or later I would have to write those we had intended to meet on our now aborted voyage. But I wasn't up to any writing of people, preferring to confine my restricted energies to these specific pages.

She went and I did what I do most of the time: lie here striving to find any clue which might suggest my sanity is being threatened. At least, I did until Keith got my new medicine. I haven't a shred of proof but I am beginning to believe the stuff is working. Even before it came I told him I was feeling stronger, but I stopped delivering these "I'm-feeling-better-and-better" bulletins when these bossy nurses started to try and get me out of bed before I felt ready for such a step.

Yesterday I had my first altercation with Nurse Rashid when I had to point out that I had been in bed for nearly nine weeks and that I couldn't start prancing and leaping about as if nothing had happened. Perhaps I shouldn't have called her an unfeeling hussy. She reported that to the senior nurse, who further chided me for attacking that chit of a girl—what a nerve!

I will only get up when Keith suggests I try. And only when he offers to assist me about my room. It will be rather like a small child embarking on its initial steps. Then that is what I feel this malaria has done to me. It has robbed me of a lot of confidence. Sometimes I lie here feeling like a child. I laugh out loud at my wicked thoughts and swear I will never tell Charley. Perhaps this is the mental loss that Keith hinted at.

No! I don't believe that. I have conquered the malaria. I will never suffer the delirium and memory lapse again. I shall stay sane. I *am* getting better!!!

CHAPTER THIRTY

On a bleakly foggy day in October we received two letters. One was from Pat Roberts in Vancouver asking whether we could find a volume of poems by Ferlinghetti at City Lights Books in North Beach. I left that to Ken, whom I preferred to let handle these things and who was, in any case, far more proficient at them. The other bore an African stamp. I assumed it was from Mama and I sought a chair where I could sit and relax before embarking on it.

It wasn't from Mama. It was from Keith McMasters in Madagascar—though it was evident from the first paragraph that his missive should have chronologically followed one from her.... "You will have now heard, etc." But that all lost significance when my racing eyes sped farther along the typed lines.

> While I am not for one moment saying your mother's life is at risk, there are certain complications from this kind of malaria of which you should be aware.... I stress this business of repetition because I have the strong impression your Mom will not!.... You know me, Davey. I am certainly no worrywart and would be the last person to cause you needless anxiety.... As if it weren't coincidence enough she should be brought up to Antananarivo and our clinic, from the south end of the island (where she had gone ashore and presumably been bitten by the mosquito), she has come down with precisely the malarial strain which is my specialty.... I have a colleague over in Mauritius and we have been in almost daily contact over the problem of potential cerebral damage.... Dr. Bruckner has been at this business for much longer than me and has come up with an antidote in medication in recent months on which we hope to start your mother.... Bruckner thinks she has already licked the initial problems of chills, fever attacks and blood irregularities which

characterize the disease. Frankly, Davey, this in itself is unusual in a person of her age. Then I hardly need to tell you what an extraordinary person your Mama is. She is as tough physically as mentally and these factors have meant far more than all the medication Bruckner and I could ever dream up.... I must mention the crucial presence of your Aunt Charlotte. So much of this kind of illness is affected by the patient's attitude and although, as I say, your Mama is an incredibly resolute woman, it was the knowledge Charlotte would be there every time she opened her eyes that determined the outcome to date. Love is indeed a powerful thing....

I gather there was no specific date you were expecting them because of freighter irregularity. I'm afraid I can't be too helpful in that quarter. I certainly don't want her moved from here in the immediate future. She is undergoing *intensive* monitoring, and as she absolutely refuses any idea of returning to England, I suggest she subsequently *fly* to you. That, of course, is most complicated from here. In any case, it would totally depend on the rate of her improvement and her eventual stamina. There is talk of convalescence in South Africa.... So don't worry unduly. What with her Charlotte and an excellent nursing staff here, she is in good hands. Rest assured, I will keep you posted.... Blessings to you both, and Davey, she's a great little lady and we've become good friends.

When Ken got home I was on my third gin and tonic. Wordlessly I handed him Keith's letter and waited for his precious verdict.

"Do you think he's being deliberately optimistic?" I asked impatiently.

"No. Why should he? He obviously thinks you've already had her letter. Probably one from Charlotte is on its way too. It's just the chancy mails from those out-of-the-way places."

I sagged with relief on the love seat. "What an incredible thing it should be Keith."

Ken went carefully over the letter for a second time. "You know my ideas on synchronicity. Nothing surprises me in *that* department. But it is nice, even so, to have it all in the family. Anyway, Keith is a darn good doctor and the most conscientious human being I know."

"Old Charlotte seems to have come out tops, too," I observed.

Ken nodded, his mouth now full of hors d'oeuvres. "As Keith says, 'Love is powerful.' It must've been something to watch. Keith isn't one to use that kind of lingo unless he was impressed out of his skin."

"Perhaps it's the tropics. To get that close to Mama is something in itself. She'll probably try and get him married off to one of the nurses while she's there."

"You're obviously feeling more relaxed or you wouldn't start inventing Mama again."

"I was just awaiting your confirmation. I personally thought he was doing his level best to be honest."

Ken looked around the apartment. "I just wish there were an elevator for Mama," he said. He looked quickly at me. "Just in case she gets a little tired," he explained.

I said nothing but I realized that at least some of my niggles over Mama were shared by my lover, even if they had existed before the malaria struck and he had tended to pooh-pooh my enunciation of them.

The following day we received two more letters from Antananarivo. The first I read was from Mama and began by informing me she had had "a bout of malaria" as a result of studying ring-tailed lemurs outside a town called Faradofay. She devoted far more space, however, to scorning the efficiency of what she described as "these native nurses." In contrast, she extolled the virtues of Dr. Keith McMasters and informed me he had saved her life at least four times. She further irritated me by stressing her good fortune in having him and not one of the many black doctors at the center who "were adequate but easily distracted."

In *her* letter Charlotte never mentioned Mama's malaria at all—only obliquely alluding to it by emphasizing how much my mother detested both quinine and institutions. In a more jovial vein she provided me with a detailed description of the delightful lemurs she'd discovered in the environs of Antananarivo, which, she said, were vastly superior to those they had seen together in the jungle on the outskirts of Faradofay, when first off the freighter. In her final paragraph she returned to the topic of Mama, telling me how proud I would have been to observe how gracious and generous she was being with the staff! No mention here of Mama's snide little racial comments. No mention either of their future plans, so we were as much in the dark as before as to the specifics of their descent upon us.

In spite of the consolations of seeing Mama's familiar handwriting, they were insufficient to dislodge my apprehension over the delayed arrival, or the vain longing for a known future.

CHAPTER THIRTY-ONE

Port Elizabeth, South Africa: January 31st, 1961

It is ages since I have made an entry! And so much has happened I shall simply have to skip some of the million details and stress only the more salient incidents that have affected both of us. Although painful, I have to start with one of the most searing experiences of my life. Charlotte and I quarreled. Not in a minor way either.

If Keith had not suddenly had to fly to Mauritius it probably would never have happened, for I would never have been put in the hands of that lisping Dr. Menatta. When I told Charley I was glad I wasn't due for an operation as I would die rather than have those black hands inside me, she looked quite put out. Chided me for my lack of Christian feelings and proceeded to lecture me about what a marvelous job Dr. Menatta had done with the little French boy on the second floor who'd been so terribly ill.

I was feeling rather down that day, what with Keith's absence and not feeling my best. In any case, I wasn't about to listen to a sermon from Charlotte Churchfield. In fact I let her have it.

I told her I needed no instruction in race relations. That my family—Poppa's ancestors, that is—were related to that William Wilberforce who had helped emancipate slaves throughout the British Empire—donkey's years before they did it in America. I reminded her of how I volunteered to join little Ali Saud during the air-raids when Charlotte had influenza and he took over the driving of her ambulance. I also pointed out that I had spent the last thirteen weeks letting those inky nurses tend me and that recently I'd spent almost as much time talking to dear Mrs. Singh with that dreadful goiter as I had with her.

But she was having none of it! She accused me of evading the issue and reminded me of some silly occasion when the two of us were shopping for shoes in Oxford Street. I had casually remarked that it looked as if London was being taken over by East Indians when some young girl in a sari let the doors into Selfridges swing right back in our faces. When she went on to point out that William Wilberforce had died years and years ago and that she hadn't seen me darken the door of a church since the Service of Thanksgiving in St. Paul's Cathedral right after the war, I ordered her away from my bedside.

I turned toward the wall and refused to look when I heard her crying. I didn't relent until I heard the door click shut.

The strange thing is what has happened since we arrived here at the opulent home of her Uncle Cyril and his Boer wife, Gerta. I ought to add first that of course we made up by that same evening. It was my initiative but I do not hold that against her. I was fortunate enough to have the influence of Poppa as a girl and one of his favorite quotations was that of St. Paul to the Ephesians: "Let not the sun go down upon your wrath," and I have faithfully followed that precept as well as urged it on my sons.

Since we came here before Christmas to the Churchfields we have not only been thrown much upon one another for company but we have come to realize—Charley in her way, I in mine—that neither this house nor this country is much to our liking.

Mr. Churchfield (her father's youngest brother) is in his seventies and made his fortune on the Johannesburg stock market. In gold, I gather. His wife, a large woman who favors much makeup and frequent visits to her hairdresser, is a *pure-blooded-Boer-from-Pietermaritzburg*—her self-description. She is also a bigot.

Not that Cyril Churchfield is any better. When I asked him politely about his weekly visits to Johannesburg which he still makes, he simply retorted that he got the hell out of "Jewburg" just as soon as possible. "Most of the problems in our country, uppity coloreds and blacks, are the fault of all those lefty Hebes."

I was too shocked to say anything. Not that my silence deterred him.

"That's why I got out of business when I did. I was surrounded by 'em, you see. Trouble is, they're English-speaking. Lots of people in the U.K. confuse *them* with *us*."

That brought his wife into the conversation and when she got excited over the subject—which was aired at least once a day in our hearing—her folds of flesh actually quivered.

"It's not just the kikes who are Commies, Cy. You're just using them to excuse your own. The English have always been soft with the kaffir. You may be the exception but I think it only fair Charlotte and Mrs. Bryant know how sick and tired we are of the British settler who pretends the blacks are the same as us." She spoke with the same squeaky tones we heard wherever we went. South African English is not attractive....

I have to confess Port Elizabeth is a quite beautiful place. You'd never know we are in the depths of an English winter. The Indian Ocean is cobalt blue here and sparkling waves roll gently in on soft sand beaches. The bougainvillea blazes everywhere and mesembryanthemum flowers in magenta profusion amid the low cliffs at the water's edge.

This iceplant carpet would seem to stretch into infinity whereas in fact paradise stops with the rocks. Laws, local by-laws and goodness knows what else decree who is fortunate enough to sit there in the sun's warm glow and watch the waves roll in. Pigmentation can make you a trespasser there, just as elsewhere in this artificial country it can make you a pariah. The scientist in me rebels at such an arbitrary—not to say lazy—form of classification!

Charlotte was revolted by the way her uncle and his wife patronized their numerous servants and was horrified to hear that for the black population of South Africa there was an inferior educational system. She spent a lot of her time probing and prodding for information over the quality of medical and hospital services available to the indigenous population. She was progressively more upset by her findings. There are times when I see old Florence Nightingale resurrected in my friend.

There are some nice things I should record here. A lovely letter from Paul with news of our ex-shipmates on the *Ijmuiden*. Another letter from Keith with a long list of do's and don'ts for a post-malarial patient. I thanked him for it before I tossed the instructions into the wastepaper basket. There is just a chance he will get home leave to San Francisco by the time we get there—whenever that may be!

Actually *things are in motion*. Like his infinitely pleasanter brother (who I'm afraid sounds frailer and frailer in every letter Charlotte gets from home), Cyrus Churchfield is adept at pulling strings. As a result, a friend of his who is a director of South African Airways is looking into the possibilities of our getting an Air India or BOAC flight via Hong Kong and Honolulu. Once we get the booking I understand we will be there in two or three days at most. Please God soon!

I have had to write so many people, like those in New Zealand, explaining we will not be seeing them after all. I feel such a fake as I am now almost back to my normal self. But Keith would not hear of us catching up with the *Ijmuiden* or finding another freighter to take its place. Unfortunately he spelled out his list of horrors over such transportation for me in front of Charlotte. And she can be even worse than my solicitous doctor when it comes to bossing me about!

As I recall, Davey could be more than a bit like that. I certainly hope he has changed as it is quite enough to cope with one at a time. Then perhaps he will be too busy to fuss over his frail old mother on his home ground.

Tuesday, February 12th. (Still with the Churchfields!)

The booking confirmation came through this morning! We leave on Friday. I HAVE NOT BEEN SO EXCITED SINCE EMBARKING FROM ROTTERDAM!

CHAPTER THIRTY-TWO

Ken saw both of them before I did. Then I often forget that he is over six foot three and I a mere five eight. When I followed his shout and saw Mama my tummy flip-flopped. With her handbag grasped tightly in one gloved hand, an overnight bag in the other, wearing a navy blue summer coat, and with her bared gray head thrust down in the effort of all that airport walking, she looked so small and vulnerable. About her milled a heterogeneous European and Asian crowd awaiting immigration officials. So many faces lined from the rigors of long flying hours. Expressions anxious as people cast about the barricades for familiar figures of welcome.

Mama looked neither anxious nor haggard, just petite and determined, as I saw her prod Charlotte with her bag when her friend started to search the waiting multitude for Ken or me. There was just time for one visual exchange between mother and son before an avalanche of mutual greetings enveloped the four of us. Mama finally looked up when all the customs and immigration business was over. Our eyes met. I was amazed to see the rare smile of a shy young girl flit across her face as she beamed in recognition. I hope I looked as nakedly loving as she did.

The trip back into the city—Ken had borrowed a car from our dentist friend, Lee Quan, who had volunteered to rustle up a Chinese meal for us back at the apartment—was all breathless questions and aborted answers. We hadn't reached Candlestick Park as we drove along the El Camino before Charlotte was describing in vivid detail the grosser aspects of yaws as she had witnessed them in Antananarivo and previously in Faradofay. It appeared the disease had imposed the most vivid impression upon her of all her experiences since leaving Rotterdam—though every now and then she would interrupt her grisly narrative to mention lemurs, deck quoits and a young man in poor health named Nick. Charlotte, I recalled from years earlier, often dispensed with surnames—most probably because she never remembered them.

Not to be outdone, Mama, who was sitting next to me in the back seat, first described the poor quality of food served in flight and the general inadequacies of air travel, particularly in comparison with sea voyages in general and the S.S. *Ijmuiden* in particular. Then she moved from the delights of that vessel and its crew to the nastiness of South Africa and its business community and the unmitigated wickedness of apartheid.

I was so delighted by this unexpected display of liberal sentiment, I think I was lulled into a state of undue relaxation and forgot Mama's capacity to spring surprises or display dramatic inconsistency. We had only just climbed the two flights to our marina apartment, shown the ladies their room and left them to take off whatever they wished when the aromas from Lee's efforts with the wok began to waft throughout the apartment. It quickly brought results.

Mama, already changed into a somewhat ill-fitting summer dress she informed us she had purchased "somewhere in Africa," was dying to know what was cooking.

"Come into the kitchen and meet the cook," Ken suggested.

The kitchen was a large L-shaped room and our dentist friend was working at the far end. Long before the group of us reached him and introductions could be effected, Mama spoke up with chirpy clarity.

"Oh, I didn't know you had a houseboy! That's excellent, isn't it, Charley. Now we can feel less guilty about imposing on you. What's his name?"

The kitchen clock ticked more loudly than usual. Ken cleared his throat. I sought invisibility and Miss Churchfield reflected on recent experience.

"It's funny, Isabella, but did you notice how Auntie Gerta treated Ah Wong much better than she did Stephen and the other Bantu? I suppose she was afraid he might poison them if she was too rude."

I came to my senses.

"Mama...Charlotte...I'd like you to meet our good *friend* Lee. Dr. Quan also happens to be our dentist."

Ken followed on my tail. "Wasn't it kind of Lee? He closed his office and came here to prepare things for your welcome-to-San-Francisco dinner."

Lee's feigned deafness over Mama's rocky opener was impeccable. With outstretched hand he approached her.

"I can see where Davey gets his good looks from! I feel honored, Mrs. Bryant, to be the first of Davey and Ken's friends to have the pleasure of meeting you."

Mama tilted her head and put out not one hand but two. It was her equivalent of purring.

As Lee shook hands with Charlotte she told him just how much she and Isabella loved Chinese food.

"Paul, our dear friend on the *Ijmuiden*, introduced us to all sorts of delicious things at Chinese restaurants he took us to in the various countries...." She tailed off.

The meal turned out to be a great success. And Mama had the usually rather taciturn Lee giggling like a schoolgirl as she described and mimicked Keith McMasters' less than successful efforts at coping with the French-speaking members of his staff at the hospital. She had no way of knowing, of course, that Lee and Keith had been lovers long ago.

Nor was I about to tell her this fact when, later that evening, we were finally alone. Lee had left and Ken had taken Charlotte down to the Marina to look out over the inky water at the darkly massive shape of Alcatraz and the electric pinpoints at the bases and towers of the Golden Gate. I sat on Mama's bed while she returned to unpacking their things and hanging them up. It was soon obvious she wasn't interested in superficial pleasantries—as I was rather hoping at this early stage.

"So how are things, darling? Is my little boy happy?"

"Very, Mama. A few little niggles now and then—but only like everybody has. We have an awful lot to be grateful for. Not least having you come to stay."

"You can have no idea just how much Charlotte and I have been looking forward to it. You know, there was just one point when I was ill when I really thought I might be a goner. I can remember thinking, 'No I *can't*. I'm on my way to see Davey!'"

"We think there's enough to entertain you. San Francisco's got plenty of attractions. I'm not worried about that. I just hope our friends prove interesting enough. At least they're all dying to meet you. There'll be lots of dinner parties—hope you don't mind?"

"You've forgotten! It was Charlotte's parents who really got me involved in dinner parties again. When you children were small, when we were still in Cornwall, it wasn't always practicable. Besides, your Daddy wasn't too keen. It wasn't really till he'd passed on I could go out more. In recent years it's been much more like in Poppa's days. I've told you, Davey, how we used to entertain when I lived at home."

"Yes, Mama. You have told me that."

She looked intently at me. "So here are you and Ken doing the same kind of thing. It's just a question of circles, I sometimes think."

She paused for a moment. I couldn't think of anything to say. In any case, I knew Mama was far from through. For as long as I could remember she had always evinced a penchant for the oblique approach.

"Ken is a kind person, isn't he? I didn't really get a chance to know him when you brought him down to Cornwall that time. I suppose the truth is I only had eyes for you after those two years of separation. And now another eleven have gone by!"

It was time for me to also do a bit of confessing. "Too long, Mama. I should have come back earlier. Ken was always suggesting we do so. It was I who resisted."

We both mulled that over.

"How are my brothers?"

But she still wasn't finished with the two of us.

"Well enough. But there'll be time to talk of Simon and Little Arthur later. Davey, did you hear Charlotte mention a young man named Paul on the *Ijmuiden*? He was our steward but became our friend."

"You've mentioned him yourself. *Several* times."

"He's unmarried too." She paused. "I don't think he ever will be."

A blind gay could see in which direction she was headed. I had a revelation: I didn't want that route. I didn't want to discuss THAT SUBJECT with her. After years of telling myself how I would love to have one of those mothers from whom nothing was hidden, I now wanted out!

"I think that's Charlotte and Ken coming up. I must put the kettle on. Still like a cuppa before bed?"

She smiled vaguely and nodded. I'd been saved by the bell perhaps—or at least by footsteps on the stairs—but Mama never gave in as easily as that....

Nevertheless, it was a couple of days before there was anything remotely germane to our bedside exchange, and that was generated by neither of us. We had been asked to that same elegant home of Reeves Fawcett and Arnold Decker where the latter had left the dinner table in a huff the evening when Mama and Charlotte's visit had first been broached and the invitation by Reeves made to us. This time Arnold was on his best behavior, was reasonably sober, and before dinner, with Reeves at the Bluthner, entertained us for forty minutes or so with songs by Schumann and Schubert.

I had never heard Mama express enthusiasm for classical music, let alone lieder, but it was quite obvious she loved the occasion of this domestic concert: the civilized aspect of it and such ancillaries as Victorian furniture, and the glow of lighted silver candlesticks flickering on the grand piano.

In the middle of the recital Charlotte leaned over and informed Mama that the chairs on which they were sitting were similar to those of her parents when they were still living at Chesney Court before removing to Cornwall. Even the singing Arnold only smiled rather than scowled at her and Reeves most subtly slowed his playing—just enough to inform us he had registered the obtrusion.

Mama didn't respond verbally, mercifully merely admonished her friend with a peremptory wag of the finger. But I was already breathing easy. If our perfectionist hosts were not to have their equilibrium thrown by Charlotte's philistinism, then it boded well for the rest of the evening, including triumphing over the somewhat strained and rarefied atmosphere which invariably hung over Reeves' dinner table.

Reeves, from his vantage point at the head of the table, waited for the entrée and what he deemed an adequate amount of unfocused conversation between seated neighbors before embarking on drawing his British guests out. It was obvious, from both the lavish fare and our host's deferential attitude, that Mama and Charlotte rated number-one treatment.

"I thought I heard you mention Chesney Court, Miss Churchfield? Is that one of your famous English stately homes?" He graciously omitted to specify *when* he'd heard Charlotte's reference to her parents' house.

Mama answered for her. "It should be," she said. "It is one of the finest houses in which I have ever stayed."

"Of course," murmured Reeves. "I was forgetting how long you two have been close friends and familiar with one another's homes."

"I, too, can vouch for the candidacy of Chesney Court as stately home," I said, smiling at Charlotte. Adding what was a considerable distortion of the truth: "I spent some of the happiest times of my adolescence there."

"Do your parents still inhabit it?" Reeves asked.

"It's now a sort of school," my aunt informed him. "For the unfortunate, you know? Little chaps? Boys and girls with that straight soft hair and rather squinty eyes?"

"Charlotte means it is now a place for the mentally retarded," Mama said firmly. "Down's syndrome, mainly."

Reeves changed the subject abruptly. "And how are you enjoying Ken and Davey's hospitality? It's a charming little flat they have, don't you think? Such atmosphere—and so many lovely books!"

I would have preferred to stay with the mentally unfortunate housed in Chesney Court.

Mama either was unaware of our host's sarcasm or chose to ignore it. "It could be your Alcatraz for all I care. It is such a joy to be with my son and his friend. I must say, what with their household and this one—all you bachelors seem to know how to enjoy life. Is there a secret you can pass on to us unfortunate women?"

"Oh come, Mrs. Bryant," Reeves riposted. "Talk of Chesney Court...a romantic cruise on a ship right out of Wagner's *Flying Dutchman*...and the obviously rich relationship you and Miss Churchfield enjoy. I find it hard to think of a better fate than that!"

Mama partook of her Chablis. "I did not intend to suggest I had cause for ingratitude."

I stiffened as I picked up on the quickening of formality in her language. She had something in mind. I was not to be left in the dark for long as to its nature.

"I was thinking more of all you boys. There's Lee, whom we met our first night here, and dear Keith, of course, who saved my life in Madagascar. And that lively chap we bumped into on the street. Dick something? I think he must be an actor or dancer."

"Sounds like Delilah," said the less voluble of our hosts as he gazed steadfastly into his now empty glass.

"Richard Carlsberg," said Ken evenly. "In fact he's an accountant."

Mama sailed blithely on. "Be that as it may. And then there was the dear boy we met on the *Ijmuiden* who took such marvelous care of us. He has proved to be such a diligent correspondent, too, since we left the ship. At the moment they are in some coconutty place in the South Pacific, and are likely to be there some time as there is much inter-island trading in those parts, he says.

"Then all of you have been so kind and generous. Wouldn't it be splendid, Charlotte, if there were more of all these boys back in Cornwall? I'm sure we could find partners for the likes of Paul and Lee. We also have bachelors, you know. The trouble is, they tend to be stick-in-the-muds like Davey's cousin Petherick or his second cousin Wesley. They never come out."

I noted that Reeves now wore an amused expression and Arnold was actually smiling.

"People come out here all the time," said Reeves. "Maybe it has something to do with the climate."

"Ah, the climate," said Mama. "Add to that the cuisine. I am sure the lovely meals you all eat has much to do with all these rich relationships."

Charlotte suddenly felt a contribution incumbent upon her. "The weather is delightful. But I miss the songbirds."

"In Port Elizabeth you complained about missing the Madagascar lemurs, my dear. You must learn to accept the nature of things."

Arnold suddenly saw his opportunity. He was at the wine flask in a flash. He held it on high. "I propose a toast. *To the nature of things*."

"To the nature of things," we solemnly responded. The dinner then proceeded on its unruffled way.

CHAPTER THIRTY-THREE

San Francisco: February 22nd, 1961

This is harder to put down than any of the stormy events on board the *Ijmuiden*, or even in Port Elizabeth with those dreadful people. Harder, because while I understand so much more about so many things, my son remains a mystery.

Oh yes, at the *chit-chat* level it all goes swimmingly. Davey rushes about treating me like a duchess or, at worst, an old lady who is a bit gaga. He is all grand gestures of leaping ahead to open doors, and on occasion as oppressively solicitous as those smothering nurses, trying to be helpful, in Antananarivo. Did you like that meal, Mama? What shall we do today, Mama? How did you like so-and-so last night, Mama? But it is NEVER *What do you think of me, Mama,* or *How really close are we, Mama?*

I know I am not the easiest of women to get on with. Poor Charlotte could attest to that—though she is far too loyal, bless her, ever to do so. But I have surely made it quite clear that I *do* like their friends. That is the simple truth. It's most odd, but I feel most relaxed with all sorts of people that a year ago I scarcely knew existed!

Of course, dear Paul was most responsible for opening my eyes in *that* direction. I do miss my silly boy. I would so like to introduce him to Davey and Ken and their friends. I am sure they would all get on famously. But that isn't what I really want to put down here. I must stick to this matter of Davey and me. I so ache to hold him—to reassure him all is well.

That can't be done without his help. And he is so terribly skilled at dodging away at the very last moment. I *think* he wants me to say certain things. To indicate, for instance, how much Charlotte and I enjoy staying here in this charming little flat—and meeting all their bachelor friends. But he makes absolutely no effort to help me. So it all comes out stagy and affected. As if we were just playing roles or something. And I mean both of us. Neither can help the other. We are so horribly powerless.

Outsiders might think it was to do with his personal life, about what he is—I mean being like Paul and living with Ken. All that *single* world, if you like. But deep down I know it's more than that. It's not just a question of giving names to all those things. I suppose I am a bit of an ostrich when it comes to dotting "i"s and crossing "t"s.

I admit I get goosepimples just thinking about discussing such subjects with Charley—who would be as distressed as I and even keener to drop the topic and return to safer things. No, what I strive to put into words here in my journal, where I hang out my heart, is to do with an identification with my second son which at times makes it hard to even remain in his presence. It's as if I shared his skin but lacked any ability to ward off his pain. When I am with him I watch him watching me. I swear we feel one another's hurt and mutually realize we are somehow *victims* of one another.

Yet I cling to the belief that this *wall* will disintegrate between us. I do most strenuously believe the same hope moves within him. I believe the ice at our mutual core was frozen into place a long time ago. I am not speaking of a specific event—not like that brutally abrupt departure so many years in the past. Nor of my blindness over his *difference* from my other two boys.

It is all more elusive than that. Part of me thinks I'll never really know what it is; what *happened* to create the barrier, which existed in the saddest way even when he was just a voluble little chap determined to get his way. Staying here under his roof, I know I must let him see I am not all that different as a loving mother from Ida Brierly and her Nick. If only Paul were here to act as a catalyst. I must try and get closer to Ken. Every instinct tells me it is he who can lead me closer to his pal.

What am I saying! His *lover*. Yes, let me say it again. Let me scream it across the housetops. MY SON HAS A LOVER WHOSE NAME IS KEN!

CHAPTER THIRTY-FOUR

Mama and Charlotte rapidly became highly popular with our friends, who vied quite strenuously to entertain them. No matter whether it was amid the comparative affluence of Reeves and Arnold, the Marin County spread of Lee Quan and his new lover, Charles (whom we met for the first time when they invited the four of us to Sunday brunch), or our younger friends who lived in more austere surroundings, the ladies were "the hit of the season"—as Delilah put it. He himself volunteered to take them to lunch at the St. Francis without us. As long as it wasn't to one of his gay haunts like the Copper Lantern or the Paper Doll I could not have cared less.

They seemed perfectly at home, even with relentlessly extravagant queens like Delilah—and as long as I wasn't along to be embarrassed or involved in overly explicit situations, that, too, was O.K. with me. What did take me off my guard, though, and perhaps surpassed all the other social events during those winter weeks of 1961, was the visit to Santa Cruz we made one weekend as the guests of Jane Lipton and Doria Lehman.

The four women hit it off as if the whole of their prior lives had been preparing them for it. Mama squared with plump, practical Doria, and Charlotte with her older lover from Oklahoma and owner of the ranch. There was nothing of the invisible line over subject matter which was inherent in even the most relaxed of situations when our visitors socialized with our gay male friends. Not that the word lesbian was ever articulated, but the flood of talk from all save Charlotte, who tended to nod and smile unless the plight of the poor or their social needs happened to come up, covered womanly topics in a degree of candor I had certainly never heard from Mama's lips before.

It wasn't that she sought to shock her prudish son so much as that she simply ignored him when enjoying the company of this forthright woman who shared his age if not his male inhibitions. Before we left it was already agreed that the girls would come to us for dinner the following week. But there was also talk of a visit from them to Mama in Cornwall.

When, on arriving back in San Francisco, I commented on the portrait-sized photograph that Doria had signed and given her, she informed me proudly that its ultimate destination would be her dressing table. I recalled the sepia photo in a silver frame of her cherished brother killed in the Great War, which had stood before her mirror for as long as I could remember....

One afternoon toward the end of the month, on coming home especially early from the paper, as Ken would be late as the result of a French Department meeting, I found Charlotte alone in the living room. She sat on the sofa with her legs up, reading. I saw that the book was *The Gallery*, by John Horne Burns. It was one of the first gay novels I had read.

The moment she saw me she began to apologize. "I just spotted this on your shelves, Davey. I do hope you don't mind. I thought it might be a jolly good read, as we did Naples when on board the good old *Ijmuiden*. Fascinating place, Italy. We went right up Vesuvius and had to win over a prudish chap who didn't want Isabella and me to see the drawings at Pompeii."

I was sure my aunt's Italian experiences would find no echo in Mr. Burns' pages—though I confess she had always displayed a voracious appetite for far less accessible literature than what she held in her hands. In my student enthusiasm I had brought her both *Ulysses* and *Finnegans Wake* and she had dutifully read each volume—although, significantly, without any specific comment. There had been other times, though, when she had embarrassed me by innocently asking the meaning of a lewd word she'd come across in a novel I'd recommended. I quickly decided to avoid the chance of that—given the narrative of gay GIs in wartime Naples on which she had cheerfully embarked.

"Where's Mama? Not out shopping in Chinatown with Lee again!"

"Oh no, dear. She turned him down this time. He won't let her spend a single penny, you see. He and Charles keep showering her with gifts! She's in the bedroom, I think."

I found her writing in a book I'd never seen before. But the minute I tapped on the half-open door and entered, she closed it with a snap.

"Have I caught you up to no good?"

"You have caught me at something very private. Now don't pry, darling."

"It looks like a diary."

"It *is* a diary. Simon gave it to me as a farewell gift for the trip."

"I'd never thought of you as a writer, Mama."

"There are a lot of things you have never thought about me, sweetheart. But don't be upset—it appears to be in the nature of things between sons and mothers." As she talked I noticed she took a tiny key and locked the ledger on her lap.

"I am glad you are home, though, as Charlotte and I have news about the *Ijmuiden* and our travel arrangements."

My mouth was suddenly very dry. "I hope it has nothing to do with your leaving early. We're all just getting used to one another and there's still tons to do. Besides, Keith doesn't get in from Madagascar until the end of the month, and I know you wouldn't want to miss the man who saved your life."

I was only half kidding. I was feeling quite desperate.

Mama put the diary in her overnight bag, got up from the rocker and came over and pecked my cheek. "Darling, we have had a *marvelous* time with you but we've been here for ages. It's time we thought of returning home, and both Charlotte and I would love to sail again on the same ship with our friends. There's only one snag. Paul doesn't mention San Francisco but only Vancouver. If it isn't going to dock here, can we get up there fairly easily? We were looking at your atlas over lunch. It seems an awful long way."

"Maybe we could all go up there," I said quickly. "Ken has spring break and I can always do an exchange with a colleague. We have a friend there. So do you. Remember Natalie Lockyer-Pope, now McGregor?"

I wasn't eager to take Charlotte and Mama to Victoria—but I was prepared to do anything that would stave off the bitterness of saying goodbye.

By the time Ken got home I was well into organizing a British Columbia expedition, suggesting we go by a rented car big enough to take the ladies' luggage. And on ascertaining the time of the *Ijmuiden*'s arrival, I arranged for a week-long exploration of what our Vancouver friend Pat Roberts had called the Lower Mainland of B.C. I was suddenly as keen to return to the site of our recent and fleeting visit as Mama and Charlotte were to renew acquaintance with the Dutch freighter. Ken offered little resistance. In fact it was his idea to contact the *Ijmuiden*'s agents in Honolulu, both to confirm the ship's schedule and to find out how practicable it would be for the two women to pick up their cabin status again in Vancouver and sail back to Amsterdam on the same vessel. Before we were to drive north across the Golden Gate Bridge all these questions had been satisfactorily answered—although the ladies would now be berthed in a different cabin, and despite the fact that Ken found it impossible to satisfy Mama's burning curiosity and procure an updated passenger list.

Was it my imagination or did I detect something of a retrenchment from Mama during those final days they shared our home?

There were the farewell encounters, of course—including a large buffet party in the apartment for eighteen people, at which Mama and Charlotte were the only straight women. (Although, in spite of my protestations, there were many—such as Reeves and Arnold—who ridiculed a heterosexual label for my mother and her friend.) On each such occasion Mama chirped and chatted with a deft assurance, and displayed a facility for bringing out the shy and giving come-uppance to the brash that made it seem as if she had been the queen of such febrile assemblies for most of her life. But I wasn't hoodwinked. I saw the faint fatigue flit over her face as the last guest departed. Then she would turn to Ken and me with renewed enthusiasm—chatting away as we all three collected glasses and ashtrays while slogger Charlotte washed up in the kitchen.

I told Ken in bed, that night of our big farewell for the ladies, that I thought Mama was a one-on-one person or at best a one-on-two. What I didn't mention to my lover—in spite of our usual practice of sharing knowledge—was that I had, with increasing frequency, chanced upon Mama scribbling away furiously in that journal she was so concerned to keep covert. It was immediately locked and put away unremarked when she grew aware of my presence.

I somehow connected it with their coming voyage and with their past life on board ship. It made me feel isolated from something indubitably central to her experience. But when I ventured to suggest that I was being excluded, she gave me one of those familial pecks on the cheek, told me not to be jealous of a silly book and asked whether I would take her shopping to buy "her" Ken a really splendid farewell gift.

CHAPTER THIRTY-FIVE

March 15th, 1961

Try as I may, this diary doesn't run as easily as before. Perhaps I am too self-conscious to come into our bedroom and make an entry while living under the roof of my son. Perhaps it is simply because of his proximity. In any case, my attention span seems to have dissolved. Or is it that I have so little *time* compared to when I was on the *Ijmuiden* or staying with those dreadful people in Port Elizabeth? Yesterday the four of us had a lovely outdoor lunch in Tiburon, across the Golden Gate Bridge. And still only mid-March! We shall be thoroughly spoiled by the weather (let alone the lavish attention these boys shower on us) before we reach home.

******

The imminence of separation hung like a specter in the wings of my consciousness during our few days in Vancouver. It was a strange fear that loomed and lapsed and made me keep darting glances at Mama as if she might abruptly vanish.

It was a delicate affair. When we four dined in the restaurant of the Sylvia Hotel (where we were staying) with Pat Roberts, who was so pleased to see us again after our earlier visit and so welcoming to us all, I felt secure with Mama at my side, her faint Yardley's perfume a balm of reassurance. I really was on top of the world—just as the roof restaurant's advertising said! Again...when we later drove the blossomed-laced streets of Vancouver's late spring, I fed happily on them and the occasional clumps of still-blooming forsythia, and the blood-red camellias blotting out dark green leaves. I soared with this seasonal high tide and became excited as the conviction grew in me that this was the place for Ken and me—somehow...sometime...when these persistent shadows had departed.

Shadows? I went right back to something dim and distant. I recalled during the war when I thought that Mama was leaving me forever. All those letters! All that childhood anguish which extended to time frames beyond childhood comprehension. As we broke free of mansions, landscaped gardens and their beacons of ornamental shrubs, into the freedom of the university campus, I had a nudge of shame. Mama and I had already reluctantly aired that subject. Had forgiven one another. But since when did mothers and sons stick with mutual forgiveness?

I thought so again when the object of my reflections suddenly addressed me. "Davey, *this* is where you two should be! Ken at the university, and you with the Canadian Broadcasting Corporation and that nice Pat who dined us in the sky-in-the-roof restaurant or whatever it was called. You have a beautiful voice for broadcasting, darling."

"That is lovely crimson ivy on the walls of the hotel," said Charlotte. "Although I am sure Queen Mary would have torn it all down with the handle of her gamp." She laughed unaffectedly at her little joke, not seeming to mind that all three of us ignored her.

"As a matter of fact, Pat was saying the other night at dinner that he knows the head of the French Department quite well. What do you think, Davey? Should I ask for an interview?"

"If Pat thinks I could get enough freelance work up here, it would be super. But for you—it's like going to another country, isn't it?"

Ken shrugged at the wheel as we drove around a headland, looking out at vast logbooms at the foot of tall cliffs. "Doesn't bother me."

"It would be neutral territory for you both!" Mama insisted. "I think that's very important for couples from different places. Your Daddy and I should have gone off to some neutral place, instead of his first dragging me to his Cornwall and then me making him live in London."

"Mama! Ken did *not* drag me to San Francisco!"

"We're assuming Canada would want us," Ken said.

"I should hardly think they'd turn up their noses at a brilliant French scholar from Stanford and my son, the star of the *San Francisco Tribune*!"

When we had finished laughing and protesting, Ken returned to his remark. "I wasn't thinking so much of our jobs as of the fact of two single men...."

He didn't bother to complete his sentence. He didn't have to.

"Let's drive that road that Pat said borders a Norwegian-type fjord and goes to Squamish," I suggested.

It was on the way there that I was again visited with foreboding about Mama and that mysterious freighter, which I imagined was already heaving its way through the swell toward the west coast of Vancouver Island. Only I spoke to Charlotte. "Looking forward to sailing out there on the high seas, Charlotte? The last leg of your trip?"

"Your mother and I will certainly miss you two boys," she began. "You've been so kind and you have such generous friends. We certainly never dreamed of the lovely life you have out here. You did the right thing, Davey."

"Davey asked you whether you were looking forward to rejoining the *Ijmuiden*," Mama said in sudden ill humor. "Answer his question."

Charlotte smiled sweetly, her survival-obstinacy in dealing with Mama unimpaired. "I tell you what I'm looking forward to, Davey. It's the dawn chorus of the thrushes and blackbirds in the woodland behind the house. These eagles and things are quite nice but they don't make up for our darling English songbirds."

All this unasked-for ornithology was frustrating.

"What about you, Mama?" I asked. "You keen to gain your sea-legs again?

"Will I be more pleased to go home—or sadder to leave my boys? That's the kind of question one answers differently at different times. Like—is the cup half empty or half full? Do you know what? I think you're trying to lay a little trap, you naughty boy!"

"Why don't you leave it alone," Ken said quietly. I did as I was told.

* * * * * *

I don't think he has the slightest notion his Mama can be homesick! Then he has his Ken and *that* is his "home," wherever he lives. Of course, I would be hard put to it to pinpoint my own feelings. I love my Charley, of course, but that isn't the same thing. And Cornwall can never mean to me what it did to Wesley. Even so, I miss it. I wouldn't go into all that birdsong nonsense like Charlotte but I totally understand the feelings behind her words. I suppose we are just two Englishwomen who are too old for transplanting—however much my dear child would love us to do precisely that.

* * * * * *

That morning came as, of course, it had to. The arrangements were simple. The local shipping agent had informed us of the specific dock on the North Shore where the *Ijmuiden* would tie up. There was a shed where we could take the baggage and there would be a few hours after we got the ladies aboard before their departure. All went well until ropes were thrown, engines quelled and the gangplank lowered. As we stood there waiting there was a flurry on the deck above us and then, suddenly, a slight figure came bounding down toward the dock screaming, "Tante Isabella! Tante Isabella!"

It neither slowed nor hesitated—obviously fully aware of its objective. As Mama raised her arms in ecstatic greeting, a young man in a steward's uniform swept her off her feet and around and around. I happened to glance at Charlotte. As Mama and this stranger grabbed one another in greeting, she was smiling seraphically. I could have slapped her face.

The palaver was soon over and she introduced us to Paul Leiden, of whom she had so often spoken, and the supervision of the baggage began. I affected normalcy, grinning broadly at all and sundry. But inwardly I screamed as the knife of jealousy, over that ridiculous steward whom she obviously loved, probed ever deeper.

When it came time to say goodbye I was unable to tell Mama that my moist eyes were the result not of a son's sadness but of a lover's torment. But perhaps she saw.

She spoke more quickly than usual—as if the boat might leave without her! "Paul has taught me so much," she said. "In a way he was like John the Baptist in the Bible, Davey. He prepared the way for San Francisco. First him, then Keith. Give Keith my love, won't you, darling. I'm so desperately sad we had to leave before he got back."

I promised.

"I've got something for you. Only there are a couple of conditions."

I said nothing.

"I never, ever want you to mention it. In a letter or talking with me. Nor are you to ever mention it to your brothers. Only—only Ken can see it."

With that she unzipped her overnight bag and retrieved her diary.

"I wondered why you didn't give that bag to Paul to take aboard," I said.

"What was in it was for you alone, my darling. Even Charlotte has no idea what's written there."

She dropped the bag to the floor and handed me the stiff-covered volume. With her free hand she pressed something into my outstretched palm. It was the tiny key.

There was a scrape of feet from outside. We were not to be left alone for much longer.

She reached up on tiptoe. This time it was our lips that met.

FINIS